Praise for *Unnatural*

"The most unique, haunting, magical, treacherous, romantic, and combative novel I've read in a long time. Action, betrayal, peoples at war, strange magic . . . a whole new take on fantasy!"

—#1 *New York Times* bestselling author Tamora Pierce

"I want to climb inside C. M. Waggoner's world of powerful trolls, cheeky wizards, and mathematical magic and make myself at home. She seamlessly weaves politics, love, and magic into a novel that challenges everything we know about fantasy."

—*New York Times* bestselling author Chloe Neill

"Within the compelling tale lie some big themes—power, magic, gender, and sexuality among them—and the author weaves them in skilfully with just the right combination of compassion, insight, and humour. This one goes straight onto my Keepers shelf."

—Juliet Marillier, author of *The Harp of Kings*

"Waggoner's debut offers fantasy readers a new viewpoint on magic, love, responsibility, and sacrifice. The themes of found family and unlikely, hard-earned trust are warmly convincing, and Waggoner's system of magic is unique and deeply satisfying."

—Vivian Shaw, author of the Dr. Greta Helsing series

"I have never read another novel that gave me so much of what I wanted so soon, and then just kept delivering the goods, page after page after page. Love, lust, magic, murder . . . this book has it all!"

—Lara Elena Donnelly, author of *The Amberlough Dossier*

# UNNATURAL
# MAGIC

## C. M. WAGGONER

ACE
NEW YORK

ACE
Published by Berkley
An imprint of Penguin Random House LLC
penguinrandomhouse.com

Copyright © 2019 by C. M. Waggoner

Library of Congress Cataloging-in-Publication Data

Names: Waggoner, C. M., author.
Title: Unnatural magic / C. M. Waggoner.
Description: First edition. | New York: Ace, 2019.
Identifiers: LCCN 2019022560 (print) | LCCN 2019022561 (ebook) |
ISBN 9781984805843 (paperback) | ISBN 9781984805850 (ebook)
Subjects: GSAFD: Fantasy fiction.
Classification: LCC PS3623.A3533 U56 2019 (print) |
LCC PS3623.A3533 (ebook) | DDC 813/.6—dc23
LC record available at https://lccn.loc.gov/2019022560
LC ebook record available at https://lccn.loc.gov/2019022561

First Edition: November 2019

Printed in the United States of Americah
4th Printing

Cover art by Tomas Almeida
Cover design by Katie Anderson
Book design by Alison Cnockaert
Interior art: Vintage frame by Ozz Design/Shutterstock

*For Xia Nan, who is always very patient*

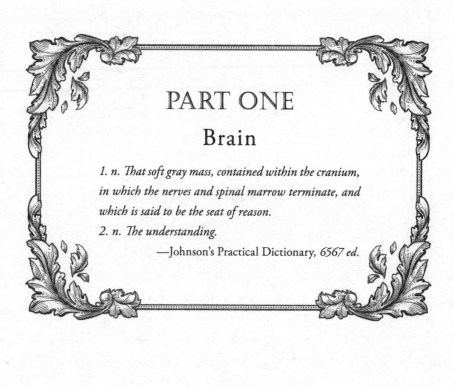

# PART ONE
## Brain

*1. n. That soft gray mass, contained within the cranium, in which the nerves and spinal marrow terminate, and which is said to be the seat of reason.*
*2. n. The understanding.*

—Johnson's Practical Dictionary, *6567 ed.*

# 1

*Since the earliest days of our nation, when Elgar was yet to walk among us and the trollfathers still guided our clans, we humans of Daeslund have been a singular people: unique in our government, in our religion, in our customs and speech. Great wizards have been born to us, and great poets: Callet Brown was rocked in a cradle of Dirnam wood, and Oneram was nourished upon good Daeslundic bread. We are a proud nation, but we must not allow this pride to be our undoing. We must not make an altar to our past and consign our future to the ash heap. From Sango, from Nessorand, from the Mendani federation, from all of these nations can we see the shining lights of progress, of bustling commerce, of scientific endeavor. Gentlemen and ladies of the Assemblage, we must not allow ourselves to be left behind. Let us look to the Sangan examination system, which has lifted so many great minds from obscurity. Let us look to the engineers of Awat and the mighty dam of Botevi. To emulate wealthier nations is not to abandon what makes us proud Daeslunders, but rather to ensure that in one hundred years our descendants will see in our history an unbroken line of progress . . .*

> *—Assemblor Elgarson H. Whicks, in a speech before the Assemblage on the modernization of the Daeslundic magical education system, Erlmonth 17, 6572*

Onna Gebowa had always liked numbers.

She could remember being six years old and watching her mother making apple pies. Her mother was very good at making apple pies. There were eight apples in each pie, apples that her mama had brought up from the cellar. Onna stood nearby as her mama rolled out dough and peeled and sliced the fruit. Onna's job was to help eat bits of apple peel, fetch anything from the pantry that her mama had forgotten, and ask innumerable questions.

"Mama, how long does it take for you to use up a whole bushel of apples?"

"Oh," her mother said. "I don't know, Onna! I suppose it takes about two months."

"We have apple pie once a week, Mama. That's sixty-four apples every two months, and there are one hundred and twenty-eight apples in a bushel. We have six bushels in the cellar. That's seven hundred and sixty-eight apples. That's an *awful* lot of apples, Mama."

"That's very clever, Onna," said her mother, and pointed to a bucket of peas. "Do you think you could help me to find out how many peas are inside of the pods?"

Her mother told this story to her father that night, one of several stories she told about funny things that the girls—there were six of them altogether, Onna the third—had done that day. Mr. Gebowa didn't laugh, but instead took off his spectacles to examine his daughter more closely. "Onna," he said, "please fetch me a piece of paper and a pencil."

She did so, and he used them to work out the sums. He stared at the paper for a moment. "How many apples did you say that there should be in the cellar, Onna?"

"Seven hundred and sixty-eight," she said. She was surprised that Papa had to ask.

Mr. Gebowa set down his pencil. "I think that we should take her to see Mr. Heisst."

Onna frowned. She didn't think she would like to go to Mr. Heisst's school. He was a very untidy-looking man, not at *all* like Papa, and his school was full of big, loud, rowdy boys.

"Oh, *Kasi*," said Mrs. Gebowa, in tones of great reproach. "But she's barely even six! She shouldn't have to worry about learning *wizardry*, of all things. And I told Miss Amelia that I would send Onna to her girls' school next autumn. And what if she gets the swooning sickness?"

"I will take her to Mr. Heisst's tomorrow," said Mr. Gebowa, and Mr. Gebowa so rarely argued with his wife—he tended toward smiling indulgently at everything she said and then retreating into his favorite chair to read an improving book—that she hadn't the heart to disagree.

In this fashion Onna embarked upon her academic career, and despite her mother's concerns, she flourished at Mr. Heisst's. By the time she was seven she was already working at the theoretical level of her twelve-year-old classmates. What made her truly remarkable, however, was her ability to invent and recall parameters. While other budding wizards were forced to write everything down, and read everything out loud again when they were ready to incant, Onna could memorize pages worth of parameters as easily as a grocery list, and she could incant entirely without speaking. Though, of course, she was strongly warned against any attempts at major magical feats, for fear of her developing the wizard swoons. Very few studies had been made of the effects of magical education on young girls, and it was generally thought that their more delicate natures would make them more susceptible to magically induced illness.

The boys, for the most part, took being embarrassed by a little girl with admirable grace, and they alternated between teasing her to distraction and making a pet of her, bringing her sweets and allowing her to come along on their romps. By the time she was thirteen she was, it must be confessed, rather spoilt by them. Though Onna was perhaps not *quite* as pretty as her elder sister Mani (who was married to the village headman and had once posed as a shepherdess for a series of pastoral tableaux by a famous painter from Leiscourt), it still pleased the boys very much to be given the honor of escorting Onna home from school in the afternoons or to pick up her handkerchief should she happen to drop it. She was a small girl, quite unlike her statuesque elder sister, but she had a spotless dark brown complexion, wide startled-looking eyes that she accentuated by keeping her hair cropped very short, and full lips that lent themselves very agreeably to smiles at the boys who surrounded her. She smiled often, and as she grew older her smiles increased with her awareness of how the boys reacted to them. They often seemed to look at her face as if it were an examination paper, and a frown at the weather or too-tight stays or indigestion was a failing mark.

Sy Carzda was the richest of all of the students at the school, and his parents the most disliked about town. They, like Onna's parents, had moved to Cordridge-on-Sea from Leiscourt. However, while Onna's parents were fairly popular and admired—Onna's mother's youthful indiscretions as a successful authoress were forgiven due to her exemplary behavior now as a frugal and fastidious housekeeper—Sy's father was thought to be "stuck on himself" for his academic inclinations, and his mother "no better than she ought to be" for her Adaptivist politics. All of this combined led the good people of Cordridge-on-Sea to conclude that they were at best very *peculiar* people, and at worst actual *Hesendis*, which was considered an eccentricity of a particularly alarming sort. Onna's parents, Leiscourters themselves, were not overly concerned by this, which was very fortunate for Onna, as Sy had been her bosom companion since she was seven years old, and he a very mature and sophisticated nine.

Sy came by to walk Onna to school almost every day, though it generally launched such a storm of shouts of "*Onna, it's your beau!*" and shrieks of laughter from her sisters that he would often tell her that he regretted it. One morning on their walk she asked him about the rumors about his family for the first time. "You know, I've never really asked if you *are* a Hesendi or not."

He laughed, but it didn't sound very natural. "Of course, I'm a Hesendi. Why else would I not eat meat?"

She kicked a stone. "All sorts of people are vegetarians now. Magister Exley says that it dampens the immoral appetites." A pause. "You don't wear all black."

"Magister Exley's a *Hesendi*," Sy said. "He just used traditional

Elgarite theology in his book because he knew that otherwise no one would read it. Vegetarianism is one of our universal principles: we're supposed to try and spread it about. And I don't wear all black because I haven't dedicated myself to the spreading of the principles. I'm not even that *religious*." He shoved his hands into his pockets. "Though I might have to dye all of my clothes and buy a riverboat if I don't get into Weltsir. After ten years of wizarding school, I'm certainly not suited for anything else."

"You'll get in. And what would you do with a riverboat?"

"Oh, I don't know. I can't be be one of the Clear Voices and heal people's thoughts if I'm not religious, can I? I suppose I'd just have to travel about in it and have adventures."

"Can I come, too, then?"

"Don't be stupid. At least one of us has to get into Weltsir. It will probably be you. You can read all of my letters about my travels when you're not working like a peat miner in the library."

She smiled. "Oh, *will* you write me letters?"

Sy nudged her with his elbow. "Of course I will. And you'll send some back, won't you?"

"I suppose I might," she said, and kicked at a rock with such joyful energy that it flew through the air and landed in the ditch at the side of the road. *All* of the boys seemed to think that her moods were directed toward them, but the thought of entering into an intimate correspondence with Sy really was enough to make her feel as giddy and light-headed as if she had just poured half the magic in her body through a particularly tricky set of parameters.

Weltsir College of Magic was in Leiscourt, and it was the best school of human magic in Daeslund—troll schools, it was said, were vastly better, but no humans were admitted to them. Weltsir also lagged woefully behind the Heijin Fa'ou in Sango, the Palace of Learning in Bene, and, of course, the great university on the wizard island of Hexos, but a degree from Weltsir was still more than enough to secure a Daeslunder a life of work in magic.

Weltsir was also the scene of a great deal of recent excitement. For centuries Weltsir had been open only to the sons of Daeslund's greatest families or to certain other boys with faultless letters of introduction from men of appropriate wealth and rank. Then, only a few years ago, the new Adaptivist government led by Assemblor Jemmis had forced the school to modernize and adopt a Sangan-style examination system. The university had protested, but the Adaptivists had held firm: How was Daeslund to maintain any sort of economic strength when its magical education system lagged so dreadfully behind that of other countries? And so the reforms came about, so that even Onna—who was a girl, and solidly middle-class, and whose family had only been in Daeslund for three generations and were therefore quite clanless— might have a chance to attend.

Although Mr. Heisst now had almost a dozen regular students, it was generally understood that only Sy and Onna had the necessary aptitude required to even sit for the exam, though Sy's father's excellent connections in the capital made him a far more likely candidate. To be a wizard required, of course, the intrinsic magical ability that most people had—enough to fire a folk incantation to keep milk from souring too quickly, or to keep your shoes dry on a rainy day—but, more importantly, it required an enormous dedication to studying and understanding the construction of safe and accurate parameters. Most of the boys at school knew they were as capable of becoming wizards as they were of successfully engineering a cantilever bridge. However, the heady vision of one day having Sy, an old school chum, with a room in Leiscourt—where one could kip, and from which one could sally forth to the jolly pantomime, or the crowded dance hall, or the glittering gin palace—was such a wonderful one that the other boys at Mr. Heisst's put forth every particle of effort to bring it to fruition.

Thus, before Sy was to take the exam, Onna and his classmates spent many a long, warm spring day sitting under the blooms of the big old apple tree in Mr. Heisst's garden, books and papers spread out in a great confusion all around them, peppering Sy with questions of every imaginable sort—what parameters would you write in order to heat one pound of copper by five degrees? If you examine this parametrical description of an onion, what linguistic errors can you identify, and how would they influence the result of any parameters you wrote including this description? What five devices are commonly used in the creation of weather analysis and prediction constructions? And so it went until poor Sy flung himself face-first onto the grass and begged them for mercy, as he could bear no more.

It was up to Onna, then, in the quiet evenings when the boys had all gone home to their suppers, to come up with a rational system of study and organize everything into neat stacks of notecards, to brew coffee and procure cakes, and thereby, as Sy said, "to cram a bit of knowledge into me, in one way or another." Sometimes she studied along with him—after all, she would have to sit for the exams herself in another year, after her graduation from Mr. Heisst's—and sometimes she played the tutor and quizzed him. And sometimes she only sat nearby and kept him company. This was as much for her own sake as it was for his. Home, with its noise and laughter and endless stream of sisters, was all very well and good, but far more delicious was the opportunity to sit in Mr. Heisst's dusty little study and read one book after another, warming her feet by the fire and eating too many cakes with no one in the world to disturb her.

She liked to read novels the most, but she also enjoyed the sort of history books where the author included entire conversations between great wizards as if they had been crouched in the corner of the room taking notes. One of her favorites of these probably-mostly-invented history books told the story of how, after many years of her clan having ruled over humans, the great troll Cynbatren traveled the earth sharing the secret of magic with all of humankind. After that trolls could no longer have dominion over humans, and humans of every nation could at any time produce a wizard great enough to lay waste to an invading army or overthrow a cruel tryrant. It was a much nicer story, Onna thought, than the much drier and probably factual versions (that magical education had either originated in modern Nessorand and then spread along trading routes over the course of several centuries, or that powerful innate magical ability began to occur spontaneously in humans as a survival mechanism in response to a global pandemic, or both, or neither; it was a very popular argument between wizards). In any case, it was very thrilling to read all of the gory stories about humans marching about sticking their kings onto spikes before the Magical Awakening (quite interesting) and the Waste of the Gauts (*wonderfully* thrilling, though Onna wasn't sure if she believed that a single wizard really could have *single-handedly* dissolved the skeletons of an entire occupying army), and all of the terribly boring laws and treaties and things that had come after it.

She was, of course, very *grateful* to have been born into an age when attempting to steal another nation's land or stick their king onto a spike or burn down their villages for having a different god or language or mode of dress would earn you the wrath of the entire Consortium of Nations. It was only that the poor benighted humans of the past seemed to have been witness to a great deal of *excitement*.

Sometimes when she got tired of reading she would work on her embroidery, and Sy would look up and tease her about making someone a charming little wife one day. She never knew what to say to that, or indeed what to think about it. She didn't know whether to be pleased, as she was proud of her embroidery and thought that she *might* make a very good wife one day, or annoyed, since it didn't seem like the sort of thing that a boy would say to someone whom he thought of as a very talented young wizard. So she settled on "Hmm!" and ignored him.

Eventually it came time for Sy to take the exam. He came by Onna's house to say good-bye before he left for Leiscourt, looking a bit wild-eyed from lack of sleep. His normally ruddy cheeks had gone a fashionably unhealthy gray, and at some point in the past few weeks he had sprouted the suggestion of a thin black mustache on his upper lip. Onna couldn't say from its appearance whether it was being cultivated, like a hedge, or was the result of neglect, like a briar patch, but in either case, as far as Onna was concerned, it made Sy look *awfully* dashing. He stood at the doorstep with his hands pushed deeply into his pockets, staring at her in such a pitiful way with his long-lashed brown eyes that she thought that she might burst into tears at once.

"I'm going to fail, I know that I will," said Sy. "I've already forgotten absolutely everything that you wrote onto all of those notecards for me."

"Listen to you talk!" said Onna. "You're just nervous, that's all. You'll do beautifully, and Fairnwell and Johnson will go to stay with you in your flat in Leiscourt when you're an important scholar, and they'll probably end up making light effects for the pantomime and falling in love with actresses and never coming home again." She paused. "I would invite you in, you know, but Mama and Papa are out, and I don't think it would be proper."

Sy managed a wan smile. "I'm sure you're right. I was about to invite myself in, but you always know what the proper thing is, as you haven't got a pair of heretical Hesendis for parents. And I suppose I shall have to try my best at the exam, just so Johnson will have his chance at the gin palaces."

"Of *course* you will," said Onna. "Here, I made this for you. For luck."

She pulled a small mirror from her apron pocket—she had been tidying up in the kitchen when he rang the doorbell—and handed it to him. "In a moment, tap on that with your fingertip and say *sister,*" she said and bustled off, leaving the startled Sy with the mirror in his hand. She hurried up the stairs and down the hall to the cramped little room she shared with her sister Gertie and snatched up another small mirror from her bedside table. She tapped it with one finger, said, "Brother," and crowed in satisfaction as Sy's puzzled face appeared in the glass. She waved at him energetically, then dropped the mirror into her pocket and rushed down the stairs again. Sy was still standing in the doorway, grinning. "It's the cleverest thing I've ever seen! But it must have taken you an *age* to make them. Could I see the parameters?"

She ducked her head, embarrassed. "Do you really like them? But it wasn't clever at all, really; I just read in a book that they have them in Hexos and thought it would be fun to make them. Of course, I can write down the parameters for you, if you really would like to see them."

He smiled at her. "Only *you* would ever think that it isn't very clever to read about some fiendishly difficult little construction they have in Hexos and then make up the parameters for it yourself, just for *fun*." He put the mirror into his pocket, along with his right hand. "I suppose that I must be going, then."

"Oh, yes," said Onna, in what she hoped was a very calm, grown-up lady sort of way. "You mustn't be too late arriving in Leiscourt. It's very important to get a good night's sleep before the exam."

He smiled at her. "All right, then. Good-bye, Gebowa."

"Good-bye, Carzda," she said. "To close the mirror you have to tap it and say *good night*."

"I'll remember. Look at it sometimes, won't you? So that I can see you."

"I will," she said. "Good-bye, Sy."

"Good-bye, Onna," he said, and left. Onna closed the door and leaned against it, crying bitterly and thinking that nothing so romantic or so terrible would ever happen to her again for her entire life.

The next day was the first part of Sy's exam, the written portion. Onna kept the mirror with her for the entire day, nestled safely in her apron pocket, and every time she checked it, she saw only her own face reflected back at her. Then, at around three, she pulled it out again and saw an exam question.

It was quite ingenious of him. He had copied the question in very heavy ink so that it bled through to the other side, then stuck it to the underside of his desk and put the mirror in his lap. She could read the backward text very clearly, flipped as it was in the mirror. It was a question asking for the student to write their own parameters to address the proposed problem. It was exactly the sort of thing that Sy always struggled with; the sort of thing that they both knew would present no difficulty at all to Onna.

She was suddenly, furiously angry, though she couldn't understand why or at whom. She found a piece of paper and wrote out the parameters that he needed—it only took her a minute or two—and then she wrote another set of parameters for flipping the writing before setting the note in front of the mirror. There was a mean shard of pleasure in adding the mirror-writing parameter. *I know what you can't do*, it said. *You know what I can.*

If Sy tried to contact her over the next few days, she didn't know about it. She put the mirror facedown on her bedside table and ignored it and set about doing her own work instead. She was thinking already of her own exam and what she would do for the practical demonstration. She thought that she would like to do an illusion. For three days she sat down every afternoon at the kitchen table—after the lunch washing-up was finished, but before anyone asked her to start slicing gingerroot for dinner—and worked out her parameters.

Sy, when he came back, caught up to her on a walk to Mr. Heisst's. He fell into step next to her, his shoulders bunched up around his ears. It had grown cooler again over the past two days, and Sy was wearing only a light summer jacket and skirt. Though she had meant to stare straight ahead and march briskly forward, Onna found herself slowing her pace to look at him. He cleared his throat. "You're vexed with me."

She didn't think that there was any need for her to answer this. He fisted his hands in his pockets. "I passed the exam."

She gave up being vexed and gave a little whoop of delight. "Really? Did you?"

He nodded. "Only because of you, though, helping me." He cleared his throat again. "Thank you. I know how you must have hated it to break the rules like that, but I just *had* to get in, and I knew that you would know the answer at once." He blew on his hands to warm them, then said, "You look very nice today."

She looked as she always did; the blue-and-white dress she was wearing was one of her favorites. "Do you really think so?" she said. She didn't know why she said it, exactly, only that it felt somehow simply, fundamentally correct in the same way that the multiplication tables were. If a young man said that a young lady looked nice, she should say, "Do you really think so?" and smile, and smooth her hands over the skirt of her blue-and-white dress. If this formula was followed, the boy would smile. Sy smiled, the one that twisted at the corner from an old scar on his lip. For a moment Onna was startled by him: by his thick black hair and decided eyebrows and that engagingly twisty smile. He was in that moment someone she didn't know at all, someone who looked at her in a way that was completely unfamiliar.

Sy left for Leiscourt two weeks later. Onna cried when he left and then shut herself up in her room and began to study. Her friends interpreted this as pining, and they attempted to lure her from her books with promises of dances, or county fairs, or a particularly beguiling set of new summer hats being sold by her father at Gebowa's Goods and Sundries. Her family at first applauded her studiousness, and then they began to fret over her neglect of herself. Her eldest aunt—who had been staying with them for several weeks—set about cooking every Awati dish Onna had ever been fond of as a child, so that the whole house was redolent with the smells of fish and nuts and spices. Her father invited her to sit by the fire while he read aloud from his latest religious book. Onna's mother drew her warm baths and suggested that she might enjoy a day of healthy tramping about in the fresh air.

Onna, however, could not be tempted. Studying would admit her to Weltsir, where Sy was. Whether it was to be close to Sy that motivated her, or to advance her own studies, or to please her parents with her scholastic accomplishments, or simply to prove that she was capable of it, she herself could not say. She didn't reflect much upon it. She simply studied out of a deep and abiding faith instilled in her by her parents, by Mr. Heisst, and by every ounce of experience she had gained in her short life so far: that all problems could be solved with hard work, a pleasant smile, and advanced mathematics.

Sy wrote to her every week, long, affectionate letters full of jokes and gossip. She responded with letters that were equally long but considerably less amusing. Often they were little more than a greeting followed by page upon page of experimental parameters. She was working, she told him, on something very special. Something that she was quite sure no one had ever done before.

It was difficult, working on her own projects while still keeping up with her schoolwork and helping Mama around the house. Her sister Mani had just had a baby, and her mother was so busy with helping with her first grandchild that many of the burdens of the housework fell on Onna. A great number of relatives came pouring in from Lesicourt as well to see the newest addition to the Gebowa family, and though Onna was happy to see them all—and eat good Awati food and see her little cousins and laugh at the old stories her uncles and aunties told— the plain fact of the matter was that with so many people about she never had a moment's peace, and she could not display any unhappiness over this fact to anyone for fear of being thought a very spoilt and selfish young lady, indeed.

Her grandparents and aunts and uncles were all very much involved in Leiscourt's close-knit Awati Elgarite Hall, and Onna often felt as if any minor misbehavior on her part would immediately attract the disapproval of at least four dozen elderly persons who believed firmly in both their Elgarite principles and their grandchildren's ability to annoy their departed ancestors even from across a very wide expanse of ocean. It was difficult enough to be a young lady of seventeen, Onna thought, without having to also feel the weight of both her Awati ancestors and the laws of Elgarism upon her not-particularly-broad shoulders.

Her father often chided her for reading his daily paper and getting overwrought over the news. She tended to ignore this—she thought that a young scholar ought to be well-informed—but lately the news in the papers was very disturbing. A horrible story about a troll massacring almost the entire population of a village called Coldstream in the northlands completely overtook all of the papers for weeks. One of the papers said that the attack had been unprovoked, while in another, local trolls claimed that one of the villagers had murdered and eaten a troll child, while a third claimed the entire massacre had been staged by the Daeslundic human and Cwydarin troll governments to cover up how people in the village had been poisoned by a leak of strange substances from a nearby matchstick factory. The stories nestled themselves into her head and created a sort of horrid wax mold into which her brain poured her own petty anxieties. She had strange dreams. She dreamed of being lost in an enormous house full of endless twisting passages, searching for something but terrified of finding it. She dreamed of walking through the village and finding it empty, everyone she had ever known murdered and gone. She dreamed, often, of being eaten alive.

She didn't mention her dreams in her letters to Sy. When she wrote of the rest of her troubles—the fantastic difficulty of her projects, the endless labor produced by her uncles and cousins and little sisters, her morbid fascination with the news reports—she wrote in an airy way that made it all sound as if she was one of those artless young brides in a story from a women's quarterly. This was the character Onna cast herself as in her letters because she suspected that if Sy knew what she was really like—her worries, her resentment, her fevered work that kept her up past the dawn—he would draw away in revulsion.

Matters of the heart, however, were eventually supplanted in Onna's mind by the increasingly pressing issue of the entrance examination. Somehow, a year passed, and the exam soon overshadowed everything; no dinners or dances or deliciously beribboned bonnets or even distant terrors in northern villages or Onna's own seventeenth birthday could obscure, for more than a moment or two, the looming threat of the exam. It sat there at the gate of summer like some fearsome dragon, and she dragged her heels through the whole of the spring until, with terrible swiftness, she found herself seated beside her mother in a twelve-hour coach headed for Leiscourt, preparing herself to face the monster.

# 2
---

*To be introduced to a troll is a very different matter than to be introduced to a human, and all usual rules are to be disregarded. First, it is essential to remember that reigs—who are usually, but not always, of the female sex—assume most leadership roles within troll society, and that trolls therefore admire strength and decisiveness in human women. A young lady who is being introduced to a troll reig should expect to be embraced and kissed briefly on the cheek: this kiss should always be returned to avoid an appearance of haughtiness. Trolls do not generally like to smile at anyone other than intimate friends and family, and a stern countenance should not be taken as churlishness. Bold eye contact, a low-pitched voice, and good posture are all considered attractive, and modesty is not thought of as a particular virtue: compliments should be accepted with a brief "Thank you," without demurral. A young lady who is accomplished in music or magic might find an excellent audience or conversational partner in even the humblest of trolls, and a fine singing voice is generally much appreciated and applauded . . .*

—Mrs. Barton's Manual of Manners, *Cordoline Barton, 6568*

When Tsira first heard about the murders, it was in a tea shop. She was picking up a new knife in Dunnhepst when she spotted another troll. A big reig, tall and good-looking. They kissed. The stranger said her name was Fyllemwydmesura. She was wearing a cloak with hems covered in the kind of embroidery that would take the vahns in Tsira's clan months to make. Tsira tried not to think too much about how long her clan could eat if they sold something like it.

They ended up sitting down in a little place near the village square. Tsira wasn't really in the mood to chat with some rich city reig, but it was in custom to share a drink with a traveler.

The owner bowed to them when he brought the drinks. Fyllemwydmesura sat back and looked pleased, like she had probably been born a reig and felt like one her whole life and never had anyone argue with her about it. She looked like someone who was used to being listened to. Not Tsira.

Tsira knew she was meant to be a reig, but people in her clan always told her she was wrong. Acted like she didn't know what she *was*. Like maybe she thought that bleeding most months or wearing a reig's torc could make her a reig without her stepping up to the tasks of leadership and caretaking of vahns and children that came with it. Like calling herself a reig when most people were vahn meant she was stuck on herself. If she wasn't so small and magicless, no one would have ever asked twice, but she was and they had, so she'd had to think it through. She could make the arguments. She was a reig because imagining herself doing vahn's work—the detail-work, the patience-work, teaching children and doing embroidery and keeping accounts and all of the other vahn-chores—made her itch. She was a reig like her ma: she had the head for books, the calm steady temper, and the will to be a leader in her clan and take care of any vahns who'd have her. If they ever would have her. That was feeling less likely by the day. Fyllemwydmesura had probably never had anyone ask her if she was *sure you wouldn't rather declare vahn and get taken to clan by a kind steady reig*. Tsira wanted to smack her for it.

"It's good to be back up north," Fyllemwydmesura said. "Moths here know how to pay their respects."

Tsira kept her face blank. "Pinks."

Fyllemwydmesura raised her eyebrows. "What?"

"Call them humans or pinks. Not moths. Pinks around here don't like it. Trolls don't much like it, either." *Moths* was what stuck-up city trolls called clanless humans.

Fyllemwydmesura brushed her chin with her fingers to show how little she thought of that. "It's sweet of you to worry about their sensibilities."

Tsira tried not to look mad. Not that she'd ever *met* her da—all her ma ever had to say about him was that he was clever, and a *sweet little vahn*—but she didn't like hearing some stranger calling his people names. Still, she didn't feel like getting into an argument. She wouldn't win with a reig like this anyway. She changed the subject. "You've been down south?"

"In Monsatelle. I was installing freezing constructs into ships' hulls. Easy work for good pay. The humans practically think you're their *Elgar* for doing advanced magic."

"You're a wizard," Tsira said. *And an arrogant ass*, she thought. "Any work down there for a troll who isn't?"

Tsira had been thinking about heading down to a human city to find work for a while now. It was the best idea she'd come up with. She was too high-ranked as a clan-head's daughter to not have taken any vahns to her name by now, but not good enough with the vahns to manage it. Not gentle or patient or good enough at detail-work to make a good vahn for a decent reig to care for, either. Shit, she had to start fights just to prove that she didn't want to declare vahn herself, and while she could find plenty of vahns who were willing to lick her for a night, she couldn't find too many who'd want a washout as a reig to take them to clan. She wasn't educated or strong or good-looking enough to make it in Cwydarin or another troll city without a lot of trouble and grief. People up there looked down on anyone from border-clans like hers, thought they were poor and backward. She'd never even been to a real school like a Cwydarin troll, just studied her clan's grandmother-books and learned what her own ma had to teach her.

Pinks, though. They might not think she was pretty, but she was strong and fast, by pink standards, and had all of a bigger reig's decisiveness. She could read and write in two languages, turn her hand to cheesemaking and woodwork, and do more mathematics than most pinks could. She could make some money, have some fun. Maybe finally do something that'd impress her ma a little. Maybe convince a good-looking human vahn or two to give her a chance. Not that many human men these days were interested in declaring vahn. Maybe she could find a woman who'd take to it. Or a man who was as odd a man as she was a reig.

That was the plan, at least.

Fyllemwydmesura looked smug. "I don't know. I never had to look into it. Bricklaying, perhaps."

Tsira wanted to tell this reig to lick her. Instead, she said, "You from Cwydarin?"

"Yes," Fyllemwydmesura said. "You could tell from my accent? I don't have much practice speaking border dialects."

Tsira took a sip of her tea and said, "No. Just a guess."

"Well," Fyllemwydmesura said, "I'll be glad to get out of here. Have you heard about the murders?"

Tsira shook her head and waited. This Cwydarin reig thought she was lavender to everyone who smelled her, but she wasn't any good at keeping her face in check. Fyllemwydmesura looked nervous. "I heard about it from the reig who came to replace me at the shipyard. Some moth's been murdering border-trolls, cutting them up like laboratory specimens."

Tsira kept her face steady. "How do you know it was a human?"

"They say there were traces of human magic on the body. But of course it was a human. Do you really think one of the *blood* would murder a child and cut her up like a goat?"

Tsira shrugged. "Believe anything of anyone who isn't my mother." She stood up and put some money on the table. "Long life to your children," she said, because her ma raised her to be polite. Then she left.

She didn't really think about the murders after that. Figured it was just gossip: you heard a lot of strange things from travelers. Couldn't believe everything you heard from every Jok or Elgarson passing through. She just lived like she usually did. Did her work. Minded her business. Milked her goats. Sat by the fire in her old abandoned cave house, thinking about how she'd moved in temporarily and ended up staying for three years. And about how she felt older than she was, some days. And about making a change.

When the news came, it came quickly, new strange rumors springing up every time she went into town. A child had been killed. The child's mother attacked Coldstream village. Some humans went after her whole clan for revenge. Tsira couldn't make any sense out of it. All her neighbors were fighting like they hadn't all been trading at the same market three weeks ago. Not that she'd ever been all that social with any of them, but still. Seemed like a long road from selling someone a jar of apple-blossom honey to killing them in their bed at night.

She made the three-hour walk to visit her ma, just to make sure that everything at the winter seat was all right, and she found everyone acting like normal. Her ma told her again that she thought Tsira should declare herself vahn and get taken under a good reig's name. Then she told Tsira she looked thin and made her eat about a pound of cheese with her dinner.

Tsira escaped at dawn the next morning. It looked like snow—they got plenty of snow this late, up here in the mountains, even if you'd hit spring just a few hours south—but she decided to risk it. Figured she'd take a blizzard over swallowing her words around her ma all day. You couldn't argue with a blizzard or with Tsira's mother, but at least the blizzard wouldn't criticize your logic if you tried.

By the time she got close to home she was doing a pretty good job criticizing herself. It was dark, and the snow was coming down hard. She had on her good Cwydarin-made boots, the ones spelled to keep the water out. It was still damn cold. She put her head down and walked. Didn't see the pink until she'd nearly tripped over him.

He was just a little thing. She thought he was a child at first, but then she remembered that humans always looked smaller to her after she'd been with her clan. He was still pretty tiny, though. Weak and helpless on the ground. Dressed like he was Daeslundic military, in trousers instead of a skirt. His skin was very pale, his hair close to black, his eyes wide and terrified. She heard the quick rasp of his breath.

"Evening, pink," she said. Then she leaned down and picked him up.

# 3

---

*Red sugar white sugar, buy a pat of butter, run to the dairy man
and make the man an offer. Red cherries white cherries pick a peck
for cheaper, you can catch a pretty bird but you can never keep
her. Cold stove hot stove, try and spare your skin, find a troll to
marry you and never work again!*

— Leiscourt Children's Skipping Song, Trad.

By the time the army got to Coldstream Village, there wasn't much
left of the place.

From what Jeckran could tell there hadn't been much to begin with.
It was the sort of town that half the men in his platoon had joined the
army to get away from: a few little shops, a cluster of houses, and a
scattering of farmers' cottages trailing into the hills. Some of the houses
had roses at the front—though they were only gray vines now, rattling
against the stones with a sound like dice in a cup whenever the wind
blew—and one could imagine someone's old maiden aunt tottering out
to tend them.

Anyone taking the new highway could easily pass by Coldstream
without noting anything out of the ordinary. From horseback a man
was unlikely to notice how the laundry on the lines was hanging too
low, heavy with a week of ice. From a passing stagecoach a traveler
wouldn't see the corpses in the streets.

The mortal remains of the citizens of Coldstream littered the ground
like so many cigarette butts. Some were still dressed in their slippers and
nightcaps; most looked as if their necks had been snapped or their
throats ripped out before they could even think to run. The village

children were the only survivors. They were staying at a camp a few miles off, cared for by members of the county Women's Charitable Legion. The children had walked for miles before anyone found them, and no living person had entered the village in the two weeks since the children left it. In that time the silence had been absorbed into the very mud of the place. Most of the two hundred men of the company didn't speak above a whisper.

They passed a dead girl lying in a ditch: an unprepossessing young woman with nothing-colored hair and a cheap cotton dress printed with blue cornflowers. She could have been a scullery maid in any kitchen in Leiscourt. She could very well have been *his* scullery maid: Jeckran remembered similar faces from his childhood. He looked away, but not before noticing a few of the men making Elgar's Circles over her body and on their foreheads. "Looks like my baby sister," one of them said.

They walked past a baker's shop with loaves of bread and cream cakes arranged in the front window, preserved like specimens under bell jars by the cold. The baker was splayed facedown on the street just past the shop's door, one arm flung out in front of him. His head was lying a bit past his hand as if he was reaching to fix it back onto his neck.

Jeckran stopped to light a cigarette and took a long drag, feeling his shoulders climb back down from their positions beside his ears. One of the enlisted men walked up to his side, a dark-haired young person with a face that suggested he had spent his entire childhood watching his bread and butter fall to the floor butter-side down. A moment later Jeckran's batman Calt walked up, glancing between his friend and his superior officer as if he was afraid that something untoward might happen.

Calt gave Jeckran a little salute. "Lieutenant." His friend followed suit, drearily.

Jeckran gestured at the baker's body, attempting to make conversation. "Was that by chance, do you suppose, or did the troll responsible have a macabre sense of humor?"

Calt flinched. The boy Jeckran didn't know screwed up his face with enough vigor to open a case of wine bottles. "Dunno what *macabre* is, sir, but I don't see nothing humorous about it."

"No, I don't suppose that you would," Jeckran said, and blew a thin stream of smoke skyward, hoping that this would encourage the boy to go away.

Instead, the boy only scowled more deeply. "Calt's pa is a baker."

Jeckran suppressed a wince. He thought of apologizing, but what would the apology be for? So he just said, "Ah." It was a very familiar-feeling *ah*. He felt that he had a particular genius for always saying the exact thing that was most detestable to his companions and then emitting a feeble, wheezing little "ah" when reprimanded, like the last pitiful gout of steam from a kettle that had been lifted from the stovetop.

"Trolls must be terrible, wicked people," said Calt, who had been raised in an old-fashioned halton and who prayed for an hour every morning at dawn. "I've heard they don't believe in God even, just *philosophy*."

Jeckran looked down at Calt's wide, earnest face and was suddenly furious, though he wasn't entirely sure why. Perhaps it was that Calt still trusted his lieutenant, despite the fact that Jeckran's role was to lead him directly into an engagement that Jeckran was increasingly sure would be a blood-drenched farce. Perhaps it was that Jeckran was fond of Calt despite the fact that Calt was manifestly a bit of a turnip.

"Most northerners would say that they're normally perfectly amiable neighbors, and that their children are excellent models of thrift and studiousness for human youth. I imagine that the residents of Coldstream might disagree. Move along, men," he said. Then he continued walking toward the muddy gray hills before them, allowing the men to direct their glares at his back, if they so wished.

The whole campaign in Coldstream was a backward, embarrassing sort of affair. His men were too green, and his orders were too scattered, and everyone involved desperately wished that their platoon had been deployed to somewhere more congenial. Back to Mendosa, for example, where they could be shot at and come down with wizard-constructed wasting diseases because Governor Bryce, the great silly ass, would rather quarrel over fishing rights with the new conservative Mendosan government than simply draw up a new contract. In Mendosa, at least, one enjoyed the sunshine and occasionally ate a few fresh figs whilst contemplating one's ensuing demise.

At the moment, an incurable flux or a back full of bullets struck Jeckran as infinitely preferable to the awful silence of Coldstream village.

All the more disquieting was the fact that no one could agree on *why* six rogue trolls had suddenly wiped out an entire human village. Rumors were that the attack was retaliation for the murder of a troll child, but that had yet to be confirmed by any authorities. The local troll clans, as a result of their refusal to pay taxes to the government in Cwydarin, didn't benefit from their excellent police force, and there certainly didn't seem to be any connection to Coldstream. The local troll clan-heads claimed no involvement, and after a human mob had gone after the nearest troll village in retaliation, the entire region had dissolved into chaos. The army, from what Jeckran could tell, had been sent to Coldstream largely as a symbolic gesture in order to prevent riots from breaking out in Leiscourt. Antigovernment hysteria among Leiscourt's lower classes continued to mount despite a recent declaration from the great-clans of Cwydarin that they supported the Daeslundic government in its efforts to arrest, try, and execute any troll found to have molested a human in any fashion. The general sense in the penny press was that the callous assemblors and headmen who ruled Daeslund would prefer to see a thousand poor human villagers die instead of jeopardizing relations with their powerful troll allies, who were, presumably, involved in some sort of wicked scheme to torment the humans of Daeslund's northernmost counties.

Jeckran, for his part, thought that risking their lives in a deadly encounter with a group of rogue trolls before the situation was clear seemed an odd way to defend the value of the lives of ordinary Daeslunders. Unfortunately, he was only a single man with a single vote for his county assemblor, and his body was likely more valuable as a lifeless symbol of the government's devotion to its people than it would be if it were enjoying a glass of beer and a cigarette at a charming seaside resort.

It had been mentioned to Jeckran, once or twice, that he had an unattractive tendency toward cynicism.

Still, the whole business really did make one uneasy. It was out of the natural order of things. Jeckran had listened to as many thrilling bedtimes stories about Lorag the Fierce, the mythic troll monster, as any Daeslundic child, but trolls, in real life, held a certain *status* within Daeslundic society. To have a wealthy troll over to dinner was a tremendous social coup for any headwife with an eye to establishing herself as a hostess of note, while third- and fourth-ranked headmen's families contented themselves with serving troll-made cheese at parties or wearing gowns with troll embroidery. Scions of the oldest Daeslundic clans tended to boast about their lines having at one point been under the name of a troll clan-head, and therefore truly "blue-blooded" in the way that no upstart three-hundred-year-old clan could ever be.

Jeckran's own mother had sometimes claimed troll connections in their clan history, though Jeckran found this highly unlikely. His father's clan had only recently risen to a fifth-ranked headmanship, and his mother's family was a mixture of beautiful, ambitious, and utterly clanless Daeslundic women and the wealthy foreign merchants who had financed their slow march into society. Jeckran, therefore, was more the product of foreign and female ingenuity than he was of Daeslund's ancient troll-blooded heroes. Still, Jeckran, as a headman's son, had been raised to think of trolls as people to be admired. They had, so the stories went, brought magic and science to the benighted humans of Daeslund and raised up great human clans as headmen in their wake.

And now Lorag the Fierce had suddenly emerged from the storybooks to destroy a village and tear a baker's head off.

When Jeckran relayed the major's orders to dig pits for the bodies and make camp for the night, his men thought themselves very ill-used: either because they didn't relish digging graves, they disliked the idea of sleeping so close to Coldstream, they were lazy as a matter of character, or they were insubordinate as a matter of principle. They sulked, and the sergeant screamed, and to keep his men from shirking, Jeckran was forced to stand by with his boots slowly sinking into the boggy ground, watching them pound tent poles into half a foot of mud. He thought to lend a hand, seeing what a dreadful time they were having, but he couldn't quite bring himself to do it. He was, after all, an officer, and he didn't see the point of making himself miserable in some transparent attempt to endear himself to a group of men who disliked him on principle and would start making jokes about his eccentric personal habits the instant he turned his back.

Once his tent was finally erected, Jeckran retired inside and looked over his maps while Calt cooked his supper. It was another five hours' march to the nearest troll village, but of course that hardly signified. The local trolls—the Dachunath, their great-clan was called—were goat farmers, and they were used to moving between seasonal villages for better pasture for their flocks. They knew their land well, and if the Dachunath were involved, they would have little difficulty packing up and moving.

Jeckran wished, not for the first time, that someone in command could have sent a wizard scout to accompany the platoon. The odds were certainly on their side—an entire platoon sent to arrest six outlaws—but infuriated trolls were still not at all the sort of people Jeckran fancied engaging in a merry after-dinner game of seek-and-ye-find-me. If the trolls had a wizard with them, Jeckran thought, his men might as well have spent the day digging graves for themselves.

At least his second set of instructions was clearer, if no more appealing. He was to take a small patrol and arrest the troll who was sheltering in an abandoned cave-dwelling a day's march northeast of Coldstream. He found the cave on the map and circled it with a pencil.

According to their local informants, the troll had been living there peacefully for years, but locals claimed that a troll matching his description had been seen beating a human to death with another man's severed leg.

When Jeckran took his small patrol to engage the troll, he did not plan to be in the van.

Having exhausted all interest from his maps, he rummaged in his pack until he found his sketchbook and a pencil and began to draw a troll. It wasn't very good; something about the limbs struck him as unnatural, as if they were constructed from earthworms. He supposed this was for the best. He preferred drawing from life, but in this case, he was rather relieved not to be in such intimate proximity with his subject.

Then Calt materialized out of the ether to announce that supper was ready, which sent Jeckran jolting halfway to the ceiling of the tent. The sketchbook dropped from his lap and fell open on the ground, and Jeckran's face went hot. It was wonderfully in line with the normal run of his luck that, though his sketchbook was composed almost entirely of pastoral landscapes, crumbling ruins, and ships at harbor, it had happened to fall open on a group of nudes.

In fact, the sketch was of the famous marble *Thasmus Attended by Death's Daughters at Bonsetti*, which was as far as Jeckran had gotten on the eastern tour before he ran out of money. Judging from the fixed look of horror on the face of his batman, Calt was not familiar with Tiorgo Fante's later works, or indeed with any works of the ancient masters. Jeckran had to admit to himself that, lacking context, it did look a great deal like a soppy young fellow lolling on a boulder without any clothes on, while a number of very immodest young ladies pranced about in the vicinity.

"You're dismissed, Calt," he said, and Calt wasted no time showing himself out.

Jeckran ate alone, as usual, and pondered whether this little episode with Calt would do any damage to his reputation among the men. He thought not. His reputation among the men was already such that an additional rumor of his wanton un-Elgarite inclinations couldn't possibly hurt it much more. It was all rather trying. The fact of the matter was that he had as much actual experience of being wrapped in the embrace of a lover as he had in riding camels—which was to say that he had done both once, briefly and uncomfortably. It was not, of course, possible to explain so much to the most fervently Elgarite men of his platoon, whom he doubted would be very interested in a spirited debate of the philospher Armund Clearmaker's theories on the five expressions of desire versus Officiant Kesper Brown's views on cleansing meditation and denial of the flesh.

Once he was finished eating, Jeckran lay down with his wet woolen stockings toasting by the stove and considered the things that were wretched about the army. The blisters, and the dreadful coffee, and the horrid, endless damp. Camp latrines. The men, with their constant snickering. Tents, cots, insufficient shaving soap, dreary rations, dead girls in the mud, and being told that one had to march off and single-handedly attempt to arrest a ten-foot troll who had recently beaten a man to death with his own severed limb. It struck him suddenly how lucky the humans of Daeslund were that trolls as a people were apparently more interested in the construction of cities and the development of fine cuisine over the past eight hundred–odd years than they were in violent conquest.

Then, because he felt a sort of perverse pleasure in dwelling upon and thus increasing his own misery, Jeckran set himself to considering things that he missed. Gas lighting, for instance. He liked wizard-lamps the best, the kind that Adomo Darvey-Huntington had recently installed at his place in Corpsir, but Jeckran thought that gas was more appropriate to the idle fantasies of a member of the impoverished headmanship. Brandy and soda. Snooker. A new skirted suit that showed the calves to their best advantage. Being conveyed by cab in the winter, and conveying oneself in a curricle in the summer. Libraries. Adomo

Darvey-Huntington had wizard-lamps in his library, and probably someone at hand to bring a man a brandy and soda while he sat in an armchair. Jeckran missed armchairs.

He managed to soothe himself to sleep with thoughts of armchairs, and he woke up in a sort of confusion, his bedclothes damp with sweat, a choked-off scream in his throat. He had dreamt of Mendosa, of warm sun and bright screams and white paving stones spattered with blood, of rotting figs dropping onto rotting corpses, and that combined with his thoughts of brandy and armchairs served only to make the icy quiet of Coldstream even more deeply unreal than it had the day before.

He had thought, in Mendosa, that he would return home when the war was over. Instead he had brought war back with him, rattling with the Mendosan coins in the bottom of his rucksack. The heat and the terror sunk into his bones.

It started to snow the morning that they marched out of Cold-stream, a heavy, steady fall that blotted out anything more than a few feet away. As was usual, no one knew whether or not any persons in command would like for them to stop, so they kept on, even as the going got rougher through the drifts.

When he got out of the army, Jeckran thought, he would never walk again. He would purchase one of those Hexian floating carts and loll about like some particularly shiftless Leiscourt man-about-town, and his life would be the richer for it.

The image of that baker suddenly intruded into his thoughts. The rigid fingers stretching out toward the severed head. *Two hundred of us*, he thought, reminding himself of the odds. A company of two hundred human soldiers to apprehend six troll civilians. The odds *ought* to be in their favor, but it wasn't as if they had any modern accounts of war with trolls to refer to in the matter. The last similar skirmish had taken place a century before Jeckran was born. He touched the butt of his pistol. They would deal with these six first, and then the one in that cave up the mountain, and then it would be finished.

The odds didn't stop him from nearly losing his breakfast when the call went up that a troll had been spotted on their left flank.

The snow was too thick to see much of anything. They formed ranks with their hands thrust out before them, stumbling about in the muck. He could hear curses, labored breathing. Then, from his right, a scream.

The troll was only a few yards away, ten feet tall at least, a dead soldier gripped in his huge gray hand like a club. He was grinning.

Everyone started shooting. They shot, and the troll kept coming, holding the corpse across his chest with one enormous hand and cutting men down with the other, snapping necks as if they were twigs and grinning all the while. He was using some sort of magic, his hands first striking like clubs and then cutting into flesh like knives. Jeckran had read about this, about how trolls would smile as they fought to show their enemies that they weren't afraid, but to *see* it was more terrifying than anything he had imagined. The troll fought like he had never done anything else. He was bleeding from half a dozen wounds, and still he came on. He came on like an avalanche.

For the first time in ten years, Jeckran thought about God.

Someone prayed, his voice a wail, the words coming out in one long breath. *"Oh blessed Elgar I commend myself to your keeping grant me ease in reliving—"*

Jeckran gasped, coughed, and found his voice. "His *head*, you asses! Aim for his head!"

The men didn't hear him, and before he could convince himself to lie facedown in the mud and pray that his next attempt at life would be more virtuous and less miserable than this one, he was walking toward the troll, firing.

Hated Jeckran might be, but not a man in his platoon would say a word against his marksmanship. The troll went down at the third bullet.

For a long moment there was quiet. One of the men went to slap Jeckran on the back. "Don't *touch* me," he said and stepped away. His hands were shaking. He tried to light a cigarette, but gave up, cursing, the shaking too violent for him to manage it.

He looked at his men. They had formed a ragged half circle around him as if waiting to receive his council. He drew in a breath. "Good God. *Might* I invite you to reform your *fucking* ranks?"

A few of the men lurched to obey him, while others just stood there, vacant. One young soldier stepped aside to vomit.

And then a blast of trumpets.

An unthinkable noise. What thunder would sound like if it screamed. Someone said, "Oh, *God*." There was some magic in the sound, something being done to them. Jeckran's head was splitting, his vision blurred.

He smelled piss. Another blast followed, and another, and another still. More than six, far more, the sound endless and all around them, and then it was madness.

The men broke ranks immediately. Some charged forward and fired their rifles at random, some raced off in the opposite direction, and all the while the roaring came closer, closer, until the trolls were among them. The dead troll rose to his feet again, wiping blood from his forehead. Jeckran sobbed.

White snow, white teeth. The crackle of magic. The snow was turning red. Calt was close by. Jeckran could see his orange beard and the rising bulk of the troll behind him.

He shouted out a warning. *"Calt! Calt, for God's sake, behind you!"*

But too late. The troll picked Calt right off his feet and removed his arm. There was screaming. Jeckran didn't know if it was him or Calt or some other poor damned creature.

The troll tossed Calt's body away and looked toward Jeckran, and in that moment Lieutenant Phillim Kail Jeckran took careful stock of his position.

Many of the men had already bolted like green horses at the sound of a shot. Raw, honest terror was not what precipitated Jeckran's decision, though he held no illusions of himself as a man of great courage. Rather, he made a simple calculation: If he ran and survived, he quite likely would be hunted down and shot by his own military as a coward, making himself utterly infamous and bringing disgrace upon his entire family. If, on the other hand, he stayed to fight, the even greater likelihood was that within moments the troll facing him would rip his still-beating heart from his chest and toss it aside like a cherry pit.

Jeckran ran like hell.

The snow was almost to his knees, so every step was either a labored push forward or an ungainly hop. Still, he supposed that he should thank his expensive scholar-hall education; years of participating in games of hare and hounds had prepared him beautifully for running away from the field of battle and leaping over the dead and dying bodies of his fallen comrades. He passed the other deserters quite quickly.

Even when his side cramped, terror gave him speed.

Eventually, the sounds of gunfire and screaming faded away in the distance until there was nothing but snow, before him and behind him and falling slowly from the flat gray sky. He had no idea where he was: the rough road they had marched along was no longer visible.

It occurred to Jeckran that he had successfully escaped the trolls only to die of exposure, which annoyed him exceedingly. If he had known, he would have stayed for the battle and made his exit in a spatter of glory.

The entire situation struck him as deeply unfair. He had never entertained dreams of glorious battle: the decision to buy his commission had been a purely pragmatic one. He needed to make a living. His father had been in embarrassed circumstances for most of Jeckran's lifetime, and Jeckran's mother had been forced to sell the last few pieces of her wedding gold in order to scrape together enough for the commission. The army was a respectable career for a headman's son, and Jeckran's parents had nurtured hopes that he would distinguish himself. And he had, in a way, in Mendosa. He had been presented with a medal for valor, which led him to suppose that by "valor" they meant "extraordinary viciousness in a pinch" or "unflagging desire to keep his own worthless hide in one piece." If the desire to not die while still young was valor, he had exhibited far more of it today than he ever had in Mendosa.

He thought of what his mother's face would look like if she was to hear of his being shot for cowardice and had to stop to catch his breath.

He could see it in the air, his breath. A little white cloud. Would he be able to watch its shape change as he died? It was the sort of topic upon which a cleverer and more patient man could base an academic study.

He wondered if it was usual to have thoughts like these as one was dying.

It grew darker, and the sweat from running turned cold against his skin. His feet burned. He knew that Coldstream could only be a few hours' walk away, but he didn't know in which direction. The mountains, once distant, had drawn closer.

He walked.

His feet went numb. He imagined them turning black and made himself nauseous. He thought for a moment of lying down for a rest, then shook himself. That was how men died, lying down to sleep in the snow. If he could keep himself moving, he might live through the night, might make it to a village by morning. The money in his pockets would be enough for a bit of food, a change of clothes, and a seat in a stagecoach to the Esiphian border. That was all that he needed. Thinking about it cheered him enough to speed his steps, until he stepped into a crevice, heard a sickening crack, felt a gut-churning bolt of pain, and found himself lying in the snow with his cheek pressed into the ground.

He tried and failed not to whimper.

He thought it rather unfair that the pain in his ankle kept him from drifting off peacefully into unconsciousness, as one was supposed to when freezing to death, but the pain in his ankle ruined even this. Instead he found himself dreadfully alert and very aware of the silence around him. The sound of his own breathing was unbearable. He tried to sing a bit, but stopped at once: he sounded less like a man laughing in the face of danger and more like someone lying alone with a broken ankle on a godforsaken ice-covered mountaintop. And then, in the perfect silence following his singing, he heard footsteps.

Footsteps of someone very large. Jeckran thought to yell for help, then stopped. If a soldier of his platoon or an enemy troll found him, they'd ensure he enjoyed a worse death than quietly freezing. He would much rather have his mother believe that he had been torn to pieces by an outlaw border-troll on the field of battle than learn he had been shot after an unsuccessful attempt at desertion. Or, for that matter, having run away from battle and *then* been killed by a border-troll, which struck him as a particularly ghastly irony.

The footsteps grew louder, and a figure appeared out of the darkness. A massive figure, heavily wrapped in furs. The figure drew closer, and Jeckran knew what it must be even before he turned his head enough to see the troll's face. It was mostly in shadow, but the moonlight gleamed on his teeth as he grinned.

"Evening, pink," the troll said, and lifted Jeckran up like a child. Pain ripped through his ankle and terror through his gut, and he had just enough time to feel thoroughly ashamed before he retched and fainted.

# 4

*When we first struck upon the idea to write this little volume, the chief difficulty that occurred to us was how we might impress upon our readers that there is nothing whatever unsuitable, in the diet of the Dachunath, that should cause a young Human bride to avoid preparing and serving troll dishes to her husband and children as readily as the fashionable set might enjoy troll dainties during an evening's entertainment. It is our belief, as Troll parents with many intimate Human friends, that our cookery is as well-suited to promote Health and Vitality in Humans, particularly in Human invalids, as it is to the strength and well-being of the most powerful reigs of our clans, and far more economical and well-suited to the tastes of Daeslunders than the Human cookery of Nessorand or Esephe . . .*

—*From the preface of* The Dacyn Cookbook: Dainty, Wholesome, and Economical Troll Dishes, Especially Adapted for Human Tastes and Requirements *by Wyramwydcuden and Wyramwyddinas*

Tsira got the pink home before she'd decided what the fuck she was going to do with him.

*Think about the grandmother-books. That's what her ma would say. Use your head, be rational. Look at what you're doing. Think about if you're in custom. If what you're doing is out of custom, try and make an argument for it. If you can't make an argument for what you're doing, stop doing it.*

Tsira settled her new pink under some blankets and sat down in front of the fire. Then she picked up her whittling to keep her hands busy. Carrying home stray pinks on a whim sure as shit wasn't anywhere in her clan's grandmother-books. She was out of custom, so she tried to make an argument.

First mark: There was a story in one of the books about a clan-head rescuing an injured droveless vahn, and the annotations all agreed that the reig had done well, that you should care for the sick and injured when you could, even when they weren't kin or if it might cause some hardship for you. This pink had a broken ankle. He was definitely injured. He'd also fainted like an inbred goat when she touched him. Maybe he was sick; maybe just nervous.

Countermark: This pink was probably a soldier, and there was all of this mess with the army coming in to arrest those rogue trolls. He might be a danger to her clan.

Countermark to that: He was injured, she was far from her clan, and there was only one of him. There was no danger, no risk to the clan. Just her doing a good deed.

There was no one around to hear her. She snorted anyway.

He was good-looking, she thought. It always took her a while to see that in a pink. At first they just looked strange and undersized. This one was scrawny and white, except for his hair, which was dark. Still, she thought pinks could look all right. This one had a good face. Symmetrical. Not handsome like her ma's vahn Marden was handsome, but good enough if you didn't mind a skinny little vahn. Or *man*, she supposed, seeing as he was a pink and wearing trousers. Couldn't really be a vahn without declaring it, but he had the feel of one to her. Like he needed a steady hand.

She shouldn't be thinking about that. Not with him asleep and helpless.

Continuing the argument: She'd been wanting to find work in a human city, but the truth was she didn't know a thing about places like Leiscourt and Monsatelle. Having a pink helping her would smooth things out a little.

Maybe this pink would be grateful for her help. Maybe he'd do a little helping back.

Countermark: This pink had just been in combat with trolls, and now he was going to wake up in a cave with one. He might take one look at her and faint again. He might figure he was a prisoner of war. He might be scared out of his head.

He had a gun on him. A little pistol. She figured she'd let him keep it. He'd probably be more frightened if he woke up with it taken away. Him the size he was, being caught by someone her size might scare the piss out of him even if he *wasn't* worried about being held captive.

Not that she knew for sure. Tsira'd never had much time for being scared.

The little pink wasn't moving. Tsira checked to see if he was still breathing. He was. She let him be, then, and started fixing supper. Just barley porridge, like usual, with a little extra meat added. She needed to kill a goat soon and check on her cheeses.

Maybe this pink could help with the milking. Maybe with an extra set of hands at home she could do some hunting, have some fun, maybe get a decent skin or two. Maybe she could read one of her books she hadn't looked at in a while.

Maybe she was getting a little fucking ahead of herself.

The porridge was almost ready when she heard the pink stir a little. She turned to look at him. His eyes were open. They were dark eyes, same as his hair. They were wide, too. Probably scared.

Pinks smiled at one another a lot, she knew. She thought it was a little embarrassing. Too intimate for someone she'd just met, but she did it, anyway. When he flinched, she realized it was a mistake. She'd forgotten about her teeth, how they made humans nervous. She ran her hand back through her hair—it was getting a little long, past her shoulders now—and touched the gold torc she wore around her neck, which was a bad habit of hers. She was always rubbing at it when she was nervous.

"Hey. You're awake," she said.

"Why?"

He had a little voice. That always startled her, when she heard them talk. Those high little voices, like children. She tried to make her own voice low and gentle. "Why what?"

"Why am I awake?"

She shrugged. "Done sleeping, I guess."

"Why am I *alive*?"

She stared at him, not knowing whether to laugh or cuss. What the fuck kind of question was that? Why the fuck would she drag him back here just to kill him? Maybe that was the sort of thing they did where he came from, just killing people in their own homes. She hoped not. She'd rather not get stabbed in her sleep.

He stared back all big-eyed. She tried another smile, then turned to stir the porridge. She heard him wiggle around behind her and then give a little cry. Hurt his ankle, probably. "Shouldn't move," she said, without turning around.

He shifted again, and she was on him before he could train the gun at her. Tricky little pink. She squeezed his wrist a little, forced his hand back. Couldn't help but be surprised by how weak he was. He'd looked shocked, at first, at how fast she moved, and then he just looked scared.

She said, "Drop it."

He swung out with his other hand. She caught that hand, too, and held him in place. "Bad idea," she said.

He took a deep breath, and his eyes went darker. Then he gagged and started to thrash. She held him and waited until he stopped. He took another deep breath and looked her in the eye.

Brave little thing.

"Will you kill me now?" he said.

Tsira wasn't sure how to answer.

"Torture or otherwise maim me, then? Any disembowelings or violent removal of limbs planned at present? I'd like to make it clear at the outset that I would vastly prefer for you to start with ripping my head off and get it over with."

Tsira kind of wanted to laugh. This pink's mouth seemed to run faster than he could keep up with. She liked it. She always wanted to have a sweet little vahn around to chatter and fill the silences while she worked. She guessed he'd been to school, which was a good sign. The richer the pink, the more they liked trolls, wanted to be like them, wanted to get a little taste of troll power. Not that a runty border-troll like Tsira had much of that.

"No," she said, then dropped his wrists and grabbed his little gun. "I saved your life. You might thank me."

He gaped. "Ah. Thank you."

"Pleasure." She grinned at him. Hadn't expected him to say that. "I won't give your gun back. Don't want to have to dig out the bullets. Fucking *hurts*. What's your name?"

He paused. Then he said, "Jeckran. Phillim Kail Jeckran."

"Jeckran. Still pink to me. Hungry?"

Jeckran nodded. She went to the fire and served him up some porridge. "Careful. It's hot."

He looked into the bowl. "What is it?"

Part of her wanted to say that it was human meat, just to see his expression. She decided to be nice instead. "Barley and goat."

He hesitated, then started to eat. "Won't you have some as well?"

"I've only got one bowl and spoon."

He finished eating and handed the bowl back to her. She filled up the bowl again and sat down on the blankets by the fire to eat. He was staring at her like she was a pile of cold goat shit. She nodded at him. "I make you nervous."

"Yes, rather. I barely survived an encounter with your friends earlier today."

She shook her head. "They're not my friends. Never even met anyone from that clan. Wouldn't go running into a fight like that, anyway. Trolls would think I'm on your side. Humans would think I'm with the trolls. I'd get it from all angles."

"Why? You're a troll, aren't you?"

That surprised her a little. "You can't tell?"

"Tell what?"

She thought it was pretty damn obvious. "I'm half."

Pink frowned. "Pardon?"

"Half-human, like you."

He stared. "Ah. I . . . see. Your mother married a human?"

She grinned at him. "Nah. Ma worked in Leiscourt for a while, didn't have so many trolls to spend time with. Found a human who was interested. I don't know who he was. Think he might've been a headman. Doesn't matter, really."

Pink nodded. "And—you were raised around here? With the Dachunath?" He was *making conversation*. Like they were at a party. She smiled.

"Yeah. I left our clan a few years back, though." She'd struck out on her own not long after the first time her ma had suggested that Tsira declare herself vahn and let a good reig take her to clan, since her ma couldn't look out for her forever. Tsira'd said no. Said she was a reig who didn't need looking after, and she could be clan-head like her ma one day, and she'd prove it.

So far she wasn't doing such a great job.

Her new pink shivered. That wasn't a good sign. Her house was warm. His little voice sounded raspy when he spoke. "Have you ever lived down south?"

"No," she said. "Not yet, anyway."

He nodded. "What's your name?"

"Cynallumwyntsira. Tsira."

"Tsira. A pleasure, I'm sure," he said, and bowed. He shivered again, and she moved closer to him to check his temperature. He shied back at first, then he settled when she rested her wrist on his forehead.

"You're warm. Fever. Should sleep."

He nodded and lay back. His eyes were shining too brightly.

He slept for a while. Then he started to talk. Babble, really. He didn't call for his ma, like Tsira would've with a fever like that. He said "please" and "stop" and "no" and "I'll shoot." He cried without making any sound. He threw all of his blankets off. She brought in some snow from outside and held it against his forehead, and he cried some more and begged for her to stop. Then he started to shake all over.

Tsira's ma always said that fear was a waste of time. Still. Tsira didn't really want to watch him die like this.

It took all night before the worst of the fever broke. Close to dawn she stripped him out of his clothes, cleaned the sweat from his body, and then dressed him again. She held him to her chest and tried to spoon some broth into his mouth. She talked to him in Dacyn. "Don't die," she said. "Don't die, Pink. Stay here. Stay with me." She held the spoon to his lips. He turned his face away and groaned. "Drink," she said in Daeslundic. "Go on."

He whined. She shushed him and tried again. "Drink. Be good."

He softened against her. Took the broth in his mouth. Obeyed.

She talked to him in Dacyn like Tsira's ma had when Tsira was small and sick. "Good. Good little rabbit. That's a good little vahn. Strong and brave."

She hadn't had so much as a dog with her, all these years. Just the goats, with their warm fur and thoughtless eyes. She liked the trusting way he settled against her body. Liked the sound of a voice, the sour smell of mouth that could speak opinions. Liked the little whistling sounds of his breath when he finally slept.

She wasn't ready to let a little company go just yet. It was in custom to save a life, anyway.

She curled up a foot away so she'd know if the breathing stopped.


He stayed like that for two days. Wandered in and out of the fever while she tried to work and not fret like someone's old grandsire. Then he stopped wandering and just slept for a long time. Even that wasn't easy for him. He had a lot of nightmares, woke up screaming and shaking. Tsira'd seen that before, from old trolls who'd been through war. She figured he was remembering his own wars.

On the third morning, she'd just finished milking the goats when she heard that little voice calling out. "Tsira?"

She grinned and pushed her way through the blankets she'd hung at the mouth of the cave, kicking the snow off of her boots before she entered. The cave smelled good: she'd crushed up some lavender in a bowl earlier. Just because she was living rough by herself didn't mean she couldn't keep things smelling good. "Pink! You're awake."

"Much to my regret," he said.

Tsira wanted to laugh again. He was a funny thing. "Seem cheery. Feeling better?"

Jeckran raised his eyebrows. "Rather. Thank you."

"Pleasure. Made you this," she said, and picked up the crutch she'd whittled for him.

He took it. Looked pretty confused about it. "You made this?"

"Try it." She held out a hand. He took it, let her lift him up. It didn't take him long before he was getting around the cave just fine. Tsira nodded. "That's all right, then. Lie down. Rest."

Jeckran hesitated. "Are you sure? I could help you to—do whatever it is that you do. I don't like feeling a burden—"

Tsira snorted. "I'm starting a new batch of cheese. I don't need help. *Rest.*"

He opened his mouth like he wanted to argue. Then he closed it and lay back down again.

That was good to see. She liked a vahn who minded.

# 5

---

Jeckran slept for almost another entire day and woke up in the morning with the peevish, aching feeling of having spent too long abed. He glanced about. The cave was flooded with sunlight, the furs at the entrance pulled back to let in the sun and air. Tsira was sitting cross-legged on a pile of furs and blankets near the fire, whittling away at a chunk of wood. He had his silver hair gathered in a tail at the base of his neck, exposing the gold torc that he always wore. His massive hands were sure and steady on the knife. He caught Jeckran's eye and nodded, his face breaking into one of those wide, sudden grins of his. His sharp teeth gleamed a bit in the light.

"Hey, Pink."

Jeckran blinked. "Pink?"

"Yeah. You know. Human."

"Is it meant to be an insult?"

"Nah. I always say I'm half-pink. Pink's just because your tongues are pink. It's friendly sounding. *Human* is what you call a pink who owes you money."

Jeckran laughed, startled, and then shivered. A breeze blew in from the mouth of the cave.

Tsira gestured with his knife to a point directly to Jeckran's left. He moved very slowly, as if wary of startling Jeckran, who wondered whether he might have lashed out at Tsira in his delirium. He had come close to shooting his batman once, when the fellow suddenly cropped up behind him. It wasn't something that he liked people to know about, that nerviness. It was common enough, he supposed, among soldiers, but it made one feel wretchedly vulnerable to be found out. Tsira said, "Put that on."

Jeckran looked to where Tsira pointed and raised his eyebrows. What he had thought was part of his bed was, on further inspection, a woolen cloak. Jeckran pulled it on, appreciating the warmth and weight of it. "Thank you. But wherever did it come from? Surely it's much too small for you."

"I made it."

"You *made* it? When?"

"Yesterday."

"And did you spin the wool and weave the fabric yourself as well— yesterday?"

Tsira gave him a look that Jeckran couldn't interpret. "Bought the cloth last autumn."

Jeckran ran a hand over the thick brown wool. "I imagine that it must have been expensive?"

"A little."

"I'll pay you back, of course. As soon as I'm able."

"No need."

He always answered so shortly that Jeckran would have thought him irritated by the questions, if he hadn't begun to suspect that it simply had never occurred to Tsira that there could ever be cause to utter sentences of much more than two or three syllables in length. Perhaps it came from living alone.

Jeckran inspected the hem of the cloak. The stitching was very fine.

"I suppose that I should make preparations to leave soon. How far is it to the nearest town?"

Tsira tilted his head back and forth. "In snow, on a bad leg? Two days to the closest village. To anywhere bigger two weeks, maybe three. I'd wait for the melt, if I were you."

Jeckran frowned. "But that will be months, surely."

Tsira gave a shrug of assent.

Jeckran frowned. "But I—won't you find it rather trying to have me under your feet for months on end? Most people find me *extraordinarily* trying when they're subjected to me for more than half an hour."

"It's easier for me," Tsira said.

"Why?"

Tsira grinned. "I ignore about half of what you say. Like the other half just fine."

Jeckran grinned back, startled, then looked away and changed the subject. "What are you making now?"

"A bowl."

"Oh," said Jeckran. "It's not for me as well, is it?"

Tsira gave him another look. "You want to keep sharing?"

"No, not particularly. But I hate to think of your going to so much trouble."

"No trouble."

"But it must be, surely."

Tsira beckoned with his knife. Jeckran took up his crutch and hobbled over to where Tsira sat, then he eased himself down onto the blankets at his side, starting when Tsira put a hand on his elbow to steady him. Tsira handed him a chunk of wood and another, smaller knife. Jeckran turned the wood over in his hands. "What's this for?"

Tsira shrugged. "Keeping you busy."

They whittled away in silence, which was only broken when Tsira repositioned Jeckran's hands on the knife and the wood. The third time that Jeckran nearly cut himself, Tsira laughed aloud.

"I know," Jeckran said. "I'm dreadful at it." The shape of a bowl was already emerging from Tsira's hands.

Tsira, to Jeckran's great surprise, mussed his hair. It made Jeckran's skin prickle. He could not recall when last he had been touched like that. He suspected it must have been sometime in his childhood. Perhaps not even then. He had no recollection of any adult touching him more than was necessary to keep him bathed and dressed and fed. Headwife Jeckran's warmer maternal feelings had largely expressed themselves through anxious twittering over the state of her younger son's health and studies on the rare occasions upon which he was presented to her in the drawing room. When he thought of her, he thought of the shoes he was made to wear when he saw her—which always pinched his toes—and of the jaundiced color of the roses on the drawing room carpet.

"Pink."

Jeckran started.

Tsira took the knife from him. "Cut yourself."

Jeckran looked down at his hands. He had somehow managed to slice open the tip of his left thumb. It was a deep cut, bleeding heavily. "Oh. Damn."

Tsira grasped Jeckran's wrist and pulled his hand up above his head. "Hold it."

As blood trickled down Jeckran's wrist, Tsira left and returned a few moments later with a few strips of cloth and a bottle. He sat again at Jeckran's side and handed him one of the strips of cloth. "Press."

Jeckran pressed the cloth hard against the cut. "I feel an absolute dolt."

"Look like one, too," Tsira said.

"You're laughing at me. I suppose I deserve it."

Tsira opened the bottle of brown liquid and poured some of its contents onto one of the strips of cloth. There was the strong smell of alcohol. "Only a little." He pulled Jeckran's hand away from the wound and dabbed at it with the wet cloth. Jeckran hissed at the sting. When he finished, Tsira gestured to Jeckran's abandoned knife and bit of wood. "We need to find something else."

"For what?"

Tsira grinned at him. "Keeping you busy."

This, over the following weeks, proved to be a somewhat difficult task. Though Jeckran was keen to be helpful—he himself was quite surprised by this, as he had never caught himself having such frequent fits of helpfulness in the past—there were few things he attempted to turn his hand to that Tsira could not do vastly more quickly and effectively. Many days passed during which he occupied himself almost entirely with drawing—Tsira had a small collection of stubby pencils and old newspapers—and fretting. There was a great number of things to fret about. Chief among them—beyond what in the wretched earth he was going to do once Tsira tired of his presence, a problem he was desperate to avoid contemplating—was the puzzle of Tsira's gender. He had, in the feverish haze of their first meeting, thought of him as *he*, but then he had woken up one night in a state of utter, gut-liquidating panic at the realization that he *didn't actually know*. He had a vague recollection of having learned from his governess when he was very small that trolls did not have *ladies* and *gentlemen* in the way that humans did, and so it was very important when one was being formally introduced to a troll to attend to which terms were used in the introduction in order to avoid causing great offense and embarrassment. He could, however, not for the life of him remember what those terms *were*, and in any case, there had been no formal introduction, either before or after Tsira had lifted his frozen carcass out of a snowbank. So far, it had been a nonissue—with only two of them in the cave, it was never necessary to use any pronoun other than *you*—but at any moment, a third party might arrive, and Jeckran positively dreaded the thought of mucking it all up and provoking great offense. Or worse, *hurt*. Tsira was so unfailingly *kind*, and that kindness stirred in him an impulse toward kindness that Jeckran was unaccustomed to. He was used to witlessly crashing about in other people's sensibilities like a wild boar in a laboratory. The thought of *hurting* Tsira by blurting out a question to which he ought to have already known the answer further liquidated his innards to the point of absolute crisis, and on many of his desperate sprints to Tsira's tidy little outhouse, he spent a great deal of time freezing with his pants around his ankles and contemplating whether it might be best to build a sledge, ride it rapidly down the mountain, ascertain Tsira's proper mode of address from the tradesfolk in the nearest village, and then hike back up in time for one of Tsira's horrible suppers.

Tsira, Jeckran thought, was aware of this preoccupation, though he—Jeckran was resigned to thinking of Tsira as *he* until he could bring his elaborate espionage project to fruition—seemed to put it down mainly to boredom. He was kind about that as well: Tsira dug up a battered deck of cards—for Crwydarinand—and a pair of dice, and they taught each other games, and he told folk stories from his clan in exchange for Jeckran's human stories. One afternoon Tsira simply handed him a broom, and Jeckran occupied himself quite happily with sweeping and spreading fresh straw from the storeroom—he amused himself, at one point, with idle thoughts of whether he or Tsira would cut a finer figure in an apron with a feather duster—until Tsira called him to eat. "Wash your hands, Pink."

Jeckran went to the basin by the fireside. "Very well, troll. How mad you are for handwashing! I imagine you'd make me wash my hands if I was at death's very door."

"Probably."

Jeckran shook the water off of his hands and took his place at the table. "Why? Is it religious?"

"No. So you don't get sick."

Jeckran raised his eyebrows. "Trolls believe that illness is caused by dirty hands?"

"Not dirt. Little bugs, too small to see. They don't cause all illnesses though, just some of them."

"Oh," said Jeckran. "I read that some wizards in Hexos believe that. I had assumed that they had spent too much time stuck indoors doing alchemical experiments."

"Maybe," Tsira said, and he ladled some stew into Jeckran's bowl. "Still true, though. Our clan's wizard has a few dozen scrolls about that stuff. What makes people sick, what the insides of bodies look like."

Jeckran frowned slightly. "The Elgarites say studying that sort of thing is in defiance of God's will. Though I suppose most foreign wizards would say that's why the average Daeslundic life span is so short." Then he ate a spoonful of stew and grimaced. "Your cooking hasn't improved."

"No one's ever complained before, Pink."

"No one but you has ever *eaten* it before, troll. Let me cook tomorrow, won't you?"

Tsira looked at him. "You know how?"

"I—well. I've done a bit of it, here and there."

Tsira looked skeptical.

"At least let me try. You've done far too much for me already. If I can produce an edible meal for you, it might be a step in the direction of thanking you properly."

Tsira shrugged. "I don't need thanks."

"But I need to thank you," Jeckran said, startled by how much he meant it. "Please?"

Tsira regarded him for a long moment, his amber eyes fixed thoughtfully on Jeckran's face. "All right," he said finally, and set to eating his porridge.

Once Tsira finished his meal, he sat back in his usual posture: back very straight, legs widespread, with one hand braced on each thigh. He trained his gaze toward Jeckran for a few breaths longer than Jeckran found entirely comfortable.

"You married?" Tsira asked.

"No."

"Why not?"

"That's a very impertinent question."

Tsira cracked a little grin. "You pissed on me in your sleep a while back."

Jeckran grimaced. "Point taken. And if I answer your impertinent questions, will you answer mine?"

Tsira shrugged. "Sure."

"Very well, then. Question for question? And I don't suppose that you have anything to drink?"

Tsira stood up and disappeared into his storeroom, reappearing shortly with a large earthen jar. He opened it before putting it down in front of Jeckran. "Mead."

"*Mead?* How very merry-days-of-yore. Why not wine or beer or a nice brandy?" He took a sip of the mead and choked. "It's absolutely dreadful."

Tsira gave him an even drier look than was his custom. "Got a bee-hive not far off. You want wine, plant grapes."

"Did you make this yourself as well, then?"

"Yeah."

"Is there anything that you *aren't* able to make yourself?"

"Yeah. Drink."

"Why must I drink?"

"You asked me a question."

"I had no idea that this was to be a drinking game," said Jeckran. He took a swig. "However did our forefathers stand to drink this stuff? Maybe it suffers from lack of proper atmosphere. We should have tankards. And trenchers. And . . . a minstrel. And dogs fighting in front of the roaring hearth. And some ruddy-faced old man pinching the wenches."

Tsira ignored him. "Why aren't you married?"

"I never found a girl who suited me, I suppose. Or whom I suited. Most of the prospects bored me. Drink."

Tsira complied, throwing back a large swallow from the jar without seeming to notice how the stuff burned. "Why?"

"I found that most of them had nothing of any interest to say. That was two questions. Drink, troll."

Tsira did. "Need to talk in bed?"

"Good God, you're rather crude, aren't you? I suppose that you don't. But one should at least be able to manage some light conversation with one's wife. There was a girl—she was to be my fiancée. I hadn't yet gone so far as to ask her father for her hand, but it was certainly known that we had an understanding. By the end she asked me to make a clean break. She said that when I looked at her, she felt that I despised her. I imagine that I wouldn't fare much better with a gentleman who might like to household me: I'm certainly not sweet-tempered enough to make a good addition to a society dinner table." He paused. "That was another question. Drink."

Tsira did so. Jeckran thought he might rattle his composure. "Have you ever slept with a troll?"

Tsira snorted. "Yeah. Ever slept with a human?"

Jeckran flushed. "No. Not exactly." He didn't think that having had his hands down Adomo Darvey-Huntington's trousers a few times should count: they had barely even kissed. He paused. "How was it? With the troll."

Tsira shrugged. "Depends on the troll. Never been with a human. Think it might be . . . complicated."

Jeckran considered the mechanics of a human woman attempting to be intimate with someone of Tsira's size and conceded, "It would seem likely to require a certain degree of . . . delicacy."

From that point they continued drinking without bothering to ask any questions.

It did not take long for Jeckran to become quite thoroughly swozzled, while the only sign that Tsira felt the drink was when, for the first time in Jeckran's presence, he removed his fur cloak. Underneath he wore trousers and a simple woolen vest over a thin shirt. He rolled his sleeves up, and Jeckran nearly choked. "You're like a damned anatomical drawing!"

"What?"

Tsira's arms were, indeed, more like a piece of classical sculpture than anything Jeckran had ever seen on a living man. Jeckran waved him over. "Come here."

Tsira obeyed amiably enough, and Jeckran stood to examine him more closely. "I ought to draw you someday."

"Yeah? You'd want to?"

"I would. I'm rather good at it. Won some prizes in school. Can you flex?" Tsira laughed and did so, and Jeckran swore under his breath. "Good God." He had never really been one for very muscular men—he associated those sorts of bodies with fellows who spent a great deal of time drunkenly arguing over local hammerball matches—but Tsira was so clever, and kind, and his body was *confoundedly* nice to look at.

Jeckran, in that moment, suddenly became very aware of the entirely inappropriate path his thoughts were leading him down.

The room gave a hard counterclockwise lurch. Jeckran lurched forward with it and found himself pressed up against Tsira's chest. Tsira gave his back a pat. "All right?"

Jeckran nodded and remained where he was. He looped one arm around Tsira's waist to steady himself. "It's a *horribly* dangerous path," he told Tsira. "With all manner of . . . cliffs and things. And that dreadfully spiky sort of hedge."

Tsira smiled at him. "What the fuck are you talking about?"

*Oh, no.* He oughtn't have said that. He was an entirely wretched, useless, and altogether ridiculous personage, and he was always saying thoughtless things and making an ass of himself. Tsira and his magnificent arms would be far better off without him. He told Tsira so, mournfully. "You shouldn't have saved my life."

He wobbled a bit. Tsira braced him with one hand at the small of his back. "Why?"

"I'm an utter reprobate. I'm a coward and a deserter. I say rude things for no reason whatever and never say pleasant things when I ought, I broke a young girl's heart, and it's been two years since I've written to my mother, and I don't even know if you're a *he* or not, which is *unconscionably* rude of me." The word *unconscionably* came out as more of a multisyllabic oat porridge. The world was shaking. Tsira was laughing, his big steady hand on his back.

"I'm a reig," Tsira said. "A *she*, in Daeslundic. You can't tell from looking. Some reigs have cocks, even." She paused. "You were worried about that? Why didn't you ask?"

"I didn't know how to do it *politely*," Jeckran groaned, torn between hot-faced humiliation and a knee-shaking amount of relief that Tsira was *laughing*. He loved it when Tsira laughed. "And now I've done it in the least polite way imaginable because I'm a dreadful wretched ass. You smell *wonderful*." He pressed his face into Tsira's chest and breathed in the warm-sun-on-straw smell of her. Tsira. "Why don't you get rid of me? You ought to toss me down the mountain."

Tsira gave a soft huff of a laugh. "You're drunk off your ass."

"But you shouldn't have saved me. Why did you?"

"Looked like you needed it."

"Oh," said Jeckran. "You smell of the stables. The hay and the leather. I used to hide in the stables when I was a boy at school. One grows tired of being thrashed, and one is never thrashed by a horse." He swallowed. "I think that I might be sick."

Tsira sighed and carried him outside.

Jeckran woke up the next morning with a grinding headache, the taste of rot in his mouth, and a sensation of impending horror weighing upon him. At first he attributed this to the usual spiritual malaise that followed an excessively riotous evening, but then he realized, to his dismay, that his current unease had a cause: he had gotten far too drunk; said any number of awful, rude, embarrassing things; and generally made an enormous ass of himself. He quite expected to be rebuffed when he offered Tsira a tentative "good morning." Instead, Tsira looked up from her whittling and grinned. Still the same Tsira, unaltered.

"Hey, Pink. Look like shit."

Jeckran grinned back, his relief making up for the fact that the skin of his face hurt. "I feel like it."

Tsira shrugged. "Sleep it off."

Jeckran was already getting up. "I think that I need a cup of water. And my pistol, to bring an end to my suffering."

After procuring a cup of water—Tsira refused to give him his gun back—Jeckran sat down next to Tsira and watched her whittle. After a time he was seized with an odd impulse to lean his head against Tsira's shoulder, an impulse that he did not act upon. Tsira looked down. "Not going to sleep?"

"No. I'm not tired in the least."

Tsira indicated her whittling. "Want to try again?"

"God, no! Once was quite enough."

Tsira stared at him for a moment, then she rummaged about in the straw basket that she used to store various odds and ends. After a moment, she handed Jeckran a few scraps of cloth, a needle, and a skein of thread. Jeckran regarded this assortment. "What's all of this for?"

"Should learn how to sew," said Tsira. "No reason not to."

"I suppose that you're right. It's only that gentlemen don't do needle-work, as a rule."

"Yeah. Don't cook. Can't use a knife. Don't sew. What do *gentlemen* do?"

Jeckran considered this. "If we're not forced to enter into gainful employment? Hunting, in the summer. With guns and dogs and horses, I mean, not in the way that you do it. Attending the theater or the opera, and balls, during the season. At night we drink and gamble our family money away." He paused. "Not much that's of any use to anyone."

Tsira looked at him in silence, then said, "Sounds like rich city trolls. They've got magic for everything, so they don't need to work. My ma told me she met a vahn once who didn't know what meat looks like before it's cooked. I'd rather be useful, myself."

"I believe that I would, too. Is it usual for vahns to be more useless, as a rule?"

That made Tsira laugh, which made him feel pleased with himself. She said, "Mostly just the rich ones."

"Maybe that ought to be my purpose in life, then. To be a rich vahn. I've already mastered the uselessness." He noticed an odd expression gust over her face, but he became distracted by his needle, which he finally managed to thread. "Look!"

Tsira grinned, clapped him on the shoulder, and proceeded to teach Jeckran a simple stitch. She then left him to it—with instructions to keep practicing until his seams stopped coming out crooked—and headed out to hunt.

Tsira was only gone for an hour or two—in which time Jeckran produced three extremely crooked seams and cursed a great deal—when she came charging back into the cave. Jeckran looked up. "Good God, whatever is—"

"Pinks coming up here. About six. I could kill them all, but I'd rather not. You want to run out and meet them or stay with me?"

"I'll stay with you, of course," Jeckran said, instantly rejecting, he realized, an opportunity to be guided back to the nearest town in order to remain in a cave with a troll who, though undoubtedly awfully kind and patient and clever and well-built, might not want to cook dreadful porridge for him in perpetuity. Tsira did not acknowledge this. Instead, she walked to the fire and used a long stick to push back the logs and stir up ashes over the coals. Next, she walked to the furs at the door and pulled them down with a wrench.

Jeckran watched, puzzled and alarmed. "Tsira," he said, "what are you doing?"

"Making us look long gone. If they think we'll come back, they'll wait for us." She glanced toward Jeckran. "Bring your things to the back. Wait."

Jeckran obeyed, gathering up his furs and his sewing and carrying them into the storeroom. Instead of waiting, however, he returned to the main room in time to see Tsira kick over a chair. The temperature in the cave had already dropped dramatically, and Jeckran pulled the cloak that Tsira had made him more closely around himself. Tsira saw him and snapped out, "*Pink*. Go. Wait."

Jeckran did as he was told, and eventually Tsira joined him with a few essential items in her arms: some heavy furs, their bowls and spoons, her knives. These she placed on the floor before turning her attention to the storeroom's entrance. The entryway was very small; Jeckran himself had to duck his head to pass through it, and Tsira was forced to practically bend in half to squeeze through the hole in the rock. Beside the hole was a large boulder. Jeckran had never paid it much attention, but suddenly he grasped its purpose. This, however, did not clarify the chief problem. "How in God's name will you move that thing?"

"Like this," said Tsira, then she picked up a sturdy stick from the floor and, with the aid of a smaller rock beside the boulder, used it to lever the boulder across the opening with one enormous heave. The door now shut, Tsira sat beside Jeckran and said, panting slightly from the exertion, "Close your mouth before moths fly in."

Jeckran closed his mouth. "When I was seven, my governess said that if I gawped, I'd catch flies."

Tsira shrugged. "True."

"Are *all* trolls so dreadfully ironical or are you a particular case?"

Tsira mussed his hair. Jeckran, by way of retaliation, flicked Tsira's ear. Then Tsira froze, pulled Jeckran tight against her chest, clapped a hand over his mouth, and whispered, "*Don't scream.*"

A moment later Jeckran heard them as well. A group of men, but no voices that he recognized; none were boys from his regiment. He could only hear what they said in snatches.

"*Gone—fucking snow—*"

"*How long—*"

Jeckran pushed gently at Tsira's wrist, taking care to not make any violent gestures that might indicate a desire to scream for help. Tsira hesitated and then lowered her hand, and Jeckran pulled away and sat beside her, casting her a reproachful look. Tsira shrugged. The voices grew louder: the men had come farther into the cave. Jeckran screwed up his face at the shrill, piping sound of their voices, before realizing to his horror that he must sound exactly the same. The voices were muffled through the stone.

"So what the hell do we do now?"

There was the sound of stomping about.

"Spend the night here, I—*mumble mumble mumble*—tomorrow morning."

"*Mumble*—castle—*mumble mumble*—have our asses."

"Well—*mumble mumble mumble mumble*—put a vest on a bear and tell him it's a troll we caught?"

They weren't proper soldiers, this was clear. No commanding officer would sound so unsure of his decisions, regardless of how utterly idiotic he might suspect them to be. Still, their lack of military discipline did not make Jeckran a whit more pleased at the thought of a gaggle of jackasses sleeping in Tsira's home while the two of them bunked in the storage room. It was, for one thing, damnably cold, and the stone walls disagreeably damp. He looked at Tsira despairingly, and almost laughed when he saw the expression reflected on Tsira's face.

Then, suddenly, came a voice very close at hand. "What's this?"

There was a pause and a tromping of feet. Then another voice. "Looks like a needle and thread." Jeckran's stomach lurched, and he looked down toward his sewing. The needle and thread were gone.

"I know *that*," said the first voice, "but what's it doing back here?"

Another pause.

"Look at that rock. Do you think that looks like you could move it?"

Jeckran thought that he might be sick. Tsira got silently to her feet. Jeckran scrambled upright as well, as quietly as he could, and started when Tsira put a hand on his shoulder and handed him his pistol. They waited.

"I'm going to try," said the first voice.

There was a muffled thump, then a groan and a peal of laughter.

"Guess you can't move it," said a third voice amidst the general hilarity. "You great dafty."

Jeckran sank to the floor, feeling as if his heart might burst from his chest. Tsira joined him, looking pastier than her usual self.

Then a determined voice spoke. "There's something back there. *Mumble mumble*—or gold. If we all push together—"

"Gold," muttered someone else. "It's a *troll*, not a fucking fire-breathing dragon—*mumble mumble mumble*—and a princess back there, too?"

"I'll help," said another voice, inspiring a chorus of agreement. Jeckran shot Tsira a panicked glance. The rock slid slightly forward. Someone said, "Harder!"

Tsira picked up the lever to the door and leaned close to Jeckran's ear. "You ready?"

Something about the sound of Tsira's voice made Jeckran want to respond with something absurd like *For anything!* Instead he gave a tight nod.

"Then watch my back," said Tsira, and in an instant she opened the door.

Everything went extraordinarily quickly. The men barely had time to draw their weapons before Tsira had grabbed two of the men by the throat. "Drop your weapons or I'll snap their necks."

"I would do as I was told, fellows," Jeckran said, sauntering around the boulder. "Or it will likely be the worse for you all."

One of the men yelped. "He's got a toff back there!"

Jeckran aimed his gun at an older man, the only one of the lot who looked as if he might know what to do with a pistol. "Go on, then," he said.

The men hissed but obeyed. The older man had a decent-enough-looking weapon, but the rest of the idiots were armed with antiques: a rusty pistol, two ancient rifles, a blunderbuss, and an actual damn *sword*, which looked as if it had spent the last fifty-odd years hanging above a mantelpiece.

"Who sent you?" said Tsira, but the men were too preoccupied with glaring at Jeckran to respond.

"Fucking *toff*," said one of them. He was young enough to have spots on his forehead. "Just *like* you fucking *headmen*. Rather mess about with trolls than honest working men. You sucking that troll's cock back there?"

Jeckran went hot, and he was about to respond when Tsira cut in, that tremendous voice of hers dropping into its deepest register. "No," she said. "It won't fit in his mouth."

Jeckran could barely suppress a cackle, though his cheeks remained pleasantly and embarrassingly hot as he contemplated the thought. The boy quailed visibly. Tsira's grin widened. "You're not soldiers. Who sent you?"

The boy swallowed. "The government doesn't give a toss about us. There's a fellow who *cares* about humans who sent us. We won't give him up."

Tsira tightened her grip around one of the men's throats. The man gurgled. The boy blanched. "Don't! I'll—" The boy broke off from whatever he was trying to say and began to choke. He put his hands to his throat, gagging, and shook his head, his breath coming in painful-sounding wheezes. It did not look at all like an act.

Tsira raised her eyebrows. "Are you cursed?"

The boy nodded. Jeckran frowned. "What on earth would a *wizard* want with you?" He was acquainted with a number of wizards, and most of them were far more interested in prattling on endlessly about their deadly boring research and ingratiating themselves with people who might provide them with free food and drink than they were in hiring gangs of bumpkins to hunt down trolls.

"Might have an idea," said Tsira, but she did not elaborate. Instead she jerked her head toward the weapons on the floor. "Gather those up," she said to Jeckran.

Jeckran did so. Tsira then ordered the men to stand along the far wall of the cave, while Jeckran stood nearby, training his pistol on them. Tsira went through their pockets one at a time. Eventually, she straightened, grasping something in her hand. "Look at this."

She tossed it to Jeckran, who failed to catch it and had to contort himself in all manner of absurd ways to pick it up off the floor without losing a clear shot at the men. It was a gold coin, though its octagonal shape was unfamiliar. Jeckran frowned and read the inscription aloud. "*Minted by order of Director Balach.* I think it's from Hexos."

Jeckran knew Hexos was an odd little city-state on an island off the coast of Esephe. It used to have nothing on it but rocks and pelicans, but it had been purchased from Esephe by an international consortium of wizards about one hundred years ago. He didn't remember all the history: judging from the name he imagined that a certain amount of alcohol was involved in its establishment as a nation. The greatest wizard in the world was supposed to be the Lord-Mage of Hexos.

"Don't suppose a fancy Hexian wizard would hire this lot," Tsira said. She looked at the men. "Someone from Hexos hire you? He give you this coin?"

"And what was that name I heard before?" asked Jeckran. He was sure he had heard something about someone having their heads if they returned without a troll. "What castle?"

Several of the men began choking at once.

Tsira shook her head. "Never mind." She glanced at Jeckran. "What should we do with them?"

Jeckran shrugged. "Kill them?"

One of them whimpered. Tsira appeared to consider this for a moment, then shook her head. "How's this," she said to the men. "I count to fifty. You start running. You still here when I finish, I rip your head off. Come back again later and I rip your balls off first." She grinned. "One."

They were gone before she got to three.

Jeckran and Tsira straightened up the place in silence. Tsira hung the skins back up at the cave's mouth and built up the fire, while Jeckran put the furniture in order. Then they both sat in their usual places by the fire and stared at each other for a long moment.

"Sorry," Tsira said. "For covering your mouth before. Should have trusted you."

"Don't mention it," Jeckran said. "I'm sorry for being such an ass last night."

"Don't matter," Tsira said, then paused. "Been thinking, Pink."

"Take care not to overexert yourself, Tsira."

Tsira snorted. "I've been planning it for a while. Since I found you.

More since I saw how we get on. I thought we could work together. Sell ourselves as bodyguards, or cover the stagecoaches. I'd do it myself, but it'll be easier with a human along. We could make money, See the world. Not have to spend the rest of our lives in a damn cave, hiding whenever someone comes to kill me." She paused and added, "It's not just me. You're a deserter. They'll shoot you if they catch you. You can't go home. Can't stay here, either. You can come with me, though."

This was the longest speech Jeckran had ever heard from Tsira. He imagined her proposition: spending the rest of his life as a person of the worst sort, selling his martial services to unsavory types with a partner from the lowest ranks of troll society.

He grinned. "Very well."

"Yeah?" Tsira grinned back. "All right. Want a bath? You stink."

"Not any worse than you do, goatherd."

Tsira laughed and mussed his hair. It made Jeckran happier than it probably ought.

It took Tsira almost two hours to melt and boil enough snow to fill the enormous tub that Jeckran pulled out from the storeroom. The tub was made of leather stretched tightly over a wooden frame; Jeckran was quite sure Tsira had made it herself. "I had thought that you used that tub to store potatoes."

Tsira glanced over at him, clearly amused. "Get in."

"Me first?"

"You're smaller. Less dirt on you. Maybe more per inch."

Jeckran laughed and began to undress, then paused, suddenly recalling his Daeslundic modesty. "I don't know—ought we put up a curtain, or something?"

She snorted. "Lived in one damn cave for weeks now. Not like you're keeping modesty in the vahns' hall." Then more gently, "I'll keep my back turned, if you like."

"That will make it more difficult to chat," Jeckran said, and continued undressing, his heart beating a bit faster. He didn't want Tsira to look, exactly, but he didn't mind if she did.

The bath was wonderful; it was Jeckran's first real hot soak in several months. He did a bit of moaning as he washed, which provoked a "hurry up" from Tsira. He did, scrubbing out his dirty hair with a bit of dreadful-smelling soap that Tsira had provided, and then he borrowed Tsira's knife and had a go at shaving and trimming his nails. Thus cleansed, he dried himself as quickly as he could with a ragged bit of cloth and sped across the room to his pile of furs, burrowing underneath them for warmth. "Your turn."

After Tsira's snorting at Jeckran's notions of modesty, Jeckran decided that he oughtn't feel any guilt when his eyes drifted toward Tsira as she undressed. She had, Jeckran thought, a very beautiful back. Other than a few small scars, there was nothing to mar the velvety gray-blue of her skin or to distract from the play of muscle underneath it. As she stepped into the tub, he forced himself to tear his gaze away, but not before he registered her pectoral muscles—she had the torso of an extraordinarily well-built human man—and the fact that she did *not*, in fact, have a cock too big for him to fit in his mouth. Not that that was something that he should be *considering*, he reminded himself, immediately feeling like an ass all over again. Tsira's cock—or lack thereof— was *entirely* beside the point and had nothing whatever to do with him, and though she had laughed at the idea of modesty, his contemplating her genitals in relation to the size of his mouth when she had not invited him to do so could only be considered the *height* of caddishness.

He endeavored to distract himself with conversation. "You never finished that story you were telling me the other night. About the wizard who taught the raven to repeat secrets?"

"Oh, right," she said, grinning, and dove back into the story, which had them both laughing as she gave herself a good scrubbing. Having finished her ablutions, she stepped out of the tub and pulled on her cloak, then stood by the fire to comb the knots from her hair. Jeckran watched her. After a long moment, he spoke.

"Do vahns keep their hair long as well, or just reigs?"

"We all do. I keep mine plainer than most. Some keep it longer, put it in braids around their head, wear combs in it, that kind of thing. Not too practical, really. I might cut mine. Shave my head."

"That would be a pity," Jeckran said, then felt his face go hot.

"Why?"

"I'm sorry. It isn't *my* business whether you cut your hair. It's just such a lovely color." It was like freshly cleaned steel.

She looked surprised. He himself was surprised that he had said it. He was generally awful at giving compliments: they usually came out all wrong, so he said nothing pleasant at all to avoid embarrassment. Tsira said, "Thanks."

"You're welcome."

She nodded. "I'll take first watch tonight. In case those fellows come back. Mind waking up past midnight?"

"Not at all."

There was a pause. Tsira spoke again. "We'll be heading out soon, I guess."

Jeckran smiled. "Yes," he said. "I suppose that we will be."

# 6

*It is never to the advantage of a young lady to accept a proposal in the first instance. This is not to say that a young lady who has received a good proposal ought to play the coquette! Rather, she must exercise prudence and caution and not worry that a sign of hesitation might be taken as an insult. It is a sign of a charmingly feminine sensibility for a young lady to beg a suitor for more time to consider, as his wonderfully flattering proposal has so utterly overwhelmed her . . .*

*. . . in the case that a young lady or gentleman receives a proposal of householdry, a greater degree of forthrightness may be required. In the case that the householdry is a love match, the householded-to-be ought to respond in the same manner as a young lady who has received a marriage proposal, though young gentlemen ought to avoid as much as possible any girlish excess of sentiment. In the case that the proposal is political or economic in nature, it is customary for the householded-to-be to request at least a week's time to discuss the matter with their family . . .*

—Mrs. Barton's Manual of Manners, *Cordoline Barton, 6568*

When Onna and her mother arrived in Leiscourt after an arduous twelve-hour journey by coach, they spent the night at the home of one of her mother's friends, a lady novelist who for twenty years had been householded with a woman who made oil portraits for a living and, in her leisure hours, somewhat alarming still lifes featuring a great quantity of animal skulls. The two ladies were very warm and very kind and had all sorts of interesting stories to tell about their travels—they had recently gone on a grand tour across the eastern continent, and they showed Onna and her mother a great number of photographic slides to illustrate their recollections—but Onna made such a distracted and unresponsive guest that eventually her mother suggested it might be best for her to have a glass of sherry and retire early. Onna did so, and then she lay awake in bed, wracked with nerves, until her mother came into the room with her to sit on the edge of her bed and rub her back.

"What are you so afraid of, Onna?"

"That I'll *fail*," Onna said. She felt sick to her stomach.

"And then what?" her mama asked.

"Then I'll be miserable, and I'll barely ever see Sy again, and I'll have to go back to Cordridge-on-Sea in *disgrace*."

Her mama kept rubbing her back. "And then what?"

"I don't *know*," Onna said.

"Well, I'll tell you," Onna's mama said. "You'll go home with me to Cordridge-on-Sea, and you won't be the very first girl from the whole county to have gotten into Weltsir. But you'll do something else that's just as good, if not better, and your grandparents will tell every Awati person in all of Leiscourt about how brilliant and accomplished you are in either case." She kept rubbing her back. "Your papa and I are very proud of you, Onna. You're a good, diligent, sensible girl, and we know that you'll make a success of yourself one way or another."

Onna suspected that her mother, who'd worried for years that her daughter was too wrapped up in academics to make an acceptable marriage, had a young man with a good income in mind as the *something else*. It was still comforting to hear it. Mama and Papa were proud of her. There would always be a *something else*. The comfort of hearing it, and the back-rubbing, and the sherry, at last managed to send her to sleep.

Onna woke up long before dawn in a blind panic and commenced desperately to turning through her notebooks in search of the parameters that she had spent so many months working on, which she was quite sure she had completely forgotten.

She had worked herself into such a state of exhaustion and nervous tension that in the final hours before the exam she found that she had become numb, and she walked through the Weltsir College of Magic's imposing gates with the dull eyes and steady gait of a murderer headed to his execution.

The building that housed the examination hall was a wonderfully grand old place, all arched passageways and flying buttresses. The famous empty plinth was even bigger than she had ever imagined from reading about it, and the low buzz of ancient magic echoed soothingly in the back of her head. Onna, however, was in no state to admire the atmosphere. In fact, she was in no state to notice anything at all, but even in this condition she couldn't help but notice the stares she attracted as she whisked down the corridors, a drop of neatly mended blue muslin in a sea of spotless dark suits. Her throat tightened. Every other person attending was wearing a black Weltsir suit, with its traditional trollish skirt: even the few other girls she saw were dressed in a female version, with the skirt lowered to the ankles. She had known, of course, that the suit was what one wore when one was a student at Weltsir, but as her frugal mother's daughter, it had never once occurred to her that she ought to purchase one *ahead* of time in order to better look the part. She supposed that perhaps most of these students were, like Sy, rich enough that buying an entire new suit of clothes simply in order to take an exam was of no consequence. Many of the attendees were accompanied by their tutors: one very grand-looking young man with his hair in gold-tipped braids came with an entire retinue, and as he passed, Onna heard people murmuring about *First Headman Greenfeld's son.*

Onna felt a brief, mean little flash of resentment: she knew, of course, that many of the greatest families of Daeslund had spent years desperately attempting to form marriage alliances with minor families in the increasingly wealthy and powerful Mendani federation, but there was something disagreeable about seeing a boy so outwardly similar to her in age, complexion, and magical education being followed about by great flocks of servants. If her great-grandparents had only remained in Awat instead of leaving during the last Halton movement, perhaps she would be sweeping about dripping in gold as well, she thought, immediately before she squelched the idea and felt dreadful for having had it. Here she was regretting that her family hadn't remained longer in Awat while simultaneously thinking ill of her departed great-grandparents, which was about as un-Awati a thing as she could imagine.

At last Onna arrived at the examination hall, but her attempt at entrance was barred by a little man holding a large ledger, who smiled at her with great condescension. "I'm very afraid that you can't go in there, my dear. There's an *examination* about to be held." He spoke very slowly and with exaggerated enunciation, as if he was under the impression that she was so provincial that she couldn't understand him otherwise.

"Yes, I know, sir. My teacher registered me three months ago, so I think that everything must be in order."

The man started slightly. "Registered! And your name?"

"Gebowa. Onna Gebowa."

He opened his ledger and turned through several pages, then stopped to stare at an entry for far longer than Onna imagined was quite necessary. "I do see a Gebowa here. An O. Gebowa, registered by a Mr. Joachim Heisst." He closed the ledger and frowned. "*You* are O. Gebowa?"

Onna swallowed hard, then smiled. "Yes, I am, sir. *Onna* Gebowa."

"It is rather irregular to have a student registered only under a first initial. How are we to confirm—"

Onna could feel her eyes beginning to string with tears and was forced to cut him off before they began to overflow. They *couldn't* keep her from taking the exam; they couldn't *possibly*, it was *illegal*. "If anyone else comes and says that he's called Gebowa and is here to sit for the exam, I shall give up my seat to him at once. *Please* let me in," she said, and the man, if grudgingly, did so. The other things that she wanted to say to him—that she imagined the authorities would take a very dim view of her being denied entry to an exam because she couldn't afford a new suit of clothes—remained caught in her throat. She hadn't the stomach to be so impertinent to someone in charge, and he hadn't, after all, *said* anything about her being a girl, or having a common-sounding accent, or not being properly dressed. Perhaps he suspected every young man who walked through the door of being a potential impostor.

There was no more time to contemplate the question, however, as only moments after she took her seat, the papers were handed out, and the examination began.

It was easy. So easy that she almost laughed when she read the first question: it was like the sort of little parametrical puzzle she would have done for fun after school when she was nine years old. The entire exam was like that; one trifle after another. She glanced up to see if the others looked as relieved as she felt, and she was surprised to find herself surrounded by drawn faces and hunched shoulders. Her fellow students, in fact, looked so dreadfully grim that she began to wonder if she had been mistaken in her first impressions. She took her time with the rest of the exam and double-checked her work. She corrected a small spelling error and added an extra defining term to a parameter, in case the first one were to break down in field conditions. Then she glanced around herself. Everyone else was still writing. She considered triple-checking her work but decided against it. She raised her hand for her paper to be collected.

Stares, coughs, and muffled hisses followed her out of the room, but Onna pretended not to notice. She had once read that they had wizard-lamps to light the streets in Hexos and that at night the city center was as bright as midday. That was how Onna felt as she left the exam. Lit up by magic.

That evening the two artistic ladies were treated not to a silent, mournful ghost of a young visitor, as they had the night before, but to a creature so electrified with relief and spilled-over nervous energy that she talked continuously for over three hours, pausing only to drink too much of their (very nice) wine and to eat too little of their (not nice at all) boiled beef. This strange mania, however, did not last for very long:

Onna was not a very accomplished drinker, and so the wine—happily enough for her understanding but overwhelmed hostesses—sent her soundly to sleep very early in the evening, and the stress and exhaustion of the preceding days kept her asleep until late the next morning.

The practical examinations were scheduled for the next afternoon, and Onna arrived promptly at one o'clock. She joined a whole crowd of students waiting outside of the examination rooms, and her nerves were now calm enough for her to notice that a great number of her fellow scholars were staring at her with great intensity. She also noticed, with some surprise, that all of them were carrying thick notebooks. She had known, of course, that it was *permitted* to write one's parameters down, but it hadn't occurred to her that anyone would need to do so.

She waited in the crowded stone hall for an absolute age, watching student after student be called into the room and then emerge a few minutes later, some looking edgily pleased, others despondent, still others pale and shaken. The crowd thinned, and the air between the gray stone walls grew cooler, the worn red carpet reemerging into view. Then, finally, her name. "Gebowa!"

The examination room was small and dim and bare, paneled in dark wood and dominated by a rough-hewn table that Onna thought looked far more suited to ancient bearded men slopping mugs of ale than to an academic setting. Behind the table sat four old men. They all looked very similar, with their thin gray hair, pinched faces, and black suits: like academic owls. Their expectant smiles withered quickly as she entered.

"*You* are O. Gebowa?"

It was like having the same horrible dream every night. She nodded, addressing the bespectacled owl who had just spoken. "Yes, sir. Onna Gebowa."

"I see." He smiled again. "Your scores on the written exam were . . . very satisfactory, Miss Gebowa. Who is your tutor?"

"I haven't my own tutor, sir. I attend Mr. Joachim Heisst's school. In Cordridge-on-Sea." As she spoke she became terribly conscious of her

Northwestern accent. She had never in her life felt so thoroughly a simple unspoilt village girl. From the way the owls looked at her she thought that perhaps they found her very charming, as if she had ridden into town in the back of a hay wagon.

It made her want to scream. It made her want to weep with frustration.

"Cordridge-on-Sea! Where they make the pencil erasers?" said another owl, a fat one.

Onna nodded. "Yes, sir. Where they make the pencil erasers."

The owls exchanged significant looks. "And is your father a wizard?"

She shook her head and bit back a flare of temper. Onna's papa was an exceedingly gentle and indulgent parent in almost every respect, but he had boxed her ears for speaking smartly to an old lady one day, and even now she trembled at the thought of being rude to a person with gray hair. "No, sir. My father owns a shop. My mother was an authoress. She wrote *The Trials of Resalind*." She supposed that they might as well know all of the disreputable things about her at once and get it over with.

"Ah," said the owl. "I *see*! How very charming."

Onna swallowed back the furious lump in her throat. "Should I begin my demonstration now, sir?"

"Her demonstration!" said the fat owl, just as amused by this as he had been by Cordridge-on-Sea.

Onna pulled in a deep breath and spoke very quietly. "Has a Morgan's wall been erected in this room?"

She hadn't really needed to ask—it was clear enough that there hadn't been—but she had thought it politely respectful to assume that they might be using magic more subtle than what she was used to. The owls stared at her. Eventually, one of them answered, "No, there hasn't been."

"Do you suppose that it would be possible for any of you to do me the great favor of raising one? I want it to be very clear that I have no way of summoning anything from outside."

The owls exchanged looks. Finally, one spoke up. "We don't have any parameters here. All examinees must provide any parameters that they plan on using during the course of the exam."

"Yes, sir, I understand that." She paused. "Have you pen and paper?"

A small, bearded owl handed both to her. She wrote down the parameters very quickly, then handed them back. "I believe that you will find that these are in order, sir."

The bespectacled owl took them and removed his spectacles to scrutinize the parameters for a moment before looking back at her. "You have Morgan's wall committed to memory?"

"I have all of the parameters in the *Reclid's Wizard's Primer* committed to memory, sir." She paused, then added, "The twenty-seventh edition."

Two owls whispered together. The bespectacled owl stared at Onna's piece of paper for a long moment. There was a strong smell of copper, followed by a furious whispered conversation. Onna supposed that they were trying to establish whether or not the Morgan's wall had gone into effect, though it was obvious: she could feel it pressing down against her like a woolen blanket. She smiled. "If you don't mind, gentlemen, I will begin my demonstration."

She reached into her blue velvet reticule and pulled out an apple. It was a small apple, slightly mottled with brown spots. She placed it onto the table. "I have been interested for a long time now in illusion. Many wizards think of it as the most frivolous school of magic, but I think that it has been underestimated." Another apple appeared, identical to the first. She switched their positions back and forth as she spoke. "To create objects that consume no matter or energy, but exist only within the mind of the observer, can have all sorts of practical applications." A third apple appeared between the first two. "The difficulty is that most illusions only withstand the scrutiny of the eye, and sometimes the ear. They can't be touched or smelt or tasted. This is the course of magical study that I would like to pursue, if I had the great honor of being accepted into Weltsir." Two more apples appeared, one on each side of the other three. She exchanged all of their positions in a few decided movements, then stepped back. Performing magic made her feel much better, just as it always did. She could feel herself smiling at the warm glow of it. "Only one apple is real. Please feel free to examine them."

The owls, with some hesitation, each picked up an apple. They squeezed them and sniffed at them. The fat one picked gingerly at the skin of his with one fingernail. The bespectacled one took a bite out of his, then gave a decisive nod. "This one is certainly real. Without a doubt."

The other owls exchanged glances. The fat one bit into his apple with a loud crunch and shook his head as he chewed. The others followed suit and looked at one another in silence. The bespectacled one and the fat one exchanged apples and tried another bite. More silence. The smell of fresh apples filled the room.

"There is only one weakness to this illusion, and it will allow you to discover who has the real apple," said Onna. "An illusion can only be created inside of each of your minds. I wrote the parameters to describe every aspect of what we expect of an apple. The way it feels in your hand, the scent, the sound when you bite into it. There is, as far as I know, nothing at all about apples that I didn't include within my parameters, which means that in written form the parameters for this illusion are over two hundred pages long. I beg your pardon." Onna took the bitten apple from the bearded owl's hand. "Because of the extent of the parameters, the illusory apple will behave just as you expect an apple to behave." She smashed the apple down onto the table, and the owls jumped as it spattered. "An apple should be crushed if it strikes a table, but the table is unharmed." She drew a small tissue-paper flower from her reticule and laid it onto the table beside the smashed apple. "The trouble is that an illusion cannot influence a physical object, unless the parameters for the illusion contain contingencies for interaction with that object, and even then, as the complexity of the interaction rises, the realism becomes more and more difficult to maintain. Sir, would you please place your apple on top of the flower?"

The fat owl did so, and the whole group of them murmured in

unison at the odd result: the apple rested as delicately atop the flower as a honeybee. Onna waved her hand, and the apple vanished. She looked to the bearded owl. "You, sir?"

His apple also perched on top of the flower. Next came the remaining owl—the oldest of them all. His apple crushed the tissue paper flower to the table. Onna waved her hand again, and the apple that she had smashed—along with the spattered remnants—vanished, too. "Thank you," Onna said and curtsied.

There was a long silence.

"Did you compose those parameters with the help of your teacher?" asked the bespectacled owl.

"No, sir. Most of it was composed over the summer holidays," said Onna.

Another long pause. The bearded owl leaned over to whisper something into the fat one's ear.

"I must say," the fat one said after a moment, "it's very *irregular* to perform illusions during the admissions examination. Why, it was banned for years, wasn't it?"

"Oh, yes," said the one in the spectacles. "From seventeen to forty-three, I think."

Onna felt sick. She tried to keep her voice from shaking. "But it—it isn't banned now, the regulations didn't—"

"Well, not *banned*," said the bearded one. "But certainly *very* irregular. An unnatural sort of magic."

Onna bit hard at her lip. The fat one looked up at her, then glanced away. "Thank you, Miss Gebowa. You may go."

She curtsied again and left. Her mouth was very dry, and she could feel her stomach churning. She had eaten nothing that morning, and had drunk three cups of strong coffee. A headache was building behind her eyes. She thought about what had just happened over and over, as if somehow she might crack the secret of it and discover exactly where she had gone wrong. It was, however, increasingly plain to her that she had gone wrong long before she had ever set foot in the room.

She walked out of the university grounds and into the street. Since a great number of anxious mamas and papas still waited outside the gates, she continued onward, walking fast, ducking through side streets and alleys out from the wide, tree-lined avenues of the university district and into the warrens of Leiscourt that held the common people.

Only once people around Onna become ordinary looking—with women in patched dresses and men with rough laborers' hands—did she pause to look around herself. She was on a poor, shabby street filled with poor, shabby people. She couldn't see a single building that was not in desperate need of repainting or a single suit of clothes without the soft grayish cast that came of innumerable washings. Some were tinged yellow from never having been washed at all. In the gutters flowed filth of a type that did not bear closer examination, and in the air was a very curious perfume: part night soil, part burning coal, part roasting meats and freshly baked bread. Vendors were tempting the workmen who walked past with the whole cast of Leiscourt delicacies. Here there were pickled whelks, and there jellied eels, here meat pies and there sweet buns. She considered the whelks, then noticed a stall offering coffee for two sen a cup. The woman selling it—a morose-looking, weary-eyed old lady—cut her a sliver of seed cake to go with it and waved Onna off when she tried to give her another sen. "You look like you could use it, dearie. Bad day, is it?"

"Yes, awfully. Though it's much better now, thank you."

She finished her coffee and cake and returned the cup. The wild, trembling energy that had driven her to now had subsided, and she was suddenly aware of how hungry she was and how her feet ached. She bought a meat pie—it tasted like, and she hoped that it was, mutton—and attempted to retrace her steps. She looked about as she walked, at the way the sunlight struck against the crumbling bricks of the buildings and illuminated the filth in the streets. The sunlight was different here than it was at home. There it was a friend, or in summer a nuisance: here it was a gossip, a betrayer.

She soon realized that she was hopelessly lost. And as the light dimmed, the streets changed. The darkness softened everything, smoothed over the cracks, swept the rubbish into the corners and out of sight. Young couples emerged. This was a place that was better in the darkness, when the children were put to bed and the gas lamps softened the hard lines of their mothers' faces. She saw one young woman walking some paces ahead wearing a beautiful green satin gown, and for a moment Onna thought that she might somehow have wandered into a fine neighborhood, where the members of the headmanship might take the night air. Then she drew closer and saw the stains on the dress and the sloppily mended tears, along with the pinched, hungry, childlike face of the girl wearing it. She paused, startled and appalled, and in the time it took her to recover herself, the girl drew away, became a grand lady again for a moment in the darkness, then turned down an alley and disappeared from view.

A blaze of light ahead: a music hall. Onna stood a few paces away from the entrance, watching the patrons walk in. They were all sorts: rough-looking fellows with unshaven cheeks and battered boots, troops of rascally boys with enormous mustaches, plump smiling couples just come from a day's work and ready for a jolly night. There were no women alone. They all filed in, and Onna, after only a brief hesitation, went in after them.

She had come this far in the desperate hope that she could forget what had happened in the exam today, and she welcomed anything that might distract her.

It cost two sen for a seat in the stalls, and only one for the gods. Onna paid a sen and climbed up to the balcony, where she was almost knocked off her feet by the clamor of the audience and the strong smell of spilt beer. She elbowed her way to a place by the rail, bought a ginger beer from a hawker, and turned her attention to the stage just as the curtain rose. The first act was a comic one, performed by a small boy billed as "Len, the Genius Infant of One Thousand Impressions." He was dressed as a fat old fishwife, and he sang a comic song about what a trial it was for a girl to grow old. With great laughter and applause, the audience joined in the chorus. Next came the Dancing Singing Lewis Sisters and a troupe of Amazing Alabian Acrobats—though at one point one of them shouted out a thank-you to the crowd in what struck Onna as a terribly strong West Leiscourt accent for an Alabian. Then, finally, arrived the Great Wizard Nephor, dressed all in black with a spangled cape around his shoulders. Onna had managed to forget about her dreadful day, but she winced at the word *wizard*, which yanked her out of her haze of enjoyment and directly back to reality, with her dreams dashed and the floor of the theater disagreeably sticky under her feet.

The Great Wizard Nephor was not, in fact, any sort of wizard at all. At best he was some kind of practical. He could do a very simple charm or two, but he had clearly not had any schooling. Still, Onna was riveted. His costume, his gestures, his thrilling way of announcing his next trick; all of it was so wonderfully calculated to amaze, to delight, to astound. Onna had always approached wizardry as an application for mathematics: a successful bit of magic was simply proof that there had been no errors in her parameters. She had always wondered at other people's reactions to her studies: the gasps or smiles or quick steps backward. Here, in the pantomime, she began to grasp what else magic could be. She watched how the audience reacted, how they clasped their hands at the buildup of a trick and sighed with pleasure at the climax.

Power. There was power in magic.

She recalled the odd looks cast between the owls that afternoon and thought she understood. The law might have forced Weltsir to allow her to take the exam, but Weltsir would only ever accept exactly who it wished. Those men had seen a pretty young village girl in a faded dress and thought her charming, harmless, an amusing little diversion. Then they had seen what she could do, and it had disturbed them. She was not what they had expected, not what they wanted, not what she was supposed to be. Not what belonged.

She would not, she knew then, be going to Weltsir. There had never been a chance. She had been a very foolish girl to ever believe otherwise.

She watched the rest of the pantomime without seeing it and drank her ginger beer without tasting it. A strange foreign ache gripped her chest.

Later, as she was attempting to find her way home along the unfamiliar streets, like someone groping their way along the walls of a darkened room, she heard a scream. A dreadful scream, with something cold and sharp and primal in it that snapped Onna's head around like a slap, looking for the source. Then there was another scream and the sound of running feet, and Onna found herself running, too, toward the sound, driven by the vague thought that she shouldn't allow a woman who sounded so afraid to be left alone in the dark.

She went skittering around a corner and came to an abrupt halt. A strange tableau appeared at the opening of an alleyway, the gas lamps casting all of the figures in deep shadows. A few men stood around, shocked and silent. On the ground was a still form, too large to be human, and a woman knelt next to it, wailing.

"She was just stepping out for a beer," the woman said, weeping so violently the words were unclear. "She was just ste-stepping out for a minute. Said she'd only be gone for a tick, she said. Stepping out, just for a *minute*—" The woman clutched a hand to her chest, a massive, blue troll's hand with a ring around the householded finger.

Onna walked away, her heart rattling in her chest but her breathing steady. She ought, maybe, to have been frightened, but instead she felt nothing at all. It was as if the hot pan of her own petty worries had been dropped suddenly into a tub of cold water: a hiss and a sizzle and everything was gone. Nothing but cold iron left, and the sting of brushing up against someone else's monumental tragedy.

This new dullness in her feelings served her well when she finally arrived home. Her mother was waiting in the sitting room, apparently having saved up her hysterics for her daughter's arrival, since she unleashed them in a torrent that lasted, it seemed to Onna, for hours. Finally, when her mother paused for breath, Onna broke in. She didn't even think to mention that she had just seen a dead troll lying in the street: her mother was already close enough to apoplexy as it was. Instead, she cut straight to the very last thing that she wanted to say aloud.

"I won't be admitted."

"Nonsense," her mother snapped. "Go to your room at once!"

Onna didn't have the stomach to argue.

She returned to Weltsir at promptly two o'clock the next day to find a large crowd already gathered at the gates. The names of the accepted had already been posted. Onna excused her way through the crowd, then looked immediately to the middle of the list, past Farren, Jonethon, and Gate, Kail. There was no Gebowa.

Onna had never had a chance. She had told this to herself, of course, but some very foolish corner of her mind had held on to a dry little currant of hope. Now even that was gone. She pulled out her handkerchief and pretended to cough: there was no reason to let this crowd of strangers see her cry. But then she wet her handkerchief in earnest because it wasn't fair, it wasn't fair, it wasn't *fair* that she could be clever and polite and work hard and mind her elders and smile prettily and mend her dresses and clean her nails and chew every bite twenty times and do *everything that every adult had ever told her she ought to do* and *still* not get what some silly troll-blooded boy with a pony and a tutor and a house in the country got just because he *wanted* it. And the more she thought about it the harder she cried, and the harder she cried the more she wanted to kick everyone around her in the shins.

Then she heard her name being shouted.

She looked up. It was Sy, rushing toward her through the crowd: Sy looking older and handsomer than ever. "Oh, *Onna*," he said, and he reached out as if he meant to touch her before he caught himself and tugged his handkerchief out of his pocket instead. "Here, take mine."

"*I worked so hard,*" she said. Or she attempted to say it, at least: the words came out more as a series of loud blubbering noises, which only served to make her feel even more horrible and wretched and downtrodden.

"I know," Sy said. "Come on, Gebowa. Let's go have something to eat."

He took her to an awfully expensive-looking little Esiphian-style chocolate shop and ordered two bowls of chocolate and a large plate of orange-scented biscuits. Sy pushed the plate toward her and said, hesitantly, "Your dress is very pretty."

"It's the *same dress* that I *always wear*," Onna said, and she teared up again because she had failed at all she had worked for, and her parents would be *so* disappointed, and she *didn't even have a nice new dress*.

"Oh, dear," Sy said, and pushed the biscuits a little closer. Then he ventured, "Weltsir is absolutely awful."

Onna brightened a little. "Is it really?"

"It really is," Sy said. "Everyone is always mocking my accent and laughing at how I don't eat meat and talking about how I'm clanless and my father made his money in *trade*. Most of them will barely speak to me outside of the lecture halls."

"Golly," Onna said, dabbing at her eyes. She knew that it was un-kind, but the thought of Sy having an awful time at Weltsir without her really made her feel a bit better. "My father has barely made any money in trade at all. I wonder what they would think about me?"

"You know, I'm not sure," Sy said. "The only thing that they despise more than people without a house in Leiscourt is people who are clev-erer than they are. But you are awfully pretty, so maybe they'd overlook your being clever and ask you to marry them." Then he said, "I'm an idiot to have risked our friendship just to get into this place. You really do mean a great deal to me, you know." He looked at her very intently.

Onna picked at a biscuit in order to avoid his gaze. She found herself oddly irritated by his sheep's eyes. She didn't see why, in a moment of great personal trial for her, he felt such a great need to talk about his feelings for her, as if whether or not he still thought she would make someone a fine wife one day must be her greatest concern. Then she said, "I don't know what to do now. Everything was leading up to Welt-sir. I can't just go home and spend the rest of my life helping Auntie Waneda with the cooking. Papa would never get over the disappoint-ment. *I* would never get over the disappointment." Though, to be sure, the prospect of having to go home and tell Papa that she wouldn't be the first in their family to attend a real university was horribly dispirit-ing. She could already see him shaking his head and patting her hand before retreating to his chair.

Sy, of course, would never understand. He was a thoroughly Daeslundic boy, and in stories about Daeslundic boys they were all generally orphans entirely unburdened by mamas and papas. Daeslun-dic boys were meant to break away from their families and get into scrapes and eventually end up draped in riches and glory and lovely young ladies. Though that did all sound very nice, Onna was a young Awati-Daeslunder, and a girl to boot. She had things to *consider*, and making sure that she did nothing to cause her parents embarrassment in the eyes of their friends and relations was chief among them.

Sy ran his finger around the rim of his cup. "You could always retake the exam next year," he offered. "What else could you do, disguise yourself as a troll and go to Cwydarin? Take a boat to Hexos and offer yourself as 'prentice to a magister?"

Onna looked up, startled. "*Hexos*," she said. "The University of Hexos has its entrance examinations every autumn. If I go now, I might just make it. They admit students from anywhere, don't they?"

Sy stared at her. "Onna," he said, "how will you possibly go to the University of Hexos? You've never been farther from home than Leis-court. And they only admit the *best wizards in the world*."

"Oh, well," Onna said, with her eyes downcast. Her heart was pounding a bit with excitement. This could be her last, best chance. A new school in a new country, a strange wizard island where people were judged by the quality of their research and not the name of their clan or the source of their father's fortune. A place where she might make a name for herself and her family, if only she was brave enough to seize the chance. She could do it, she thought. She *could*. She was already reviewing her notes in her head, thinking of how to improve her illusions. She was already thinking of how to break the news to her mother. She was already imagining Weltsir at her back. "I suppose it's fortunate that I'll have the entire sea voyage to prepare my demonstration."

# 7

*Great riots broke out in Leiscourt today upon the news that the Fynechun troll clan agreed to pay a mere twenty tocats per head to the families of those who were killed in the Notorious Coldstream massacre of three months ago, in which more than one hundred innocent Human souls lost their lives most brutally and Horribly. Humans of all ages, mostly belonging to Leiscourt's conservative Elgarite halls, took to the streets to call for justice for the poor people of Coldstream from the wealthy trolls and troll-blooded headmen responsible for this vile Agreement. It is the opinion of this Newspaper that this insulting payment is yet more proof of how many Daeslundic headman reject the Principles of Elgar in favor of Trollish Thought . . .*

—Leiscourt Crier, *Mornmonth 5, 6572*

Two days after the gang of humans came to the cave, Jeckran woke up to a blast of cold air.

He sat up. There was enough of a dim glow from the banked fire that two things were suddenly and dreadfully clear: The furs at the mouth of the cave had been left pulled aside, and Tsira was gone. He licked his lips. "Tsira?"

There was no response.

He stood and went to look outside.

It was very dark, and he could hear snow falling. There was nothing but that for a long moment: the darkness and the whisper of the snow. Then an odd scraping.

He saw her a few yards away. She was walking away from him very slowly, her feet dragging. The gait wasn't hers.

Needles pricked at his neck. "Tsira!"

She didn't respond. He raced to snatch up his pistol, then stumbled out into the snow, heedless of his stocking feet. "Tsira, wait!"

He ran after her and caught at her wrist. She ignored him. He punched her. She didn't so much as look down. He looked up at her face. Her eyes were fixed blankly ahead of her. Snowflakes were melting on her cheeks. His stomach lurched.

He punched her again, harder, and looked in the direction that she was walking. Something was out there in the darkness. A still, quiet figure.

He shivered.

"Hey!" he shouted out. "Hey, you there! Who are you? Come forward and show yourself!"

The figure didn't move. Tsira continued to shamble forward, her movements utterly unnatural, as if she were being operated by strings. He punched her again and shouted her name, but she kept moving like a cart on a track.

He reached for his pistol, aimed, and fired. The figure jumped and said "*Shit*," and a sudden, searing pain ripped through Jeckran's hand. He dropped his pistol, swore, and rummaged blindly through the snow on the ground as Tsira continued her slow march forward. He glanced up and saw the figure growing closer. He tried to concentrate on finding the glint of metal in the snow, to swallow back the ball of terror that was forming in his throat. He could hear his own shallow breaths in the silence.

His fingers brushed against something hard and then closed on the butt of the pistol. The pain was like grabbing on to the wrong end of a hot iron. He bit the inside of his cheek until he tasted blood. The man was within sprinting distance and walking quickly toward them, his hand stretched out toward Tsira as if preparing for a caress. This time, at such close range, Jeckran didn't miss.

Tsira gasped and stumbled. Jeckran grabbed at her arm. "Tsira! Are you all right?"

"Yeah," she said. "Yeah." She clutched at his shoulder. He could feel her hand shaking. "He was going to kill me."

"How do you know?"

"He told me. In my head. Said it wouldn't hurt."

"Well," Jeckran said. "I think he's dead now."

"Yeah," she said, and released his shoulder. "Yeah." She drew in a breath.

He looked up at her. "Are you all right?"

"Yeah," she said again. "Fuck. Sorry."

He licked his lips. "Don't apologize."

"You saved my life."

He started slightly. "I suppose I did, didn't I?"

"We're even now."

He tried a smile. "We are, aren't we?"

She slapped him on the shoulder, then nodded in the direction of the corpse. She had already regained her composure.

"We should go look at him."

The man was rather a disappointment. Medium height, medium build. A beard that did a poor job of disguising a weak chin. Large blue eyes that must have been his best feature, while he lived. Jeckran looked away.

Tsira went through his pockets in her calm, methodical way and came up with a five-sen piece and a single cigarette, slightly bent. "Not much on him."

"What," said Jeckran, "no villainous note with his employer's name and address at the bottom?"

Tsira shot him a look and handed him her loot. "Employer?"

"Well, I suppose that he could be a lone evildoer, but it seems unlikely, doesn't it? I mean, he doesn't look the type. No long, lank hair or lurid scar across his right cheek or anything of that sort." He looked at his new cigarette. He felt odd, almost giddy. "Good God, this is lovely. I'd kill him again, just for this."

Tsira ignored him, still crouched down beside the corpse. He had fallen on top of one of his arms. She worked it out from under him with a degree of gentleness that Jeckran found surprising, nodding toward his hand. "That mean he's married?"

The man was wearing a ring. Tsira pulled it from his finger and handed it to Jeckran to inspect. He frowned. "No. It means he's a wizard."

It was a class ring from Weltsir, the school's crest in gold around a small emerald. Tsira shrugged. "We knew that, didn't we?"

"We knew that he was doing some sort of magic. We didn't know that he was a Weltsir wizard." He slipped the ring onto his finger, then realized what he was doing and jerked it off again. He rubbed his finger against his trousers. "He must have fallen on hard times. Weltsir wizards all come from good families. If someone's paying people to hunt down trolls, then a gentleman neck deep in debt might be induced to murder easily enough, even if a wizard commands a higher premium than the merry band of dunces who invaded your home." It made perfect sense to Jeckran: he himself had joined the army purely in order to get out from under his father's debts, and the men he had killed as a soldier in Mendosa were no less dead than any murderer's victim. To a man being relentlessly dunned by his creditors, a pile of corpses could begin to look like a pile of banknotes very easily.

"Maybe he just likes killing people."

"Possibly. But look at his cuffs." They were filthy and visibly fraying. "A gentleman of means wouldn't let them get into such a state, even if he *was* a murderous fiend."

Tsira leaned over the corpse and sniffed. Jeckran wrinkled his nose. "Must you?"

Tsira stood. "Smells funny."

"I would imagine so."

"No. I don't know what it is. Funny." She went quiet. "Can't hear anything. Can you?"

"No," he said, and gave a violent shiver.

She looked down at Jeckran, spat out something in her language, and scooped him up in her arms, cradling him like a child. He struggled a bit. "Put me down, Tsira, I'm perfectly all right!"

"No," she said, and wrapped one massive hand around his left foot. He hissed at the heat of it and tried to squirm out of her grasp, but she only gripped him more tightly. "No." Her gaze was hard and unreadable and stayed locked on his face for a long moment before she looked away.

She carried him back into the cave, depositing him beside the fire. "Warm up. Then put your boots on. We're leaving once I've packed. Not safe to stay any longer. Murdering fucks coming after me every fucking day."

He obeyed, though it took him some time. He was shivering so badly that it was difficult for him to fasten the laces. She watched him in silence for a time, then she handed him the knapsack. "Put that on."

He did. She knelt. "Get on my back."

He recoiled. "I will *not*."

"You fucking will," she said. "It's snowing out there. Up to your knees. You'll slow us down. I won't die for your pride, Pink."

He got on her back. She slung her fur cloak around both of them and left the cave without a glance behind her.

It was a long, strange night. Tsira moved quickly, the only sound the creak of wet snow under her feet. It was wonderfully warm under her cloak, and the smell of her was heavy in Jeckran's nose. He could feel the muscles of her back moving between his thighs. It almost was like being on horseback.

While being nothing at all like that.

Jeckran fell asleep pressed against her body, and he woke up in the daylight in a place he didn't know. He was damp with sweat all down his front and realized that it must be mostly hers. He gave a little shiver and tried to pull off the cloak. She did it for him and draped it over her arm. The snow had mostly vanished—whether from a sudden change in the weather or because they had descended from the mountains, Jeckran couldn't say—and it gave his memory of the frozen, silent night an oddly dreamlike quality.

"You're awake," Tsira said.

"Yes. Have you been running all night?"

"Yeah."

"Won't you rest?"

"No."

"At least let me walk. I certainly won't allow you to carry me all the way to—where on earth are we going?"

"Monsatelle," Tsira said shortly. "You talked about it, a while ago."

"I did," Jeckran said. "It's just the place I would have chosen myself." He was surprised that she remembered Monsatelle, out of all of their conversations. He was fond of the city for how decidedly *cosmopolitan* it was—a troll wandering about in Monsatelle would not at all be a remarkable sight—though as a child his county hall officiant had interpreted this noble quality as "the rich and dissolute ignoring the evil that surrounds them, consumed by the pursuit of their own base pleasure." Even Jeckran's elder brother, Jokwin, who generally was perfectly content to nod his disinterested way through a Friday meeting, had found this to be, "*Rather* strong stuff, wouldn't you say, Pip? Any fellow listening in might think that everyone in Monsatelle was drinking the blood of virgins instead of just throwing a few sen at the races, what?"

Tsira only grunted in response to Jeckran's approval of her scheme, and she did not see fit to set him down and allow him to walk on his own. After another hour or so passed, the air grew warmer and Tsira knelt, saying with surprising cheerfulness, "Stretch your legs."

From where they stood, Jeckran could see the mountain and distant hills spreading out in front of him like a carpet, with its quick little streams and jumbles of bracken and sudden bolts of rabbits from burrows. It felt good to be walking in the clean air with Tsira at his side, here in the foothills where the spring had well and truly come, far from the ice of Coldstream. His ankle was a bit sore, and his boots kept slipping in the mud, but somehow this was more an amusement than an annoyance, and Tsira's hand was always at his elbow to keep him from falling. She seemed in good spirits as well. At one point she bounded off for a moment and returned with a little purple flower gripped between two fingers. "Found this."

He laughed. "Lovely, Tsira."

"Want it?"

"Not particularly," he said, but she stuck it behind his ear, anyway.

"Suits you."

She hummed a bit, then sang a short bar in her own language. Her singing voice was as beautiful as her speaking voice, and she held the melody quite capably. Jeckran glanced at her, startled. "I had no idea that you sang."

Tsira shrugged. "Doesn't everyone?"

"No, I wouldn't say that they do. Not well, at least. What was that you were just singing?"

"A walking song."

"Is there—" He slipped in the mud again and nearly fell, pinwheeling his arms madly.

Tsira grabbed his shoulder. "Slow down, Pink."

He wriggled out of her grasp, careful to put his feet somewhere relatively dry. "Maybe I need a walking song. To keep the pace."

She began to sing at once, without any of the modest demurrals that he would have expected from a human. The song did create a fine rhythm for walking, and they marched along to the beat for several minutes. Then it was over, and she mussed his hair. "Your turn."

"I don't sing."

"Sure you do."

"Truly, I don't," he said, grabbing at a bit of gorse for balance as he slithered his way down a small incline.

"Human soldiers sing when they march, don't they?"

"Enlisted men sing. I've always considered it to be one of the privileges of my rank that I can choose to abstain from subjecting any-one to my tin ear." He caught himself then and shook his head. "My former rank, I suppose I should say."

"No," said Tsira. "You're still an officer. Left because of your leg."

"Oh," said Jeckran, understanding immediately what she meant. "Of course. Wounded in battle and discharged from duty. I suppose I should consider myself fortunate that I won't have to pantomime the limp."

Tsira squeezed his shoulder. "It's not so bad."

"What?"

"The limp. Getting better all the time."

He changed the subject. "I should have an assumed name as well. What would you suggest?"

"I don't know. Something ordinary."

"Smith, then. Something Smith. Jeck, maybe. Or Janus." He glanced at Tsira. "It might make things easier if we allow people to think that you're a man. If you don't mind. In terms of finding work and sleeping in the same rooms in boardinghouses, that sort of thing."

"All the same to me."

"Well, that's good to hear. Any number of human men wouldn't like to hire a woman bodyguard, even a troll, and I don't know how most people would react if they knew we were unmarried and traveling about together." In Elgarism, all sexual relations were considered a distraction from focusing on spiritual refinement. However, relations between a male and a female that weren't sanctified by an officiant were considered *especially* bad conduct, as this might potentially result in children whose conception had not been overseen by God.

"Not a woman, exactly," she said. "I'm a reig. It's different. Don't really care if humans think I'm a man, if it makes things easier." Then, a moment later, "I can still be Tsira, though."

"Yes. You can still be Tsira." There was an odd clenching sensation in his throat as he said it, and he had a sudden, wild urge to grip her by the hand. He resisted it and picked up his pace instead. Jeckran felt the beat of his heart rising in his chest. Tsira stayed at his side, her movements as effortless as his were labored, and he wondered if she noticed a change in the air between them. He was very aware of her; how her color was up from the wind and how it tinged her face indigo, how bright her silver hair was in the sunlight.

He was, he thought, almost certainly going mad.

His ankle began to throb, and his limp got worse. He kept his eyes trained ahead, as if he were still enjoying the sweeping view down the mountain, though his only focus was walking without her noticing. He flinched when she spoke. "Pink."

His face heated a little. She always seemed to fit a great deal of softness into that word. "Yes?"

She sank to one knee, pulled off her pack, and jerked her chin over her shoulder. "Get back on." He wasn't used to seeing her face like this, from above. He wondered why he had never noticed the little freckles over the bridge of her nose. "Faster this way."

"I'll walk."

"If you want." She paused, then added, "It's too slow with you walking, Pink."

He eventually acquiesced, though not without further argument. "You should put me down at once if you feel tired."

She laughed again. "I won't."

"Put me down or feel tired?"

"Both."

It was comforting to hear that. It was comforting to feel her body close to his. He was quiet for a while, watching things pass by. Gorse, mostly, and birds.

"Tsira?"

"Yeah?"

"I don't suppose you know *why* you've been hounded out of your home by humans attempting to murder you?"

Tsira paused before she spoke. "There's been someone trying to kill us for a while. A few bodies have turned up. Poor trolls from border-clans who the bigger clans don't care about. It's why all those humans died at Coldstream."

Jeckran craned his neck to look at her face. "What do you mean?"

"Human wizard killed a little reig, thirteen years old. They found her all cut to pieces. Heart cut out, brain cut out, liver cut out, all the blood drained out like a butchered goat. Her ma killed those people at Coldstream. Just wanted to punish the first humans she could get to, I guess. She killed herself, after. Walked into a river."

Jeckran swallowed. There was a sudden eruption of birds from the hillside, a thick thrum of wings boiling dark against the sky and then settling down again into the grasses. His heart sped against her body. "I never knew." He resettled his arms around her neck. "Why would anyone cut out a child's heart?"

She shrugged. "Some magic project, maybe. Or because they liked doing it."

A flutter of something like panic settled just below Jeckran's collar-bone. He said nothing.

A long time passed. Jeckran tried to keep his mind blank. The birds kept rising and falling in writhing clouds, spreading thin and then twisting into black knots. Once one of the knots flew overhead, and the sound was terrible, a thousand little cries tangled into a thunderclap. Tsira came to a stop until they passed.

"Not so nice," she finally said.

"Good God, no. Like a legion out of the land of wandering dead."

"Thought they might shit on us."

He laughed, and she laughed, too; his panic eased. It was getting darker. Tsira quickened her pace. "We need to make camp soon. Keep an eye out."

He did, though he couldn't say with any degree of certainty what he was meant to be looking for. Tsira found it herself, in any case, quickly enough; a flattish, dryish area beside an enormous boulder. She knelt, allowing Jeckran to slither off her back. "Can you make a fire?"

"Of course I can," he said. "If I have a flint or a match I can, in any case. I suppose that *you* can make a fire by giving some logs a severe look."

She laughed and gestured toward her pack. "I've got flint and steel in there. I'm going to hunt now."

"Very well," he said to her back. She was already leaving.

Jeckran spent a few minutes stumbling around in the bracken and cursing as he attempted to gather up kindling, but he managed to outclass himself with the fire, producing a small blaze in minutes and thoroughly impressing himself in the process. Then he must have drifted off because next thing he knew Tsira was squatting by the fire and skinning two rabbits. It had gotten much colder. He untangled himself from his seated position with difficulty—his whole body had gone stiff—and went to her side. She glanced up.

"Tired?"

"Rather."

She nodded to the rabbit she had just finished skinning. It was a pink lump, limbless and pitiable. "Can you gut that?"

He shook his head. She didn't sigh or roll her eyes, only nodded. "Wait. I'll show you."

She finished skinning the second rabbit and then gutted it with a few quick movements, slitting it open with her knife and then pulling the organs out with one hand. He looked at the rabbit and thought of the little troll girl. He imagined her looking like Tsira. Brain cut out, heart cut out. He looked away.

"Pink."

He looked up as she handed him the knife. "You try."

He made a hash of it, of course, puncturing some bit of innard, which immediately leaked greenish ooze. Even at this juncture, Tsira remained patient. "That's all right. Finish it. Like I did."

Jeckran swallowed and did so, nauseated but triumphant, and was rewarded with a smile. He had to look away again.

Tsira cooked the rabbits until they were well past done, charred on the outside and near-leather within. "It's safer this way," she told him. He ate his with relish and gnawed at the bones.

It was quite dark by then and very cold. Tsira tossed her rabbit bones into the fire, lay down, and pulled her blanket over herself with a soft sigh. Then she said, "Come here."

"What?"

"Sleep here. With me. We need the heat."

He sat up. "I couldn't."

"Sure you can. Come here."

He obeyed. He had thought to maintain some space between them, but she laughed and used one arm to haul him closer. "Warm?"

"Yes. Thank you."

"Good. Shit, I'm tired." She yawned. "All right, Pink?"

"Yes. All right."

For a few minutes they were both quiet.

"Tsira," Jeckran said, "are you ever afraid?"

"Of what?"

"Of anything. Of dying. Of those people trying to kill you."

"No. I'm never afraid." It didn't sound at all to Jeckran like bravado, just plain fact. "Go to sleep, Pink," Tsira said, and he did.

He woke up with his hard cock pressed against Tsira's leg. She was grinning and said, "Morning."

He jerked away, awake all at once and utterly aghast. She must have noticed. He wondered if she could read the thoughts on his face. "Good God, I'm so sorry! I was—dreaming." The dream had been terribly real. He had tasted her skin in it.

She was laughing at him. "All right, Pink. It doesn't matter." She smiled; a genuine smile, not a baring of her teeth to tease him. "Must have been a good one." His stomach lurched. He knew that he shouldn't think too much of it. Only she sounded gentle when she spoke, and he wanted her so badly that he was going mad. He leapt up, pulled his boots on, and walked away as quickly as he could, though his ankle sent bolts of protests. Once he deemed himself suitably hidden by rocks and gorse, he paced, not quite able to bear stillness.

It was, he thought, only because she was a troll that he hadn't seen it for what it was weeks or months ago. Humans did not become infatuated with trolls. Ancient human clans had sometimes been under the headmanship of a troll clan-head, but there were no great love ballads about humans wooing troll reigs. In particular, a gentleman was meant to *emulate* trolls, not *marry* them, which no one ever even considered. An occasional tryst was one thing. Most of the time, human-troll unions were barren. But what human man would choose to court a woman who could fling him about like a hammerball? Gentlemen were meant to pursue *dainty* women.

He supposed he could pretend that it was noble of him; a man loving someone for her qualities and not her physical appearance. It was also nonsense, of course. What he felt for Tsira was not noble admiration for her pure and virtuous spirit, and he'd spent too much time mooning over her muscles and her cheekbones and her freckles to delude himself on that point. He suppressed a nervous giggle and realized that he badly needed to piss. As he did, he recalled Tsira's doubts concerning the mechanics of sex with a human. No doubt she would find him woefully inadequate. He imagined that he must look very puny and ridiculous to her. Though he supposed it was presumptuous to be even considering the issue, as Tsira had demonstrated nothing but a sort of soldierly camaraderie for him for the duration of their acquaintance. Since, by now, she was probably wondering what was taking him so long, he buttoned himself up and headed back, preferring not to cultivate the impression that he suffered from loose bowels along with his other faults.

At their little campsite, Tsira was crouched next to the fire, stirring something in the pot. She saw him and said, "Hey, Pink."

"Hey," he said back, trying out Tsira's preferred mode of address. He liked being inside of the things that she used: borrowing her bowl, crawling under her blankets.

"I made breakfast."

"What have you made?"

"Fried bread."

She had sliced some flatbread and fried it with foraged wild onions and eggs in some of their precious store of goat fat. It was better than he had expected: her cooking was improving. All it really lacked was salt. He squatted next to her and stabbed at chunks of bread with his knife. "I would happily shoot a man," he said, "for a cup of coffee and a cigarette."

She didn't respond, nor did she touch the food. He glanced up at her. *I want you*, he thought. He said, "Thank you for cooking."

"Pleasure."

"Why aren't you eating?"

"Not enough for both of us."

He stopped eating, stricken. "But of course you should have half, at least! Good God, you should have all of it! You *carried* me yesterday."

"Carry you today, too. I don't mind being hungry."

He put his knife down. "Absolutely not. I'll throw it away before I'll eat it all."

She stared at him for a moment, then shrugged and began to eat. "We're goat farmers, in my clan. Not much money. We had some bad years. I went a little hungry sometimes, growing up, if the trading went bad or the goats got sick. I didn't mind it. Ma always found something then, and I always find something now."

Jeckran stared at his hands. They were almost as calloused as Tsira's now, and there was dirt caked under his nails. They didn't look at all like a gentleman's hands.

"I did as well. Went hungry, I mean. My father went to Aufdom Mare for six months and gambled away everything that we had. There was nothing left to pay the bills with. My tutor left, and the cook, and the damn housemaids. My mother sat in the sitting room and embroidered as if nothing was wrong. I lived off the jam and pickles and stale biscuits I found in the cupboards for two weeks. Then it ran out, and I had to beg my mother to sell some of her jewelry so that I could have something to eat. She acted *surprised* that I was hungry, as if she thought that I would be fed by pixies when the cook left and the grocer stopped taking our credit. Eventually my father came back with a bit of money he had won, all apologies, and mother was so *vexed* that I didn't seem pleased to see him."

He had never told anyone that before. He wasn't sure why he had told Tsira now, except that there was an intimacy in telling her his secrets. He snuck a glance at Tsira; she was shaking her head. "They didn't tend you like they should have. If it were my ma, she wouldn't have rested until I got fed."

He shrugged. "It's over and done with, in any case. My talking about it doesn't make my father any less of a disgrace or my mother any less of a simpering twit."

She ate her bread for a time in silence. Finally, she said, "It's good we're together now."

"Why?"

"We can look out for each other. Make our own little clan on the road." She stood and stretched, then extended a hand to Jeckran to help him to his feet. "Want to scrub out that pot?"

They set about breaking camp. Once everything was neatly bundled into their packs, Tsira knelt next to him. "Come on, then."

The idea of riding on her back again, after his realization of the morning, provoked such a dreadful combination of naked desire and abject horror that Jeckran flinched. "I think that I should be able to manage walking today."

She looked at him. "Saw you limping this morning."

"Well, I *do* have a bad leg, don't I? I *will* limp. That doesn't mean I can't walk." He paused. "I suppose that I should find a stick to lean on."

"Won't find any up here. The trees are too small." She rose to her feet and held out her arm to him, and he stared at her, not grasping what she was doing. She threw her head back in an impatient little gesture that hit him like a punch to the stomach. "Lean on me."

He put his hand on her forearm, then laughed.

"I feel as if you should have given me a nosegay and filled out my dance card."

She raised her eyebrows, and he shook his head. "Don't mind me."

"Never do."

They continued walking after this, with very little conversation. It was rough going, picking their way around boulders and sliding down muddy patches; the pleasant side was that the exercise kept them from feeling the chill. Tsira would occasionally dart away and then return with some toothsome little thing she had found: three large tubers that she called "ground pears," a small grouse that she knocked down with a slingshot, and finally a large number of enormous beetles, which Jeckran begged her not to thrust into his face so eagerly. She only laughed. After a few hours the endless descent began to bother Jeckran's ankle, and Tsira dropped to one knee without comment.

They made camp that night as usual and ate what Tsira managed to forage, though Jeckran rejected the beetles with all of the politeness he could muster. Then Tsira lay down to sleep, and Jeckran, after a moment's hesitation, lay down beside her. She slung an around around him. "Night, Pink."

"Good night, Tsira," said Jeckran. They were both quiet until almost dawn, when Jeckran's nightmares woke them both.

The days over the next fortnight or so began to run together, after that, with very little to separate one from the next. They walked, they ate, they slept, and they walked again. They covered a great deal of ground, though, and eventually they began to pass by little human villages. Before long they could see the highway in the distance, but they gave it a wide berth: they agreed that they were probably better off in the wilderness than they would be at the mercies of highwaymen. Jeckran was down to his last two bullets.

The weather grew warmer, and Tsira brought back bigger game from her scavenging excursions. One night she returned with a deer slung over her shoulder, and they gorged themselves sick on it, both deeply aware of the fact that it might be many days until they could eat their fill again.

Then, one morning at dawn, they arrived.

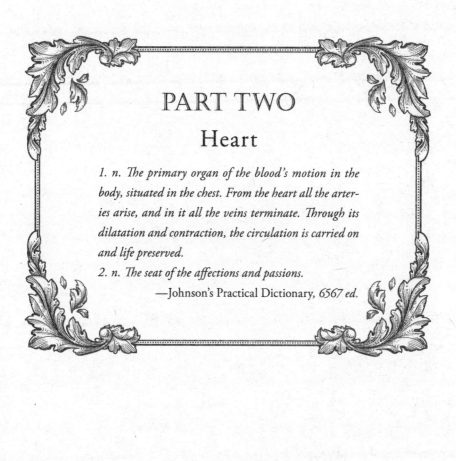

# PART TWO
## Heart

*1. n. The primary organ of the blood's motion in the body, situated in the chest. From the heart all the arteries arise, and in it all the veins terminate. Through its dilatation and contraction, the circulation is carried on and life preserved.*

*2. n. The seat of the affections and passions.*

—Johnson's Practical Dictionary, *6567 ed.*

# 8

---

*It's the custom of Cynallum to travel between our summer and winter villages every year as the seasons change. Why is this the custom? Some might say it's to better browse the goats. This answer is too simple. Why not build a barn and fill it with hay? Why not move to a city and buy cheese in a shop?*

*Why do we move with the seasons? Because we prefer not to swelter in the summer and freeze in the winter. Because to stay all year round in one place increases the difficulty of maintaining an attractive and sanitary environment in our village. Because a long walk is healthy and gives us time to think.*

*There is custom that rises from happiness.*

*—Grandmother-book 9, clan Cynallum, annotations*
*by Cynallumwynsurai, page 22*

It was wonderful what one could accomplish when one threw everything away.

Onna threw away her dreams of Weltsir, Mr. Heisst's promises to speak to the dean, the thought that tests could be retaken. She threw away her mother and father and their shabby, comfortable house in Cordridge-on-Sea. She threw away Daeslund, and even before she stepped on board the ship, she could see home receding in the distance.

There was, of course, a bit of bother with her parents. At first they said that she would not be allowed to go at all. She pleaded her case. She was a good girl and would wait for their blessing, but they *must* see that this was the best opportunity for her to achieve the sort of success they had intended for her when they first sent her to school with Mr. Heisst.

"I *have* to go. I'll *rot* here if I don't," she told her mother. "I'll go *mad*." She was annoyed when her mother made a face at this that struck her as far more amused than it should be. She herself thought that she was bold and tragic in equal measure, but not in the *least* amusing.

At last it was agreed that she could go, under three conditions: she would travel and stay with a chaperone to be selected by her parents; she would turn around and come back to Daeslund if she couldn't find a suitable placement at the university; and she would write letters every day to assure them that she hadn't been abducted by pirates or tumbled into the Hexian Sea. To these terms Onna agreed very readily. As far as she was concerned, the chaperone made no difference whatever. She could easily make polite conversation with some upright spinster for the duration of the voyage to Hexos, and as she did not have any notion of not being admitted to the university, the return voyage was not a matter for concern.

While Onna threw herself back into her studies, her mother set out in search of a suitable chaperone. Mrs. Gebowa inquired first with her literary friends, but alas, none of them had any plans to visit Hexos in the near future. She then prevailed upon Mr. Heisst for his assistance, but he told her with great regret that none of his wizarding acquaintances had any business in Hexos. Finally, with all other avenues exhausted, Mrs. Gebowa sighed, put on her nicest bonnet, and went to pay a call on Mrs. Gregs, secretary of the Cordridge-on-Sea chapter of the Women's Charitable Legion.

She returned from this venture exhausted but triumphant. Between cups of tea and several extremely lengthy stories about the difficulties Mrs. Gregs had been having with her newest plantings—Mrs. Gregs was an avid gardener and the winner of a great number of local prizes for her rosebushes—Mrs. Gebowa had acquired some valuable information. Recently the Women's Charitable Legion had invited a worthy by the name of Mrs. Cordram to speak to them about her life as an Elgarite messenger in Mendosa, where she had lived for many years. There, by her own accounts, the widow Cordram had convinced scores

of Mendosans to move to Daeslund and join her beautiful seaside halton in Aufdom Mare before she was cast out by the new anti-Elgarite
Mendosan government. She was was now making a brief lecture tour of
Daeslund before departing to Hexos in order to convince the shock-
ingly atheistic wizards of that notorious city to give up their godless
ways and take up the simple and contemplative halton life. She would
be leaving Daeslund in two months. Despite harboring a degree of dis-
trust for anyone calling herself an Elgarite Messenger—Awati Elgarites
believed that new conversions to the faith should only occur naturally
as a result of a message from ancestors who were still among the releft—
Mrs. Gebowa knew an opportunity when she saw one dressed head-to-
toe in black crepe. Mrs. Gregs, that charming woman, had agreed to
write Onna a letter of introduction.

Onna received a letter two days later, written on crisp paper and in
plain language. Mrs. Cordram would be pleased to accompany Miss
Gebowa on her journey, provided that she was a polite, sober young
woman who eschewed fine clothing, sensual dalliances, and strong
drink, and who was devoting her study of magic to the further advancement of the Laws of Elgar.

Onna's family had always been somewhat slapdash in their religious
observances. Though Mr. and Mrs. Gebowa had both been raised as
strict Awati Elgarites, both of them were far more liberal in their own
observances, and they had been known to quietly encourage com-
muning with God personally in the out-of-doors, as the Reenvisionists
recommended. With their children, Mr. and Mrs. Gebowa were firm
that it was essential to attend Hall every Friday, but they were lackadai-
sical when it came to strict adherence to the laws about plain food and
dress, and any reading that Mr. Gebowa did from *Elgar's Passage* in the
evenings was balanced with Awati stories and songs that he had learned
from his grandmother. This was very within the Awati Elgarite tradition: Onna's great-grandparents had left Awat in order to live within a
Daeslundic Elgarite Halton, but they insisted upon their own children
knowing the language and customs of their homeland. The language,

at least, had not made it past Onna's grandparents' generation, but Onna was still quite proud to be an Awati Daeslunder with connections—albeit distant ones—to the great Mendani federation, especially when a princess of the federation received particularly effusive praise for her beauty and sophistication in the Daeslundic press.

Onna herself was rather a disgrace as an Elgarite, as her fondness for well-trimmed bonnets had only recently been eclipsed by her fondness for a small glass of sherry in the evening before bed. She was, however, irreproachably polite, and she thought that one of the essential abilities of a polite and genteel young lady was to create pleasant fictions in order to preserve her companions from unpleasant truths. With this in mind, she wrote to Mrs. Cordram a letter that depicted Onna Gebowa as a girl of such simple tastes and fervent piety that Onna found herself quite intimidated.

Mrs. Cordram responded to this in tones markedly warmer than those of the first letter, and they exchanged another few messages on topics such as suitable clothing for the hot Hexian climate. Between this thrilling correspondence and preparations for her journey, the two months passed much more quickly than Onna had anticipated, and in what seemed like a matter of a very few days it was time for her to go.

Her mother cried when she left, and presented her in a small but solemn ceremony with her very own version of the carved wooden Elgar's Circle worn by adults in the Awati Elgarite faith, so that it could bring her luck and protection on her journey. At this Onna began to cry as well, which nearly undid her poor father, who shook her by the hand like a mayor congratulating a returning war hero; told her that he trusted her to be a good girl, mind her manners, and be a credit to the Gebowa name for as long as she was abroad; and then darted quickly into the next room and the safety of his favorite armchair. Onna sniffled quietly all the way from Cordridge-on-Sea to Del Sem Berg, where Mrs. Cordram was waiting for her at the station.

Mrs. Cordram was not at all like what Onna had expected. She had imagined a spinsterish person in her twilight years, in an old-fashioned hat and black widow's crepe. Instead she was a tall lady in her forties, with high cheekbones, blue-black hair, and an energetic handshake. She held a sturdy carpetbag in each hand and refused assistance from the porter when climbing aboard the coach to Leiscourt. Onna shot a guilty glance toward two porters struggling with her own enormous trunk, and she scrambled as quickly as she could into the coach in the hopes that she would not be discovered as the hopelessly spoilt wastrel that she suddenly found herself to be.

Onna seated herself next to an elderly gentleman who was puffing disconsolately on a pipe that looked to have long since gone out. Mrs. Cordram sat down opposite Onna, set her carpetbags next to her feet, and fixed Onna with a look of great intensity. "Miss Gebowa," she said, "when I look at you, I fear that you may not have been entirely truthful with me in your letters."

Onna thought for a moment of leaping from the coach. Instead she assumed an expression of polite surprise. "Why, Mrs. Cordram, whatever do you mean?"

Mrs. Cordram leaned forward and seized one of Onna's hands in both of her own. "You told me that you wanted to dedicate your life to study and the advancement of the Laws of Elgar, and that you had no suitors to divert you. But I can't believe that such a lovely young lady could ever lack for beaux."

This comment was so entirely unlike anything that Onna had anticipated that she could only gape. Mrs. Cordram smiled a very fervent smile. "Shall we pray together for safety on the journey?"

The elderly gentleman gave a despairing groan. Mrs. Cordram squeezed Onna's hand even harder and launched into a very emotional recitation of the Prayer for Summer Travel. The elderly gentleman glared and puffed ever more furiously on his extinguished pipe, and Onna attempted to look as if she knew the words to the prayer and was only silent because she was so overcome with religious feeling.

At last the prayer was over, and Mrs. Cordram—seeming to have entirely spent herself on her spiritual exertions—fell asleep. Every few minutes she emitted a delicate snore, to which the elderly gentleman responded with a number of furious ejaculations. "Dreadful woman!" he said. "Religious zealot! Very worst sort! Halton nonsense! Unbearable!" Onna hushed him every time, but she only managed to eventually secure his silence by pointing out that, if Mrs. Cordram was to be awakened by his insults, she would surely retaliate by praying all over again.

Between the religious conflict and the deplorable condition of the Del Sem Berg–Leiscourt highway, it was an altogether uncomfortable journey. Onna passed the time with calculations. By observing the rate at which they passed road markers, she judged their speed at approximately five miles per hour. From this and the frequency of jolts, she estimated that there were, on average, thirty small ruts and twenty large pits per mile of highway, and that they would therefore be jolted more than two thousand times before they reached Leiscourt. This great quantity of jolts did not have any effect whatever on Mrs. Cordram, who continued to snore at a rate of twenty snores per hour until she woke up of her own accord and began to read her battered copy of *Elgar's Passage*. Mrs. Cordram read at a speed of approximately two pages per minute, which was rapid enough that Onna suspected her of either having memorized the text or of being inattentive.

Though it was early when they left Del Sem Berg, it was long after dark when they reached the capital, and neither Onna nor Mrs. Cordram had any inclination to do anything but sleep in their appointed Elgarite women's boardinghouse.

Their ship was to sail the following afternoon, and at breakfast that morning Onna was so dreadfully excited that she could barely think of eating. The unflappable Mrs. Cordram fixed her with a stern look. "Now, this will not do at all, Miss Gebowa. I cannot abide the sort of woman who fusses and fidgets and picks at her food. We sail to Hexos this afternoon, Miss Gebowa; we are not shrinking, sighing women. We are bold, and the bold always take a good breakfast." Following this speech, she ordered a great quantity of kidneys on toast, of which Onna was surprised to find herself quite glad to partake.

The dockyard was a loud, confusing riot of great bales of freight, shouting red-faced men, and the pervasive odors of salt, fish, and urine. Onna stuck closely to Mrs. Cordram's side as she made her way through the crowd, across the gangplank, and aboard. Soon enough they were snugly ensconced in their little berth, with their trunks and carpetbags safely stowed away, leaving Onna enough time to hurry up to the deck and watch as the sailors rushed about and swore and shouted until the ship pulled away from shore.

After this initial burst of excitement, Onna quickly realized that a two-week-long sea journey was much less thrilling than her mother's novels led one to expect. Indeed, life was so terribly dull on board ship that she thought she might actually die of it. Mrs. Cordram, with her constant placid knitting, fervent prayer, and cheery injunctions to "Chin up and make the best of it" only served to make Onna annoyed as well as dreary. The only thing for it, she decided at last, was to work so hard that she would have no time to consider how terrible it was to be trapped for days and days on board a dreadful ship that made one feel listless and seasick. So Onna set herself once more to writing parameters, working every day from just past sunrise until after nightfall, and she was almost frightened by the strength of the work she could see developing on her bundles of cheap notepaper. She noted only vaguely how the air grew warmer as the days passed and they traveled farther south, and how the time displayed on her little pocket watch grew slowly out of step with the dusk and dawn.

Then, at long last, she heard shouts that land had been sighted.

Hexos, from a distance, was a blurry mass very much like Daeslund. Then it grew closer and emerged into focus: the narrow white and blue and yellow buildings crammed close together and stacked on top of one another higgledy-piggledy over the narrow cobblestone streets. These streets were full of very curious people: they almost all were dressed in what looked rather like the traditional knee-length tunics of Esfona, but in bright gaudy colors or dripping in trollish embroidery of mathematically perfect geometric patterns and endless spirals. Others wore

Weltsir suits in shocking pinks or greens instead of the traditional black, or they were dressed in the clothing of their home countries in similarly unusual shades. The crowds resembled nothing so much as the display in the window of a milliner's shop, a burst of colorful ribbons and notions and frills. And there, above it all at the center of the city, was the Wizard's Lamp.

She had read about the Lamp and seen illustrations of it in books, but to see it in real life was a different matter entirely. The most expensive structure built in modernity, it was a frightfully tall and slender tower—she hadn't believed it when she saw in her book that it was two hundred feet high, but now that she saw it herself she was completely convinced that this was quite possible—and contained such a great number of rooms that it was rumored that the Lord-Mage himself hadn't been in all of them. An iron staircase led from the bottom to the top, and it was the longest such staircase ever built. Most extraordinary of all, however, was the workshop at the very highest level. Every inch of its walls and ceiling was made of glass, glass that was said to appear thick and swirled and mottled from without, but perfectly transparent from within, allowing the Lord-Mage to look out over all of Hexos from within his study. Onna stared at the Lamp, squinting at it in the distance as the night drew in. Then, all at once, the glass dome at the peak of it lit up from within, and along with it blazed every lamppost in Hexos, so that the whole city was as bright as morning and the Lamp gleamed over it like the sun.

The Lord-Mage, Onna thought, must be in there at this very moment, watching the city below him.

When they disembarked, Mrs. Cordram once again took the lead, pushing her way with great confidence through the jostling crowd, and flagged down a cab at the street corner. The cabs in Hexos were quite the most wonderful things that Onna had ever seen. They were like tiny carriages with no wheels or horses, just large enough to seat two passengers and the driver at the front. Each cab was decorated as per the tastes of its individual driver, and some were very fine indeed, with carved

wooden railings and silken canopies in the bright colors of which Hexians all seemed so fond. Once seated, the driver would stomp his feet
on the floor, the cab would rise into the air, and they would float gently
down the street, the driver steering by leaning his body to the left or
right.

Mrs. Cordram showed the driver of their cab a slip of paper with an
address on it written in Nessoran—as the standard language of magical
parameters, Nessoran was also the common tongue of Hexos—and he
nodded his vigorous comprehension and stomped his feet with such
energy that the cab practically leapt into the air. The driver was very
young and attempted to chat a bit with Onna, but she found to her
dismay that all of her Nessoran lessons and ability to read and write in
the language were quite useless. All she could manage was to say, "I'm
sorry, I only speak a little Nessoran," over and over until the poor boy
gave up. The driver, for his part, snuck another glance at her, accidentally caught her eye, and broke out into giggles. He struck Onna as
much more like the village boys who gawped at her and her sisters when
they strolled through town on fine Friday afternoons than like a dashing foreign rake, which was disappointing. She was confident in her
ability to firmly reject the advances of a dashing foreign rake, but
thought that having the opportunity to do the firm rejecting would be
very thrilling.

When at last they arrived at what Onna dearly hoped was the correct
address, Mrs. Cordram paid the driver with several little bits of paper. This
seemed to please him very much, for he smiled broadly—giggling a bit
when he looked at Onna—and then clambered out of the cab to help
them with their luggage. Onna took the opportunity to take a good look
at him. His tunic was a cheerful bright blue, and he wore his brown ring-
lets loose to his shoulders in the trollish style that the magazines said was
perennially popular in Hexos and had recently come into fashion in Monsatelle. He was, she thought, rather handsome. He seemed to notice her
staring, and he smiled and then busied himself with the luggage while
Mrs. Cordram knocked at the door. The door soon opened, and in the

flurry of greetings the young man departed, though not before giving Onna a very charming bow.

"Good-bye!" she called after him, and he laughed as he floated off.

After this brief, tantalizing little adventure, Onna was quite mad to see the rest of the city, but Mrs. Cordram and the other ladies of the boardinghouse were not at all inclined to allow her to wander about as she wished. She was allowed, at least, to go along on a trip to the wonderfully clean and well-lit market, where she gawped wide-eyed at the sheer variety of fruits and vegetables available for sale. They came in every conceivable shape, size, color, and flavor: purple potatoes, pink-and-green spinach, and blood-red oranges among them. It was very difficult to tell which were the ordinary foods of some faraway country and which were the result of a fanciful wizard's greenhouse experiments. Onna was gravely disappointed when the ladies of the Elgarite Women's Boardinghouse purchased only the most unoriginal and Daeslundic of vegetables in order to make the dullest and most ordinary of roast mutton for their tea: they told her that it was because food in Hexos nowadays was far too dear to waste a crumb in culinary experimentation, but Onna found this explanation less than satisfactory. After the sad ending of this venture, Onna rededicated herself to preparing the practical demonstration she would give to the proctors of the University of Hexos after her appeal for a special audition was accepted.

The one luxury that she allowed herself in those two weeks was to take little afternoon strolls about the neighborhood, attempting to look like a sophisticated young Hexian wizard and not a wide-eyed provincial. She found, to her somewhat confused pleasure, that most people took no note of her whatever: the streets were so drenched in brilliant sunlight and extraordinary people that she faded into obscurity and could observe the locals like an ornithologist observing woodpeckers from within the protective cover of a hedge. They were all so wonderfully dressed in their knee-length tunics and oddly shaped hats, and spoke so loudly and quickly in their distinctively slurry Nessoran—utterly different from the standard accent she had studied at school—and went about together so happily in their international flocks, that she began to think of Hexos as a sort of paradise, utterly removed from the petty Daeslundic concerns of class and sex and clan name.

This view of things was disturbed one day while she was on her walk and happened upon a noisy gathering in a nearby square. A squat gentleman in a black tunic was on a platform giving a speech to an assembled crowd that roared its approval after every few sentences. The gentleman was perhaps in his sixties, but the crowd was mostly made up of young people dressed in simple brightly colored tunics made of cheap-looking fabric, without a hint of the expensive trollish embroidery that was otherwise so popular. Onna listened as carefully as she could to the speech and managed to make out a few words: "wizards," "Lord-Mage," and "to permit." She spotted a handsome blond boy of about her own age wearing a bright pink Weltsir suit and walked up to him, thinking that he might speak Daeslundic. "I beg your pardon, but would you mind very terribly telling me what it is that man is talking about?"

The young man gave her a slow smile and ran his hand back through his blond curls. "I never mind talking to a pretty girl," he said. He spoke Daeslundic with a Hexian accent. "He's exhorting the Lord-Mage to ban trolls from his auditions for an apprentice."

"Ban trolls? But whyever—" She paused, as what the boy had just said suddenly caught up to her. "The Lord-Mage is searching for an apprentice?"

"Of course he is," the boy said with great surprise. "Why else would Hexos be this flooded with foreigners? They're all here for the audition on the morning after next. Aren't you?"

"I suppose that I am now," Onna said, smiling so widely that it was difficult to speak. The Lord-Mage. *The greatest wizard in the world.* Whoever was chosen to be his apprentice would be the subject of envy from absolutely *every* young scholar of magic. She thought it must be very wicked of her, but in that moment the greatest wish in her heart, beyond any hope or dream she had ever contemplated, was to become the youthful protégée of the greatest wizard in the world, drape herself in acclaim, and then return to Leiscourt and parade herself before every wretched old man and smug preening boy who had ever attended Weltsir.

Thus energized, she got the rest of the details of the audition from the boy, and then she recalled why she had approached him in the first place. "Why *don't* these people want trolls to be allowed to audition?"

"It's a matter of fairness," the boy said. "They don't allow us into their learning halls. They withhold their research from us or demand enormous amounts of money for it. Why should they be able to take *this* position as well?"

"I believe," Onna ventured, "that humans aren't admitted to the troll schools in Daeslund because there were religious riots over human children being taught necromancy, and the troll great-clans signed an agreement that full-blooded humans wouldn't be instructed in troll magic in the future without the express permission of the first headman." Onna had read several books on the history of the study of magic, and she personally felt that the type of medical magic trolls performed was very frightening, indeed, though she didn't know if its theoretical study really ought to be forbidden *entirely*.

"You see!" the boy said. "They're in alliance with the landed classes; they always have been. They're already bigger and stronger than us, and live longer, and have every advantage, and won't even allow us to study their magic. We ordinary humans have to stick up for ourselves against them."

Onna felt an odd cold slither in her gut. She remembered what she had seen the night of her exam in Leiscourt. The screaming woman kneeling in a dark street, her hands wet with blood. The troll who had only stepped out for a moment before she was killed. "I don't think that can be right," she said slowly. She didn't know exactly *how* it was wrong, but something about the way he said *stick up for ourselves against them* struck her as nasty and sneering and *mean* in a way that she didn't like at all.

The boy snorted. "You talk like you were born on a pile of diamonds," he said. "You'll see, though, in time." Then he walked away before she could formulate a satisfactory response.

For the rest of that and the next day, Onna abandoned all pretense of studying for the university entrance exam and threw herself with all of her strength into practicing for her demonstration for the Lord-Mage. It was difficult to eat or sleep or think about anything else: when she tried to rest, her head was flooded with parameters, and her heart pounded hard against her ribs. The night before the audition, she stayed out by the front door for hours with her hand clasped over the Elgar's Circle that connected her to her family's faith and her ancestors, feeling the warm breeze against her skin and waiting for the sky to turn from black to gray before she set out in search of a cab.


She arrived at the Lamp at dawn, almost five hours before the appointed time, and was surprised to find that a very large crowd had already gathered at the open gates. This fancifully dressed crowd was quite unlike the gathering of rich Daeslundic boys she had found herself in competition with at Leiscourt. Many looked to be natives of Hexos: they came in a wide array of shapes and colors, but one could identify them by their outlandish robes and elaborate hairstyles and loud, oddly accented Nessoran. There were also Daeslunders, looking prim and nervous, and dashing Nessoran fellows with swords at their waists. One group of people seemed to be from some part of the Mendani federation, though their clothing and the language of their murmured conversation were completely foreign to her. It made her feel a bit self-conscious. She imagined that they might very well look at her complexion and think that she, too, was a citizen of the federation, and be gravely disappointed to discover that she was only a simple village girl from an admittedly somewhat backward nation who could only speak Daeslundic—and that with a *very* provincial accent.

She fretted over this thought for a time and then gathered herself up again. Her great-grandfather had brought their family to Daeslund: it therefore followed that he would like her to be as proud of being a Daeslunder among Mendanis as he had taught his family to be proud of being an Awati among Daeslunders. Bolstered by this thought, she caught one of the gentlemen's eyes and nodded, and was very gratified indeed when he smiled and nodded back.

There were also many more women in the crowd than she had expected, including a number within the Mendani contingent, a personage of uncertain origins wearing an enormous feather in her red velvet cap, and one very grand-looking Hexian lady with a monkey at the end of a silk lead. The ladies, Onna noted, did not tarry near the back, but put themselves forward just as the men did. Onna, emboldened, pushed herself to the front of this miscellany of wizards, and stopped at the gates to see what everyone was looking at.

It was, it turned out, a Morgan's wall, or something very like it. She could see people pushing against it, trying it with their fingers as if they thought it might bite. The wall seemed to give a bit, like a piece of rubber, before springing back. It had completely filled the gate, barring anyone from entering the Lamp. Onna wondered if perhaps it was to prevent eager applicants from storming the place before his grace the Lord-Mage had so much as eaten his breakfast.

As if in response to this thought, words made of smoke appeared above the gate.

*Enter*, they said, in what looked like more than a dozen languages.

This, of course, caused a bit of a scrum. Onna stepped aside and watched with great interest as several hundred wizards attempted to force themselves through the same small entryway, though the barrier spell remained. One particularly clever young Nessoran man attempted to scale the walls and get over that way, but he was forced to clamber back down again in defeat: the barrier, it seemed, covered the whole of the Lamp like an inverted soup bowl. A few people tried to break it down by running against it, which ended predictably enough in injury and embarrassment. Others began writing elaborate parameters in an attempt to dismantle it, an attempt which struck Onna as a waste of energy: she doubted very much that anyone present would be able to outmatch the Lord-Mage of Hexos with a few hastily written parameters. There must be some sort of trick to it.

She inched closer to the gateway, murmuring apologies to people as she pushed past them, and got close enough to press her finger against the barrier. It felt very much like a Morgan's wall, which struck her as significant: a Morgan's wall was meant to keep out *magic*, not people, which made it an odd choice for something that was intended to prevent people from entering. As she pondered, an irritated Daeslundic wizard flung a messily constructed ball of energy at the gate. It passed through harmlessly, sputtering out on the grass on the other side. The crowd groaned. "It's impervious to magic," said the wizard, his face even redder than it had been previously.

"Or it was just your damn sloppy work," said his friend, who set about working on the parameters for a more sophisticated energy ball.

This, of course, was the wrong conclusion entirely. It seemed perfectly obvious to Onna. The barricade wasn't impervious to magic: it was a Morgan's wall written in reverse. It let only magic *in*.

From there, things were relatively simple. She recalled the parameters for a bit of magic that would encase her entire body—she used the same little construction when she was caught in a sudden rain without overshoes and umbrella—and increased the amount of energy that she put into it to match the strength of the barrier. Then she walked through.

There was a roar of surprise and shock from the assembled wizards. She thought for a moment of waving at them, and then was quite ashamed of herself; no one liked a young girl who crowed over her accomplishments. Instead, she soon found herself far too engaged by the beauty of her surroundings to think any more of her competitors.

The Lamp was surrounded by a garden, one unlike any garden she had ever seen before. It was a vision of what nature ought to be if nature was as pleasant in reality as it always was in novels. She followed the path, which lead her around a small lake covered in white water lilies, then through a stand of apple trees in full bloom—which was odd, since at home it was usual for either water lilies or apple blossoms to be in season, but generally not both at once—before depositing her at a fork in the road. Directly before her was a brook surrounded by ferns, with a little bridge over it. To the right was a lovely little mountain complete with twisted, wind-blown trees and a path that looked to take one through a cave at the center. To the left the path was bracketed with willow trees. She stood for a moment at this crossroads, rather confounded.

Someone spoke directly next to her ear. "Beautiful, isn't it?"

She thought she might have screamed a bit while jumping about a foot into the air. The young man who had spoken took a step backward. "I'm dreadfully sorry! I shouldn't have crept up on you so suddenly."

She took a deep breath, embarrassed by herself. He was a very handsome young man, and she thought it quite dismal that his first impression of her would be that of a cat leaping after a moth. "No, it's perfectly all right. It was very silly of me to scream." She smoothed her hands over her skirt, waiting for him to introduce himself.

He bowed at once. "My name is Haran Welder."

She curtsied. "Onna Gebowa. I'm very pleased to meet you." She paused. "Everyone must be coming in now, then?"

He smiled. He had a very engaging smile. "Not everyone. A few of us realized how to get in after we saw you do it, but not all of us could manage to put so much power into it. I only pushed through by the skin of my teeth." He spoke Daeslundic very well, with only the barest touch of a Hexian accent. He wore his brown hair to his shoulders, in the Hexian fashion, but was dressed in a plain black Weltsir suit.

"Oh," said Onna, embarrassed. She hadn't noticed that it took much power at all to walk through the gate. She changed the subject. "You speak Daeslundic terribly well."

He laughed a little at that. "My mother is Daeslundic." He gestured toward the willow trees. "The Lamp is this way. Shall we walk on together?"

They did so, and the willows rustled conspiratorially above them. It seemed to Onna that this was very much like taking a turn through a garden for reasons quite different than going to a wizarding audition, and she tried to turn their conversation toward academic topics.

"Were you at Weltsir, Mr. Welder?"

"Yes. Though it was a very near thing. I swear that I heard one of the proctors at the exam calling me '*that clanless boy with the dreadful Hexy accent.*' They quite changed their tune when they found out who my father is. I started growing out my hair and wearing a Hexian tunic to lectures, once I got in, just out of spite."

"Your father—"

"Magister Alric Welder. He's fairly well-known for his work in constructive theory."

"Oh," said Onna.

He smiled. He had, she noticed, very bright blue eyes. "I'm glad to be here. It's a much more cosmopolitan place than Leiscourt."

"Did you just come for the audition?"

"No. I've been at the University Hospital doing independent research since I graduated from Weltsir. When I heard about the audition, I thought that I might as well try my luck. At least I'll have the fun of seeing Magister Wuzan's face when I turn up!"

"Do you know him, then?"

"Oh, yes. He's known my father for years, and he used to come by Weltsir to take me for tea before my exams. I'll warn you now that he's a very odd fellow! And a bit of a controversial figure in Hexos."

"Golly! But whatever is he like?"

"Indescribable. But you'll see for yourself, soon enough."

They turned a corner and came suddenly upon the open stone courtyard that surrounded the Lamp itself. The Lamp's great blue doors were closed, and when they stepped into the courtyard two chairs appeared, along with more smoke words in many languages.

*Please wait.*

They did, continuing to converse as the day grew brighter and more wizards trickled into the courtyard. Onna asked Mr. Welder about his research, which he was very happy to speak about at length: he was doing research into new protocols that doctors and nurses could implement to reduce the likelihood of patients contracting new illnesses while in the hospital. "I know it sounds *terribly* dry, just establishing standard parameters for magical hand washing, but it really can save lives, and one really feels like a detective sometimes, tracking down how disease is spread throughout the hospital grounds. And when things do get dull, I usually pop into the children's ward to read stories for a while. You ought to come by the hospital for a visit. It really is wonderful, *far* more modern than anything they have in Daeslund."

Onna couldn't help but think of Sy, who had needed to cheat to get into Weltsir; Sy, who studied magic so that he could earn money and please his father, Sy who was so miserable and adrift at Weltsir. Sy, who was clever and charming and had never in his life been dedicated to a thing outside of himself. She smiled. "I would like that very much, Mr. Welder."

He smiled back at her. "I'm very glad, Miss Gebowa."

At this point, about fifty wizards were sitting on little chairs or milling around the courtyard, waiting for something to happen. Then something did. The smoke words shifted, changed from *Please wait* in all of the different languages into three words in an unfamiliar script. One of the waiting wizards gave a little yelp and rushed for the doors, which opened for him. He entered.

He emerged a few minutes later, looking disconsolate. This happened a few more times, with the examinees entering and exiting at fairly regular intervals. Then Onna's own name appeared.

*Onna Gebowa.*

She was obscurely pleased to note that it was *Onna* and not *O*.

She walked through the heavy blue doors and found herself in a reception hall made of wood, with elaborate carvings decorating the ceiling. They seemed to be depictions of stories; she could make out people and horses and ships and a number of strange beasts. There was, however, no time to stand and stare. At the end of the hall, in three carved and painted wooden thrones, three people waited for her.

At the center was a man with a stern, craggy face and a military bearing, dressed in a plain blue robe. His skin was about the same brown as Onna's, and his hair was silver and cropped very short. To his right was a plump, neatly dressed middle-aged lady, with a round pale face, brown curls, and a kind, motherly expression. On his left was a young man wearing a Hexian tunic in rumpled black silk. His long black hair was in disarray, and the look on his face suggested that he would much rather be still abed than sitting through dozens of wizarding auditions.

Not one of these people looked even remotely, to Onna, like the Lord-Mage of Hexos. It struck her, however, that Mr. Welder had said that the Lord-Mage was eccentric; disguising himself as someone else to determine whether an applicant was the sort to make assumptions based on appearances seemed exactly like what an eccentric wizard nobleman would do in a novel. With this in mind, she curtsied to each of them in turn, starting with the lady, and said, "Good morning. My name is Onna Gebowa. Thank you very much for seeing me."

This seemed to please the lady. She smiled. "Good morning. Please, go ahead with your demonstration."

She spoke in Nessoran, but Onna somehow heard it in Daeslundic. The effect was disconcerting. She curtsied again and began.

"Watch my hands," she said. "Watch my face." She clapped her hands. A double appeared, another Onna. "I live," said the second Onna. She clapped her hands, and a third Onna appeared, saying, "I breathe."

At this point the illusions grew more complicated. Onna breathed slowly, riding the crest of it, making adjustments as she went. All three Onnas clapped their hands, and there were six. They clapped again, and there were twelve. Twelve illusions, twelve sets of parameters. One of the Onnas sneezed. They walked to the center of the room, mingled together. Two of them bumped into each other, and one caught her breath. They pulled apart, formed a wide circle. Clapped their hands again so there were twenty-four. Onna's head was splitting. It was almost too much to bear, at this point. One of the Onnas drew a ball from her pocket. She threw it into the air and caught it. "What determines the difference between illusion and reality?" she said. Another Onna scratched her nose. The Onna with the ball tossed it to a different Onna, who caught it. "Is it intelligence?"

Onna pulled a knife from her pocket. "Is it the capacity for pain?" she said, and dug the knife into her palm. She winced, as did some of the other Onnas, watching her. She held her hand out, and the blood dripped onto the floor. For one dreadful moment she thought that she might drop the illusions from the pain, but they stood, lived, breathed. She passed the knife to Onna on her left, who imitated her gesture. Her blood dripped onto the floor just as the real Onna's had. One of the other Onnas coughed softly and covered her mouth with her hand. A second cleared her throat. A third stepped toward the three people watching. "Is it the warmth of our blood?" she said, and reached out her hand to the stern older man. He touched it and started slightly. Onna knew that it was warm, and that the skin was rough from washing dishes. It was, after all, her own hand—or close enough to it. Then that Onna rejoined the circle.

"Only one of us is real," said half of the Onnas.

"Pick the right one," said the other half, and then they were silent and still, though some of the Onnas fidgeted slightly. This was the hardest bit of all, to keep all of them looking alive at once without one of them doing something interesting to direct all of the attention. She had to keep all of the Onnas breathing and blinking, while some occasionally subtly stretched their necks or shifted from foot to foot. She was floundering, struggling to keep up, exhausted by the expenditure of energy and distracted by the pain in her hand. A drop of sweat trickled down her back. She swallowed and had one of the others do the same. She willed the three seated in the thrones to pick quickly.

"Her," the older man said, pointing to the Onna who had touched his hand.

"Her," the lady said, pointing to the Onna who had scratched her nose.

"You," the young man said, pointing straight at Onna herself.

Her heart sunk. She nodded and allowed the other Onnas to wink out of existence. Her hand was throbbing. She curtsied again. "Thank you very much for your time," she said to all three of them, though she was sure now that the young man must be the Lord-Mage.

The young man nodded, speaking in the drawling Daeslundic of a headman or assemblor. "Well, that's more than enough for *me*, certainly."

She swallowed hard, feeling tears spring up in her eyes, curtsied one last time, and replaced her knife in her pocket before she turned to go.

"What a wonderful idea this audition was!" said the young man. "It isn't even lunchtime, and I already have my assistant selected. I always find it so gratifying to get important business settled before noon. The entire day simply opens up in front of you."

Onna stared at him. "What?" she said, and then quickly corrected herself. "I beg your pardon, sir?"

"Didn't I just tell you? I'm very pleased to make you my new assistant."

She felt, suddenly, as if she could leap into the air and fly directly to the ceiling. "But—you knew who I was. The illusion failed."

He raised his eyebrows. "Heavens, you do hold yourself to dreadfully high standards. I *am* the greatest wizard in the world, after all." He stood from his chair and rolled his neck around his shoulders. "That was perhaps the most technically impressive piece of illusionary magic I've ever seen, and one does like to see a hand-slicing level of devotion and a well-developed sense of theatricality in one's assistants. I am altogether completely charmed, enchanted, and *delighted* by you, and in any case I have seen enough barely-above-average wizardry today to last me a lifetime. I see no point in subjecting myself to any more. What was your name again?"

"Onna Gebowa," said Onna. Her head was spinning.

"Onna. How perfectly charming. Come along, then," he said, and he strode quickly toward a doorway at the far end of the hall. He continued talking as he rushed along, occasionally glancing back over his shoulder to look at her. "I do hope you don't mind the walk, as there are quite a few stairs, but I get so little healthful exercise that I feel I must attempt to exert myself from time to time."

They passed through the door into a long covered walkway that ran along the edge of an interior courtyard. Onna had only enough time to give a few passing glances to the pretty little garden in the courtyard and the paintings that decorated the ceiling of the walkway before they were back indoors and heading up a spiral staircase. Following behind the Lord-Mage she noticed how gracefully he carried himself. He was tall and very slender, but not at all gawky or awkward in his movements. His dark brown eyes, when still, were large and long lashed, and he could transform his entire face with his expressions; from moment to moment, he would flit from being decidedly handsome to being quite the oddest-looking man Onna had ever seen, like a very smug cat on very tall stilts. Now he was smiling at her in a confiding way that made her suddenly far too aware of where her hands were and how often she was meeting his gaze.

"I feel that I must begin by enumerating my faults, so that you won't be taken by surprise and run out in fits of hysterics. I have truly dreadful personal habits: I smoke, I drink, I keep unhealthy hours, and I have been known to entertain lovers in my offices. I'm also *dreadfully* affected, probably because I grew up on the stage. I'm told that it grows quite unbearable at times. If you begin to find me insufferable, you may kick me soundly in the shins."

"I'd rather not kick you soundly in the shins, sir, if it's all the same to you," Onna told him. "I imagine that you must be a dangerous person to surprise or injure."

He stopped on the stair above and cast her an admiring look. "You know, I *might* do something I would later regret if I were startled enough by a sound kick to the shin. You're terribly clever, aren't you? How *very* charming. You're clever like me, and theatrical like me, and one always finds it so *wonderfully* enriching to spend time around people who are almost exactly like oneself." He gave her another of those smiles and headed up the stairs again. "Are your parents wizards as well, Onna?"

"Oh, no. My father is a shopkeeper."

"Wonderful! You're almost as common as I am, then. My parents are farming people, back in Sango. Ah, here we are!"

They had arrived at a door at the very top of the staircase, which immediately struck Onna as extremely odd, as it certainly wasn't possible for the few stairs that they had just climbed to have reached all the way to the top of the Wizard's Lamp. She had no time, however, to ponder the practicalities of this particular piece of magic, as her new employer was already walking through the door.

Despite the fame of the Lamp, and the enormous sum of money that had been spent on its construction—the glass alone, Onna once read, had cost more than a year of Daeslund's entire military budget—it was furnished with extreme plainness. It took the Lord-Mage only a moment to show her around the room. The only substantial piece of furniture was a long wooden table, which was equipped with hundreds of drawers: the largest were big enough for a grown man to crouch inside, and the smallest were so tiny there was barely room for a single needle. There were a few chairs as well, all made of plain wood. The view, at least, was every bit as spectacular as she had imagined, though after a few moments of standing near the glass, she was so overcome with vertigo she had to step away. Onna had never in her life been so far above the ground, and she found that it did not quite agree with her.

"It is rather dizzying at first, isn't it? You'll get used to it soon enough," said the Lord-Mage.

"I do hope that you're right, sir," said Onna. He shook his head at the *sir*.

"You must call me Loga."

"Loga?" said Onna, trying to get her mouth around the sound of it. "I had thought that your name was Woosong Zuylong."

His nose wrinkled slightly. "*Wuzan Zilon.* Not—whatever it was that you just said."

"Wuzan Zilon," she said again, trying to pronounce it as he did. This time he flinched visibly. "I really would be *delighted* if you were to call me Loga. It started as an intimate nickname among my Sangan friends, but I assure you that it's what *everyone* in Hexos calls me now. It came about because it sounds, in the dialect of Sangan that I spoke as a child, like what one calls an elder student at school."

"It seems very unconventional," said Onna, nervous at the thought of calling such an important man by an *intimate nickname.*

Loga raised his eyebrows. "Well, Onna. I'm a very unconventional wizard."

She found herself avoiding his gaze, embarrassed. It had suddenly and uncomfortably occurred to her that she was currently completely alone at the top of a tower with an alarmingly sophisticated foreign man she had only met a few minutes earlier. Then she remembered how giddy she had been at the thought of meeting a real authentic dashing foreign rake and felt her cheeks heat. She thought that perhaps rakes were more intimidating when one encountered them at the tops of towers in foreign lands instead of in one's own sitting room in the pages of a particularly thrilling book.

When she glanced up again, the Lord-Mage had moved to stand at the other end of the table. She tried to sound light and airy, as a young lady should when speaking socially to a gentleman of high rank. It wouldn't do to take on an anxious or complaining tone, she reminded herself, when she had worked so hard and come so far for this opportunity. "Loga, who were those other two people downstairs?"

"Oh! That was Mr. Doran Bierce, commander of our navy. He held a dinner at his house last night—I was invited primarily because he wanted to ask me endless questions about how I might create a more terrifying class of cannon—and after a few glasses of wine I suggested to him that he might enjoy watching a few young wizards give practical demonstrations this morning. To my great horror he agreed that it sounded very amusing. He's one of those old men who are always doing healthful exercises at ghastly hours of the morning, which is absolutely the last sort of person one ever wants to encounter before noon, don't you agree?"

"And the lady?"

"She is my housekeeper, Mrs. Macosti. She's a local Hexian, but I've taught her to cook some simple Sangan dishes, and she dragged me back from the brink of despair with her porridge this morning. It's all due to her that I made it down to see you at all, even if I didn't manage to change my clothes. I was so desperately grateful for her succor that I invited her to join us."

Onna stared at him, trying and failing to keep a censorious note from creeping into her tone. "Do you mean that you were *drunk* last night, before you were to judge the demonstrations?"

He smiled and raised an eyebrow. "I'm afraid that it's very possible that I'm still drunk now. Would you like to see your rooms?"

Her first instinct was to say yes at once: Onna had spent her entire life sharing a cramped little room with her elder sister, and the thought of having *rooms* of her own was almost unbearably thrilling. Then, after a moment's thought, she stopped herself. It was already foolish enough of her to have followed Loga alone up into the Lamp; to go with him to a *bedroom* would be utterly impossible.

She stood in silence for a long, agonized moment. Loga gave her what seemed a very knowing look, then put a hand to his hair. "Actually, if you don't mind too terribly, I might call up Mrs. Macosti and ask her to take you. It would give me a chance to refresh myself, and she could fix you a little luncheon. Would it bother you dreadfully if I abandoned you for some time?"

She shook her head, so grateful for the delicacy of his suggestion that her eyes stung. "Oh no, not at all. You mustn't put yourself out over me."

He smiled at her. "I'm very glad to hear you say that. I've been told that I rarely put myself out over anyone at all. We can start work after you've finished eating," he said, and strode rapidly out of the room.

Mrs. Macosti arrived a few moments later—Onna felt rather faint at the thought of the cunning little parameters Loga must have set up in order to summon her so quickly and quietly—and she brought Onna to look at the rooms that had been provided for the new apprentice. The bedroom and sitting room were clean and spacious and well aired, furnished with lots of simple, elegant furniture that would be equally suitable for either a male or female wizard. The bookshelves in the sitting room were crowded with fiendishly dense-looking books and scrolls of magical theory, though the majority were in languages that Onna did not understand. Best of all was the balcony, which provided her with a lovely view of the lily pond in the garden below.

Mrs. Macosti soon came bustling in with her luncheon: a casserole of vegetables and mutton in a thick sauce. She was halfway through her meal when Loga sauntered into the room. He did, indeed, look vastly better than he had that morning. His hair was neatly combed and plaited, and he had changed into a fresh black tunic. He looked very elegant. Onna was grateful for Mrs. Macosti's presence.

He seated himself in a chair opposite from Onna. "I know that I said 'after you've eaten,' but I wanted to speak to you a bit about the sort of work you'll be doing while under my tender tutelage. Is illusion your main area of research?"

Onna cast her eyes toward her plate. "It was what I had thought I might study if I had been accepted into Weltsir. I would be very glad to help with any little tasks that you might have for me."

She risked a glance at him. Loga raised his eyebrows. "First, Onna, though modesty is a great virtue, I feel as if you lack faith in your own work. You are a *wizard*, darling, and you have an *area of study*. Of course, often you will be asked to do things outside of that area by your superiors and sponsors, and it will be up to you to manage them without abandoning your own interests. What do you know about fireworks?"

Onna was somewhat taken aback by this abrupt change in topic. "Not very much. Why do you ask?"

"Because of the murders," he said, as if it was all very obvious. Then he noticed the look on her face and elaborated. "A wizard somewhere in Hexos has murdered four impoverished trolls in the past two months. As Lord-Mage I am held responsible for the investigation of any crimes committed by wizards within my jurisdiction, since it's rather beyond the abilities of the ordinary Hexian police force to arrest a competent wizard who would rather not be arrested. I also must answer to the Directress, who is very annoyed with me at present for having allowed some ill-intented wizard to run wild in the year before an election, when I continue to serve in this office at Madam Directress's pleasure. Unfortunately, I have seven examinations to administer, three schools in Sango to build, an entire navy's worth of cannons to upgrade, and fireworks to design for a jubilee commemorating the foundation of Hexos. Since my doctor has been cautioning me about overexerting myself magically, I will require your assistance in the matter of the fireworks display. I imagine it will be an excellent use of your skills as an illusionist, don't you?"

Onna nodded, then swallowed, remembering again. The kneeling woman, and the gas lamps, and the screaming and the blood. *She only stepped out for a minute.* "I'm sure you're right, sir," she said, "and it's terribly kind of you to think of it. But if you think that I might, and it isn't too much trouble, I think I'd much rather try to help stop the murders."

# 9

*A crowd gathered at Leiscourt's West Dock yesterday to greet Princess Ame Mbato of Kep as she arrived for her inaugural visit to Daeslund. Several young orphans from the West Leiscourt Foundling Home, where the princess later paid a visit to distribute new Nessoran-language textbooks and fine Mendani sweets to the children, assembled to sing a song of welcome to the princess. Her highness, who has been widely hailed in the Esiphian press as "the loveliest girl in the world," and by the poet Sir Willian Reppon as "the ruby of rubies, the silk of silk," was a vision of beauty in an Esiphian gown of brilliant red crepe. . . .*

—Leiscourt Crier, *Erdmonth 16, 6570*

At first the city was just a dirty smear on the horizon. Then came the smell of burning coal. Then Monsatelle itself, a dreary tangle of crumbling houses and muddy alleyways that seemed to grow darker and denser the closer Jeckran and Tsira came to it.

"I don't remember it being so . . . gray," said Jeckran.

Tsira shot him a look. "Said you'd been here."

"Well, yes, of course I have. But I came in a carriage, so I suppose that the view of the outer districts was rather less—intimate. But then—"

"Pink," said Tsira. "Got a problem."

They had entered the city, and the narrow, muddy track that led through the city wall had matured into a narrow, muddy cobblestone street that cut between dilapidated buildings. It was quiet and still, so early in the day. The few people about were mostly stone-faced men with their caps pulled down low and their eyes trained toward their feet. Tsira, however, gestured toward a young girl standing on the opposite sidewalk, her fists bunched up against her mouth, her eyes wide as she stared straight at Tsira.

"Hey," Tsira said.

The girl screamed.

Within a few moments the street was in near pandemonium, with shouts of "Troll!" mingling with the hysterical shrieking of the girl. It seemed that they had stumbled into a poor Esiphian quarter of the city rather than a Daeslundic one, so that the already great level of confusion was compounded by the fact that Tsira clearly couldn't understand a word anyone was saying. The appearance of a man in a nightshirt holding an antique blunderbuss and of a mustachioed fellow with a pistol prompted Jeckran to put his hands into the air with great alacrity, though he had to kick Tsira in the ankle and hiss "Put your hands up!" before she did the same.

Jeckran shouted to the crowd, stumbling a bit over his Esiphian. It had been years since he had spoken the language, and shouting down an armed mob was not the ideal environment in which to remember the gender of one's nouns. "Stop! Please! My name is"—for a moment, he panicked, then recovered himself—"Jeck Smith. I understand that my appearance is alarming: we were lost in the mountains during the spring blizzards and have been sheltering in a cave for several months." The guns were lowered: Tsira had been right about the power of Jeckran's one-house-in-town-and-one-in-the-country way of talking.

"What about the troll?" someone called out.

Jeckran did his best to adopt the imperious, drawling, dim-sounding accents of his elder brother. He regretted the lack of props: he could, at this moment, make wonderful use of a walking stick and a monocle. "The troll is my companion. You need not fear him."

Tsira gave a little wave and smiled, which only served to rattle the crowd further. Jeckran continued to sound as aristocratic as he could manage, which was somewhat less aristocratic than he might have achieved were he not exhausted, filthy, and attempting to find a room for himself and his troll companion in a shabby corner of Monsatelle. "May we pass?"

The crowd seemed not at all amenable to the notion. Jeckran considered the possibility that they might have to run.

"Cousin!" a voice cried out in Daeslundic. "How very tired you look."

Tsira went tense and whispered, "*Shit.*"

Jeckran looked about wildly for a moment, half expecting to see one of his relations popping out of a passing carriage. Instead a tall, thin man with a delicate bone-white face appeared. He was wearing a neat gray suit and a blue cravat and leading a white horse by its bridle. His hair was the reddest that Jeckran had ever seen, like the very center of a hot fire.

The stranger stopped in front of Tsira and gave an elaborate bow, like something out of an earlier century. "Well met, cousin."

Tsira, to Jeckran's great amusement, bowed back. He had never seen her move more stiffly. "Well met."

The stranger leaned forward to whisper. He was, Jeckran thought, almost too delicate to be a man at all; in a dress he would have made a very beautiful woman. He spoke Daeslundic with what Jeckran thought a very charming southern Esiphian accent. "I saw you were having trouble. Your new friends will depart now."

As the stranger promised, the crowd seemed suddenly to remember pressing appointments elsewhere. Everyone seemed to avoid looking at the stranger's face, some going so far as to put up a hand to shield their eyes as they left.

The stranger put out his hand. "I'm called Mon Del Ras."

Tsira, after a moment's hesitation, shook it. "Tsira. Thanks." Jeckran noticed that she refrained from giving her full name.

"I'm glad to help a cousin," said Mon Del Ras. He looked toward Jeckran. "Might I have your name?"

His eyes were bright green, and when he smiled he showed his sharp white teeth.

Jeckran was about to answer when Tsira grabbed him by the shoulder and wrenched him to the side. "Cousin," she said to Mon Del Ras. "Don't do that. And he's called Smith."

Jeckran listed slightly to the right. He was rather dizzy. Mon Del Ras stepped backward and redirected his gaze to a point past Jeckran's head. "I'm sorry. I make myself rude." He paused. "He has a sympathetic nature, is it not?"

"Hadn't noticed," Tsira said, which struck Jeckran as funny. "Tired as hell. Know where we can stay?"

Mon Del Ras smiled. "At my place."

"What?"

"I am running a boardinghouse. It is a new house, very clean, and my wife makes the cooking. I ask for two tocats a week, with clean sheets every week and hot water every morning. Meals are accounted separately."

Tsira and Jeckran exchanged a look. Jeckran raised his eyebrows. Tsira shrugged. Then they both looked at Mon Del Ras and nodded. He laughed.

"You are like a double act! Come on, then," he said, and turned to go, pulling his horse away from the wan blades of grass it had been yanking from the cracks between the cobblestones. Jeckran fell into step beside him. "That's a beautiful little mare."

Mon Del Ras smiled. "Is it not? Her sire won the Elmsbridge ten years ago. I won her in a game of twenty-one."

"You're joking!"

"I do not." He cast a considering look at Jeckran. "Do you play?"

Tsira interrupted. "Not with you."

Mon Del Ras grinned. "You allow me no sport, cousin." He gave Jeckran another look. "You *are* a gambling man, though, is it not? Billiards?"

"A bit," said Jeckran.

"A few times a year, for high stakes."

Jeckran stopped walking. "You're a cousin to Tsira in what way, exactly? You're not a troll, surely?"

"No. In Monsatelle they call us *the good neighbors*."

"A *fairy*? But they're all dead," said Jeckran. "Oh God, I'm sorry. How horrid of me."

Mon Del Ras did not seem offended by this misstep. "Not dead. Just not always present. There is business to attend to in other places. But it is like so: you're a gambling man because of how your breath speeds up when I say I won my horse at cards, billiards because of this Headman-Mimsywell-Feathergoode accent you have, and high stakes a few times a year because you are too poor to play more often, but too proud to play for a sen or two."

Jeckran flushed. Tsira gave a short little laugh.

"Can you do me?"

Mon Del Ras looked at her.

"You? You are a dark hole, cousin."

Tsira showed her teeth. "Good guess."

Mon Del Ras led them to a large, neat brick building that stood out among its more weather-worn neighbors, and as soon as they drew near, three extremely redheaded young boys came tearing out of the front door, shouting with all of their strength.

"Papa! Papa!"

Tsira and Jeckran exchanged startled looks. Mon Del Ras laughed and allowed the boys to rifle through his pockets, speaking to them in Esiphian. "Jerome! Albert! Yves! I haven't brought anything for you this time."

This was shouted down immediately, and Mon Del Ras was forced to concede defeat and produce a few boiled sweets for each of them. The boys went into raptures of excitement. Then one of them noticed Tsira. "Papa," he said, "where did you get that monster from?"

Jeckran was suddenly very grateful for the fact that Tsira spoke no Esiphian. Mon Del Ras, for his part, smacked the offending child sharply across the mouth. The child began to wail, at which point a young woman emerged from the house, wiping her hands on her apron. She was very plump, decidedly blonde, and exceedingly pretty. Her dress displayed a broad expanse of freckled bosom, which struck Jeckran as extremely fortifying after his long trudge across the mountains and plains. Perhaps he would at last be treated to his tankards, minstrels, hunting dogs fighting by the fire, &c. "Jerome!" said Mon Del Ras's wife, whom Jeckran was at great pains to avoid thinking of as "the tavern wench." "Stop screaming!"

She smiled at Mon Del Ras and kissed him on the cheek. "You're home! What have you done to Jerome?"

"He was rude," said Mon Del Ras. "Tsira," he added in Daeslundic, "this is my wife, Bette, and our boys." He switched back to Esiphian. "Bette, this is my cousin Tsira, and her"—he paused for a moment, then continued smoothly—"business partner. Bette, what rooms have we left?"

"Number two and number six."

"Put them in six," he said, and led his horse away with a yank at the bridle.

Bette led them into the boardinghouse. There was a sitting room with a few yellow armchairs and cheap prints of seaside scenes on the walls, and the dark-paneled dining room was crowded with men reading their newspapers over their breakfasts. Some of them looked up when Tsira and Jeckran passed, then looked down again quickly. The whole room smelled strongly of coffee and cigarettes. Jeckran's mouth began to water. Bette glanced at him and smiled. "I'll bring a pot of coffee and some breakfast along with your washing-up water," she said. "You look as if it would do you good."

Their room, number six, boasted a large bed, a single chair, a wash-basin, a slightly warped mirror, a chipped chamber pot, and a small window with a view of the dismal-looking tenement next door. Jeckran stared about for a moment. "Good lord."

Tsira edged into the room and shut the door behind her. "Real white in here," she said. The walls were whitewashed and only peeling in a few small patches.

"It is," said Jeckran, marveling at the richness of the setting. "God. It's like a dream."

He walked to the glass to look at himself and started a bit. He had expected the wild stubble and the long hair, but not how his skin had turned browner and his hair had picked up a hint of red from the sun, or how his face had grown thinner and his shoulders wider. He looked quite a stranger.

Tsira stood behind him and examined her own face in the glass with enormous interest. "So that's what I look like now."

"You've never seen yourself before?" He moved out of the way to allow her a better view, and she squatted down on her haunches to get a closer look.

"Not so clear as this for years. We don't keep mirrors in our houses. Look more a pink than I thought." She glanced at Jeckran, then back at herself. "Bigger, though."

"A bit bigger, yes."

"Got a nose like a pink." She ran a finger down the bridge of it.

He reached to touch her elbow. "I'm sorry for that scene outside. All of those brutes with their guns."

She shrugged. "Don't matter." She sat down gingerly on the bed, as if afraid of breaking it. "I'll sleep on the floor."

"Don't be absurd. I imagine that the bed is big enough for both of us." Tsira was about a foot or so taller than Jeckran, and significantly broader: it would be a tight fit—he imagined that she might hang off the end a bit—but he couldn't in good conscience let her sleep on the floor. He could, he supposed, volunteer to sleep on the floor himself, but the fact of the matter was that he didn't want to. The floorboards looked *exceedingly* uncomfortable.

"Don't mind?"

He managed not to blush. "Not at all."

Bette appeared with coffee and toast, and a younger girl behind her had a pitcher of hot water, a basin, a sliver of soap, and a thin towel. As soon as the two women closed the door behind them, Jeckran went at once for the coffee, scalding his tongue and groaning with pleasure. Tsira poured some hot water into the basin. "That good?"

"Heaven," he told her, and he took a piece of toast, which had been spread with a somewhat stingy amount of marmalade. At first bite it was so tremendously sweet compared to Tsira's bland cookery that he almost spat it out in shock. He soldiered on nonetheless.

Tsira sauntered over, stripped to the waist and slightly damp. It was a testament to the toast that he hadn't noticed her undressing. She smelled of soap. "Didn't wash your hands."

"I hope you'll find it in your heart to forgive me," he said, stepping over to start washing up at the basin himself. "Have some toast."

She took a bite and pulled such a face at the taste of it that Jeckran laughed aloud. "You must hate it."

"Nah," she said, and picked up another piece.

"Do you like sweets, then?"

She took another bite. "Yeah," she said. "Ma used to bring me honeycomb. When she found it."

Jeckran had always classed listening to anecdotes from other people's childhoods as one of the more detestable possible uses of his time, but the thought of Tsira having ever been a child who had eaten honeycomb filled him with sensations of such tenderness that he was quite embarrassed by himself.

It was a confoundedly uncomfortable thing to be in love.

She demolished the toast within seconds and then tried the coffee, which she seemed to find unimpressive.

"Strange."

"One grows used to it. You might like it better with sugar."

She shrugged and finished her cup as he put his dirty clothes back onto his freshly washed body. "What now?"

"I thought I would go and order some clothes, and visit the barber. Then maybe speak to Mon Del Ras about finding work."

"Careful."

"With what?"

"Mon Del Ras. Don't speak to him alone."

"Why not?"

"Pale cousins take what they like."

"I haven't got anything he would be interested in, surely?"

She stared at him levelly for a moment, then she gave him a long, appraising up-and-down look. Jeckran bridled.

"Good God, Tsira, he's a married man with three children."

She shrugged. "Cousins like pretty things."

"And am I a *pretty thing*, then?"

"Want a compliment?"

"Don't be an ass, Tsira. I imagine if Mon Del Ras was interested in pressing his attentions upon me it would be within my power to refuse them, but I can wait to talk to him until you're with me, if you would prefer it."

"I would," Tsira said, and sat down on the bed. "Think I'll have a nap. Money's in my pack. Take what you need."

"Are you sure?"

She didn't bother to respond. Jeckran went into her pack and retrieved the little leather bag from the bottom. He had known, in a sort of abstract way, that she had some money, but he swore when he opened her purse. There was enough inside to keep them richly equipped with coffee and toast for a year or more. "Good God, Tsira, where did all of this come from?"

"Earned it trading in the villages. Selling cheese, mostly. Never spent it."

"But—you're *quite* sure you don't mind my spending some? It's your money, after all."

"Yours, too, now," she said, and lay down, putting an end to the conversation. Jeckran carefully counted out what he thought he would need into his own purse before he turned to leave.

"Jeckran."

She never used his name. He liked hearing her say it. "Yes?"

"Got pretty eyes."

"What?"

"Compliment you wanted. Your eyes are pretty."

He fled to the sound of her quiet laughter.

When he returned several hours later, Jeckran was in excellent spirits. Bette jumped a bit when he walked in, and addressed him as "sir." Even Tsira looked somewhat startled by his appearance. She sat up when he entered the room and grinned.

"Look at you."

He had shaved his beard off entirely, but he had decided to only have his hair trimmed a bit: long hair was the fashion now in Monsatelle, and it made him look less like a soldier. He had also managed to borrow a suit.

"The tailor lent me this, which is why it fits so dreadfully. He'd been using it for display, but I think he was horrified at the idea of me continuing to go about dressed as I had been. It's just for until what I've ordered is ready. I'm afraid it was all rather expensive, but if we're to be taken seriously—you're laughing at me. I must look absurd to you."

She shook her head, though her eyes were alight with amusement. "No."

He ducked his head. "I—ah. Shall we have some lunch?"

She nodded.

Lunch was vegetable soup, roast chicken, bread, and cheese, with a bottle of the cheapest red wine that Mon Del Ras had on offer. The dining room was quite empty at this time of the afternoon, which to Jeckran was a relief; he didn't relish the idea of Tsira being subjected to a crowd just yet. He suspected that she was already overwhelmed enough. Even the food was a bit of a struggle. The butter dish was particularly confounding, and she made an attempt to dip her bread directly into it before he interceded and showed her how to spread it on her bread with the butterknife. It was to her credit that she took this incident completely in stride, thanked him for the instruction, and set about eating enormous piles of buttered bread with utter equanimity, as Jeckran worked every last shred of roast chicken from the poor beleaguered creature's bones.

Mon Del Ras appeared with another bottle of wine and an empty glass while they were having their wine and cheese, pulling up a chair to their table. "Are you enjoying the food, cousin?"

Tsira nodded. "Yeah. Thanks."

"I'm glad," he said. "I wondered, Mr. Smith, what are your plans in Monsatelle?"

Jeckran wiped his mouth with his napkin. "We had discussed trying to find work in private security."

Mon Del Ras raised his eyebrows and poured himself a glass of wine. "The Bastennes won't like that, with you new in town."

"The detective agency, you mean? We had thought more of covering the stagecoaches."

"It is all their line. They do most of their business in what they call *property recovery*, but they like to keep their hands on everything. I should not like to cross them. You'd be better waiting for them to come to you."

Tsira and Jeckran exchanged glances. Jeckran spoke. "You're saying that there's no way for us to work without their say-so."

"There are other ways to make a living."

"Such as?"

Mon Del Ras leaned back in his chair. "You play billiards, is it not?"

Jeckran recoiled. "You mean become one of those wretched creatures who's always inviting himself to parties and trying to force all of the gentlemen into a game of twenty-one."

"It does sound unpleasant when you put it this way," said Mon Del Ras. "I did it myself, for years."

"It strikes me as like prostituting oneself."

"It is different, in fact." He poured himself a glass of wine. "Of this, I can give you assurance."

"Ah," said Jeckran. "I—oh. I don't play well enough, in any case."

"Ah, well. I can get you a job as a waiter. A friend of mine manages a very good hotel. You'd be perfectly suited for it; all you need is a mustache to really look like the fallen aristocrat. You'd make enormous tips. Monsatelle is full of lonely old women with too much money who want to buy a handsome waiter diamond cuff links. Do you think you could manage it?"

"I don't want to sell myself," said Jeckran, "in any capacity whatever."

"You pick a hard road. Do you draw? Paint?"

"Well—a bit."

"That's something, then. You could make some pictures and try to sell them at the galleries for a few sen. Better would be to set yourself up by the river promenade with an easel, make pictures, and look very tragic—yes, like that, just so—so that the passersby stop to talk and buy your pictures." He lit a cigarette. "You must look a bit less tragic. You have many good advantages. Think of the poor hungry man who hasn't your face or your accent and has to work with his hands for his bread."

At that moment Bette came walking by, staggering under the weight of an enormous basket of laundry. She stumbled over a rough patch in the carpet, but Tsira leapt to her feet and snatched the basket with one hand and Bette with the other before either could hit the ground.

She set Bette gently upright. "All right?"

Bette giggled breathlessly and responded in Esiphian. "I don't understand Daeslundic!"

Jeckran translated for her, and she nodded. "Oh yes, perfectly all right."

Jeckran relayed this to Tsira, who hefted the laundry basket against her hip. "Want help with this?"

Jeckran asked Bette, who giggled again. "How kind of you!"

They went off together, leaving Jeckran and Mon Del Ras to sit in silence. Mon Del Ras was the first to speak. "Did you know that your friend could move like that?"

Jeckran nodded. "I did."

"That should not be possible, for a gray cousin."

"Tsira is special."

"Is it not?" He leaned forward slightly and looked Jeckran in the eye. "What *are* you?"

Jeckran felt something warm spread his chest. His tongue was thick and heavy. He could hear his words slur. "I beg—I beg your pardon?"

"I think that we perhaps have the natural sympathy. Do you feel this also, Mr. Smith?"

Jeckran closed his eyes, then opened them. It took a long time. "Yes."

"Are you fucking my cousin?"

He felt as if he was floating in warm water. His thoughts were coming slowly. "No."

"Really? I had wondered. What's your real name?"

"Phillim Kail Jeckran."

"Thank you. Are you promised or bound to any one of the free folk?"

Jeckran shook his head. "What?"

"He is," said Tsira.

Mon Del Ras started, and Jeckran could breathe again. Tsira stood beside them, massive and cool. One of her hands closed around Mon Del Ras's throat. "Told you not to do that."

Mon Del Ras scrabbled silently at her hand, his eyes wide and frantic. Tsira loosened her grip, and he pulled in a breath. It was a moment before he could speak. He bared his teeth at her. "Cousin. I apologize. I was only curious."

"Don't be."

"Yes. Of course." He nodded to Jeckran. "Please forgive me." He paused, then said, "I wanted to suggest something to you, cousin."

Tsira looked unimpressed. "Yeah?"

He rubbed at his throat with one hand. "Have you ever heard of boxing?"

# 10

---

*A visitor from Sango might note with interest the large number of Daeslunders whose surnames originate from Sango's southwest, or who claim at least one ancestor from the southwestern state of Waizo. This is due to a unique property of the local religion. Two centuries ago, Daeslunders known as "Elgarite messengers" traveled abroad in order to encourage all they met to convert to Elgarism and be welcomed into their Daeslundic religious communities, which were known as haltons. An immigrant who entered into a halton would be provided with free food and housing until they were able to provide for themselves in their new home. One of the most charismatic of these messengers was a young Sangan man named Wen Caro, an early Sangan convert to Elgarism who famously convinced more than two hundred citizens of Waizo to leave their homeland and form a new Sangan-speaking halton in Daeslund's Morbreak County. This halton was intended to allow Sangan Elgarites to practice their religion with little outside influence or government interference, but over the generations intermarriage between members of the Waizo halton and Daeslundic Elgarites has left Morbreak with a unique local culture . . .*

—*Bak Wendun,* Notes on the Eastern Nations,
*translated by Laster Cordus*

Pink took her out that night.

They went out into the city, and the people on the streets made way. That was all right. Tsira didn't mind them being scared.

They should be.

The pink city was about like she had imagined it. Houses built up like cliffs and streets running like thin streams between them; no broad green avenues like her ma said they had in Cwydarin. Pinks everywhere all packed in together, too many too close for it to be safe or clean. The smell of shit in the gutters. Thin baby cries spilling from the open windows. A man selling sausages, licking grease from his fingers.

Pink was taking her to a fight. That's what he called it. *A fight*. What it sounded like to Tsira was something between a blood sport and a children's game. Neither of those things was in custom for a full-grown reig to be getting into. Tsira couldn't so much as make a decent argument for it. Her ma'd be mad as a wet cat if she found out.

Part of Tsira liked that.

Pink was excited. She could tell from looking at him. Blood rushing, cheeks dark. They walked past places lit up like the daytime, so bright it hurt to look. They didn't look like wizard-lamps. She pointed at one.

"How do they make the light?"

"Gas lamps," he said. "Aren't they wonderful? I always thought that I wanted them for my own home one day. When I was a boy we were forever running out of candles."

Tsira didn't know about them being that wonderful. Too bright by half, for a troll's eyes at night. Their blaze made her head ache.

The place Pink brought her to was even brighter inside than out. Wall behind the bar was all mirrors, light beating off it, the slick drunk faces of the crowd shining back twenty times over. She liked the crowd all right. A few of the men looked at her and nodded, then looked away. There was a strong smell to the air, tobacco and sour sweat and alcohol and bitter new plants. Loud metal-sounding music coming from the corner. She nodded at a man banging his hands on a big wooden box.

"What's that?"

"A pianoforte. Do you like it?"

"No."

He laughed. "As you shouldn't. It sounds as if they tuned it against an angry cat."

She sniffed and squinted. The thick air stung at her eyes. Pink noticed.

"It's gin, what you're smelling. They call these places gin palaces." He looked around. "I've never been inside one of them before."

She snorted.

"What?"

"Don't seem like your kind in here." She meant it as a compliment. He was just her Pink, when they were alone, but here among fifty other Daeslundic pinks he stuck out like a dark boulder in a field of pale grass. Special.

He raised his chin. "I don't suppose that I know what kind I am, not anymore. Would you like a drink?"

"All right."

He brought back two glasses of something that looked like water and smelled half like pine needles and half like her own throat-burning mead. She drank. It tasted fine. Pink wiped the rim of his glass with his handkerchief first, then noticed her watching and went dark.

"I *do* wish you wouldn't always laugh at me."

"Not laughing," she said, and threw back the rest of her drink. It went down warm. She thought she liked it. She licked the last drop from her thumb. Pink stared.

"Your tongue is purple."

"Your face is red."

He went darker. "I'm sorry. It's only that I hadn't noticed before."

She clapped him on the shoulder and finished his drink for him. Handed the glasses back.

"Ask him to wipe them this time."

He looked toward the man behind the bar, then back at Tsira. The fellow was big enough, with a smashed-up nose and half a finger missing. He looked like he'd seen a few fights himself, and not the kind that you planned ahead of time. "I think that if either of us is to make demands of the barkeep, it should be you, Tsira."

She took the glasses and shoved her way to the bar. A few men swore, then backed up quickly when they saw her. The barkeep gave her a steady look. Didn't want her to know she made him nervous. "Two more?"

"Yeah, thanks. Wipe the glasses for me."

He looked at the glasses, then back at her. "You won't want me to once you've seen the rag I'm wiping with."

She showed her teeth. "All right. Long as no one's died yet."

"Not from the glasses, at least."

She carried the gin back to Pink. Traded a few more nods as she went. Handed Pink his glass. He took a sip and screwed his face up. "Terrible stuff, isn't it?"

"Not so bad."

He took another drink. "You're much better at being a man than I am."

She shrugged. "I'm a lot bigger than you." It seemed like that counted about as much for human men as it did for reigs. She didn't mind being the biggest person in the room for a change.

He shook his head. "I don't think that's it. Not entirely. You always seem so—easy. I'm always talking too much and trying to be clever and putting my foot in my mouth and insulting people inadvertently."

"I like how you talk."

He went quiet, then pulled a metal case from his pocket. Opened it up and took a cigarette out, then made himself busy lighting one. She grinned. She liked hearing him talk all right, but liked shutting him up even better.

He took a drag on his cigarette. Did a little trick with it, let the smoke trickle out from his mouth and up into his nose. She watched him. He noticed. "Yes?"

"How'd you do that? With the smoke?"

"I can teach you, if you like."

He lit another cigarette, handed it to her. Took another sip of gin. "Here. Take a drag, but don't inhale. Stick your lower lip out a bit and breathe in through your nose."

She tried. He laughed. "Oh, God! Please never make that face again."

She grinned at him. "You look at my face all the time."

"Not like that. You looked like one of those rainspouts with a lion's head for the water to run out of," he said, and blew a smoke ring.

She didn't know what the hell he was talking about, so she ignored it. Watched him blowing smoke rings instead. She always liked a vahn who was good with his mouth. "Showing off now."

"I must confess I'm delighted to have discovered there's anything in the world that I'm better at doing than you are."

Someone stumbled up against Tsira's back. She turned to look down at him and he threw his hands up. "Sorry! Sorry! Just slipped, is all! No harm meant, sir! No offense!"

She showed her teeth. Dropped her voice as low as it could go. "None taken."

The empty space around her and Pink got even wider.

A little fat man started pushing his way through the crowd, shouting louder than you'd think such a little man could. "Five minutes, gentlemen! Five minutes!"

Pink jerked his chin toward a door in the corner of the room. "Shall we?"

She followed him down the stairs. The crowded basement was packed close enough to make the air heavy and wet. She looked the room over and hung back near the staircase. Let the crowd push past her toward the platform at the center of the room. Pink gestured toward it. "Don't you want to get closer to the ring?"

She shook her head. "There's only one exit."

"Ah. I suppose that's right." He coughed and dropped his cigarette to the floor, grinding it under his heel. "I should pace myself. It's been so long since I've smoked that I'm quite out of the habit."

"There's enough smoke in here already, anyway," she said. Pink nodded and pulled out his handkerchief to wipe his forehead.

"It's beastly hot in here, isn't it?"

She hooked a finger behind his cravat. Gave it a tug to loosen it. Watched how his breath quickened and his eyes turned darker. She ran her hand over the shoulder of his jacket. "Take this off."

"In *public*?"

She laughed.

The little fat man climbed up into the ring. Started yelling about rounds and weights, with Pink trying to explain it all in her ear. She ignored both of them. Waited. Two other pinks climbed up onto the platform then, and the fat man rang a bell, and the fight started.

It was more fun to watch than she'd expected.

Tsira would go for the knees, herself. Get them on the ground and then get them in a hole. Instead they were hopping around and hitting each other with their little fists. She elbowed Pink.

"Why don't they use their legs?"

His eyes didn't leave the ring. He twitched his shoulders like he was throwing punches. "It's against the rules. Fists only."

She watched their feet and saw the rules in it. Watched their hands. Seemed simple enough. She saw that there was labor in making a frail pink body move like that. Could see that there were parts of it that would suit her own body better than the way of fighting her ma had taught her. Thought she could learn quick enough. Her body did what she told it to.

They had good little bodies, the two pinks. She could hear them panting, smell their sweat. Their punches got bigger and looser. They leaned into each other, pressed up against the ropes. She let the heat pass through her, then banished it. The little fat man pulled the fighters apart, sent them to rest at opposite sides of the ring. They sat with their heads low. One of them was bleeding from a split lip, the other from his knuckles.

Tsira looked down at Pink.

"You know how to do this?"

He nodded. Licked his lips. "I fought a bit in school."

"Teach me."

He laughed. "I'm not good enough to make a worthy instructor. Besides, you might kill me accidentally."

"I could teach you a bit," said another voice. "But I'd ask a favor for it."

Tsira looked down. It was the bartender from upstairs. He held out his hand, the one with the missing finger. "Angus Bastenne. At your service."

She thought she'd heard that name. Pink had for certain. His tail nearly wagged at the sound of it. She shook the man's hand. "Cynallumwyntsira."

Pink stepped forward and held his hand out. "Jeck Smith. Tsira's partner."

Bastenne shook his hand. Looked like he was squeezing harder than he needed to. Jeckran didn't flinch. He was taller than Bastenne, but their hands were close in size.

"And what sort of business are you fellows in?"

Pink took a sip of his gin. Tsira noticed for the first time how softly he spoke. Bastenne had to lean in to hear him. "This and that."

Her pink could look tough enough, when he wanted to. She put her hand on his shoulder. "Just got into town this morning."

Pink pulled a cigarette from his case and lit it. "What sort of favor did you want?"

"Might be in your line. An exhibition match. Tsira here against a few local boys. Five, say. I've been looking for a new troll to work with. Had one for a while, but he lit out for the northlands after that mess at Coldstream. Wanted to check on his family, I guess."

"And what would the benefit be for Tsira to enter into such an arrangement?"

"I'd train him up a bit, first, and he'd be paid for his trouble. Five tocats a match, say."

Sounded all right to Tsira. Pink took a drag on his cigarette. He held in the smoke while he spoke. "Will you be selling tickets to this exhibition match?"

Bastenne didn't like that question too much. "Yeah, we will be."

Pink let the smoke trickle out from his nose. "A percentage of the sales. Thirty?"

"Ten."

"Twenty."

"*Ten*, you miserable fuck, and it's better than you've got any right to be asking for."

"Fifteen, then. Tsira?"

She nodded. "Sounds all right."

Bastenne rubbed his broken nose, looking like he'd rather she give him a damn break. "You're a puny one, too. Half-human?"

"Yeah. Big like a troll and mean like a pink," she said, and showed him her teeth. "When do you want me to come by?"

He grinned. "That's what I like to hear. Be here at ten tomorrow." Then they shook on it.

The fight started up again. Bastenne walked off to "speak to some business associates." Tsira watched the two little pinks hitting each other and thought about which one she'd rather fuck. She thought she liked the darker-skinned one better than the paler one. He kept licking his split lip as he fought. She liked the look of his tongue.

Pink went off to get another gin. Came back looking mad, knuckles white around the glass. Tsira watched him. Waited for him to say what was wrong.

It didn't take long. "That fellow over there just trod on my toe and then called me a mewling little puke."

"You mind?"

"I did, rather."

"You hit him?"

"I didn't."

"Why not?"

"I—I suppose it didn't occur to me."

"Go hit him," said Tsira. She took his gin from him. "I'll wait."

He went off. She waited. After a few seconds there was some shouting. She gave him some time to get some punches in, then went over to have a look. He was on the ground, straddling the other fellow's chest. Working his face over pretty good. She let him go until she thought both of them looked like they'd had enough. Grabbed him by the collar and pulled him off.

"Time to go."

They left. Went out the door and down the street laughing. Pink's eye was swelling shut. She grinned at him. "How you feeling?"

"*Fantastic,*" he said. She put her arm around his shoulders.

"Good."

They walked down the street for a while. People stared as they passed. She showed them her teeth. "I'm a little drunk, Pink."

"Are you really? You don't seem it. How much did you have to drink?"

"Four glasses."

"Good God. We were barely in there for an hour."

"Yeah. Not bad."

"I daresay not. In an hour we drank half a bottle of gin, smoked three cigarettes, broke a man's nose, and secured paying employment. An hour well spent."

"Good job bargaining. Would have taken the five a fight."

"Well, I have to earn my keep somehow, don't I?"

She smelled something then. Something familiar. It was coming from an alleyway nearby. She headed for it, with Pink running up behind her. "Tsira! Where in the releft are you going?"

The smell was coming from a doorway with a small lamp beside it. She walked in.

The room was dark and even thicker with the smell inside. Pinks were sitting in chairs along the walls, slumped over onto tables. A few of them looked at her when she walked in. They looked pretty far away. The kind of look people got when they were trying to outrun their own head.

Pink was tugging at her elbow. She backed out, closed the door behind her. "That was it," she told him. "The smell on that wizard. One who tried to kill me."

"Oh, in that case, if it was to *identify a smell*, it was well worth it for you to go charging into a dripping parlor."

She shrugged. "Didn't look like they could do much harm. What's a dripping parlor?"

"A place in which people use drip. It's a sort of altered laudanum they make in Monsatelle. It's meant to be mixed with liquor and fortifying herbs, but from everything I've heard it's just as likely to be full of turpentine. Shall we return to the main thoroughfare, or do you have more business to attend to in this alleyway?"

She didn't have any more business in the alleyway. They returned to the thoroughfare. Pink was limping again. Tsira offered her arm, but he looked around him and didn't take it. Tsira could understand that. Didn't want to look weak in front of other pinks. He said, "I suppose that's something, though. Now we know why a Weltsir wizard would be in such a pitiful state."

"Stuff they were using that bad?"

"They call it *the wolf of Monsatelle*. It's been eating up the young men for years now."

"Should get a good reig to sort it out." She was only half joking.

Jeckran smiled. "I'm sure that if you were put in charge of things, you would resolve the scourge of drip in Monsatelle within a day or two."

"Not me. My ma could, though."

They walked for a while without talking. Got back to Mon Del Ras's place and took the stairs up to their room. Tsira started to undress. Pink hung back at the doorway. "I think I'll talk to Mon Del Ras. Thank him. The boxing was his suggestion, after all."

"Suit yourself," said Tsira, and pulled off her shirt.

His eyes flicked down to her belly, then up again. "I'll be up later. You should sleep now. You have to go to work in the morning, after all."

She lay down on the bed and waited. The bed was too short. Her feet hung off the end of it. She fell asleep, anyway, then woke up when Pink crawled into bed with her.

He lay still for a while, then said her name. "Tsira?"

She didn't respond; too drowsy for talking. Felt him moving around. First like he was trying to settle, then with a rhythm to it. It took her a bit to realize what he was doing. She hadn't ever heard him before. Thought of letting him know she was awake, then thought better of it.

He was very quiet and came fast. Cleaned himself off and went still. She fell asleep again soon after.

Woke up to a scream.

She nearly fell out of the bed from the sound, like someone being murdered. She grabbed him by the arm. "Pink. *What?*"

His right eye was nearly swollen shut and his hair was like something a rat had made. Face as white as the walls, except for the eye, which was about the shade that Tsira was normally. Looked a mess. "Tsira, are you all right? What happened? There's blood *everywhere*."

She looked down under the blanket. There was blood everywhere. "Oh. Yeah. Happens."

"What—*oh*." He drew back a bit, but didn't scream again. "You—that happens to *you?*"

"Sometimes." It had been a few years.

He was looking at her funny. Wished he would stop. "Are you sure that you feel quite all right, Tsira?"

Definitely funny. She shrugged. "Sure. Bit hungry."

"I'll go get you some breakfast. And tell Bette to come up to change the sheets," he said. He was suddenly awake and getting dressed like he had somewhere to be. She watched him pulling his boots on.

"How's your eye?"

"My eye?" He looked in the mirror. Winced. "I suppose that I'll live."

He headed for the door. She sat up. "Pink."

"What?"

"Bring some clean rags."

Bette came up a few minutes later. Brought hot water and a washbasin and clean sheets. Kept talking all the time as she cleaned up. Tsira couldn't understand the words, but got the feeling of it. Sympathetic. Cozy. Like they were two girls together. Sweet of her, even if Tsira always thought pinks were funny with how they divided themselves up so strict by what they had up their skirts. She knew a few big tough reigs who'd never bled in their lives; didn't seem to have slowed them down any.

Bette left, and Pink came creeping back in with food and coffee and a box of shaving things. She'd gotten herself cleaned up pretty well by then. He put the breakfast on the dressing table and poured out two cups of coffee. "Will you still be able to fight today, do you think?"

Tsira shrugged. "Sure."

"Really? You don't have to, if you feel unwell."

"Yeah? I'll tell Bastenne. Sorry, can't fight, bleeding from the cunt."

Pink winced. Tsira grinned. "I feel fine." She slapped him on the back. "Thanks."

There was an ache starting in the space between her groin and her navel. She sat down in one of the chairs and began to eat her breakfast. Pain would get better once she started moving for the day. "Good talk with Mon Del Ras?"

He looked away. "Yes, perfectly fine."

Probably thinking about Mon Del Ras when he jerked himself off. Two of them looked all right together. Two pretty little things. She thought about snapping Mon Del Ras's neck. Thought about tearing his belly open with her teeth. Choking him hadn't been enough. "Ask him next time if he knows who sells that stuff."

"What stuff?"

"Stuff I smelled."

"Drip, you mean? Why—oh, to see if anyone knows our wizard?"

She nodded. "Smart."

"I do my best."

They headed out after breakfast. Back to the gin palace. The city stunk worse in the daytime. All of those chamber pots emptied out into the gutters and warming under the sun. Was going to be a hot day. Pink looked worse in the sunlight, with the swollen eye and the limp.

"We're being stared at," he said.

They were, a bit. More than a bit. Some folks were stopping and turning around to see them go past. Pink smiled a tight little smile. "Don't we make a pair."

A cart went by with a young fellow in a tall hat driving it. Pink swore and looked down. Looked up again once the coach was gone. "I think I know him. Or knew him, I suppose. From my club in Leiscourt."

He was hurting. She could see that now. Hurting pretty badly. Limping worse than ever, like it was spreading from heart to ankle.

"When you getting your new clothes?"

He brightened up at that. "At the end of the week, I expect."

"All right," she said. "How much does a cart like that cost?"

"The little curricle, you mean? Good God, a fortune. I don't like to think about it. I've only ever driven a friend's."

"We'll get you one."

He grinned. "Will we?"

"Yeah. Get you whatever you like."

He laughed. That was all right.

When they got to the gin palace Bastenne was waiting for them. Sitting on the front step with a pint of beer in his hand. "Two of you beat on one of my customers last night."

"Wasn't me," Tsira said.

"He deserved it," Pink said.

Bastenne rolled his eyes. "Show me a man in my place who don't deserve to get beat on and I'll show you one who took a wrong turn on the way to the Elgarite Hall. Don't drive off my paying fucking custom, boys, that's all I ask of you. That goes double for you, Blue. You could do some fucking damage to my revenues."

Tsira liked him just fine.

First thing he taught her was the rules. No biting, first off. No kicking. No hitting a man when he was on the ground. No grabbing a fellow below the waist or hitting him in the stones. All well enough. Next he picked up a pair of leather things to show to her.

"See these? These are boxing gloves. Now, in most instances, I take for my authority on the sport Mr. Arimi Marlow, the Hesendi Hellcat, and he supports the use of gloves. In stance and footwork, Blue, all you need to do is follow the rules that Mr. Marlow sets down and you won't go too far astray, but I won't have fucking gloves in my establishment.

Without them, fellows have to consider their knuckles as much as the other fellow's face. With them we see all manner of dreadful violence, and no mistake. Tried them for a week, and half of the fighters left feet first. What you've got to learn is how to punch *proper*."

Learning to punch proper took some practice. She couldn't even stand right at first. Bastenne kept smacking her on the chin. "Keep your chin tucked in. Fists up. You're not biting folks in my joint. You're not an Elgar-fucked crocodile. And don't fucking stare at me like that. Makes you look like a jackass. Are you a jackass, Blue?"

Pink was tittering at her from the side of the room. Having a fine time. She glared at him. Bastenne smacked her chin again. "Don't fucking glare at your friend, either."

He showed her how he wanted her to punch. Made her do it over and over. Asked her to do it faster, and swore. "Shit. You ain't slow."

He let her have a rest and some water. She sat next to Pink to drink. She could feel the wet between her legs. Needed to change the rag out. She jerked her chin at Bastenne. "Need to piss."

"Privy's out back. Up the stairs and to the left. Don't run off. Got your friend here for a hostage."

"Keep him," she said. Almost meant it.

They kept up like that for about two weeks. Bastenne working her hard in the basement, Pink coming along to watch. After the first few days he started joining in, trying to keep up with her training. Only had to stop sometimes when his ankle bothered him. They went home at night and ate everything that Bette could find to feed them.

Tsira slept like the dead, but Pink kept staying up to talk to Mon Del Ras.

She thought she'd kill that fucking fairy any day now.

They met a few other people, too. Gamblers and fighters, big tough men, loud-talking girls. Tsira liked the working girls she met, liked how they took Tsira as she was and didn't ask too many stupid questions when she stopped by to chat. Liked a woman Mon Del Ras was friends with, a madam who ran girls out of a dripping parlor near the river. Her name was Catleen. She was a tall, pretty girl, pale hair, pale eyes, and an easy smile, silk on her back and emeralds on her fingers. She liked Tsira, too. Sought her out to have a drink together the first time they crossed paths in the dining room and told her that she'd always thought it'd be useful to have a troll for a friend. Tsira liked the honesty. Catleen taught her how to speak some Esiphian, taught her how to throw dice so they came out right. They ate dinner together, drank wine, and laughed loud.

Catleen was a different kind of reig than most Tsira had met. Little and soft but rock hard in the bones.

"You're not like other human women," Tsira said to her one night.

Catleen smiled. She had a smile that looked like it tasted good. "How do you figure that, then?"

"You're tougher," Tsira said. "Don't simper."

"Ah, well, that's where you're wrong," Catleen said. "I'll simper with the best of them, when it serves me. Humans aren't trolls, Tsira. We human women don't have so many weapons. I'll use the first that comes to hand, when it comes to that."

Sometimes when Tsira came back late from a dinner with Catleen, Jeckran smelled like gin and acted like he didn't want to talk.

Tsira didn't know what she should think about that.

Bastenne kept smacking her while she trained. Kept calling her *Blue*. One day he did it and she stopped moving. Looked down at him. "Red."

"What?"

"Don't mind if you can't say my name. *Cynallumwyntsira*. Hard for folks who don't speak Dacyn to pronounce. But my name's not Blue. My name's Tsira. That means red."

He stared at her for a bit. "If you're done talking, I'd like to see you punching, Red."

Pink was in a good mood when they walked home. Wearing his new suit, the one he'd had made. She hadn't understood the fuss about it until she saw it on him. You could see the whole shape of him in it, with his calves showing in their new white stockings. They were nice calves. It was a nice shape.

He'd gotten himself a stick, too. Other pinks had them for the look of it, just swinging them when they walked. He did that most of the time, but leaned on it sometimes, too. She could see the relief when he did. Leaning on the stick and feeling like himself. Like he lived in a body that didn't hurt.

It was too hot to sleep that night. Pink brought up a basin of cold water and dipped his head in it every once in a while. Tsira tried it, too. Laid on the bed and stared at the cracks in the ceiling.

She had her first fight the next day.

They didn't talk much that morning, just ate breakfast and stayed away from each other. Tsira went out for a walk. Tried to work some of the nerve out. It didn't work. She came back mad and sweating.

Pink was getting dressed when she got back. Kept knotting his cravat over and over. She put a hand to his hip. "Hey."

He shuddered when she touched him. Didn't move away. He said, "It was a mistake. To do this. It's dreadful. It's a dreadful sport. I'm sure that trolls never beat each other senseless in front of screaming crowds for the sake of entertainment."

"We don't," she said, and smiled at him. "It's all right, though. Learning something new, that's all."

She slid her hand from his hip to his waist. Watched his face in the mirror. "You look good."

Always pushed that thought down, but it came running back up like a hungry dog. Knew it wasn't right. Not when he watched other pinks on the street. Not when she was a sad excuse for a reig, and he was the kind of man any human would want. Not when she was twice his size. Not when he thought he owed her his life.

Didn't stop her from thinking it.

Bastenne's place was crowded that night. Crowd started yelling as she walked up. Friends of the other fighters, some of them. Someone shouted, "You think you're better than us, troll? We don't need you *or* your dirty fucking magic!"

One fellow reached out like he was going to touch her, but Pink

cracked him over the knuckles with his stick and jerked his chin toward
Tsira. "I've done you a favor, sir. If you had managed that, he would
have taken your arm off."

Bastenne met them at the doorway, walked ahead of them, and told
the drunks to fuck off. Led them past the bar to his office, which was
what he called the room where he spilled beer on his ledgers. "You can
change in here." He punched her in the shoulder. "You're going to flat-
ten some local boys tonight, Red, and I'm going to enjoy seeing it."

He left. Closed the door behind him. It was dark in his office.
Smelled of gin even worse than it did in the bar. She started to unbutton
her shirt and noticed Jeckran staring. She stared back at him.

"I make a habit of tearing arms off, now?"

"I'd like those beasts outside to believe that you do, if it keeps their
hands off you."

She took off her trousers and traded them for a looser pair.

"Tsira," he said. "Tsira. There's something that I must say to you."

A roar rose up from outside the door, followed by a pounding on it.
"Troll!"

"Later," she said, and rubbed her torc for a second before she opened
the door.

The crowd parted for her. Always did. They might scream, but they
weren't stupid.

There were steps up to the ring, but Tsira jumped up to the edge of
it instead, then stepped over the ropes. The crowd screamed harder at
that, and for the first time, it didn't have a mean sound to it. She had
practiced that jump. Fallen onto her ass a few times. Worth it, now, for
the cheers.

The boys came in. Five of them. All big, as pinks went. Umpires
stepped up, too; Bastenne for her, tall skinny fellow for the boys.

She waited with her hands up, to make Bastenne happy. Knew she
could move quick enough that it wouldn't matter so much. Waited for
the bell.

One of the boys couldn't wait. Rushed her before the bell had rung, swung wide and sloppy for her head. She stepped to the side, and he kept going. Practically ran into her fist.

The crowd liked that all right.

Then the rest of them came at her. These were smarter than the first. One throwing punches at her face, another at her chest, another at the kidneys. Too much at once to act smart, so she just started hitting. Aimed for the chest because she didn't want to kill them. Got one hard enough to wind him, drove her elbow back into another. Got punched in the cunt. Lost her temper. Broke his jaw. Felt her knuckle split and kept hitting through it.

She wanted to use her legs and her teeth, get them on the ground and tear out their throats. She didn't. Just kept working the combinations that Bastenne had taught her. She wouldn't bite anyone in his joint.

Someone pulled her fucking hair.

She reached behind her to try to get him off, but he was stuck in there like a burr, and he got a few hard punches up under her ribcage with his free hand. The umpires ran up to try and shake him loose, but she was quicker. Her heel grinding his toes, her fist in his stomach, her knee on his chest.

"Want to fight for blood, you'd better be good at it."

There was a buzz like bugs on a summer night.

Cheering.

Bastenne was pounding her on the back. She stood, jumped out of the ring. Found her pretty little pink. He was at the edge of the ring, sweating and laughing. Put her hand to his back, took him with her through the crowd. Got back to the office and shut the door behind her. "Tsira," he said, and she put her hands to his shoulders, shoved him up against the wall. Slid him up higher and kissed him.

He scrabbled for a hold. Looped a leg around her waist. Pressed his palms against her chest. Gentle at first, then harder. "Tsira, stop—"

She put him down. Backed away. Buzzing was back in her ears. Grabbed her shirt and pulled it on. "Sorry."

"Tsira, I only—"

"Sorry," she said, and left. She could hear him calling after her, but she didn't look back.

She went out into the hot night and walked.

She wanted him. Wanted him with his face between her legs. Wanted him screaming for her. Wanted him her vahn and no one else's. Wanted it whether he wanted it or not.

She leaned up against a building to wait for the nausea to pass.

She came to the city wall. Climbed up. She didn't think too much of it, just wanted to work the fear out of her muscles. She cursed herself when the guard came up. Had to climb back down real quick. She dangled from her fingers, then dropped. Felt the shock in her knees when she landed. Felt old, and tired, and lonely. Felt shame climbing up her throat. Felt sick with it.

She wanted her vahn.

When she got back home, Mon Del Ras was sitting alone in the dining room, smoking.

"He's asleep. I fed him brandy until he passed out. Catleen sent a bottle of wine for you, by the way. To compliment you on your victory."

"Better not have touched him."

"I have no interest to touch him. I'm a married man, cousin."

She stopped before she got to the stairs. "She know you're of the blood?"

"Bette? Of course she does."

"Why pick her? Why not another fairy?"

He ground out his cigarette and smiled. "Why else, cousin? Because I fell in love."

Tsira went upstairs. Lay down on the floor and tried to sleep.

"Tsira."

She opened her eyes. It was morning. That surprised her—that she had managed to sleep. The floor was harder than sleeping rough outdoors. She tried to move and regretted it. Lay still instead.

Pink squatted down next to her. "You look absolutely dreadful."

"Thanks."

"Last night—"

"Sorry. Won't do it again."

He opened his mouth, then closed it. He didn't look like he hated her at all. "Shall we talk about the fight?"

"Yeah."

"You were wonderful."

It hadn't felt wonderful. Felt normal. Not easy, but not hard, either. "Thanks. Try six of them next time."

She sat up and winced. Hits to the face looked bad, but there was nothing like a gut punch for the ache the next day. The hits to the ribs weren't feeling too great, either.

He stood to grab a small bottle off of the dresser, then moved around behind her. "Take off your shirt."

"Why?"

"Bastenne told me that I should rub this into your muscles for you. I was meant to do it before you fell asleep last night."

She pulled her shirt off. He gave a little hiss. "You're hurt."

"Happens when you fight."

The tips of his fingers touched the tenderest place on her back. "This one looks rather nasty. You've gone a little green."

She heard him twist the bottle open, and he started rubbing her shoulders. The liniment made her skin heat up. He didn't seem to mind touching her. She thought she should tell him to stop. She couldn't manage it. It felt too good. He got his thumbs deep into the knot at the base of her neck. She couldn't help a soft grunt. He jerked back.

"Did I hurt you?"

"No. Don't stop."

She thought maybe he sucked in a little breath, but when he spoke again a few moments later his voice was easy. "We were offered another job last night."

"Yeah?"

"*Yeah*," he said. Mimicking her. "One of Bastenne's associates runs a card game a few nights a week. He lost his bodyguard a few days ago, and he asked if we'd take the work on."

"Lost?"

"Well. He was killed by a disgruntled punter, which is why he thought he'd hire a troll. I imagine that even the most ambitious of gamblers would be unlikely to want to annoy you. And we'd be well paid. You could still fight at Bastenne's if you wanted, and we could keep our room here. Though I thought that we might rent a flat." He was still working out that spot in her neck.

"What's a flat?"

"A small home inside of a bigger house. We could have a sitting room and a kitchen. I think that it would be about the thing for two young bachelors."

She could hear the smile in his voice. "We'd live in it together?"

"Yes. We would have our own bedrooms, of course, so you would be able to escape me whenever you wished."

"And a room for sitting."

He laughed. "Yes, exactly."

"How much did we make last night?"

"Eleven tocats and two sen, and Bastenne seems convinced you'll draw a bigger crowd next time. He was talking about holding the next fight out of doors, somewhere just outside of the city. We could make more than twenty tocats in a night." He paused. "We hadn't talked about splitting the money."

Tsira shrugged. "Don't matter. Mine is yours."

"But it *should* matter. You're the one putting yourself in danger. I put eight tocats in your purse and kept three for myself. I also spent the extra two sen on a glass of gin when you ran off last night. I hope you don't mind."

"Don't," she said. "I don't need that much." She kept waiting for him to push her away again. Instead he kept rubbing her shoulders. "How much they paying for the card game job?"

"Twenty tocats a week," he said. "Ten for each of us. He didn't want to pay for me at first, but I took him outside and shot a glass of gin off a hitching post. He thought I might be worth a sen or two then." He moved her hair out of the way and worked his fingers into her neck. The sun was coming clean and bright through the window. She felt fine.

Pink rubbed her neck a little harder. "Your friend Catleen sent a bottle of wine for you."

"We should drink it tonight," Tsira said. Maybe he'd rub her neck like that some more after a few glasses.

"You don't want to drink it with Catleen?"

She frowned. "I want to drink it with you."

"Ah," he said. Then he stayed quiet.

She was quiet, too, for a while. Then she said, "When do we start work?"

"Tomorrow evening, if you agree," he said, and she did.

Soon they were almost always working. The card games kept them busy when Tsira didn't have a fight, which was usually twice a week. Three weeks went by. The crowds got bigger every time, and so did the number of fellows she had to fight. She got her face beat up badly enough one night that they decided she needed some time off. She spent it reading every book she could find and teaching Pink some Dacyn. Just a few words, the basic syllabary, and the alphabet. Pink wasn't too good at it yet. One day he left her a note in it, his handwriting huge and shaky like a child's, the words all broken up in the wrong places and the wrong punctuation at the end.

*Tsira|writing b ad*
*I w ant di nner?*

When she saw it, she laughed until her stomach hurt, and then she put it into her purse to keep.

A few days later they were on a walk when they stepped into a crowd.

There were two pinks at the center of it: a tall, pale woman and a young man. Both dressed all in black, both with hair cut close to their skulls. Pink was at her elbow. A little nervy. Didn't like these pinks or what they were doing. She put her hand against his back and felt him settle.

"Who are they?"

"They're Hesendis," he said. "It's a sort of fringe Elgarism. They think they can cure melancholy and heal the sick with conversation and vegetables and prayer. It's all absurd fanatical nonsense, but every city has enough people who are desperate enough to come to them for help. And as often as not they'll feel better, probably because they want it so badly, and give the Hesendis some money for their trouble."

"I'll watch," Tsira said.

The young man was speaking. Good-looking pink. Thick black hair and big dark eyes. A scar on his lip. He was speaking to a plump woman, talking about breathing deeply with him and concentrating on God and letting evil thoughts pass through her and away. Tsira moved a little closer. It sounded mostly all right.

Then he stopped talking and started to shake, his eyes rolling back in his head, a low moan coming from his chest. Shook so hard he started to fall, and Tsira reached out to catch him.

He looked up at her. Smiled. "Thank you."

It was a woman's voice. Not his own at all. She heard the crowd hiss and let her own shock run through her. Didn't drop him. Set him back on his feet. "Pleasure."

He smiled. She could smell the magic dripping off him like sweat. Not the copper smell of a human wizard, or the cool water of her clan's wizard Marden when he was working. This was something else. Like turned earth and green wood and clean cunt. He looked at her. His eyes were all black, the lighter part eaten up by the pupils. "Your mother," he said. He touched her cheek. "I'm so sorry."

Then he moved off into the crowd.

Pink came up. Her little vahn. His hand closed on her wrist. "Tsira, what is it? What did he say to you?"

She put her hand to his back again. "Nothing."

When they got back to Mon Del Ras's place, a troll was waiting for them. A big reig Tsira didn't know, sitting in a tiny chair and drinking tea out of one of Bette's tiny teacups with the flowers on it. When they walked in, she set the cup down in its saucer and stood. "Cynallumwyntsira," she said.

Tsira lifted her chin and put her voice as deep as it went. She spoke in Dacyn. "Who are you?"

"Cynallumwyntresal sent me to track you down. You don't make yourself easy to find. Next time you decide to move to a human city, you might send word to your clan first. Lucky for me that one of my contacts saw one of your fight notices in the paper."

Pink edged up against her side. Scared, maybe. She put an arm around him without thinking about it. "What does Ma want?"

"For you to return to your clan seat. She has things to discuss with you." The reig's eyes went to Jeckran. "Is this your vahn?"

Tsira didn't know why she said it. Maybe because of how that reig sounded when she asked. Like she thought she was better than Tsira. So she said, "Yeah."

The reig just nodded. "I'll tell your mother to expect you both," she said. Then she put a coin on the table and left.

Jeckran stared up at her. "What on earth was that all about?"

Tsira sighed. "Guess you're going to meet my ma."

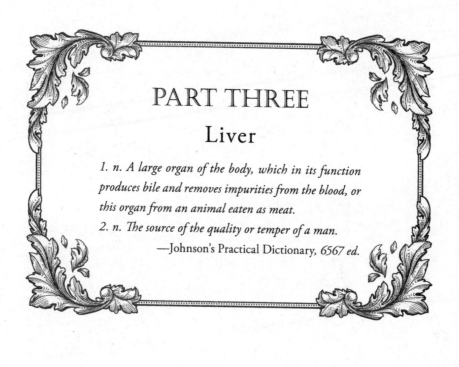

# PART THREE

## Liver

*1. n. A large organ of the body, which in its function produces bile and removes impurities from the blood, or this organ from an animal eaten as meat.*

*2. n. The source of the quality or temper of a man.*

—Johnson's Practical Dictionary, *6567 ed.*

# 11

———

*We have seen this season many young headwives of Leiscourt wearing frocks in what is being called the Hexian mode, that is very short, with trollish embroidery, such that it suggests the appearance of the tunics worn by Hexian wizards. This looks very fresh and charming on ladies under the age of thirty, with narrow figures. The daring young woman with good features might choose to also dress her hair in a Hexian crop to complete the effect. Mature ladies who wish to include elements of the Hexian mode in their dress this year might ask for trollish patterns to be embroidered onto the hem of a full-length gown with a high neck and short sleeves, with the hair worn in a "tuck" to the shoulders . . .*

—Ladies' Sketch, *Fall 6572*

On her fifth full day of employment—after speaking to Mrs. Cordram, writing several letters to her family, moving into the Lamp, and trying as best she could to grow accustomed to the singular personality of her employer, the Lord-Mage of Hexos, as well as to his home, his habits, and his methods of study—Onna found herself in a fish market with Loga.

It was inside of an enormous wooden structure like a giant barn, which Onna imagined was meant to keep the sun and rain out but served just as well to hold the smell—something between a tide pool and a charnel house—in. Of the hundreds of stalls inside the enclosure, some appeared to specialize in one type of fish or another—maybe eels or shark—but many looked exactly like their neighbors. Hexians wearing canvas aprons over their tunics gathered in great crowds around the huge tubs of fish, shouting at one another in a dreadfully energetic manner while spurts of blood erupted from the unlucky creatures that had been selected from among their brethren. The eels, in particular, were killed and gutted with great speed and efficiency, their heads driven onto a nail, which was then dragged down the length of their bodies. Other fish were simply tossed into sacks while still alive. She wondered what good a live fish could possibly do anyone: her mother had always said that fresh ingredients were the most wholesome, but Onna thought that certainly there must be *limits* on this philosophy.

"Whatever are they fighting about?" Onna asked Loga.

He looked surprised. "Fighting?"

"Yes," she said, picking her way carefully around a pool of entrails. Loga followed her more boldly: she supposed he was rich enough to not mind if his expensive clothes were spoilt with fish guts. He was in blue silk today, with a floral pattern in silver thread. Onna found it all rather excessive—though the colors were much more muted than what she had seen on some other men in Hexos—and it struck her that the neat black silk that she had thought so elegant when Loga wore it around the Lamp was the Hexian version of a morning dress, suitable only for wearing indoors. "They're all shouting at one another."

"Oh," said Loga. "They're only bargaining. Trying to get the best price. You'd hear about the same in a large fish market in Daeslund."

Onna supposed that this might very well be the case: there was nothing very large at all in Cordridge-on-Sea, other than the pencil eraser factories.

"Have you a strong stomach, Onna?"

This struck her as ominous. He hadn't yet told her what they were doing in the market, or what it had to do with trolls being murdered. "Middling, I suppose."

"I'm delighted to hear it. If you were squeamish, you would be of very little use to me at the moment."

"If you don't mind my being inquisitive, what *are* we doing, at the moment?"

"I don't mind in the slightest, darling. We're going to the icehouse to look at a corpse."

The icehouse was a small, windowless room in the farthest corner of the market. It was used, said Loga, to store the more expensive and delicate of the wares available at the market: pufferfish, caviar, good oysters. At the moment it also held the body of a troll who had been found murdered in a nearby alley two days earlier. They were let inside by a guard who nodded when he saw Loga, unlocked the door, then shut it behind them.

It was pitch-dark inside and as cold as winter. Loga created a light, and Onna saw the corpse and screamed aloud.

He gripped her by the elbow. "I know that it's dreadful, darling, but we do have to look," he said, and she gathered herself together and did.

"Tell me what you see," said Loga.

"A troll," she said. "Very tall. I don't know how tall. Ten feet or so. I suppose we could—measure."

"The police already did all of that. You can look at their notes later, if you like. What else?"

"He's naked. Was he when they found him?" The troll had obviously been moved and autopsied, judging by the stitches holding him together.

"Yes. The clothes were found next to the body."

"What did they look like?"

"Why do you ask?"

"Because it might help us to know where he came from from."

"Very good. A woolen skirt and vest, heavily embroidered. They were brought to the troll quarter and identified. His name is Aorwyn-bahnoc, from a small Daeslundic clan called the Nasen. He was a widower. He came here with his children four months ago, just after the Coldstream massacre, because he'd heard of trolls being harassed near his home and thought that they'd be safer here. Hexos has a large troll population already, including some distant relatives of his, and he thought he would be able to find work in the embroidery markets. He's the fourth victim we've found in Hexos so far. From what I've heard, the count is over a dozen in Daeslund."

It hadn't occurred to her that the trolls of Daeslund could be so terrorized by what was happening that they might flee abroad as refugees. That they would have wives and children. That they would pursue embroidery as a trade. She hadn't stopped to consider the messiness of death beyond a single corpse, the wide web of beating hearts stretching away from every heart cut out. "What will happen to the children?"

"They've been taken in by one of the local clan-heads for now."

She moved closer. Looked at the wounds. "Whoever did this was an academic wizard."

"Why do you say that?"

"The incisions are very neat." They were so neat that it was hard to tell at first look what had been done by the killer and what came after, during the autopsy. "Was there—much damage to his insides?"

Loga shook his head. "The surgeon who examined the body said that it was very neatly done."

Onna licked her lips. "He must have studied anatomy. I suppose he could also be a practical who works as a butcher or a surgeon."

"How do you think he was killed?"

She looked at the troll's face. His hands. "He must have died before he was cut open, don't you think?"

"Why?"

She swallowed. "There isn't much blood on him. Was there a great deal of blood where he was found? Or on his clothes?"

"No. A large portion of blood had been removed—he was almost completely exsanguinated, in fact—but there was very little on the ground."

"There would have been, wouldn't there? If he had been—flayed open while he was still alive." Like the fish having their heads hacked off in the market. "He must have been killed first, then undressed, then—cut." She hadn't thought of herself as squeamish before, but the thought of it—of the poor man being treated like that, like *meat*—made her stomach give a rebellious lurch.

"Any suggestions as to how he might have been killed?"

"His heart is gone, so I can't say for sure. But if I had to do it—not that I *would*, of course—but if I did, it would be with a jolt of energy directly to the heart. He would have to be a very talented wizard to manage it, I think. All of that power at once." She paused. She felt strange. There were many things that she had studied here in front of her, and there was also a person who was dead. She tried to put the person aside, make him still and flat like a picture in one of her books. It was easier. Perhaps it was easier than it really ought to be.

"That matches nicely with what the surgeon said as well," Loga said. "That if it weren't for the mutilation after death, he would have thought he died of natural causes. What else?"

"There aren't any singe marks," she said, "so the wizard would have been touching him, wouldn't he? He couldn't just fling a ball of energy. It would burn the victim, set his hair on fire." She was conscious of herself talking too much, thinking too quickly, acting like a little professor. This was the point at which someone should be laughing at her, or raising their eyebrows, or taking her aside to ask if she didn't think she might like to let the boys get a word in edgewise. But no one did, and so she continued. "But how would he get close enough to touch him?" She considered for a moment. "Do you think it could have been another troll? Someone he trusted?"

Loga looked at her. "This magic is very academic, though, you just said. Wouldn't that eliminate troll wizards?"

"There are troll wizards, though. They're meant to be the best."

"There are. What do you know about them?"

"That they have their own style of magic. That should *feel* different, shouldn't it?"

She closed her eyes and tried to concentrate. She had always been able to sense magic, but she tried to push it back when it wasn't needed. Loga's presence alone would have driven her to distraction if she had attended to it: he was a roar where other wizards were a hum. She turned her attention to the corpse, tried to feel if there was anything lingering there. And there was, if only barely: a silvery thread, the hint of parameters, a sensation of deep familiarity. She opened her eyes, startled.

"I think he must be a Weltsir wizard. A very good one, too. But then how would he have gotten so close? Are there any humans in Hexos whom trolls particularly trust?"

"Good question," said a woman's voice. Onna *shrieked* from horrible icy shock, and then she whirled around. Two people stood in the entrance.

They were both dressed in dull soot-colored robes, but that was where their similarity ended. The woman was tall and slender—but for a round belly that indicated that she was going to become a mother in the near future—with pale skin powdered to bluishness, dark eyes, and straight black hair in a neat Hexian crop. The man had a dark, ruddy complexion, round boyish cheeks, and his hair in an abundance of long braids gathered back neatly at his nape. The woman winced as she said, "Oh, sorry. I didn't mean to startle you. I just have a tendency to get excited when I hear someone talking sense."

"Ah, you're here, Captain Run!" said Loga, infuriatingly enough.

Onna endeavored not to glare too pointedly. "Were you expecting *anyone else*, Loga?" Her heart was pounding from the shock.

"Oh, no, only these two," Loga said. "Onna, I'd like you to meet Captain Run and Sergeant Bato. They're detectives of the Hexos Watch, and they will be introducing you to what they know of the case. Officers, this is my new assistant, Onna Gebowa."

"Nice to meetcha," said Captain Run, whose accent sounded so much like the countryside near Cordridge-on-Sea that Onna could practically cry from homesickness. "Where are you from, Miss Gebowa? Near Aufdom Mare?"

"A bit farther west," Onna said. "Cordridge-on-Sea."

"Gosh, who'd have thought!" Captain Run said. "I went to the four-year fair there once, when I was little. It's a nice place. Bit of a funny smell, though."

"That's from the pencil eraser factories," Onna said hurriedly, as if Captain Run might have otherwise suspected Onna of being personally responsible for the odor.

"You're from Daeslund?" said Sergeant Bato. He had an accent like Onna's grandfather, and a similar air of disappointment in her. "Your name's Awati."

"Ah, yes," Onna said, embarrassed. "My great-grandparents are all from Awat."

Sergeant Bato brightened and released a veritable storm of Awati upon Onna, who withstood the torrent until she could find an opportunity to gasp out, "I'm awfully sorry, I don't speak any Awati," which made him collapse back into a puddle of ennui.

"Too bad," he said, "that your parents never taught you."

Onna swallowed. Even if he hadn't meant it as a criticism, it stung like one, and she was momentarily torn whether he would think her an even worse exemplar of a good Awati girl if she agreed with him—as she thought *might* be proper, as he was an Awati man much older than herself—or if she defended her parents, which also seemed as if it might be the correct course. Instead she took the coward's path of ducking her head and saying nothing at all, which left her feeling all the worse.

"Now that you've all been introduced," Loga said, "shall we repair to somewhere more conducive to conversation?"

After they left the icehouse and the fish market, Onna took great gulps of the relatively fresh air of the street. Loga clapped his hands together. "Lovely! Is anyone else hungry? I could do with some lunch."

It was absolutely mystifying to Onna that Loga would still have an appetite, but the two officers of the law also expressed an interest in a meal—especially after Loga made it clear, in a circuitous sort of way, that it would be his treat—and so Onna trailed after them as they walked briskly down the street and turned into a dingy little Sangan restaurant.

There was a spontaneous outburst of "Loga!" from the waiters when they entered, and they were ushered to their seats by one waiter as several others cracked their washrags in the air and set about a furious scrubbing of the already spotlessly clean table, punctuated by more cheerful conversation. The chief waiter handed Loga an enormous book, which he flipped through in a few moments before entering into an extended discourse with the young man.

Onna stared at him. "What on earth is that book for?"

Loga smiled at her. "It's a menu, darling. We have them in most restaurants in Sango. It lists all of the different dishes available to order."

"Oh," Onna said, though her imagination failed her when she tried to think of what could possibly take up all of the space in such a large menu. All of the restaurants she had ever visited in Daeslund had offered no choices more diverting than the joint or the chop.

At last everything seemed settled to Loga's satisfaction, and the waiter departed. The other waiters leaned against the wall to drink tea and chat with one another—there were no other customers in the restaurant—though not before one of them poured tea for Loga and Onna and the officers as well. Loga said something to their waiter, who positively *giggled*, and responded using Loga's name before departing.

Captain Run looked about with keen interest. "I had no idea that there was a Sangan restaurant in this neighborhood, Loga."

"Oh, yes, I come here constantly," Loga said. "I'm particularly devoted to the braised pork." This set the two of them off into a little discussion about Sangan food—it transpired that Loga had been raised in the southeast of that country, while Captain Run's mother was from the far north, so they had what struck Onna as somewhat violently opposed opinions about noodles—until enough time had apparently been spent on idle chitchat that Captain Run asked, "So, Miss Onna. I'm curious to know what *you* think that the guard ought to be doing about these murders."

She took a sip of her tea, considering, then had to stop and look into her cup. The liquid inside was bright yellow and tasted very strongly of roses. She took another sip and spoke carefully. "I think—if I were in charge, the first thing that I should like to do would be to try to make sure the other trolls in the city are safe before trying to hunt down the murderer."

Sergeant Bato gave a quiet but clearly audible snort. Captain Run only nodded. "Well, miss, usually we try to tackle both at once, as it were. We've already assigned more foot patrols to troll neighborhoods. The hope is that we'll catch the fellow before all of our standard purse snatchers start galloping around like it's Aufdom Mare on race day because all of the cops are wrapped up trying to keep any more trolls from getting turned into gigantic fillets. If you'll excuse the turn of phrase."

Onna murmured something to the effect of "of course, of course." Captain Run continued.

"It's in the other aspect that we thought you might be able to help us, miss, when Loga said you were interested. My sergeant and I are the closest things we have to wizards on the force, you see, but our faces and magical signatures are pretty well-known to the criminal elements, and we need another wizard for this job. Right now we've got a strong suspicion that a certain gentleman here in Hexos knows something about these murders. What we'd like you to do is to see if you can mix with his set a little. See what you can pick up from him and his friends. Have you ever heard of a longeye construction? For talking to someone far away?"

"Yes," Onna said immediately. "I made one while I was at school. Out of hand mirrors." It occurred to her only belatedly that this might sound boastful of her.

"Oh, good," Captain Run said. "Then you'll be all right if anything goes wrong on your end with yours. I'll be sending you in with a one-way longeye in your buttonhole, so I can watch and listen to what's happening to you."

"Golly," Onna said, her eyes going wide. "How do you make a longeye construction small enough to fit into a *buttonhole*?"

"Captain Run was involved in the creation of the longeye," Loga said cheerfully. "She's one of the most accomplished wizards in Hexos in terms of construction work."

"*Only* construction work," Captain Run said. "I'm a *parametrist*, not a wizard. Not a speck of active magic in me. I build the raw constructions and make my sergeant here fire 'em."

"But that's *wonderful*," Onna said. "I've never met a parametrist before." They had the reputation of being brilliant, if not somewhat mad, since they pursued complex parametrical work without experiencing any of the fun of doing magic themselves.

Captain Run shook her head. "I'm not the sort you're thinking of," she said. "I'm not some sort of clever dick academic theorist. I just got mad at wizards giving me the latest in whizzbang magical police equipment that didn't do a single useful thing even when they worked like they were supposed to, so I got out a pile of books from the library and started making 'em myself. The best part of it is that if I write the things wrong, I'm not the one who gets blown up." Then she said, "Only joking! I haven't blown anyone up yet."

"*Yet*," Sergeant Bato said in an ominous tone. "Still plenty of time for me to lose a hand in the line of duty."

A plate of greens was delivered to the table. Onna eyed the dish as the two officers of the law fell upon it like it was the first food they'd seen in weeks. "What is it?"

Loga smiled at her. "Clover. Try it, it's lovely."

Onna ventured some. It was very good. "It tastes much nicer than it sounds. I never knew that you *could* eat clover."

"It's all up to the skill of the cook, really. I have a friend who always says that a truly accomplished cook can make a fine meal out of anything that can be digested and can't fire a gun in self-defense. I always feel dreadfully sorry for Daeslunders. Everything that you eat is either boiled until gray or covered in *syrup*."

Onna meant to argue with this but was distracted by the arrival of more dishes. After they had all eaten for a while, she addressed Captain Run. "Might I ask—who *is* the gentleman you suspect of involvement?"

"You can certainly ask," Captain Run said. "Might be hard to cozy up to him, otherwise. His name's Artravius Wail."

"Golly," Onna said, impressed.

"I know," Captain Run said. "A moniker for the ages. This is him," she added, and drew a small photograph from her pocket to show to Onna. "We took this after we arrested him last month for attempting to incite a riot over trolls being admitted to the university."

In the picture, a vaguely handsome young man smirked in front of a white wall, one eye blackened, his curly hair making a pale halo around his head. "Oh!" Onna said, startled. "I *met* him." Then she briefly explained running into him at the odd gathering in the square and how the young man—Mr. Wail—had told her about Loga's auditions.

Captain Run, whose posture was very upright to begin with, perked up so much she practically floated an inch above her chair. "Well, *that's* something," she said. "You might be able to get right in with him, then. Have an excuse to chat a bit. Will you be all right attending a party unchaperoned? They're sort of *artistic* types, his crowd. A few of 'em we've arrested for trying to blow up the government, and the rest of 'em just like drinking wine and arguing about etchings and pretending they want to blow up the government because they think it makes them sound clever. I got to know some of 'em when I was doing undercover work a few years back. Tiresome fellas, but mostly harmless. It's just this Wail. He publishes pamphlets with his friends about throwing the trolls and headmen out of Hexos and holding their goods in common, all the usual stuff, but his columns have a real *air* about 'em. Talking about how in Mendosa they just drew and quartered a fella for stealing from the crown, and if the common people of Hexos could draw and quarter the rich for stealing from the workers, then we wouldn't have all of these trolls coming here anymore."

"Golly," Onna said again. "It sounds very thrilling. But—will it be safe? And what if they want me to blow up the government with them?"

"Then you say no," said Sergeant Bato. "You're just going to a party, not infiltrating a revolutionary cell. You have a glass of wine, you chat, you get their faces on the longeye, you leave. That's all."

"I see," said Onna, though she felt doubtful about it. "But—I don't mean to question you, I'm sure you know your business far better than I ever could—isn't there something that I could do to help keep more trolls from being hurt?"

Captain Run glanced toward her sergeant, and they seemed to communicate with each other silently. Captain Run turned to Onna and shrugged. "I'd say that's up to your employer. If he doesn't mind you spending your time on it, and you don't do anything without me signing off, then I figure it couldn't hurt."

Loga gave Onna a lazy little smile. "It sounds like a perfectly marvelous little educational project to *me*, darling. What exactly do you have in mind?"

Onna chewed on her lip before she answered. "We could put a protection spell on all of the trolls in Hexos."

"Good heavens, darling, there must be thousands of trolls in Hexos. Do you have the energy to maintain so many protection spells simultaneously? I might, if I drank lots of nourishing chicken soup and laid in bed and didn't do anything else, which might interfere somewhat with the execution of my duties. Take a little of the cucumber: it's good for you in this weather."

She obeyed. It was very nice and crisp. "A wall of protection around their neighborhoods?"

"Helpful, if they stayed inside their homes and never left. Significantly less helpful for the trolls who work at the docks, or in the silk markets, or the young half-troll gentleman whom I've heard is currently employed as a letter writer down near the textile district."

Onna, who had never in her life met a half-troll person, endeavored to look as if she was not at all impressed by the idea of making this young gentleman's acquaintance. "Is there such a thing as a spell that could sense violence? If a troll was being attacked?"

"I suppose that there could be. The parameters would be difficult.

First, you would have to define a troll, and then you would have to define violence."

The officers watched the discussion as if Onna and Loga were two hammerball players galloping up and down the field. Onna frowned hard, then sat up straighter in her chair. "But what about blood?"

"What about it?"

"What if a spell alerted us if any troll blood was shed? Do you have any samples of troll blood?"

"Loads," Captain Run confirmed. "In little vials back at our offices. A few from each victim. Figured they might come in handy." She looked pleased with herself. Onna felt the same.

Loga seemed intent on spoiling her enjoyment. "There would still be difficulties, darling. You would have to go and investigate every time a troll in Hexos bit his tongue or removed a splinter from his toe. And it wouldn't save a troll who was killed in the same way as the one we saw today. As you observed, that troll was dead before he was cut."

"They've all been killed the same way, so far," Captain Run said. "Done with magic every time, nice and neat."

"But it would be something, wouldn't it?" Onna said. "If the troll managed to fight back. And I would be able to add something to the parameters to specify volume. Something about the amount of blood being oxidized in a given volume of air. It will be absolutely *horrid* to write," she said, with a certain amount of relish. She *did* like to work on difficult parameters, so she thought that she would quite enjoy this project, despite the circumstances. "Do you think that I could start this afternoon? And do you have any books about trolls I could read?" She turned to Captain Run. "Is there anyone who could translate for me if I wanted to speak to some of the trolls myself?"

Captain Run looked amused. "You're sounding like my kind of girl, Miss Onna. We could have a sewing circle for awful fiddly parameters. And I usually just use an awful fiddly construct for translation. Doesn't work as well as a person, but it does the trick in a pinch. I could lend you one, if you like."

"*Oh*," Onna said, a bit flustered. "That's very kind, but—I'd much rather learn how to do it myself."

There was an awkward moment of silence before Loga laughed. "If you're willing to drop by the Lamp after your usual work hours, I would of course be delighted to pay you for your time."

Onna's cheeks flamed hot as the officers exchanged glances again. "Don't look at *me*," Sergeant Bato said. "It's *your* mother who keeps complaining about how we never have her over for dinner."

Onna blinked, shocked despite herself—not only was Sergeant Bato's superior a woman, but it seemed that he was *married* to her—but Captain Run agreed to come by the Lamp the evening after next, and Onna composed herself in time to stand and shake hands with the officers before they headed off for their afternoon's business.

Once they were alone, Loga clapped his hands together. "Wonderful! We can get started on your little project this afternoon. We'll just have to take care to be done by about six. There's going to be a dinner this evening at Magister Kasur's estate to greet the Nessoran delegation, and I must *insist* that you attend."

Onna's eyes went wide. "A dinner with a *delegation*? But I just *couldn't*!"

"But of course you could, darling. It will be lovely. And you need the practice socializing in Hexos in advance of your little adventure in espionage, in any case."

"But what will I *wear*?" said Onna, envisioning herself in her faded muslin slinking shamefaced amongst the glittering throng.

Loga gave a dismissive little flick of his wrist. "Oh, don't worry about that. I'll have something made for you."

She could only goggle. He cocked his head and raised one eyebrow. "Yes, darling?"

"The dinner is *tonight*."

"I know, darling, but I don't think that we should allow such petty details to distress us. We are *wizards*, after all. More tea?"

She nodded.

Back at the Lamp, Onna and Loga retreated to separate ends of the enormous table in the study and set about their work. Loga produced several enormous books on the lifestyles, habits, language, physical attributes, and magical techniques of trolls for Onna, and she began working through the first one—*The Habits and Manners of the Great Trolls of the North*—when she realized that she hadn't any paper to write on. She glanced up. Loga was assembling an odd little sculpture out of bits of wire, looking very intent, indeed. She cleared her throat. "Loga?"

He started, and the sculpture collapsed. She gasped, covering her mouth with her hands. "Oh gracious, but I'm *terribly* sorry, I never meant to—"

He held up one finger. "Please, don't apologize! If my spellwork is as delicate as all that, I certainly should know about it earlier than later."

She leaned forward, interested. "Is that a set of parameters, then, that you're making?"

"Well, in a manner of speaking. I tend to work either in models or in physical movements that represent already established parametrical sets, instead of working up from the raw numbers. It's what you would call common magic, I suppose, except that I build the preliminary parameters myself, and then I write a few simple sets to associate them with a representative object—which in this case is each little bit of wire—so that I can focus more on the general look of the thing than on making sure that it doesn't cause the universe to collapse in on itself. Didn't you notice how I made that light this morning?"

She decided that it would be better for her peace of mind to ignore the sentence that had preceded his last. "I had thought it was a little construction, like a portable wizard-lamp."

"No, I despise carrying constructions. I hate having mounds of rubbish rattling about in my pockets. And to be quite honest, I *loathe* building the dratted things. It was this," he said, and he snapped his fingers and cupped his palm, where a little light bloomed. Onna stared.

"And you don't have to think about it at *all*?"

"Only to remember what action I've associated with what set of parameters. I once set my hair on fire, forgetting, and had to attend a party wearing an absurd Dennestoki–style hat pulled down over my ears."

"But that's *wonderful*."

"It only requires a certain degree of dedication. And genius. What was it that you wanted?"

"Oh. I haven't anything to write on."

"There's paper in the second drawer down on the far left of the north-facing side of the desk. No, Onna, north is the opposite side. We shall have to practice your cardinal directions. Brushes and ink directly above, and pencils to the right. You can't work for too long, though. The tailor will be here soon, and we should begin preparing to leave by dinnertime," he said, and went back to fiddling with his bits of wire.

Onna frowned slightly. "When exactly?"

He looked up at her. "Well, you know. The time at which one eats dinner."

"But that might vary, mightn't it?" Onna said, endeavoring to remain as polite as possible. "The time at which any person might be accustomed to eat dinner, I mean. Was there a time that you had in mind?"

It seemed that he hadn't, but eventually Onna extracted a "sevenish" from him, with which she convinced herself to be content. Not long after that a servant announced that Loga's tailor had arrived, and she went downstairs to be pricked with pins. When they arrived in her rooms, Onna was astounded to see that her sitting room table had been freshly ornamented with a vase full of white orchids. There was a note beside it, which she picked up and read.

*To Miss Gebowa,*

*With my fondest regards and congratulations on your success.*

*I remain yours truly,*
*Haran Welder*

*P.S. When you have the time, my supervisor and I would like to invite you to call on us at the hospital, so that you might see a little of my work.*

Mr. Welder. The handsome young gentleman she'd met while waiting to audition. She had quite forgotten about him in all the excitement. Now she felt a sort of warm twist in her chest. No gentleman had ever sent her flowers before.

There was no time, however, for girlish fancies. There was dressmaking to be done, and hair to be dressed, and a general flurry of activity that left her quite dizzied. Loga's tailor was a wizard himself and threw together a very elegant Hexian-style tunic—longer than the Hexian standard, to preserve Onna's Daeslundic modesty—in less than three hours, while a woman fussed over which jewels would best suit her hair and match the green-and-gold silk of her tunic. Onna happily submitted to being treated like an Esiphian princess and gave a delighted little gasp when she at last saw herself in all of her new finery, looking every inch the sophisticated young lady of Hexos. She would have happily spent the entire evening admiring herself in the glass but was forced to abandon her reflection when Loga knocked at the door.

She started at his appearance. He was wearing a beautifully cut Daeslundic suit, with a white silk cravat and ivory buttons. His hair was caught up in a conservative knot at the back of his neck, and he was holding a little white flower that smelled absolutely tremendous, as if it had been dipped in perfume. He smiled at her. "You look lovely, Miss Gebowa."

"Oh. Thank you. You look—like a gentleman," she said, and clapped her hands over her mouth, horrified at herself. He smiled again, as if he found her amusing rather than dreadfully rude.

"Thank you, darling. It was a difficult effect to achieve, I must say, but I thought that on the occasion of escorting a Daeslundic lady, I should endeavor to assume the appearance of her counterpart. Shall we?" he said, and pinned the flower to her sleeve before offering her his elbow. She took it and tried not to giggle out loud.

When they arrived at the estate's gate, Onna could hear shouts of laughter emanating from within; the party had already begun. "We're late!"

"Of course we're late, darling. Punctuality is a dreadfully Daeslundic virtue."

They entered and found the garden full of people: it was a fine, warm night typical of autumn in Hexos, and the party had spilled into the out-of-doors. Some were seated at lovely little tables and chairs scattered about, while others strolled arm-in-arm in the light of the carved wooden wizard-lamps hanging from the trees. As Onna and Loga passed through the gardens, they were waylaid several times by guests who, almost invariably, informed Onna that her employer was their *very* best friend, like a *brother* to them, *really*, and that she should be *enormously* happy to be his assistant. This gauntlet of good will continued until they reached the manor's grand hall.

The hall's courtyard was the scene of a grand feast crammed with any number of people—mostly young, mostly wizards—drinking and laughing and talking. It all struck Onna as an incredibly chaotic affair—the noise, the shouting—though terribly jolly. Fisticuffs practically broke out over where she and Loga would sit. Finally, Loga was lifted bodily off his feet and carried to the head of the nearest table.

Once they were seated, everyone ate with great energy. One wizard, a young lady, very kindly cast a translation spell so that Onna could follow the conversation, which was very lively, passing quickly from poetry, music, and art to arguments about magical theory. At one point everyone started playing what Loga said was a popular Sangan game: one person would spontaneously compose a couplet, and another had to respond with another couplet to match, sparking many cries of "Good!" or "Well said!" But Onna could not tell which were better, as the translation spell reproduced the poetry very flatly.

Onna swiftly felt remarkably dull and uneducated among this assemblage, her mood only somewhat bolstered by the little old lady on her left, who continuously held out plates of sweets to Onna and chortled merrily whenever Onna ate one, patting Onna's hand very kindly. Then Loga stood and held out his cup of sweet herbal liquor, motioning for Onna to stand with her own cup.

"To my new assistant," he said. "May she grow ever wiser and more beautiful!"

Then Loga threw back the entire cup at once. After this *everyone* toasted Onna, and one another, in such dreadful number and with such clever phrases that Onna was left feeling quite giddy and delighted.

Everyone else seemed to feel quite the same. One young lady began to tell very ribald jokes, sending the table into gales of laughter. Even the old lady cackled her approval. Onna tried to imagine her own grandmother—her mother's mother, the Hall officiant's wife—being amused by such crass levity and gave it up as impossible. However, all this nonsense didn't keep Onna from noticing Loga, who became distracted flirting with a beautiful blonde lady on his other side. The blonde lady kept putting her hand on his elbow, which made Onna rather cross. She knew it really oughtn't—Loga was her employer, not her young man, and he was far too old for Onna in any case—but already in their short acquaintance she had grown quite accustomed to basking in the bright rays of his undivided attention, and she didn't at all like to see it turned on others.

After a time a group of Sangan musicians mounted a small dais. Loga nudged Onna with his elbow. "This is the sort of thing that I used to sing, darling."

Onna wasn't quite sure what to make of it. The music was unlike anything she had ever heard before, though she recognized some of Loga's graceful little gestures in the singer's performance. Loga, at least, seemed to enjoy it very much, and he applauded wildly.

Next came a group of Esiphian toe-dancers, and then the musicians returned, accompanied by a Nessoran drummer. The music, which had previously flitted between humor and plaintiveness, settled into a beat that set the audience to nodding their heads. Loga smiled. "I never sang like this, with the drums. It's all the fashion now in Sango, along with reciting Carendic poetry and learning to shoot a Nessorand short bow. Because of the prince, you know."

Onna nodded. The Daeslundic papers wrote quite breathlessly about Nessorand's crown prince, who in the five years since his coming out— in Nessorand, young people avoided society until after their twentieth birthday in order to focus on their studies—had evidently done a great deal to make a name for himself by being *tremendously* handsome and charming.

Then someone called out for Loga to perform. Soon everyone was shouting for the same, and Loga shook his head, laughing, calling back polite demurrals. He was pushed up onto the stage despite his protests, and after conferring hastily with the musicians, he launched into a song.

Loga was, despite his claims, extremely good at singing with the drums. Onna wondered if perhaps he had practiced in secret. She thought his voice was much better than the other singer's, and something about the way he smiled when he sang made one want to touch the curving corner of his mouth. She also thought she had had far too much to drink. She stood up and darted out into the garden for a breath of fresh air, where she stumbled directly into one of the Nessoran guests.

He steadied her by her shoulders, laughing, before retreating a step and clasping his hands behind his back. She laughed, too, then got a better look at him and nearly bit her tongue. He was of an average height, but his shoulders were very broad, and his thick hair fell across his forehead in a wonderfully becoming sort of way. When he smiled his teeth gleamed white against his neat black beard. He gave her a little bow. "I know that in Daeslund a gentleman ought not speak to a lady before he's been introduced. I hope that you'll forgive me as a foreigner. Are you Lord Wuzan Zilon's new apprentice?"

"Yes," she said. "I'm Onna Gebowa. Who're you?"

She was most certainly going mad. And drunk. Mad and drunk. Speaking to gentlemen in such a way! Foreign gentlemen! In a garden!

He smiled. "I've known Loga for years. He said that he would introduce us. Is he singing inside now?"

The man really had the most *wonderfully* sophisticated accent, even if he was avoiding telling her his name. A *mysterious* handsome foreign gentleman.

She really was *frightfully* drunk.

"Oh, yes. He's singing like *mad*. I think he enjoys the attention."

He laughed. "He does like it when people look at him, doesn't he?"

As if on cue Loga came sailing out into the garden toward them, the general expansiveness of his manner suggesting that he, too, had been enjoying a great deal of that odd Hexian liquor. "Kosson! You're here!"

Loga fell upon the mysterious handsome foreign gentleman, who greeted him with a sound kiss on each cheek. "Hullo, Loga. Your apprentice and I were just talking about you."

"*Were* you? Various comments about my good looks and charm, I imagine."

His friend smiled at him. "Mostly the charm."

Loga smiled back. "And I'm sure that you haven't properly introduced yourself, you beast. Kosson, Onna Gebowa. Onna, Kosson Zahir."

"Oh, no," said Onna. "Oh, *no*."

The crown prince of Nessorand put a hand to his mouth to hide his grin. Onna wailed.

"Loga, why didn't you *tell* me?" She turned to the prince. "I'm *dreadfully* sorry, your highness, I *never* meant—"

"Please, don't apologize, Miss Gebowa," said the prince, who was laughing in earnest. Loga pulled an indignant face.

"And how was I meant to know that I would emerge from dinner to find you furiously flirting with him in the garden?"

Onna made a strangled sort of sound. The prince held his hand up in a pacifying gesture. "I am afraid that I must leave you both now; I owe Magister Fen a game of twenty-one. It was my pleasure, Miss Gebowa," he said, and bowed very prettily before returning to the courtyard.

Onna stared after him. "I think that I shall die. I shall die at this very instant. You shall have to bury me here, Loga."

"He does have that effect on young ladies."

"I shall die of *humiliation*," she said, and sighed. "It isn't *fair* that he should look like that, when our Governor Bryce is all jaundiced and spotty and First Son Haran hasn't any chin."

"Well, Onna, I suppose that one of the advantages of encouraging your nobility to marry highly accomplished commoners as they do in Nessorand is that you end up with kings who look like Kosson, instead of with frog-faced unfortunates who must call their own uncle *Grandpapa*."

As he spoke, a very tall, burly man stepped up behind him. He was wearing a black Hexian tunic—similar to the type Loga wore at home— and a Weltsir ring where most men would have worn a wedding band. His face was broad and pleasant looking, with dark eyes, a coppery complexion, and closely cropped, tightly curled red hair. "Loga, you're awfully rough on poor bug-eyed First Son Haran."

Loga froze.

"*Jok*." He swallowed. "I didn't—when did you come back to Hexos?"

The other man smiled. "I got here last week. You don't seem so glad to see me." He spoke with a soft Gallen lilt, which paired with his size made him seem to Onna more like a kindhearted crab fisherman than a wizard. Onna was quite taken: she always thought that Gallen accents were very sweet, and she liked the gentle way he spoke to Loga, as if he was very fond of him, indeed.

Loga spoke to him quite stiffly. "Of course I'm pleased to see you. I'm just surprised. You've been here for a week? Why didn't you write? I read your last letter two days ago, and it didn't say a thing about your visiting Hexos."

"Thought I might drop by the Lamp and surprise you. I haven't seen it yet, you know."

"I certainly would have been *surprised*."

"And *mighty* pleased to see me." He smiled. "You look fine, Loga. Your color's good. I'm glad."

"Thank you. So do you. *What* exactly are you doing in Hexos?"

Loga didn't sound at all like himself. There was no charm or flirta-
tiousness: he was almost brusque in a way she had never heard from him
before. Jok looked taken aback. "I'm starting to feel as how I shouldn't
have come down to speak to you."

"Don't. I'm sorry. I wish that you had written."

"I'm sorry that I didn't. And I'm working for Judge Schutts."

"Judge Schutts?" Loga smiled for the first time. "You poor creature."

"He's not that bad, once you get used to him."

Loga suddenly seemed to remember himself. "Oh, Onna, darling,
how terribly thoughtless of me! Jok, this is Miss Onna Gebowa, my new
apprentice. Onna, this is Mr. Jok Finnbair."

He shook her hand, smiling. "Loga's assistant! Funny to hear that.
All the honor I'm feeling to meet you, Miss Gebowa." He glanced over
at Loga. "Only the one, then?"

Loga said something very rapid in Nessoran. Mr. Finnbair reached
out and grabbed him by the wrist. Loga pulled away. "What are you
doing for Schutts, Jok?"

He paused. "Medical research."

"Is it more of his immortality quest?"

"I've convinced him to start more modestly. We're aiming for him
to live past one hundred."

Onna listened with wide eyes. "But isn't it dreadfully wicked to attempt immortality?"

They both turned to her. Loga raised his eyebrows. "Why would it
be? Isn't it a wonderful thing to live?"

"Not for Elgarites," Mr. Finnbair said. "They think trying to live
past your natural span's an affront to God. I thought the same before I
came here. That's why medicine's so backward in Leiscourt."

"Ah," Loga said. Then he lowered his voice. "Tell me that working
in medicine again doesn't have anything to do with your brother."

"My working for Judge Schutts doesn't have anything to do with
Elgarson. I'm just trying to earn an honest living. Not all of us are famous officials who live in castles." He paused. "I wish you'd forgive me."

"There's nothing to forgive. I *worry* about you."

"Don't you bother, duck. It's been sixteen years."

"You've been counting."

"And you haven't? I don't believe that for half a minute." Mr. Finn-bair glanced at Onna again and smiled. "I look forward to talking more to both of you when I come down for lunch tomorrow."

Loga raised his eyebrows. "I must have drunk more than I thought this evening. I don't recall having *invited* you to lunch."

"One o'clock, then. Grand to meet you, Miss Gebowa," he said, and walked off.

Loga drew in a breath. "Well. Shall we have another drink?"

They did.

# 12

*This week, only months after the opening of the Leiscourt–Del Sem Berg railway line, there has been a report of a new victim of progress: Mr. Rocard Blecks, an aged Hall officiant of three and sixty, was, according to reports from his wife and daughter, frightened to death by the passage of a steam engine during his customary morning walk. The roar of the new engine, residents of the village of Holcam say, disturbs them in their rest at night, rattles crockery from their shelves, and has stopped the cows from giving milk . . .*

—Leiscourt Crier, *Hetmonth 6, 6572*

Tsira'd had just about enough of fucking rain.

It rained on the stagecoach that squeezed her like a fresh cheese in cloth on the three-day journey all the way up to Coldstream. It rained on the highway once they traveled past where the coaches ran. It rained on the hills and fatted up the streams and slowed their passage on the two-day slog to Tsira's ma's land.

"At least we have a tent now," Pink told her on one night when it was coming down harder than ever. She ignored him. The tent had been his idea. Didn't want him getting too cocky about how clever he was.

She wanted to put her mouth on that cocky smile of his too damn much.

One day when they were high in the hills, Tsira held up a hand. "You hear that?"

He frowned. "What is it?"

"Singing," she said. Nice pretty chords without much melody to them:

a classroom song for memorizing a story, probably. She couldn't help smiling a little. "We're almost home."

They turned off onto the village path, and they saw it after they got to the top of the hill. It was good to see it. A warm, calm feeling. There was the white smooth stone and black slate of the buildings, of the reigs' and vahns' halls. There was her mother's house set back from the rest. There was the airing rack out front with her ma's robe on it, that same damn purple robe she loved so much and would never get rid of even though the gold at the sleeves was half worn off. There were the goats up the hill—more of them since she'd last been home, which was good—and the children having their lesson outside the schoolhouse, and everyone bustling around like always. Like she'd never left at all.

Pink was gawking. "I thought you said your clan was *poor*."

Tsira was startled for a second. Then she saw how Pink would see it: clean and bright and well built. In pink villages, only village halls compared. "We are, by troll lights. Our food mostly comes from our work, and the money we make from selling embroidery and leather goods. These buildings are old. Full of old magic. We don't have enough strong wizards to build like this now." She gave him a little smile. "Our poor is different from yours."

She called out to the village and went bounding down the hill, grinning when she heard people shouting her name and saw them pouring out of the halls to greet her. She always got a good welcome when she first got home. It was just when everyone remembered that she wasn't a third the reig her ma was that things started going badly.

As soon as she neared the buildings, she started feeling worse. Everyone was dressed so well. Them in their good robes and skirts and their hairpins and thick bracelets, and her in her shirt and trousers. She could see Pink looking them all over. Noticing how shabby she looked next to the rest of them, maybe.

Then her ma stepped up. She looked good. Older, but she always looked older now. That big broad body of hers just as firm and straight and tall as ever, just her face a little more weathered. The scar across her left cheek the same as ever, and the broken right front tooth. Just her ma.

Tsira went up to her for a hug and a kiss. It felt good. "Ma," she said. "Been a while."

"That's your doing, not mine," her ma said. Then she looked down at Pink. "This is your vahn?" She wasn't smiling, so Pink probably couldn't tell, but Tsira could see her approving straightaway. She figured her ma had always had an eye for humans, otherwise Tsira wouldn't exist. Still, it wasn't bad to see that she approved of the one that Tsira'd picked out.

"Yeah," Tsira said in Daeslundic. "His name's Jeckran. He doesn't speak Dacyn. Jeckran, this is my ma, Cynallumwyntresal. Call her Tresa."

Pink looked too shy to be calling her much of anything. Tsira saw the corner of Ma's mouth twitch. She thought he was sweet, ducking his head like a little virgin vahn straight from some crystal-covered tower in Cwydarin. Tsira put her hand to his shoulder and felt him settle for her. It took a lot not to kiss the top of his head.

Fuck, she'd lost her brains over this pink.

Her ma's mouth twitched again. Then she said to Pink, in her softest voice, "Come here."

He looked scared shitless, but he went to her, anyway. Tsira felt a little bad. Hadn't really warned him about how big and tough-looking her ma was, with the scars and the broken tooth.

"How old are you?" her ma asked.

"Four and twenty," he said, ". . . madam."

It took Tsira a second to stop mooning over how funny he was before she realized what he'd just said. "What? Thought you were older."

"Why? How old are you?"

She looked at her ma, who answered. "Almost fifty."

Jeckran made a choking noise and turned to look at Tsira. Looked like he'd just gotten a snowball up his skirt. "*Fifty?*"

Tsira shrugged. "Young, for a troll."

Tsira's ma gave her a look. "I thought he was your vahn."

Tsira tried not to roll her eyes. "He's mine, Ma. Just never asked his age."

"Have you broken him in yet?"

Tsira winced. "No. Not yet. Want to wait, give him time." Then she changed the subject. "Could use some food. He's hungry."

"You haven't fed him?"

This time she really did roll her eyes. "Didn't have time this morning."

"You have to find time to feed your vahn," her ma said, then frowned and went off to talk to some young reig who'd just come by with a dead goat slung over her shoulder.

Tsira glanced down at Jeckran. He was watching some children playing nearby, his face looking softer than normal. She put her hand on his shoulder. He jumped. She frowned.

"You all right?"

"I—well, I suppose that I am. Only I hope that I won't make myself a nuisance. I'd hate to interfere with your . . . family reunion."

She shrugged. "They'll be glad you're here. Think you're my clan-vahn."

"What does that mean, exactly?"

She was a little embarrassed to say it. Wasn't like they'd talked about this before. "Bit like my wife."

"Husband," he said, and blushed.

"No, wife," she said. "Reigs take care of vahns they've taken to clan. That's the point. Closer to . . . *householded*, I guess. And the reig's the householder." She couldn't meet his eyes. She felt like a jackass. "Ma's pleased. Thinks I've started my own clan. Rather let her keep thinking it."

"Of course," said Pink, his face going sweet with a smile. "I'm surprised she seems so calm. My mother would take out a banner advertisement in the evening post if she thought that I was to be married."

He lowered his voice. "Is there anything that I should do to make it convincing?"

She hunched over a bit to whisper back, like they were two children planning mischief behind the reigs' hall. "See him?" She pointed to a troll nearby who was playing with a child, tossing them into the air to make them laugh. "That's Marden. My ma's favorite vahn." Marden was one of her only friends in her clan, or close enough. He was a gentle, pretty little vahn with smooth blue skin and wide bright eyes who always loved kids: it bothered him that he couldn't give one to her ma. "What Marden does with Ma, you do with me."

Pink looked at him. "Would you say that he's a handsome troll?"

Tsira was a little surprised. Pink had a real eye for trolls. "Marden? Yeah." She changed the subject. "We'll split up for a while before dinner to clean up and change. Vahns and reigs. You can go with Marden in the vahns' hall."

"Sit by myself in a building with a dozen strange trolls when I've never learned the etiquette? Do you really think that's advisable? I can barely make it through a brandy and soda in a Leiscourt gentlemen's club without some fellow expressing the desire to punch me in the teeth."

She grinned at him. Funny little thing. "Don't worry. I'll introduce you," she said, and dragged him over to Marden. "Hey, handsome," she said in Dacyn.

Marden put the kid down and pushed a few strands of hair from his face with the back of his hand. "Tsira!" he said, and they kissed. Tsira put a hand on Pink's shoulder. "This is Jeckran, Marden. Jeckran, this is Marden."

"Jeckran," said Marden, like he was testing the flavor of the name.

Pink held out his hand. "Mr. Marden. I'm delighted to make your acquaintance."

Marden smiled and leaned forward to kiss him hello. Pink kissed back just fine. Tsira wasn't surprised—he knew *how* to be polite, just didn't bother to do it sometimes—but he looked at her afterward. "Do you always kiss in greeting?"

"Yeah. You're unranked, though, so you let other people kiss you first." Then she turned to Marden. "Mind looking out for him before dinner? Show him how to get cleaned up in the vahns' hall?"

He nodded, sweet as ever. "Of course. Does he have anything clean to wear? I could find him some children's clothes, if he doesn't."

Tsira laughed and translated. "He says he'll give you some children's clothes to wear."

Jeckran looked down at himself. He was muddy from the road, wearing his oldest shirt and a skirt that was worn-out at the hems, though he'd brought a clean suit in his bag so he could look decent when he met her ma. Vain little thing. She liked that about him. "I suppose I'm not dressed for dinner, am I? Though I think I'd prefer to wear my own clothes, if he has no objections."

She laughed and sent them off together, then went back to her ma. Ma gave her a squeeze. That was all right. She let her head lean against Ma's shoulder.

It felt nice. Familiar. She'd spent most of her childhood in her mother's arms. She'd been so small when she was born: Ma'd been scared she'd lose her. Since she'd been grown, her ma'd found plenty to criticize about Tsira, and they'd passed long days without exchanging kind words, but her ma had never held back her touch.

It made her sad sometimes, thinking about how Pink had never had that. Made her want to bundle him up to her chest and keep him there.

This was turning into a real damn problem.

Her ma led her into her house. She'd kept some of Tsira's good old clothes in a leather box in the nightroom. Tsira washed in the little pool in the dayroom and then moved into the back to change. Her ma watched her.

"You look good."

Tsira tried not to look surprised. "Yeah? You think so?"

"You do. You've gained weight. Your vahn is taking good care of you."

Tsira grinned despite herself. "He's always after me to eat more."

"Good," her ma said. "He should fit in with the other vahns when you come home."

Tsira frowned. "When I what?"

"We need you back," her ma said. Her voice was even as well-hung cloth. "We've lost too many people to the cities. We don't have enough hands to care for the flocks and keep the children in school. You're young and healthy. You're out of custom leaving your clan when we have need of you."

Tsira bit the inside of her cheek and tried to measure her words. "You never seemed to have much need of me before. Had me cleaning goat shit and taking words from low-ranked vahns all day."

Ma just looked right back at her. Hard and steady as ever. Always a rock, her ma. A fucking hunk of granite. "You're my child. Do you think it'd make you loved in the clan if I gave you honors you hadn't earned?"

"And how the *fuck* was I supposed to earn a damn thing when everyone thought I was too small and weak and stupid to do anything that fucking *mattered*?" Tsira snapped back.

Her ma's expression didn't change. "You earn the right to do things that matter. You shovel the goat shit and you hold up the custom until you can shovel shit better than anyone in the clan. That's how you rise. You work."

"So that's what you want," Tsira said. "For me to spend my life shoveling shit until you think I'm good enough for something better. I'm earning good money with Jeckran. I'm getting respect. I don't need to beg for scraps in a border-clan. Just because you stayed here all your damn life doesn't mean I have to go the same way."

Her ma shrugged. "No," she said. "You don't. You can get respect out there all that you want, Cynallumwyntsira. But here you can be of good service to your clan in a time of struggle. That would be in custom." She paused. "You should break in your vahn, at least. Respect him and the custom enough for that. Maybe he could give you a child when trolls couldn't." Then she stood and walked out.

Tsira took a minute to dress and stew. Service. *Shit.* That was all right for her ma to say, when her service had been in leadership, since she was the biggest, strongest, smartest, best-looking young reig in the clan in a time of plenty one hundred years ago. It was all right for her to think shit-shoveling was noble when it had never been her damn walk. Easy enough to be in custom when custom didn't keep you in shit up to your fucking ankles.

She pulled her cloak on and went to find Jeckran. Maybe he wasn't really her vahn, but at least he didn't look at her and see a walking lapse in custom.

She stopped at the entrance to the vahns' hall and called into it. "Am I welcome?"

"No!" A few voices called out, and she waited for them to get their clothes on or put their secrets away or whatever the fuck they were doing until she got the word that she could enter. She took her boots off and went in, then looked around. Gwyma was there, sitting right near Jeckran, which was just what she fucking needed right now. She ignored him and smiled at Jeckran instead. He looked good. Clean and shaved and pretty.

"Hey, Pink." She let her eyes drag over his body. Let Gwyma see her doing it. "Look nice."

"Thank you. You look . . ." He stopped and blushed. "You look very nice yourself."

She laughed at that, then looked at Gwyma and spoke to him in Dacyn. "Hey, Gwyma. Doing all right?"

He nodded and stood. When he spoke, it was in that honey voice of his, that voice that made her forget the sting of his temper. "I'm well, Tsira. I've missed you." Then he stepped in to kiss her. She kissed back. Gwyma was a plain little thing, squat and pale and ornery, but he'd always been able to drive her a little wild. His mouth tasted sweet with herbs. She figured he knew it.

From the corner of her eye she could see Jeckran's face. Looked like he'd just swallowed a big bit of gristle.

Huh.

She crossed the room and sat at Jeckran's side, with Gwyma following her. "Marden taking care of you?"

"Yes, he's been very kind." He paused. "You never told me that your clan's wizard was your own stepfather."

Took her a second to figure out what he meant. Then she realized: Marden was clan wizard, and Jeckran figured he was married to her ma. "Nah. Not like that. Ma's clan-head. She can't take vahns to clan because the whole clan's under her protection. Grandmother-books have lots of writing against it. She and Marden just love each other."

"Oh," said Jeckran. "I had no idea that troll family relations were so . . . anarchic."

Gwyma snorted. He'd sat himself down to listen to their conversation, which was just like him. He spoke in his perfect Daeslundic. "You don't know anything about us."

Tsira gave him a long look. "Knows enough to please me."

He sneered at her. "Have you broken him in, Cynallumwyntsira?"

Tsira shook her head, and put one hand to Jeckran's back. "Not yet."

"Why not?"

"He's young."

"*I* was young," Gwyma said. "Wasn't *dainty* enough for you, I suppose."

She couldn't catch herself before she winced. She switched to Dacyn. "Rabbit, you know it wasn't about how you look—"

"I suppose *he* thinks you're very impressive."

Tsira flinched again, but before she could answer, Gwyma stood and walked from the tent.

Jeckran nodded after him. "He's rather a nasty fellow, isn't he?"

"Not really," said Tsira, even though he was. Mean as a slapped wasp. Didn't mean she wanted a stranger to him saying it. "Not you he's mad at. Mad at the whole world." She paused. "I'm sorry."

"Whatever for?"

"Should have thought of Gwyma being here. Should have known he'd start a fight. He's got trouble being around people he doesn't know, especially humans. Don't think much of me, either. Used to fight like dogs after I broke him in. Told me he hoped I'd die in the mountains when I left."

"Tsira," Jeckran said. "What does that *mean*—you broke him in?"

Well, shit. Now she'd have to explain. "Took his—what's it called." She paused, half to think of the Daeslundic word, half because she didn't want to say it. Then she gave up and shrugged. "His first time with a reig."

He got a funny look on his face. Like he'd taken a big gulp of milk and realized it was sour. "Virginity. You took his—" Pink stopped. "Your mother was talking about *me*—"

"Yeah. Keep telling her I'm waiting. Try to hold her off until we leave tomorrow, at least."

He looked a little rattled. "And how on earth could Marden *help*?"

She shrugged again. "Don't know what vahns do before."

"Is it a sort of ceremony, then, that you do?"

"Yeah. The reig gets talked to ahead of time, too. The whole clan feasts the next day."

"It sounds like a wedding," Jeckran said. "And how is it different from being taken to clan?"

She grinned at him. "You're taken to clan already, or close enough."

"What? I thought—"

"You've been under my protection for a while now. That's usually enough, for two trolls. You're mine until one of us says you aren't."

"I don't know that I like having made some manner of contract with you without being fully aware of it first."

That worried her a bit. Thinking that maybe she'd done something to him that he didn't want, even though she'd tried not to touch him except like a sister could. Maybe he saw the worry in her face because, when he spoke again, his voice was gentle. "Could you tell me what it means?"

She shrugged, relieved. "I owe you protection. Keep you clothed and fed. Won't let anyone hurt you. Anyone touches you or bothers you, it's my job to make it right."

"Would you kill them?"

She took a second to think about that. She wasn't a *murderer*, but . . . "If they needed it, and you wanted me to."

Tsira could swear he smiled a little. "And what do you get in return?"

She just stared at him and grinned. He swallowed. "Ah."

She laughed. "Cheesemaking, gardening, sewing, teaching children after they're weaned. Vahn and reig are just—*jobs*, really." It was hard to explain. Men and women hadn't made any damn sense to her when she'd first heard it explained, either. Illogical. *Messy.* Vahn and reig were about what people *did*, not about what they looked like before they even knew their own grandmothers. She wasn't about to say that to Pink, though. The grandmother-books had *plenty* of things to say about arrogant young reigs trying to dictate to other clans about their business. "You're a vahn if you do a vahn's work, a reig if you do a reig's. Or you can just refuse declaring, if you want: some people do that. If you're my vahn, you work in my name." She shrugged. "I mean, not you. You're human. You didn't grow up with the grandmother-books, don't know how anything works. We have a word for that, when a reig takes an outsider to clan. You don't belong to the clan. Don't have any rank. You're just mine." That was a nice thing to say out loud, even if it didn't have any damn truth to it. Just her playing pretend like a fucking child.

Jeckran looked like he was chewing that over. "If you did a vahn's work, would that make *you* a vahn?"

"Sure. Some people switch every few years. My ma wanted me to declare vahn for years. I always had to work twice as hard as the other reigs to keep up. I *like* being a reig, though. Never wanted to be different."

Jeckran frowned and said nothing. A cry went up outside. Tsira gave him a little thump on the shoulder and stood. She hoped he couldn't tell how much she hated his frowns. "Dinner."

When they left the building, the sun was setting and a cool wind was pouring down over the mountains. Tsira led him into the dining hall. A vahn rushed past with a tray of onion bread. Marden had come out of the vahns' hall with them and headed straight to Tsira's ma, who was already seated by the stove on her favorite rug. Tsira picked up another rug from the stack near the entrance and picked a spot across the stove, far from her ma. Pink settled in next to her like the good little vahn he was.

"Did you speak to your mother, while I was in the vahns' hall?"

"Yeah."

A vahn came by to hand her a bowl of cip and a big onion flatbread. Jeckran gave the food a sad shin-kicked look. Tsira elbowed him. "We share."

"Oh," he said.

She tore off a piece of bread and handed it to him. He took a bite and looked surprised. "It's good."

She grinned. "Yeah. Just me that's an awful cook. Not my whole clan." She used part of her bread to scoop up some of the cip. It was good: ground goat and root vegetables and their clan's special autumn pickles to season it and get their bellies ready for the winter. Jeckran ate like he hadn't tasted anything so good in years. Tsira was pretty sure she hadn't either.

By the time they finished eating the sun was almost down. It was a clear night. The stars were starting to show up through the clear roof of the dining hall. A vahn came to gather up their empty bowl. Across the way Marden was cuddling up to her ma. Ma glanced down at him and stroked one hand over his hair, and he pressed his face into the crook of her neck. Tsira looked away.

When she looked down, she saw Jeckran inching up on her. Wanting to do like he'd said and make it look like they were really fucking, maybe. She liked that he was doing it. Before she could think better of it she pulled him into her lap.

He stiffened up in her arms. "Sorry," she murmured. "Should have asked first."

He relaxed a little. "There's no need to apologize. You're like one of Bette's more comfortable armchairs."

She laughed at that. Seemed like a compliment. Bette's armchairs were pretty damn comfortable.

The clan passed a flask of mead around. Celebrating Tsira being home, maybe, or maybe everyone just felt like a drink. Her clan had never minded having a good time when they had the chance. Jeckran hesitated when it got to him. "What is it?"

"Just mead. Take some. Rude not to, for the first taste. Pass it later if you hate it."

He gave her a look, then took a sip and went all fish-eyed. "It's wonderful." He handed her the bottle. "Why on earth is yours so awful, then?"

She was in the middle of drinking when he asked. Almost choked from laughing at him. "Told you. First time making it." She mussed his hair and he leaned back against her chest. She hoped to shit he couldn't feel her heart pounding.

After that they just settled in to drinking for a while. Jeckran got happy pretty quickly. Curled up in her lap and smiled at everything going on like he was the clan-head and they were all children giving their winter singing show. It was the real children he smiled at the most: she could see him watching as the vahns carried them off to sleep, his gaze all woolly after them. After the children were put to bed, the adults starting getting lively. A couple of vahns got a little too close for public, sliding their hands up each other's skirts until a reig scolded them, and they went off to find some privacy. Tsira's own ma started kissing Marden all over his face, him all loose and sweet for her. Tsira was so busy watching and feeling all twisted up in her gut that she didn't think to expect it when Jeckran kissed her throat.

She put her hand to his side, embarrassed. "Don't have to do that, Pink. No one's watching."

He looked up at her and laughed, his eyes a little droopy from the drink. She looked back at him as steady as she could. "All right?"

"Yes. I'm drunk."

"Should learn when to stop."

He pulled back. "I know my own limits. If I choose to keep drinking, it's my own concern."

She decided to let it go. Then she caught a glimpse of her ma out of the corner of her eye. Watching them and looking pleased. "Ma's happy."

"How can you *tell*? And what about?"

"She's my ma. I can tell." There was a moment's pause. "She thought I'd be alone. Never have a clan. Not many vahns want to fall in with a tiny little reig who never went to school and can't have children."

He turned to look at her. "What?"

She shrugged. "Like a mule." She hadn't meant to tell him that. The mead made it easier. It was an old hurt, a scab that had healed over, but it didn't do her any damn good to go picking at it. She hated when people fucking pitied her for it.

"Oh," he said. "I'm so sorry. I mean—I'd heard it was common, for half trolls, but I didn't—are you quite sure?"

Didn't bother her too much when he said he was sorry for it. Maybe because he sounded like he really was sorry and not just feeling glad it wasn't him who was barren. Maybe it was because she was so ass-up face-down wild over him she'd think it was sweet if he spat in her eye. "Sure enough. Haven't gotten pregnant yet. Not that I haven't been with enough vahns who could get me that way." And almost as many who couldn't. She'd been with all kinds of vahns, sweet and mean and gentle and prickly, big ones and small ones, lazy and clever and pretty as could be. None of them had given her a child, and none of them had wanted to stay. "You're right about it being common. Why most of the great troll-human lines split into two. Guess I'm not one of the lucky ones." She paused. "Ma doesn't know. Doesn't want to know, maybe."

"Maybe you *will* be one of the lucky ones, still. Even some actual *mules* can foal," he told her. "There was one in Monsatelle six years ago. I remember reading about it in the papers."

She smiled at him. She could drink him down in one swallow. She could lick him up like honey. "Thanks."

A younger reig tapped Tsira on the shoulder and handed her a lit pipe. Choke. *Thank fuck.* She took a long drag, held it in, then breathed out. Felt her whole body start to heat and loosen. She handed the pipe back and sighed, then looked down at Jeckran. He was so little. She laughed. She liked him so fucking much.

"Hey, Pink."

"Hey, troll," he said back, smiling at her. Stupid, how they'd made *troll* and *pink* into something like pet names. "Whatever is in that pipe?"

"It's called choke," she said.

"And it's some sort of intoxicant?"

"Yeah," she said, and laughed again.

"You didn't share it with me."

"You're drunk," she told him. "Don't want you sicking your guts up."

"Ah. How terribly considerate of you."

It was dark. Just a little glow from Marden's wizard-lamps. The wind was coming in through the windows. Tsira stared up at the moon. The clouds were blowing across the sky like a mouthful of smoke through a crowded hall. It made it look as if the moon was crashing to the ground. Jeckran saw it, too.

"Look," he told Tsira. "The moon's falling."

"Yeah. You're right."

She lay on her back and pulled him down with her so that they were lying together on the rugs. Tsira felt a little dizzy. Jeckran groaned and tucked his face into the crook of her neck. Tsira wanted to kiss the

warm skin-scented top of his head. Instead she rubbed his back with
one hand.

"First time I saw you, you were all by yourself in the snow. Looked
like you fell from the moon."

"I feel that I must have, sometimes."

She didn't say anything to that. Then he fell asleep in her arms.

She stayed there for a while, watching the stars and smoking choke
and thinking, until her ma came by and told her to take her vahn to the
clan-head's house to sleep.

He woke up while she was carrying him to bed. Blinked up at her
like a new kitten. "Oh, damn. I do make a fool of myself."

"You do."

She laid him down on the bed and started to unlace his boots.

"I'm *perfectly* capable of—"

"No, you're not. Drunk as a headman." She laughed. "*Are* a headman."

"I am not. My father is, and that only *nominally*," he said. Or tried
to. Came out more like *nominiminally*. She tried not to laugh again.
"Our family only has a fifth headmanship. My father is Headman Jeckran, and my brother will be, too, when he's gone. I'm nothing at all."

"I'd say you're something, all right." She lay down next to him and
pulled a blanket over them both. "This is Ma's house."

"Where is she?"

"In the reigs'. Wanted us to be alone."

"Good God. She is persistent, isn't she?"

"Yeah." She grinned at him. "Night, Phillim Kail Jeckran."

"Good night, Cynallumwyntsira," he said. She worked up the nerve
to kiss his forehead, but by the time she did it, he was already asleep.


Tsira woke up warm.

She was in bed with Jeckran. He was soft and hot and still in her
arms. Awake, and trying not to wake her, too. She stretched a little and
pulled him closer against her chest. She figured she could get away with

it in the first heartbeats of the morning. "Morning, Pink," she said. Her voice came out a little raspy. Smoked too much last night.

"Good morning, old goat," he said.

She smiled. Took a lot for her not to nuzzle at him. She tried to let her face drift close enough to smell his hair without him noticing. She fucking loved how he smelled. A good filthy living smell. "Don't want to get up."

"Me, neither. I suppose that everyone must feel that way on a cold morning."

"Don't think my ma does."

He chewed that over. "I expect that you're right."

She yawned. "You're like a hot stone."

"Thank you, I suppose."

"How's your head?"

"Perfectly well. And yours?"

"Fine." She paused. "I let the fire go out."

"It doesn't matter."

"Stupid of me." Her ma would never let the fire go out like that.

They just lay there for a while. She didn't pull away and neither did he. It was nice. Warm and cozy. Jeckran stirred a little. "Tsira," he said, just as her ma called her name from outside the house.

She sat up to call back and Jeckran squawked like a chicken.

She looked down at herself and snorted. She'd forgotten that she'd stripped down to her smalls before she'd fallen asleep last night. "Sorry. Because of the choke. Warms you up." She stood. He looked away.

"Good *God*, Tsira."

"Wait," she said, and scrambled around to pull the rest of her underclothes on. "All right."

He looked back at her. She ran her fingers through her hair, jerking at a knot. *Pain in the ass.* "Hair's a mess. Don't have a comb."

He laughed. "You do sound like a human girl sometimes, don't you?"

"Sound like someone who doesn't want her hair to look like it's got swallows nesting in it." She gave up. "Ma's calling us for breakfast."

He got up and scrambled to pull on his robe and hand her hers. She took it.

"Thanks."

"You're welcome. I don't suppose that you might have seen—"

She handed him his boots. "Took them off you last night."

"Oh. Thank you."

"Pleasure." She shrugged her robe on and pulled on her boots before heading toward the door. "Come on, Pink."

He followed her, hopping to get into his boots. Outside there was a cold wind and dew on the grass. Tsira's ma looked mad. Hung over, probably. She nagged Tsira in Dacyn all through breakfast, going after her for all the same shit she'd been bothering her about the day before. As soon as she'd finished eating, Tsira grabbed Jeckran's shoulder and dragged him back into her ma's house.

He shook himself free once they were back inside. "I don't appreciate being hauled about like a workman's lunch pail, Tsira!"

"Sorry," she said. Then she said, "Ma's half up my ass."

"Well," Jeckran said. "She *is* your mother. What does she want?"

"Me to stay here," Tsira said. "With the clan. Shorthanded, now, with the murders. Had a few big reigs fleeing up to Cwydarin because they figure it'll be safer there. No one was begging me to stick around *before*. Want me back now that they got no choice." She paused. "She wants me to break you in, too. Get a grandchild off you, maybe."

Jeckran went dark in the face and stammered a little. Then he stopped and looked thoughtful. "When you talk about breaking in . . . does anyone witness the proceedings?"

She gave him a look. Thought she knew what he was thinking and didn't like it too much. "No."

"So one could, theoretically, simply *tell* one's mother that one was about to break in one's business partner, and then simply fall asleep instead? And would that, theoretically, cause one's mother to look upon one somewhat more charitably, for the time being?"

Tsira stared at him. Felt a little mad. Like this was all just a fucking game to him. Like fucking her wouldn't mean a damn thing. "One could. And it would."

He started stammering again. "I mean, that is, I only meant—"

She stepped in closer. "That what you want?" she said. "Want the vahns to talk to you? Want to get fixed up so you look pretty first? Want to go in that tent and have me come in and *fall asleep?*"

He swallowed. He said, "Yes, exactly."

# 13

---

*Many humans, when attempting to make a success of themselves in Cwydarin society, produce a very unfavorable and embarrassing impression and spoil all their hopes for a gleaming society debut by insisting upon behaving as if our Daeslundic thinking about the sexes ought to be applied within troll society. Though my dear Wendarumwyntset, like most reigs, uses the Daeslundic word* she *in place of the Dacyn* wys *to refer to herself when speaking in Daeslundic, a reig is not a woman or man, but a reig. A vahn is not a man or woman, but simply a vahn. To say that a reig is the troll version of a human woman is as absurd a folly as to claim that a hedgehog is the rapid version of a pincushion.*

—*From* My Life in Cwydarin: The True Recollections of a Human Woman who Rose From Low Birth to be Taken into a Great Troll Clan, *by Wendarumwynrosella*

Tsira's ma was pleased, at least.

That was the best part of this whole fucking thing. Having her ma pleased with her for once. Doing what her ma wanted, even if it was all nothing but shit.

She wouldn't mind a fight right now.

They had to take a week to train Jeckran up first. They kept him in the vahns' hall, brought him his food to him in there and all. He'd be naked, probably. They'd be washing him, whitening his teeth, rubbing the callouses from his feet. Her mouth went dry whenever she thought too much about it. She thought about it all the time, even when she should be thinking about her work. She dropped cheeses, spilled milk, nearly ruined a good piece of hide. The other reigs laughed at her.

"Little Tsira," they said, "no one ever thought we'd see you this hip-deep for a vahn."

And here she'd thought she'd been real fucking subtle about it.

The day finally came. She thought she might climb out of her skin. Her ma talked her through it, said all of the old words. Some of the other young reigs helped dress her. Then she went to the clan-reig's house.

She walked in and saw him waiting on his knees.

He looked good. Just in his shirtsleeves and skirt, so it'd be easy to undress him, his hair brushed and caught up at the back of his neck. He looked up at her and then looked down again. He was smiling a little. "Cynallumwyntsira," he said. "I was told to wait like this."

He'd learned to pronounce her name right.

She moved in close. "Stand up."

He obeyed. She felt a hot jolt. "You look good."

"Thank you. So do you."

"So now we'll go to sleep."

He licked his lips, then nodded. "Yes, of course. As agreed."

"Because that's what we want," Tsira said. "What we both want."

He opened his mouth. Then he closed it. His cheeks went dark.

She grabbed him and kissed him.

He reached around her neck and held on tight, kissed her back. She pulled away and swallowed. "Last time I did that you told me to stop."

"Tsira," he said. "You never let me explain." He paused, and his face went even darker. "I had only wanted to tell you that we should lock the door."

She grinned at him. She couldn't help it. She slid a hand to the small of his back and kissed him again. He tasted like the herbs they'd made him chew on. What a virgin vahn was supposed to taste like. He smelled like milk and lavender. "You know what you're supposed to do?"

He nodded. She cupped his cheek in her hand. "I'll listen to you.

You know that? Tell me to stop and I will." She pressed her face into his neck and breathed in. "You don't have to make me chase you. Lots of vahns don't, if they don't want to. It's just tradition. Supposed to be fun." She put her hand to his cheek, ran her thumb over his mouth, pressed it between his lips. He closed his eyes and sucked, obedient. She had to think about her breathing to keep it even. She drew her hand away. "You say *stop* and I'll stop right away. Or tell me and we'll do it gentle."

"No."

"What?"

He drew in a breath. "Gwyma and Marden told me what to do. How to make my submission." He said that last part on Dacyn. She hadn't thought about what it would do to her to hear him speaking her language, Dacyn words in that pretty little mouth. "I want to do it properly." He smiled. "I thought it sounded amusing."

She swallowed, then took a step back. "Do you make your submission?"

He tilted his chin up. "Take it from me," he said, and made like he was going to bolt.

She caught him by the shoulder and spun him around. He threw a punch, a little slow, letting her see it coming. She caught his wrist. He swung with the other arm and she caught that, too. "Want me?"

"Yes," he said. Then he grinned and tried to drop his shoulder to throw her. She laughed, hooked her ankle behind his knee, and yanked. He went down on the rugs with a soft "oof."

She put a knee on his chest and a hand to his throat, then leaned down to whisper to him. "All right?"

"Yes," he said. He was panting, breathless, laughing.

"Sure?"

"Yes."

"Want me to stop?"

"No."

"Do you make your submission?"

He bared his teeth at her and spoke in Dacyn. "Fuck off."

She wrapped her hand around his throat, squeezed a little, then released him.

"Do you make your submission?"

He was struggling under her. "*Fuck off*," he said, and bit her on the wrist.

She moved back so that she was straddling his groin, gave him a little slap on the cheek, and got him by the hair to force his head back. Licked at his throat, then bit down a little. He yelled at that.

She licked the place she'd bit, then kissed him. She put her hand up his skirt.

"*Phillim*. All right?"

"Yes." His eyes were dark and wandering past her face. He was working his hips up against her hand.

"Look at me. Sure?"

"Yes."

"Do you make your submission?"

"*Fuck*, yes."

She laughed, then picked him up and carried him to bed. Felt the quick rabbit-beat of his heart. He was sweating, but there wasn't the sour smell of fear in it.

"Tsira," he said. "Please."

She went still. "Want me to stop?"

He smiled. "*Fuck*, no."

She undressed him and kissed his throat. Put her hands against the basket of his ribs, the thin bow of his shoulders. She kept talking to him. Told him how pretty he was, what a good sweet thing he was, how she wanted him to use his tongue. He learned quick enough. She came harder and quicker than she thought she would.

She laid him down on his back and straddled him. It wasn't like it had been with others. She always liked fucking, but this was different. She looked at him and she couldn't stop smiling.

He came even faster than she had, and called out her name when he did.

They lay still, a few inches apart. He shivered, and she pulled a blanket over him. "Thank you," he said, still speaking in Dacyn.

"You've learned some Dacyn."

"Just eight variations on a theme of *fuck off.*"

She snorted and ruffled his hair. He tugged the blanket up a little higher. "This is, ah."

"Strange."

"Well, yes, rather. I mean, it all got out of hand very quickly, didn't it?"

She said, "You regret it?"

He was quiet for a while. "No. We enjoyed ourselves, didn't we?"

She said, "Sure."

Then they fell asleep.

When she woke up again, it was in the midsleep hours, still quiet and dark. Jeckran was curled up at her side making soft whistling noises as he slept. She shifted a little. Normally that might wake him, but he'd walled the world out tonight. Good. He needed sleep. *Poor tired little rabbit.*

Probably wasn't a good sign that she was thinking about him like that.

Still. She thought she was allowed to let herself feel good about it right now, in the midsleep calm. He'd liked it, she could tell. She'd made him feel good. Good and happy and safe, safe enough to sleep still and soft as a hank of wool. How a reig was supposed to make a vahn feel.

That was dangerous, probably. Made her start thinking about things she shouldn't think about. The future. Settling down. Maybe here with her clan, him learning more Dacyn and making himself useful in the village. He liked to draw. Maybe he could learn to embroider. Or shit, they could forget her clan and head back down south again. Get that *flat* he'd talked about. He could do his art and she'd—well. Figure something out. Something that wouldn't wear her body out as quick as fighting, she hoped.

He stirred. She pressed her lips to his hair. "*Shh, rabbit,*" she whispered.

He cracked his eyes open enough for her to see the warm dark of them and smiled. "Tsira," he said. "Mm." Still half-asleep, seemed like. He put his head onto her chest and wrapped an arm around her. Her stomach went tight from it. She wanted to wrap her whole self around him like a thick vine. "S'it time to get up?"

"*Nah, dolly,*" she whispered. "Go back to sleep."

"If you say so," he mumbled. "Love you." Then he did what he was told.

She held her breath until he seemed far into sleep. Then she followed after him.

She woke up to a wail that sounded like pain.

She jolted up and ran out into the night and followed the screaming. The whole clan was out, some shouting, frantic, some on the ground and still. At the edge of her mind she felt something familiar. A tug.

She turned, searching for the source of it. There. A small figure on the hillside, running faster than a human should.

She ran after it, feeling an acid sting in her chest, remembering that cool voice in her head. *This won't hurt.* This wasn't the same man, couldn't be, couldn't possibly be. That man was dead and rotting on a hillside. This man was too far ahead of her, the metallic stink of human magic fading into the distance, the screams of her people fading behind her.

She turned back. She turned herself back toward what she didn't want to see and made herself look. She ran toward it.

Marden was there, crouching in the dark. His hair was loose down his back and hanging in his face. He was crying. He was crying and screaming and his hands were covered in blood. There was a body beside him. She could make it out a little from the light of the moon.

Ma.

The front of her cut open. The top of her head cut off. Turned into meat. Tsira's ma. Still and dead.

Tsira felt her knees go loose under her. She fell hard. Tried to breathe and couldn't.

Ma. Her ma. Her mother. Her mother, her mother, her *mother*, but it couldn't be, couldn't be her ma because she was huge and endless, and Tsira wasn't anything without her ma, couldn't be here at all without her ma always there to annoy her, and *shit* they had argued, and what the fuck had Tsira last said to her? And would they throw Ma's purple robe away now, with no one left to want to save it?

"Tsira." Jeckran was touching her. "Tsira, I'm so sorry—"

She pushed him away. Did it without thinking. Knocked him off his feet. He scrambled back again. Knelt by her side, grabbed her hand in both of his. "Look at me. Tsira, I'm so sorry. I'm so *sorry*."

She shook him off and stood. She felt like she'd been skinned. She felt like there was nothing keeping the cold wind from her guts. "I have to go," she told Marden. "Alone."

Marden bowed his head. "Aye, Maem."

A sound came out of her. A kicked, hurting sound. "Marden. Don't do that. I'm not head."

"Maem," he said. "Forgive me. But we don't have anyone else."

She pushed past Jeckran and went out into the hills alone. Glad to be away from him. Needed to be away from him. She couldn't stand his being sweet. It was like pouring milk in vinegar.

Grief curdled everything.

She slept. Lay on her back in the tall grass and let the insects crawl over her body. Didn't think. Didn't think.

She tasted blood in her mouth. It dripped down her chin. She'd bitten through her lip. She hadn't felt it.

She stayed out in the hills for a while. Ate what she found, drank at the streams. Didn't think.

She tried to remember how to breathe without hurting. Wasn't sure if she could. Wasn't sure if she ever would.

Ma. She'd been a rock. A fucking piece of granite. She'd always been there. She was going to live for another five hundred years. Wasn't another reig in a thousand miles who could match her.

What would happen to her cedar chest? What would happen to her faded purple robe? What was happening to her body now? She should be too strong for worms to eat her. She should be too strong for flames.

She'd died so disappointed in her daughter. She'd died still giving instructions on the custom.

When Tsira went back to the village after a day and night alone,

Jeckran was sitting in the front room of her mother's house, on the cushions by the fire. He jolted up when she saw her, went to her, wrapped his arms around her. Didn't hold back his touch.

"Thank God," he said. "Thank God. I thought—how was I to know you hadn't flung yourself into a river?"

She pressed her nose into his hair. "Sorry," she said. "Sorry, Pink."

He just squeezed her tighter.

"I'm going back to Monsatelle," she said. "Not to work. Need to ask some questions. Find out who killed my ma."

"Why *Monsatelle*?" Jeckran asked. "So far all we know is that there is a great deal of wizarding involvement. Why not Leiscourt, that's where Weltsir is. Or why not *Hexos*, if we're going to be traipsing all over the earth on a damn fool's errand?"

"It's not a fucking *fool's errand*," she said. "It's my *ma*." She took a deep breath. "Could be in Hexos. Could be in Leiscourt. But Coldstream's closer to Monsatelle. Aren't any highways that'll take you from here to Leiscourt without passing through Monsatelle first. I figure any human who's killing Cynallum trolls and using that drip stuff would have passed through Monsatelle, at least. So I'm going to Monsatelle. I'm asking questions. If I don't learn anything, I'll ask questions in Leiscourt next. At least Monsatelle's a fucking *start*."

"And then what? What will you do when you've finished *asking questions*?"

She sat down and pulled him into her lap, curled herself around the good living warmth of his body. "Don't matter."

"It does, rather."

She kissed his neck. "Kill them."

"You can't."

"Sure I can."

"If you're caught killing humans, the masses of Monsatelle will want to see you executed for it. Even if you were human yourself, they would. You can't just *kill* people. They'll hang you for it, if the murderer doesn't get to you first."

"They can try."

"You're right. I doubt that they'll manage hanging you. They'll try to arrest you, and you'll attack them like the great brave dolt that you are, and I'll have to watch you die in a rain of bullets."

"Then I won't get caught."

"Being inconspicuous isn't one of your stronger suits. Just *leave* it, Tsira. We can get away from here, go somewhere safe."

"I can't do that."

"*Why?* You aren't a *detective*. You're unlikely to even be able to find whoever's doing this."

"Ain't Bastenne a detective? Might help."

"He's a Bastenne. I don't know if he's at all involved in that area of the clan business."

"Don't matter if he ain't. Can't just let them keep killing my people."

He shook his head. Squeezed her tight. "Why not the police?"

She snorted. "You're not that stupid. Human police don't want to get mixed up in a fight between trolls and wizards."

"Not the police, then. Have another troll do it."

"*Who?* I told you, the big clans don't give a shit about a bunch of poor unschooled border Dachunath. I'm a clan-head's daughter. Who else is going to do it?"

Jeckran huffed out an exasperated breath. "I don't know. I don't particularly care. I *need* you, Tsira. You're my—" He stopped, then went on. "Partner. I'd have nothing at all without you. You don't have to sacrifice yourself for a bunch of people who by all accounts were never very pleasant to you to begin with."

"Yeah," she said. "I do." And she did. She knew that now. She was her mother's daughter. She couldn't run out on her clan. Couldn't run away from her duty, couldn't sit around feeling like she'd been hard done by because no one wanted to hand her everything she thought she deserved. She'd been stupid to think she could, all those years.

He sighed. "I know. You're dreadfully noble. If I was more like you, I would have died at the white rocks, but as it is I'm entirely too craven and self-interested to relish participating in any ventures that seem likely to end in either a hanging or a rain of bullets."

She kissed his throat. "Bit craven, yeah. Clever. Like you like that."

"I'm glad. I like you alive."

She looked at him. "You're lying, anyway. Care about the others."

"Do I?"

"Sure. Marden, Gwyma. Mind if they got killed."

"Ah. Well, yes. But not as much as I'd mind if you did."

She smoothed a hand over his hair. "I'm going to Monsatelle, Pink. I'm going to find the fucks who killed my ma. You can stay here, if you want. Or I can settle you in Monsatelle and go my own way."

He flicked her ear. "Don't be an ass. I'll be participating in this absurd venture right along with you."

"Be dangerous."

"Of course it will be. That's why I'll go. If you were going to Monsatelle to buy some boiled sweets at Visette's Confectionery, I might chose to remain here and concentrate on my sewing, but I'm not going to stand on the hilltop waving my handkerchief while you march off to put yourself in mortal danger. In any case, you'll need me to act as interpreter when you perform all of your planned interrogations, as you don't speak a word of Esiphian, and half of the population of Monsatelle speaks nothing else. You won't be able to manage without me."

She kissed the top of his head where the hair parted. Kissed his thumb where he'd cut himself learning to whittle. Kissed the vein in his neck where the life moved under his skin. She needed to touch him, needed to feel that he was warm and breathing, needed to feel something that wasn't screaming, endless hurt. She couldn't think about what it meant. What would happen if she put him into danger that she couldn't get him out of.

"Just as well," she said. "Your sewing's shit."

They left a few hours later.

# 14

## THE GREAT-CLAN MARRIAGE

*The Residents of the Village of CORDRIDGE-ON-SEA, are Respectfully informed that on Erdmonth 16, being the date of the marriage of FIRST BROTHER WILLAM TURNGROVE to PRINCESS WEN LEGUN of SANGO, there will be a DINNER held by the family of FOURTH HEADMAN WESTGARTEN at WESTGARTEN MANOR. Tickets to be purchased at the VILLAGE HALL for 15s from OFFICIANT LANTREE no later than Erdmonth 14.*
— Village announcement, Cordridge-on-
Sea Village Hall, 6545

Onna woke up practically dead.

She had never in her life been so vile, so wretched, so completely oppressed in both body and spirit, and never—no, never!—never again would she be induced to venture out to a party with Loga. He was an *awful, horrible, terrible man*, and as she dragged her arms through the sleeves of one of her old dresses with her brain battering itself against her temples, she thought that she would like nothing better than to board the next ship away from Hexos and never see his horrid face again.

She was mentally composing the letter that she would send to her parents to inform them of her imminent return when Mrs. Macosti came in bearing a platter mounded high with food: a whole array of cheeses and pastries and eggs and fresh fruits that quite turned Onna's stomach at first look. Mrs. Macosti, however, could not accept this dismissal of her good work, and, without speaking a word of Daeslundic, she managed to communicate to Onna in no uncertain terms that she would get out of bed at once and have a good nourishing breakfast.

Onna, ever disposed to pleasing her elders, managed to drag herself to the breakfast table, and at almost the first bite found her spirits improving. By the end of the first dish she felt quite herself, and by the time she had worked her way through half of the platter she was so full of good cheer and inclination to throw herself wholeheartedly into a day of productive work that she practically skipped up the stairs to the study at the top of the Lamp.

Once in the large, bright room, however, she was confronted with a disagreeable sight. There sat Loga, looking dreadfully debauched in his shirtsleeves with the cuffs undone. He was applying himself with grim determination to a bowl of what looked like milk and a number of pieces of fried bread. Beside him sat the very beautiful young blonde woman Onna had noticed him flirting with the night before, wearing the clothes she had worn to the party and dragging a spoon listlessly through a bowl of plain porridge.

Onna stopped in the doorway, unsure as to the proper response when confronted with such a blatant display of bad conduct. There could, of course, be no doubt as to what had occurred, with the girl here at this hour in those clothes.

Loga looked up. "Ah, Onna. Good morning, darling. Or is it afternoon? How *can* one tell?"

"It's half past ten," said Onna. She didn't mean to say it so sternly, but it came out that way nonetheless. The girl, clearly noticing her tone, stood and said something to Loga in Nessoran. He raised his eyebrows and stood as well, looking briefly toward Onna.

"I'll just walk Ledia out."

He did so, returning to flop back down onto his seat with a dispirited moan. "Do you know, I've never managed to come up with a set of parameters to cure a hangover. The best I've ever managed is to drink seven cups of weak tea and then spell myself into unconsciousness." He leaned over, folding his arms on the table to pillow his head. He looked tired, and his face was an odd shade of gray.

Onna took her seat from the day before at the table and tried to put some order to her notes, which had become very scattered. She suspected that girl of having leafed through them. "You must be very fond of her."

"Of whom?"

"Of your—young lady."

"Ledia? She's not my *young lady*. She's the Directress's grandniece, and at the moment I amuse her."

"But don't you think at all about her—about her reputation?"

"Good heavens, darling, don't you know anything at all about Hexos? We don't shut our women up in towers like they do in your country." At this he returned his attention to his breakfast, giving Onna time to regain her composure. Her face felt very hot.

A minute or so later he cleared his throat. "I know that this sort of thing isn't quite . . . *regular* in Daeslund. I'm afraid that I'm not very accustomed to having another person staying in the Lamp, as you're my first apprentice, and I do have a number of habits that might strike you as somewhat . . . unusual. I suppose that I ought to amend them, now that you're staying here with me. I certainly shouldn't like to make you uncomfortable in the place that you live. I hope that you don't think too badly of me?" He sounded strangely anxious, as if the opinion of some foolish little girl from Daeslund might actually matter to him.

Onna tried to school her expression. "I'm sure that it isn't my place to think anything at all. I am your *assistant*, after all."

He looked, she thought, not very happy at this response. He continued eating his breakfast in an uncomfortable silence. Then his face suddenly twisted up with discomfort, and when he pushed his chair back and stood, he swayed slightly. He grabbed at the table edge and gave her a very rigid smile. "I'm afraid that I'm . . . not feeling well. I'll just—" Loga practically staggered from the room, waving his hand in a peculiar little gesture as he exited. She made to follow him, but a servant appeared and shooed her back in, indicating through his brisk, cheerful manner that everything was very well in hand and taken care of. So she settled back at the table to work.

It was a very curious feeling, to be all alone at work in the Lord-Mage's tower. She indulged herself for a few moments in imagining that she was the Lord-Mage herself. One of the owls from her examination begged her servants for an audience, and she had him turned out on his ear. It was one of the most wonderfully satisfying daydreams she had ever had.

Her headache crept back, so she decided to rest a little by writing letters home: one for Papa to read out to her mama and sisters to tell them about some of her adventures since she sent her last letter, and one to Sy. The one to her family was very detailed, with good long descriptions of the Lord-Mage and Hexos and all of the lovely exciting things that had happened, along with plenty of details for her mother about how she was eating well and going to bed at a decent hour every night. At the end of it she wrote: *Please do write back quickly: I miss you all awfully, and I want to know all about everything in Cordridge-on-Sea, and how everyone is, especially the baby. All my love, Onna.*

Then, as she started to write a letter for Sy, she found, to her irritation, that she was all out of paper. She rummaged in the drawer that had contained paper the last time, but it was now full of nothing but very mushy oranges. All of the drawers, in fact, seemed to have somehow shifted about since her last examination, though why and to what purpose she could not imagine. Perhaps some security measure of Loga's that he had neglected to mention.

She searched through more drawers without finding anything of use and was about to give up entirely and retire to her rooms for an afternoon nap when at last she found a drawer full of notebooks.

She pulled one out at random, opened it, and stared. It was full of Sangan writing in a small, cramped hand. Interspersed with the text were sketches, pictures that she recognized from her cursory anatomy lessons at school. Pictures of the human heart.

She took a deep breath and continued flipping through the book. There were other charts and diagrams and here and there a page of parameters written in Nessoran. These, at least, she could decipher to an extent, though they were difficult to understand. The parameters quite clearly dealt with the heart while also having something to do with *lightning*. Then, as she stared at the pages trying to work it out, she grew suddenly and terribly convinced that Loga would come leaping out at any moment and catch her rifling through his things, so she shoved the notebook back into the drawer and shut it.

The next drawer she opened contained paper, so she set to writing her letter to Sy, which contained much less information about her meals and daily habits and much more about the exciting and important work she was doing for Loga, including the exciting and important young wizarding gentleman she had met. Then she felt as if this was rather mean of her, and she crossed out several flattering references to Haran and Loga before immediately writing them back in again. She soothed her guilty conscience with the thought that it could practically be considered deceitful to *not* mention that the Lord-Mage was very young and handsome and that a famous wizard's son had sent her a bouquet of orchids. Perhaps, she thought, in a secret wicked corner of her heart, Sy might be inspired to send some flowers as well, or at least a letter filled with something more thrilling than endless dry parameters.

When she finished, she was startled to find herself with tears in her eyes. It was wonderful, of course, to have the opportunity to be in Hexos and learn from the greatest wizard in the world—even if he *was* getting up to very suspicious things without her knowledge—but all the same she had never in her life been so long without her mama and papa and sisters and Sy and the awful-familiar smell of the pencil eraser factory in the wind. She became so gloomy that, for a moment, she thought of writing to invite Mrs. Cordram over for tea just to hear a nice familiar Daeslundic accent and to argue politely over who was the most useless gentleman in the Assemblage, until she remembered that Mrs. Cordram always made her feel as if she were the most disreputable young lady who had ever sailed to Hexos, and Onna would rather not invite her over to tea until it was absolutely necessary for politeness's sake.

She then remembered, with a renewed burst of good cheer, that she was already planning to spend time with a fellow Daeslunder: Captain Run would be coming tomorrow evening to teach her about how she made the longeye constructions. This would also provide her with a welcome respite from her exhausting original research. It would be very disrespectful of Onna to ask Captain Run to spend her evening teaching Onna about her parametrical work without doing a jot of preliminary review of the literature of miniaturized constructions. So she went to Loga's bookshelves, retrieved a few likely looking volumes, and started to study.

It was all very slow going. She was shocked to realize that, for the first time in her life, she was confronted with parametrical concepts that felt above her head. She was glaring furiously at what was meant to be an illustrative diagram—that she found *decidedly* unenlightening— when Loga came floating back into the room, looking enormously refreshed in a new indigo tunic, his eyes bright and his hair neatly combed. "Good heavens, darling," he said. "If I didn't know better, I might suspect you of being a fire witch and attempting to set my reference books alight with your gimlet eye."

"I'm sorry," she said automatically. She was in the habit of apologizing for making faces that men thought weren't very pretty. It occurred to her, very briefly, that she resented being made to think about her face when she was trying to focus on the contents of her *mind*. "I'm afraid that I'm not clever enough to understand this."

"Don't be ridiculous," Loga said, and sat down beside her. "You have every right to be cross. And it isn't that you aren't clever enough. These particular concepts are just a bit like Daeslundic beef: they take an *exhausting* amount of time to chew through."

This time Onna's glare was deliberate. Loga laughed and pulled her notebook toward himself. "Here, remember what I was telling you about how I assign parametrical sets to movements of my hands? Try not to think of what you see here as ordinary language. Think of it as a gesture that triggers a parametrical set. Or as a proverb. The words as written are some pastoral Daeslundic fiddle-faddle about birds and bushes, but we know that the actual meaning is about not spending a man's inheritance until you've convinced him to become your house-holder." He started drawing his own diagram, explaining as he went. "Look, let's take a Morgan's wall as an example, and then write this to assign the wall to this smaller set. Now, here, could you please write me a minor illusion?"

Onna did, and he guided her through writing the parameters to assign her work to a shorter set. "Now, could you imagine a way to concisely combine our two new sets without corrupting the param-eters?"

Onna chewed on her lip. "I could try," she said, after a moment.

"Wonderful," Loga said. "Hand me that other notebook, and I'll look over your research while you have a go at it."

They both worked quietly—with Loga marking up her notes a great deal, which Onna tried and failed not to find horribly distracting—but eventually she managed to put together something that she wasn't too ashamed to show him, and they traded their papers. Her notes on troll blood were covered in more notes in Loga's tiny, crowded-up handwrit-ing. He looked over her new sets and smiled.

"Very good! I've nothing in particular to add, but that's largely be-cause I confess to being far from an expert in this particular field. I like to write parameters like Esiphian romantic novels where nobody does anything but pine languidly for three hundred–odd pages. You could use them to press all of the water out of a large block of tofu. Captain Run has an absolutely *stupendous* gift for editing down her sets, though, so she'll be able to take you where I can't lead." He sat back and stretched out his back in a way that struck Onna as overly dramatic. He always seemed to be enjoying himself more than he ought to be. "I think that it's about time for lunch." Then he paused, adding, "Jok should be here any moment."

"Yes," she said. She wasn't sure why he would say it in that odd tone of voice. "I suppose that he should be."

Loga busied himself with some papers on his desk, though Onna noticed he was less working than fiddling with bits of wire between glances back at the door. Onna tried not to stare, as she couldn't help but find it exceedingly odd that, while they were investigating a wizard who was stealing the hearts of trolls, Loga had failed to mention that he himself was studying the heart. She couldn't quite bring herself to suspect him of anything *too* awful, but she did think that if he was conducting his own research into the matter, he really ought to share his findings with his assistant.

Loga also darted little glances at her, and the look on his face was strangely familiar. All at once, Onna realized he reminded her of Louina, one of her sisters, trembling with nerves as she was about to go to work as governess for a third headman's children. "Loga," she said on impulse. "That tunic's *awfully* smart."

His smile was unlike any she had seen from him before, startled and unguarded. "Oh," he said. "Thank you. That's . . . that's very kind of you, Onna."

She knew that he was *dreadfully* rich and sophisticated, but at that moment she was quite sure that he was just as silly and nervous and worried about looking nice in front of his friend as she had ever been when Sy came by for tea.

After what seemed an age, a servant stepped into the room and announced something very loudly in Nessoran. This was not, apparently, the announcement that a fire had broken out, as in the next moment Mr. Finnbair walked in with his hat in his hand. He was wearing a Daeslundic trouser-suit in a military fashion that Onna thought quite suited him. He was also looking rather shy. "Hey now, Loga. Good afternoon, Miss Gebowa," he added, with a little bow.

Onna nodded. "Good afternoon."

Mr. Finnbair glanced back to Loga and gave a little smile. "You look like you had a rough night."

Loga looked embarrassed. "I'm afraid I slept poorly. And what do you think of my Lamp?"

"It's grand. Can I—" He went to the window to look out, but backed away very quickly indeed. "God's name. I don't much like that."

"I had forgotten about your trouble with heights," said Loga, some of the strength returning to his voice. "Are you hungry? There *is* lunch, if you really meant to eat, and your inviting yourself here wasn't just a pretext to come by to see the Lamp."

"It was a *pretext* to come down and see you and your lovely assistant. Though I can't say I wasn't hoping you'd feed me, too."

Loga smiled, another very natural smile that made him suddenly sweet and boyish. Onna reminded herself sternly not to admire him. "I think that I can manage that."

Lunch was eaten in the garden, as the weather was fine, with the trickle of the stream and rustle of the trees providing a soft hum when the conversation flagged. This it did only infrequently: Loga, as always, managed a steady stream of chatter, and Mr. Finnbair had a way of quietly egging him on and then laughing in what seemed like very genuine pleasure at his clever little pronouncements. Loga was different around him: more relaxed, less artificial. Sometimes when Mr. Finnbair smiled at him he looked startled, as if being smiled at with such warmth was a very peculiar thing, indeed.

Onna finally thought of something to say. "Loga, were you and Mr. Finnbair at school together?"

Loga shook his head. "We were apprenticed together to my predecessor, Lady Bawu."

Onna tried to hide her surprise. She had assumed that Mr. Finnbair must be an ordinary journeyman wizard—there wasn't the crackle in the air around him that there was around Loga—but to have been apprenticed to the former Lord-Mage, he would have to be very good, indeed. Mr. Finnbair himself spoke up: "We would have been about your age, then. Seventeen?"

"Eighteen in three weeks," said Onna. She stole a glance at Loga, who seemed, as usual, to find her amusing.

"Quite the mature and sophisticated woman. I was only barely fifteen, myself."

"And did your predecessor hold auditions, like you did?"

"Oh, no," said Loga.

Mr. Finnbair snorted. "You can put that on Loga's background on the stage."

"How dreadfully unfair of you!" Loga replied. "I would say that the way in which we were selected was *far* more theatrical."

"We were found," said Mr. Finnbair, in response to Onna's puzzled look.

"Plucked from obscurity," added Loga. "Magister Bawu had let it be generally known that she wanted to be alerted of any spectacular displays of talent from young people under the age of twenty."

"And what did you do?"

"I turned a man into a toad," said Loga.

Onna stared. "And you weren't *arrested*?"

"Well, my dear, he had just attempted to rob me, so I believe it was generally thought that I was justified."

Onna looked at Mr. Finnbair. "And you, Mr. Finnbair?"

He had just taken a large bite of roasted lamb and waved a hand in an embarrassed way until he finished chewing. "Pardon. Me and my twin brother levitated the empty plinth at Weltsir."

Onna couldn't help but gape. "You levitated the *plinth*?"

She knew at once, of course, what he was referring to: the plinth was both enormous and extremely famous. She remembered rushing past it before her written exam and thinking it was even bigger than she had imagined. It had originally been intended for a giant sculpture of some kind, but the founders of the school had not been able to come to an agreement over who the sculpture should commemorate—there had apparently been some question of Elgarite versus Republican political allegiances—and in the end nothing had ever been erected. The idea of levitating the plinth struck Onna as similar to levitating the first head-man's wife in terms of its violation of stately dignity—though of course, considering the greater mass of the gigantic granite plinth, much more difficult.

Mr. Finnbair looked something between proud and rueful. "We were terrible reprobates. They nearly didn't take me back, after I left Hexos, even with Magister Bawu's recommendation."

Onna frowned. "Only you were selected, and not you and your brother together?"

A brief silence fell over the table. "No," said Mr. Finnbair, "it was both of us." He paused, then said, "Elgar died when we were eighteen."

The sound of trickling water from the stream became suddenly very loud. Loga was staring resolutely at his bowl, and she saw his throat work when he swallowed.

"I'm so terribly sorry," said Onna, and she meant it.

Mr. Finnbair smiled and said simply, "Thank you." After another moment of silence, he said, "So what does Loga have you working on?"

She explained about the trolls and the miniaturized constructions, grateful to have anything else to talk about, even if she thought it was very callous to discuss murders over an informal luncheon, as if they were of no more account than the latest in Esiphian hats or hammerball scores. She thought it must be something that happened to you when you grew powerful. As you rose higher, everything below seemed smaller and of less consequence, just like the buildings of Hexos looked like dolls' houses from the top of the Lamp.

Though she was often very careless with remembering her evening prayers, Onna thought that tonight she should say a prayer for the ease-ful reliving of the murdered trolls.

Mr. Finnbair listened very attentively, then said, "That's a bad busi-ness. I'm glad to hear that you're looking into it. Actually, I might be able to help you out a little, if you want to talk to some of the trolls in that neighborhood near Magister Corbray's place. They know me pretty well there."

Loga looked up sharply. "Why?"

"For my work. Trolls live a long time, which is what Judge Schutts wants to know about. I've been trying to interview them a little about their magic, and since a lot of the folks here don't care all that much about all of the Cwydarin regulations, they're giving me a little information. It's good stuff, Zei; I think that you'd be interested. From what they tell me, the way they write parameters is miles beyond what we've got, and they know more about anatomy than our whole medical library. Problem is, the difference in troll life spans seems to be mostly biological. I've been wondering if it's something in their blood. I was planning on going back tomorrow afternoon, if you'd like to come along."

Onna listened with an awful sinking sensation in her stomach and glanced toward Loga to see how he was reacting. His expression was blank, which struck her as strange. She couldn't see, if he had no knowledge of the murders that he didn't share, why he wouldn't be thinking as she was.

An academic wizard. Someone whom trolls knew and trusted.

Someone interested in their hearts and blood.

Onna, in that moment, did not trust herself not to immediately begin making wild accusations toward either of them, and she was grateful when Loga responded in quite his usual manner. "I think that would be perfect, Jok. I rather fancy coming along myself, if you don't think that it will alarm the trolls to have such a great number of humans tramping about in their neighborhood asking delicate questions."

"They're not so easy to alarm! I mostly talk to a reig named Teiran-wynartur who could probably glare a charging bull into feeling ashamed of itself. Now that I think of it, she'll be pleased to see that I've brought you, Miss Gebowa! She doesn't think too much of males going around all unsupervised. In her clan they think that females are better suited for leadership. Males are meant for handcrafts and minding the food production, that sort of thing."

"Is it true that the women beat the men?" Onna asked, her curiosity getting the best of her unease. Murderer or not, she had never met anyone who had spent any time around trolls. One of the books she was reading made a great number of coy references to violence in troll marriages, though the authors of some other volumes denounced this as dreadful slander.

Mr. Finnbair shrugged. "I've never seen it, but I've never seen a man beating his wife, either, and I won't say that *that* never happens." He then added, "I should warn you, Miss Gebowa, that trolls are sometimes pretty rough in how they talk, by Daeslundic lights. If you feel too uncomfortable, you could tell me. I wouldn't like you to feel embarrassed."

Onna drew herself up slightly. "I'm a wizard, Mr. Finnbair, like you. I certainly hope that my sensibilities won't keep me from my research!"

Mr. Finnbair smiled. "You sound like Zei. He always was pretty radical."

Loga shrugged expansively. "If believing in the rights of ladies to publicly engage in serious scholarship and of gentlemen to publicly wear a delicious magenta taffeta in the summer makes me a radical, then I can only embrace the label."

"Zei," Mr. Finnbair said, "if using the phrase *delicious magenta taffeta* doesn't make you some sort of radical, then there's no reason for the word!"

A servant stepped forward then and announced, "Magister Haran Welder."

Onna jumped to her feet, then recalled that she was a lady and sat down again, then said, "I'm so sorry, I never sent you a card!" and then felt very foolish. Mr. Welder entered and bowed, and to his credit, did so without laughing. "Good afternoon, Miss Gebowa. And please, don't mention it! Flowers were the least that I could do; I can't tell you how pleased I was when I heard. I was just passing by and wanted to congratulate you again in person." He nodded to Loga and said something in Nessoran. Loga laughed and responded in Daeslundic.

"Well, I'm very sorry to have ruined your little surprise, darling! You know Jok Finnbair, don't you?"

"Of course I do," Mr. Welder said. "I didn't know you were back in Hexos, Finnbair!"

"No one did. I didn't put an announcement in the papers. And what are you doing here? I thought you were supposed to be writing your thesis."

"And I am! I'm working out of the Hexos University Hospital."

Mr. Finnbair raised his eyebrows. "What for?"

"Oh, it's all very dry. Sanitation protocols. I thought that if I plan on indulging myself in spending another five years as a student, I should at least dedicate myself to something useful."

Mr. Finnbair gave a low whistle. "Sounds dense enough to me. Who's your supervisor?"

Mr. Welder made a little moue. "Loga will laugh. It's Magister Dorabri."

"Ha!" Loga said. "And how many stirring speeches against me has he given so far this week?"

"You really think too much of yourself, Loga," Mr. Welder said, though he said it fondly. "People do have conversations about topics other than you. And his comments about you on the day before the auditions weren't all that bad, really, though I stopped listening after the first five minutes or so."

"Can't be as bad as the comments I heard him making last week when he learned that he had to pay for his guest to enter at the Fraternal Order clubhouse," Mr. Finnbair said, and Mr. Welder snickered.

Loga gave an indelicate snort. "Really, you Daeslunders with your *clubhouses*. I'm surprised that Magister Dorabri would ever be interested in something so ridiculously outmoded. Harro, darling, we really must get back to work, but if you don't have any plans for tomorrow afternoon, Jok was going to bring us to meet his troll acquaintances in the neighborhood out by Riagli Square."

Mr. Welder laughed aloud. "What an invitation! Why are the three of you tramping about harrassing trolls, and why do you insist on calling me *Harro* as if I were still three years old?"

"I *refuse* to ever call you anything else," said Loga, and Onna explained about her troll research and Mr. Finnbair's familiarity with the neighborhood. Mr. Welder expressed, in his gentlemanly way, that he would be interested in coming along and meeting some troll wizards himself, and so at one o'clock sharp the next day they all climbed into Loga's elaborate floating carriage and headed off to the troll's quarter in the west of Hexos, the population of which had recently rapidly increased in response to the less-congenial environment for trolls in Leiscourt.

Onna hadn't known exactly what it was that she expected from a quarter full of trolls who had fled their homeland seeking employment in Hexos. She had vaguely imagined something like the poor neighborhood she had inadvertently wandered into in Leiscourt, but when she peered out from the palanquin, she found a very prosperous-looking neighborhood, with many buildings painted in crisp white and blue. The streets were very quiet, which struck her as odd. "Where are they?"

"Mostly inside, I should think," said Mr. Finnbair. "Most trolls that I've met like to go home and have a proper dinner and nap around noon. They should be waking up about now."

The palanquin landed with the lightest of bumps, and Loga fairly leapt out like a small dog springing forth from its master's carriage. He seemed almost to shake himself and bounded a few steps with an air of enormous pleasure. "What an interminable ride! But isn't it lovely out today?"

She glanced at Mr. Finnbair and noted, with a jolt of unease, the intense gaze he focused on Loga. He smiled, his eyes crinkling up at the corners. "Isn't it surely."

Their little party made its way to a particularly large townhouse, with Mr. Finnbair in the lead and Loga at his side. Mr. Finnbair knocked, and Mr. Welder and Onna lagged behind on the street, exchanging quiet pleasantries about their work. It seemed to Onna a very nice thing indeed to walk with a handsome young man on a warm afternoon. Still, she mustn't make herself too comfortable: there was work to be done.

"Have you known Mr. Finnbair long?"

Mr. Welder cast her a quick glance. "Yes, for years. Why do you ask?"

"Oh, just wondering. I know that Loga is very fond of him."

"They were boys together. I think he's a very good sort and a fine wizard. How do you find working for Loga?"

She paused long enough in formulating her response that Mr. Welder smiled. "Can it be as bad as that?"

"Oh, I didn't mean that at all! I've been learning ever so much."

"I'm glad," said Mr. Welder. "I had wondered if you might find him very odd."

"But I do!" said Onna, quite without thinking. Mr. Welder laughed, and before Onna could utter something even more foolish and wretched, a troll appeared in the doorway.

Onna had, somehow, not anticipated how large a living troll would be. She realized now that the corpse she had seen was like a stuffed lion in a museum, its size and power neutralized by death. This troll filled almost the entire doorframe and was more decidedly *alive* than any person she had ever met. Her blue skin was set off by the vibrant reds and blacks of her clothing, and her silver hair was dressed in an elaborately braided collection of plaits wound about her head. Onna also noted the troll's torc, which she had seen illustrated in *The Habits and Manners of the Great Trolls of the North*. She ducked her head in what she hoped was a properly respectful fashion and said, "*Maem.*"

The gentlemen all looked at her with expressions of surprise. The troll did not smile, but nor did she—Onna knew from the torc that this must be a clan-head or eldest daughter, and therefore a reig—look displeased. "Ta beit, little sister. Are these your men?"

It took Onna a moment to construct a response to this inquiry. The shock of hearing such an astonishingly ordinary-sounding northwest Daeslundic accent in the troll's extraordinarily deep voice made the strange question itself seem almost ordinary. "I, ah—I am acquainted with all of them."

"They're on your name in this house. I'm Teiranwynartur," she said.

"I'm Onna Gebowa," Onna said, uncertainly.

The troll seemed satisfied with this, for she jerked her head toward Mr. Finnbair and said to Onna, "I've met the red-haired one. You want to take our blood, too?"

The skin prickled on Onna's arms. Mr. Finnbair objected. "I only took samples, Miss Teiranwynartur, and your vahns were paid for them. There's no need to talk like I'm a vampire!"

Teiranwynartur ignored him and looked expectantly at Onna. Onna felt a guilty little thrum of pleasure at this. She had many times throughout her life been similarly overlooked while some important personage spoke to her father, or Mr. Heisst, or even Sy. To be put in the position of speaking for a group of men was as thrilling as it was disconcerting. "No," she said. "Magister Wuzan and I are tying to find out who has been killing your people in Hexos."

"I'm surprised you care," said Teiranwynartur. "About dead border-trolls. Not like our clan has the money to thank you."

"I care very much," said Onna, and meant it. Meeting Teiranwynartur and looking her in the eye made everything suddenly, uncomfortably real all over again: the trolls being killed had family, friends, and clan-members who mourned for them. "Please, could you tell me if there are any humans whom you think the trolls in your clan would know and trust?"

Teiranwynartur's mouth turned down slightly at the corners. "There's that half-human vahn. He's friends with some of the younger reigs. Then there are a few we do business with. Shop owners, that sort. Some Elgarite messengers who always give us religious tracts and tell us that we should go back to Daeslund to join their haltons. And this one," she said, jerking her head again toward Mr. Finnbair. "He's all right."

Mr. Finnbair smiled at this, but said nothing. Onna struggled for what to ask next, then said, "Do you know if anyone has ever seen the murderer, or been nearby when someone was killed?"

Teiranwynartur, to Onna's astonishment, nodded. "That letter-writer. He says he has, at least."

"I beg your pardon?"

"That half pink. He says he saw the murderer," said Teiranwynartur, and Onna knew that she would have to speak to him.

She and Loga bid farewell to their retinue at that point, though not without some protestations and lingering glances—Mr. Finnbair's directed toward Loga, and Mr. Welder's directed toward Onna. Though, she supposed, she should think of Mr. Welder as Haran now, as he insisted.

It was very quiet in the palanquin as Onna and Loga made their way to the street of red doors. Eventually Onna convinced herself to speak. "Mr. Finnbair seems very fond of you."

Loga's response was brusquer than she had ever heard him. "He was in love with me, if that's what you mean."

Onna's throat constricted. "I beg your pardon."

"No. I'm sorry. That was rude of me. And unfair to Jok. He had some very—romantic notions about me when we were younger, but he's *quite* past them. We're only very dear friends. I'm the nearest thing he has to a brother now."

"Ah," Onna said, and then she went quiet, hoping that he wouldn't notice how the skin of her arms was prickling with unease. People, she thought, often went to very great lengths to help and defend their brothers. She supposed plenty of men would think nothing of lying on a brother's behalf. Or killing, perhaps. In books, at least, good men were often driven to kill for their brother's sake.

For the first time in her life, Onna hoped that her life might bear *less* resemblance to a thrilling three-volume novel.

# 15
------

*If there is one error that I see more than any other from frugal young housewives, it is the thought that old-fashioned methods in cleaning and cookery must always be superior to any process involving magical assistance, or that magical constructions are only to be found in the homes of grand headwives. In truth, in this modern age of widely printed magical parameters, most women can learn a few simple spells to aid them in their daily tasks, and anyone at all can purchase one of the sundry little domestic constructions now available in any well-stocked general store. Take, for example, the wizard-lamp, cheaply made Daeslundic examples of which may be purchased for only five tocats, which will emit as much light as a candle for two hours, without wizarding assistance, with only two minutes of cranking . . .*

—Ladies' Sketch, *Fall 6572*

Tsira was becomingly increasingly unmanageable.

Jeckran was frightened, sometimes, to go out with her in Monsatelle. One day they were walking down a narrow street and a man bumped against her. She turned on him, snarled, and might have killed him if Jeckran hadn't launched himself at her. The poor man was frightened into hysterics, and they ran for it before he could gather his wits enough to yell for the police, scrabbling down alleyways and jumping over fences until they were nearly a mile away. The mad dash bothered Jeckran's ankle so much that he could barely walk without his cane for days afterward, and she was sweet and solicitous, regretful of anything that might have hurt him. "Sorry," she kept saying. "Stupid of me."

"I don't want you to apologize," he told her. "I want your assurance that you won't try to murder the next unfortunate Jok or Elgarson who treads on your toe."

She only shrugged.

It was strange being back in the city like this. It had been the scene of so many private little fantasies. The flat they would have together. The hearth with a new kettle. Tsira wearing slippers and reading by the fire. Ordinary domesticity, which was an idea he had constructed from books, having never experienced it for himself. He thought that a little flat and a warm hearth and a bed with Tsira in it might be what *home* might feel like, but he would settle for nothing but Tsira, Tsira as she used to be, the stout walls and sturdy roof of her. He'd grown so used to sheltering in her. Now, back in their little room in Mon Del Ras's place, he endeavored to put together a sort of schedule to keep them focused on their goal, to hammer together some scaffolding to keep her from crumbling entirely.

"We'll find who's behind the killings," he said, "and you'll kill him, and then we'll be done with this." *And then you'll feel better*, he thought. *And then we can make a home.*

They went to the parts of Monsatelle where the dripping parlors gathered thickly, places that crackled at night but had burned down to a smolder by dawn. They knocked on doors, greeted the bleary-eyed and suspicious, the annoyed and the quietly exhausted. They followed suggestions from Mon Del Ras: criminals of his acquaintance, or men that Tsira's friend Catleen had encountered, men who liked to get drunk and start fights or hit her girls, men who might easily take money to kill a troll or know someone who would. Jeckran did the talking, with Tsira standing a few paces behind. It was always the same few questions.

*Do you recognize this ring?*

*Have you ever seen one like it?*

*Do any wizards ever come here?*

After four days of asking the questions and three doors in a row being slammed directly in their faces, Tsira was so infuriated that he had to herd her into a quiet alley and croon at her like he would to a spooked horse. "They're only frightened, Tsira. This isn't the sort of place where strangers go knocking on people's doors just to pay a social call. They might think that we're here to collect the rent. Trolls and headmen's sons don't come to places like this without reason."

Tsira didn't seem to want to listen to reason.

One night they lay together in bed, curled up close, Jeckran's face tucked into Tsira's neck.

"It doesn't feel better," she said. "Just hurts the same every day."

She'd never talked like that before. Never admitted to hurt. He threaded his fingers into her hair and scratched gently at her scalp. "I can't imagine," he said.

"Pink," she said. Her voice was a deep rasp. "Don't leave me."

He pressed in closer and slid his knee between her thighs. "Not for anything, Cynallumwyntsira."

The next evening they went to a pub: Jeckran thought that a drink would do both of them good. They sat in a dark booth in the back of the room to nurse a beer each and watch the regulars shout and gamble. She was wearing a loose jacket and a cap that she pulled down low over her forehead, and Jeckran had hoped that this would be enough to make her relatively inconspicuous in a bar full of rough men. His efforts, however, were in vain. Just as they were about to leave, Jeckran spotted a few men looking in their direction. One of them, egged on by the others, stumbled toward them and leaned on their table, craning his neck to get a better look at Tsira's face. Once he got a glimpse he jerked backward. "Are you really a *troll*, then?"

She tossed the cap onto the table and stood to her full height. The man stumbled backward, but she caught him by the collar and lifted him off his feet, pulled him close to her bared teeth.

"I'm what you pray to your cuntless god to keep you safe from, that's what I fucking am."

She looked at Jeckran, dropped the man to the floor, and stepped over his prone body to walk out.

He found her leaning against the wall of a nearby building. "Pink," she said. "I might have killed him. Might kill someone else."

"You *didn't*, though," he said. "And you won't."

She didn't respond.

They started their search again the next morning, with results no better than the day before. After a few hours Tsira's expression shifted from "calm and unflappable" to "barely suppressed fury," and fearful for the well-being of the next person whose door they knocked upon, Jeckran suggested that they repair to the nearest coffeehouse for a rest.

On the next street corner, they found a very typical Daeslundic-style coffeehouse with high-backed wooden booths and the specials of the day, such as they were, written in soap on the mirror. Jeckran found its very ordinariness wonderfully calming to the eye. Tsira was ill inclined to enter, but she acquiesced when he said he would order cake for her so that she wouldn't have to say anything to the waiter. Tsira had what struck Jeckran as a morbid fear of Esiphian waiters, who tended to be either visibly frightened of her or overly fascinated, goggling at her in a way that he understood must be rather trying.

Their waiter—an underdeveloped-looking young man of twelve or thirteen, with a piping little voice to match his diminutive person— proved to be of the goggling type. He nevertheless managed to keep his wits well enough to bring Jeckran his pot of coffee and his bread and butter and, for Tsira, a cup of chocolate and slice of raisin cake. He seemed ashamed of his silent gawping, for he said, "Here you are, sir!" with enormous vigor when he placed the cake in front of Tsira.

"Polite," she said, after the young fellow left. Jeckran nodded.

"Yes, rather. At least, he seems enthusiastic in executing his duties. I'm always heartened to see such industry in a young person. It bolsters the Elgarite argument for the continuous perfection process of man, to which I have always been sentimentally attached despite all evidence to the contrary."

She stared at him in a familiar way, the one that signified she found everything he said too absurd to acknowledge, and took a bite of cake. "Not bad."

"I thought that it might be what the afternoon called for." Tsira's great fondness for sweets had once been amusing, but Jeckran later realized that Tsira was almost constantly hungry, and anything with a great deal of grease or sugar acted like a balm upon her nerves. He now forced her to take a proper breakfast in the morning, rather than letting her, in her impatience, set off for the day after gulping down a cup of coffee and a bit of bread. He liked watching her eat, in any case; he liked the flashes of unguarded pleasure that crossed her face when she bit into something she liked. She otherwise was only ever so expressive in bed, or when she was breaking some poor devil's bones. She wolfed down her cake, drank her chocolate in two enormous gulps, and eyed Jeckran's bread and butter with such intensity that he had no choice but to push the chipped plate across the table to let her devour that as well.

When she finished eating, she sat back in her chair. Her posture was as erect as ever, but the skin under her eyes looked bruised, and the lines framing her mouth were more firmly sketched than they had been a few weeks earlier. She spoke in Dacyn. "Don't know what to do."

He responded in Daeslundic. "We'll just have to continue as we have been, I suppose."

"Isn't working."

"We've only just started. And you heard Mon Del Ras say that it will take time to learn anything, even with him asking around as well. You just have to be patient."

"Let me get my hands on someone. They'll talk then."

"That would be deeply inadvisable. They might have guns. We just have to keep asking."

Their homunculus of a waiter came to take the plates away—though Jeckran had to energetically defend the half-full coffeepot from his enthusiastic clearing—and in the spirit of demonstrating to Tsira the sort of patient dedication he was encouraging, Jeckran pulled the wizard's ring from his pocket. "Boy, wait there a moment. Have you ever seen a ring like this before?"

"Yes sir," said the boy, appearing quite pleased at his ability to make himself so helpful. "I have, sir."

Tsira sat up straighter. "Where?"

He nearly toppled over backward at the sound of her voice, but recovered himself quickly enough. "It's a wizard's ring, sir. All of them have them."

Tsira looked faintly murderous. Jeckran intervened. "I mean more specifically. Have you ever seen a ring *just* like this? Say, on a man with brown hair and a weak chin?"

"Like Mr. Chastonne, you mean, sir?"

"*Yes*," said Jeckran at once, trying not to shout. "*Just* like Mr. Chastonne. Does he come here often?"

"Sometimes, sir. Always orders a cup of tea and two slices and picks over it for hours, sir. Tight-fisted, sir. Looks like he misses a few meals, too, sir; scrawny-looking fellow. Hasn't come by for a few weeks, though."

Jeckran refrained from pointing out the irony of such an exceptionally scrawny person commenting critically upon the figures of others. "Indeed. I don't suppose that you would happen to know where the gentleman lives?"

The homunculus grew guarded; apparently the local disinclination to speak to strangers had finally found root within his diminutive breast. "Begging your pardon, sir, but I couldn't say, sir."

Jeckran and Tsira exchanged glances. Tsira's glance seemed to contain a suggestion of violence. Jeckran endeavored to imbue his with remonstration: the waiter was, after all, only a child, albeit an exceedingly trying one. He looked to the boy. "Never mind, then. What do we owe you?"

They settled the bill, and Jeckran magnanimously presented the homunculus with an additional sen for a tip, which he accepted with a smart salute.

Once they were out on the street again, Jeckran made an effort to avoid looking excessively pleased with himself. "I think that went well, don't you?"

Tsira did not seem inclined to indulge him. "Chastonne's the same name they said in the cave. Knew it when I heard it."

"Was it? Then they were all connected, the men in the cave and the wizard. That simplifies things, doesn't it?"

"Yeah. What now?"

"We return to our room and you reward me for my efforts?"

She cracked a smile at that. "Later."

"What a coquette you are! Very well. Then I would suggest that we pay a visit to the Fraternal Order of Wizards. I believe that they have their club on Gedard Street."

The wizard's club was in one of the better parts of town, necessitating a long walk. It was at such moments that Jeckran regretted Tsira's size: she couldn't fit comfortably in a cab. He occupied himself on the way by trying to tease her into a smile. It was difficult. She was so often so terribly low now. He hadn't heard her sing in ages or laugh in almost as long. He had hoped that simply trying to find her mother's killer would make her feel better, but it only seemed to make matters worse. To distract her, he chattered without pause for several minutes, until her silence weighed upon him too heavily, and he stopped.

When they finally arrived at the grand old building that housed the wizard's club, Jeckran came to an abrupt halt and glanced up at Tsira. She shrugged and said, "I'll wait here."

"I'm sorry," he said. Apparently, on her own, she had come to the same conclusion he had—that her presence would make the humans inside even less likely to talk. Of course, Tsira had never been stupid.

The man behind the desk was a slight, slope-shouldered fellow with a drooping mustache. He looked at Jeckran for slightly too long, then looked away, then looked back again. "Yes, sir?" He spoke in Esiphian, his voice high-pitched and tentative.

Jeckran leaned one elbow on the counter, partially to shift the weight off his ankle, partially to loom a bit. He was at least a head taller than the clerk. He said conspiratorially, "I was wondering if you might be able to help me find a man."

Tsira had lately begun teasing Jeckran about his soft voice. As a pettish adolescent reaction to his elder brother's constant hearty bellowing, Jeckran had always spoken gently, and through force of habit, this had turned into his normal manner of speech. However, he used it very consciously now, forcing the other man to lean in to hear him.

"A man, sir?"

"Yes." He looked from side to side, as if fearing being overheard. "I'm afraid that a young lady of my acquaintance has recently found herself in some difficulty. A man by the name of Chastonne may have some involvement in the matter. I don't suppose that you would know how I might speak to him?"

The man's mustache drooped more dramatically. "I'm afraid that I'm not able to allow any nonmembers to enter the club, sir. If you would like to leave your card—"

"He *is* a member here, then."

The man winced slightly. It seemed to Jeckran that this fellow was somehow familiar to him, that they had met before. "He hasn't come by for months."

Jeckran looked into his eyes. "Might I beg you to at least tell me where I might find him or any of his intimates?

The man looked down at his desk, then fixed his gaze somewhere near Jeckran's mouth. "There's a public house on Lavette Street that takes a few lodgers on the upper floors. He was—indisposed, one evening, and I had to call him a cab. He asked to be brought there."

"My *dear* fellow, I am in your debt!" said Jeckran, adopting a bit of his brother's heartiness. "I don't suppose that you might remember the name of the place?"

"Hort's Beer and Cheese, I think. Or Hart's Cheese and Beer." His lips curled disdainfully around the Daeslundic words. "Something like that. One of those Daeslundic places with a name that tells you exactly what you can eat inside it."

He realized, then, why this fellow seemed so familiar. Jeckran was, of course, very intimately acquainted with a highly educated, socially uncomfortable young fellow who wore suits with worn-out elbows and sometimes stared dreamily at other gentlemen. Jeckran swallowed. "Ah. Yes. Thank you very much."

The man smiled tentatively at him. He had wide green eyes and a sensitive-looking mouth under the mustache. His eyes flicked back down to Jeckran's own mouth, then up again. "Don't mention it, sir."

Jeckran fled. Nothing but embarrassment could ever come of his attempting to flirt back.

Tsira hadn't moved an inch since Jeckran had gone inside, and her face was so blank that he wondered if she had perhaps learned the trick of shutting her mind off entirely as she waited. Her eyes flicked toward him when he approached. He gave his report. "There's some pub that we could check on Lavette Street."

"Where's that?"

"Six-Bend Island. It's not a place I would very much like to visit after dark. Half of the thieves and murderers in Monsatelle have their bolt-holes there."

He had hoped that she would say something soothing in response to this about how they had tramped about enough for one day and should repair back to Mon Del Ras's for a restorative glass of sherry and a few hands of whist, but she predictably only gave a short nod. "Got two hours before sunset."

Six-Bend Island was not an island as such. Or at least, most of it wasn't. There was a bit at the center that was an island of the usual type, but the rest of it, the two square miles of crumbling tenements and makeshift shacks, the narrow alleys and the brothels and the fence shops and dripping parlors, was built upon a bed of garbage. Five hundred years of what the good people of Monsatelle had thrown into the river so that they wouldn't have to look at it had collected and risen up out of the black water, and now people went to Six-Bend Island when they, too, had been thrown away by the rest of the city.

It smelled terrible.

Most of the purveyors of food and spirits on Six-Bend Island were of the Esiphian sort, selling glasses of sour wine and plates of hard cheese and olives with day-old bread that had been discarded by bakeries on the mainland. This was the sort of place toward which Jeckran felt naturally inclined when he was taken by what his brother, Jok, often criticized as "moony Esiphian sulking." Indeed, at the moment, Jeckran thought a bit of moony sulking with a few olives amongst the other dregs of society sounded just the ticket. But alas, they had other business to attend to.

Hurt's Beer and Bread—which was the place that Jeckran thought the man at the wizard's club must have meant, as it was the only Daeslundic-style pub on the street—proved to be a particularly dismal-looking place with its windows covered over with grease paper. It appeared to be closed for business, but the door handle turned easily when Jeckran tried it. He glanced up toward Tsira. "I think that perhaps you ought to wait here."

"Right."

"Please do come if I call," he added, and stepped inside.

Though the sun had not yet set, it was very dark inside the pub, and the air was heavy with the smells of sour beer and sawdust. The faces that turned toward him were not friendly. One man stood up from his chair and addressed him in a broad Gallen accent. "What business you got here?"

Jeckran found himself irritated. He didn't see why it should be necessary for everyone in Monsatelle to address strangers with such unrelenting *hostility*. "My name is Jeck Smith."

"Do I look like I give a shit what your name is?"

"Not particularly, but my mother raised me to be polite."

"You insulting my mother?"

The cordiality of their discourse seemed to be degrading with extreme rapidity. "That was not at all my intent. I merely wished to inquire as to whether or not any of you were acquainted with a man called Chastonne."

Several more men stood, each looking more hostile than the next. The first man said, "What the *fuck* business of yours if we are? And why don't you speak the hell up? Can't hear what the fuck you're saying."

"*Tsira!*" said Jeckran, making a point to speak loudly and enunciate clearly.

She stepped in. "All right, Pink?"

The men who had risen found reasons to take their seats. She nodded at everyone in an amiable sort of way. "Evening."

"Evening," one of them said back.

Jeckran swallowed back a giggle of masculine triumph, crossed his arms over his chest, and said in his softest voice, "*Chastonne?*"

The first man looked sullen. "Haven't seen him in an age."

"No, I wouldn't expect that you would have," said Jeckran. "He's dead, and we are attempting to discover who is responsible." This was not entirely a falsehood; Jeckran held anyone who would pay a drip addict to murder trolls fully responsible for the man's demise.

The bartender spoke for the first time since Jeckran had entered. "You might talk to his wife."

Jeckran felt a curious wrench in his chest. "His wife?"

The first fellow scowled. "Why the fuck'd you have to bring her into it?"

"She won't give a toss about you either way, Mott, so it's no use your playing the hero," said the bartender. He nodded toward the doorway at the back of the room. "Chastonne's place is upstairs. First door on the left. She should be there now. You've got five minutes before I come up after you."

Jeckran nodded. The bartender was not a large man, but even from across the dark room, Jeckran could make out the large revolver on the counter in front of him.

They headed up the dim, stinking stairwell, and Jeckran's heart picked up its pace. A wife. He had never thought there might be a wife.

He rapped at the door. After a moment it opened a crack, eyes looking out, and then the door slammed shut. Tsira, as usual, was faster than Jeckran. She pushed the door back open and stepped into the room before he had time to react. The woman tried to dart away, but Tsira caught her by the arm. "Shh. Don't be scared," she said. She pitched her voice lower than usual. "Not going to hurt you."

Mrs. Chastonne gave a panicked little scream.

Tsira barely flinched. "I'm a woman," she said in that soft, soothing timbre. Jeckran could feel the muscles in his neck unknotting. "Hey. *Shh*, now. My name's Tsira. Not going to hurt you. You're safe."

Mrs. Chastonne drew in a shuddering breath. She relaxed slightly as Tsira spoke. "You ain't no woman."

"Sure I am."

They looked at each other for a moment, Tsira's gaze as steady and honest as ever. Mrs. Chastonnes looked as if she didn't know quite what to do. Tsira moved in a bit closer and set her hand gently on Mrs. Chastonne's upper arm. "Hey," she said. "All right?"

The curtains were drawn in the cramped room, but as his eyes adjusted to the light, Jeckran could see that Mrs. Chastonne was very young, with thin blonde hair, large blue eyes, and a face heavily pitted by pox. She shuddered and burst into tears. "There's no one left to help me now."

Jeckran wanted very much for Tsira to see his panicked glance, but her entire attention was focused on the girl. "I'll help you," she said, in that purr of a voice. "What's your name?"

The girl sniffed and wiped at her eye with the back of her hand. "Violet."

"*Violet*," said Tsira. Violet had gone almost slack, gazing up at her. "Violet," she said again. "You know about your husband?"

She gave a little jerk of her head. "He's dead, isn't he?"

Tsira nodded.

The girl collapsed as if someone had kicked out her struts. Tsira caught her and stood very still as Mrs. Chastonne wept quietly, her tears making jagged tracks down her pockmarked cheeks. Jeckran had never in his life felt such a worthless brute.

Tsira steered the girl to an armchair and squatted beside her. She waited, utterly still, until the girl sniffed back her tears. Jeckran, thinking to make himself useful, produced a handkerchief from his trouser pocket. Mrs. Chastonne took it, mumbled "Thank you," and blew her nose.

"The men who killed your husband," said Tsira. "They killed my ma, too."

Mrs. Chastonne looked up but said nothing. Tsira gazed back evenly. "You know who they are?"

"I—no," she said.

"Sure?" Tsira didn't avert her gaze. "You love your husband?"

The girl bristled, her eyes welling up again. "Of *course*, I do! You think I don't? With me sticking by him through all that?"

Tsira shook her head. "No. Thought you did. Loved my ma, too. Want to do right by her. Want justice."

Mrs. Chastonne had looked away, and Tsira put a finger to her chin and forced her to meet her gaze. "I can get justice. Look at me. You know I can. Need your help, though."

Mrs. Chastonne looked at her lap and spoke in a rush. "It was them bastards he worked for. Know it was. They had him doing something bad. Don't know what it was. Know it was bad. Algad, he wanted to stop. Didn't want to do it no more. They came here once, talked real rough. He was just dreadful scared, know he was. That were right before he went off."

Tsira nodded. "Who were they?"

"Don't know. Just a couple of toughs, and this other fellow. Hexy sounding."

Tsira frowned. "What?"

Jeckran interjected. "Mrs. Chastonne, do you mean that he spoke with a lisp, or was he *Hexian*?"

She scowled. "Meant what I said. *Hexy*. He was a young fella, a bit thin. Handsome."

He remembered the Hexian coin that they had found on the men who had come to kill Tsira in their cave. It seemed like ages ago. "I don't suppose that you might have heard his name?"

She shook her head. "Algad just called him 'sir.' Don't know nothing else. Algad don't—" She paused, stricken. "He—didn't like talking about them."

Tsira nodded and stood. "Thanks," she said, then drew her purse from her pocket and placed it into the girl's lap. "Here."

Jeckran swallowed back a squawk of consternation. Mrs. Chastonne sat upright when she felt the weight of it, then looked inside and gasped. "But I—I can't, it's too much," she said, but even as she spoke, her fingers tightened around the pouch.

"Don't waste it," said Tsira. "Need any help from us, go to Mon Del Ras's boardinghouse on Cooper's Lane and ask for the troll. Someone will find me."

Violet looked up. "Mon Del Ras," she said. "He's a kind man. My old boss, she knows him."

Jeckran frowned. "Your old boss? Who is she?"

Violet ducked her head. "Don't matter," she said. "Quit working when Algad married me. Suppose I'll have to see if she'll take me back, now."

Tsira nodded and thanked her for her time. Jeckran choked out, "I'm so sorry for your loss," which seemed to drop with a heavy thud to the floor as they left the dark room.

Neither spoke for some time. They walked quickly away from Six-Bend Island as the sun set. Jeckran eventually broke the silence. "Did you just give the entirety of your savings to that girl?"

She glanced at him sidelong. "No. Just ten tocats. Have five more in my pocket, and fifty that Bette is keeping for me. For you, if I get killed." She looked away. "What's *Hexy*?"

He tried to pretend it didn't bother him that she had made preparations to provide for him in the event of her own death. "She meant Hexian. From Hexos. I doubt the man she saw was anything of the sort. Probably just a man who spoke a little oddly."

"Don't know. Seemed like a smart girl. Think she knew what she heard."

"But what would a *Hexian* want with a washed-up wizard like Chastonne?"

She shrugged. "Dead trolls."

He acknowledged this with a sigh, then said, "I'm about ready to drop."

"Want me to carry you?"

"I didn't mean literally. Would you mind terribly if we went home, ate, and went directly to bed?"

"No," she said, and in that moment the thought of speaking so much as a single additional word seemed to exhaust both of them. Jeckran felt divorced from his own body, as if the force propelling him forward was not his own but some kind of clockwork mechanism that kept his legs working.

They were silent until they arrived at Mon Del Ras's place, when Jeckran knew at once that something was terribly wrong.

A crowd was gathered outside the front steps of the boardinghouse, and the whole place was lit up like the daytime. This, more than the crowd, was what pushed Jeckran toward the ledge of panic. A crowd might gather to watch a fight, or a wandering preacher, or a three-legged dog, and Mon Del Ras would ignore it. What he would not ignore was the appalling waste of lighting so many candles.

Jeckran and Tsira glanced at each other, and they both started running at the same time. The crowd parted for Tsira, but the policeman at the door held his post. Jeckran admired the fellow's bravery, even if his voice cracked when he spoke. "You can't go in there."

"We live here," she said, and pushed past the man as if he were a scrap of silk. Then they saw Mon Del Ras.

*I won't be able to forget*, Jeckran thought. *I won't be able to forget.* A terrible thought, a selfish thought, but it came to him before grief or horror at the death of a friend. Instead, the horror was knowing he would see this every night until the day he died. The white, thin body, the staring green eyes, the red hair in the red blood. The black words written on the floor beside him.

*Ask no more questions.*

Jeckran knew that he moaned.

"Bette," said Tsira. "The boys."

She turned to the policemen. "Where are the children?" she asked, and she was off before they could finish shaking their heads, ripping doors off hinges as she went. Jeckran ran after and finally caught up to see her kneeling at the closet under the stairs. Bette was silent, and the two elder boys were silent, but Jerome, the youngest, was weeping. "Papa?" he said. "Papa?" His mother was silent and still and combed her fingers through his red hair.

Tsira knelt beside them. "Who did this? Who hurt your papa?"

Jeckran translated. Bette closed her eyes. "I heard him screaming," she said. "I heard him screaming and I hid the children. When the screaming stopped, I heard them talking. One of them said her name. She *came* here, I *cooked* for her, that witch sat at my table—"

"Who?" Jeckran said.

"*Her*," Bette said. "*Catleen.* They were working with *Catleen.*"

Tsira stiffened when she heard the name and gripped Bette's arm. Jeckran felt his heart beat harder. Catleen was Tsira's friend: they'd eaten dinner together, gotten drunk on cheap gin together. Tsira's face was very still. "Stay here," she said. "Police will watch you. Keep you safe." Then she stood. "Pink. Come with me, or stay and help guard them."

"It's a trap," he said. His mouth had gone dry. "It's a trap, Tsira. No hired killer is moronic enough to say his employer's name at the scene of the crime. We're meant to go after her. She won't be waiting for us alone."

She gave him a long look. "Set a trap for a rabbit," she said. "Won't hold a fucking bear." Then she said, "Go upstairs and get my pack and a box of matches."

He went. He obeyed. His hands were shaking.

When he got back downstairs Tsira was in the kitchen, pouring sugar and a large quantity of pepper into a pot over the stove. Bette appeared a moment later with a ragbag and several chipped teacups. Tsira extracted a small pouch from her pack and tipped some of the contents into the pot, then continued to stir. "I need you to make strips from the rags."

Jeckran made close to a dozen strips before he realized what she was doing. "You're making grenades. In teacups."

She cast a look at him. "We call them *baby boys*. They make your enemies cry."

There was a plume of smoke from the pot. Jeckran's eyes immediately began to stream, and Tsira hurriedly lifted the pot from the heat and poured the sludge inside into the cups. Jeckran added the fuses. Then they took a moment to look at each other. Tsira said, "They might have a wizard with them. The body smelled like magic. Ready for a fight, Pink?"

"Never," he said.

She snorted. "Least you're fucking honest."


They went to the brothel a few hours later. It was very strange. The streets were still fairly busy at that time of night. Monsatelle never seemed to go completely to bed. It reminded him of Mendosa. The beaches were always loud at night from the crash of the waves.

When they arrived, they each took a few teacups. Tsira struck a match. "Ready now, Pink?"

*I love you*, he thought. He said, "I suppose, if I must be."

She grinned and lit the first fuse, then smashed the window in.

The first few moments after they started tossing in the teacups were fairly quiet. Then the screaming started.

The girls came pouring out of the building, choking and coughing, clutching shawls and handkerchiefs over their faces. Jeckran swallowed back a little thrill of guilt and waited for the men and Catleen, his pistol at the ready, but the only men who came out were yanking up their trousers, buttoning their shirts, and wiping at their streaming eyes as they raced away from the scene. Then Catleen was there, with a scarf tied about her mouth. Jeckran was about to say *something's wrong*, when the girls all drew their pistols.

There was a terrible clap of gunfire, and Tsira roared in pain. Jeckran only had time to give a muffled, terrified shriek and take cover behind a lamppost before everything descended into utter chaos.

Tsira ran at them hard and fast, and Jeckran fired as quickly as he could, picking off a few girls before they could shoot Tsira again, swallowing back the horror of it. He had killed boys in Mendosa, soldiers barely old enough to shave: Was it really so different to shoot at girls? They were all nothing but flesh in the end, he thought, and then Tsira was among them like a cleaver through a chop.

They were firing at her and missing, too terrified to aim. She seized one and ripped her throat out with her teeth, then she kicked another girl in the chest. One girl got off a decent shot, and Tsira screamed, and Jeckran tried to focus, tried not to think, tried not to let his hands shake. Tsira ripped the girl's arm off. Another fell to her knees to vomit. Tsira snapped the girl's neck and then went still, swaying on her feet.

By the time Jeckran got to her, Catleen was reloading her pistol. Jeckran pressed the muzzle of his own against the back of Catleen's head. "Don't move."

She went still. She said, "I never killed a troll."

Tsira took a step closer to her. "You killed Mon Del Ras."

"No," she said. Her voice was very steady. "I received, stored, and shipped what they brought to me. Boxes, heavy, very cold to the touch, like fresh-food crates. I didn't inquire about what was inside. They told me they would be capturing you tonight and replaced my girls with theirs. I never killed a troll. I knew nothing at all about what was in those boxes until two nights ago."

"No," Jeckran said, "but you made yourself dreadfully useful to whomever did. Who's paying you?"

"I don't know," Catleen said. "I'm not given names."

Tsira wrapped one hand around her throat. "*Think harder.*"

For the first time, Catleen's voice shook. "When they're asked about their employers, they start to choke. I don't know anything. Only that some of them are men from Hexos."

"Shit," Jeckran said, and Tsira fell, and in the light of the street lamp he could see that her shirtfront was soaked in blood.

He knelt by her side, terrified, and tore off his jacket to press it to the bullet wounds in her chest, heedless of the fact that Catleen was bolting down the street. "*Tsira!* Tsira, look at me, *please*, open your eyes, *shit, please—*"

She wasn't breathing. She wasn't *breathing*. He screamed for help, not caring if the police came, not caring about anything but Tsira. Tsira, whose face was going pale. A boy came running up and said he would fetch a wizard for a price. Jeckran gave him what money he had, not knowing how much, not knowing whether or not the boy would keep his word, and then felt Tsira move under his hand.

She drew in a breath. Then opened her eyes. "Hey," she said.

"Tsira?" He choked back a sob. "Thank *God*."

She drew in another breath. "Pink. Tired."

"I know." He wiped his sleeve across his eyes and shuddered when he realized that he had smeared his face with her blood. "I know. Please, stay awake. Talk to me. There's a wizard coming soon."

"What should I"—she closed her eyes, opened them—"talk about?"

"Anything. Does it hurt you to speak?"

"Yeah."

"Just listen, then. You refused to listen to me before when I tried to speak to you, and now—" He stopped and seized her hand. Thinking about her dying was an enormity that he couldn't commit. She would live. He needed her to live.

She took another breath. "Don't. Not dying. Don't say anything stupid."

He shook his head and pushed some hair back from her face. She had such beautiful hair. And a beautiful face. A beautiful everything, really: he thought that was quite objectively clear. "I'm—you must know that I'm very fond of you, Tsira."

"Yeah. Partners. Fond of you, too."

"I'm sorry. You're in pain. I'm sure that hearing me talk is making it worse. I'm afraid that I can't help myself."

"Might try."

"I love you."

She was silent.

He laughed, or sobbed. He couldn't be entirely sure which. This was absolutely dreadful. He thought he might scream. "Good God, *say* something before I shoot myself in the head."

"No good for you."

"Suicide?"

"Saying what you said."

"I said that I love you. Because I do."

"Stop."

"I'm afraid that I can't."

Her voice was a terrible rasp. "Want to marry me? Have children?"

He felt his face go red. "We've been . . . we've been intimate. For weeks."

She met his eyes. "I like to fuck."

It was a very peculiar sensation. Like waking up from a nightmare of war to find oneself back at the front. Like tripping and falling and seeing the ground approaching. Like being sick enough to vomit. "Well, then that's that, I suppose," he said. "And if that's what you'll give me, then I'll take it."

"No. You won't."

"*Why?*"

"Too hard on both of us. A city human and a border-troll clan-head. Spend the rest of your life getting funny looks. Running back and forth between my clan-seat and the city. Rankless in my clan. Never get to have your own children. Staying with me out in the hills, nothing to do with yourself. You'd hate it. You'd hate me."

He shook his head, then pressed her hand. "I couldn't," he said.

Her eyes rolled back into her head.

The wizard came: a dreadful, greasy, drunken fellow. Jeckran paid him. A constable came: a dreadful, greasy, contemptible fellow. Jeckran paid him. He got her safe, concealed, hidden in a wretched, mildewed, unwholesome little room. She woke up as the wizard was digging about in her shoulder. Her scream was the worst sound that Jeckran had ever heard.

"Laudanum!" said the wizard.

Jeckran held her hand, watched her face. Pain turned her into a pale stranger. He glanced at the laudanum bottle. "Is it safe?"

The wizard snorted. "For a big girl like her? It will barely slow her down."

He squeezed her hand. "Do you want it, Tsira?"

"Yes."

She squeezed his hand while the wizard dug out the first two bullets, and at the third she mercifully passed out. Then everything was cleaned and bandaged, and Jeckran crept into the dreadful slanted bed in the dreadful mildewed room and pressed himself to her side and slept.

When he woke up in the morning, her eyes were open. She said, "Hey."

"Hey."

They looked at each other. He reached to touch her, cupped her cheek in one hand. "You're alive."

"Yeah."

"Good," he said. He kissed her, and Tsira kissed back.

She pulled away first. "You're not just a fuck, Pink. You're not."

"I know," he said, and kissed her again.

"Hey." Her voice was raw. "My fault. Mon Del Ras."

"No, Tsira—"

"You know it was." She drew a breath, and he thought he could hear the air catch in her chest. "They won't stop."

He shook his head.

"Where's Hexos?"

It took him a moment to feel capable of responding. "It's far, Tsira. It's terribly far. We would have to travel to Leiscourt first, by either riverboat or stagecoach, and then it would be at least two weeks by ship. Then once we got there, I'm afraid we would be in rather wretched straights. It's a very expensive place with peculiar laws, and they don't speak Daeslundic or Esiphian."

For the first time since he had met her, he saw Tsira look afraid.

"By ship?"

"Yes. We would have to cross half of the Osten Sea."

She swallowed. "No other way?"

"No—I'm sorry. I can't—" The air stopped coming.

She put her arms around him, even though he knew that it must be hurting her dreadfully. "Hey," she said. "Hey."

He was laughing, which was mad, but he couldn't stop. "They took his heart out. They took his *heart*—"

She held him. After he managed to calm himself, she kissed his cheek. "Pink," she said. "Have something to tell you."

"What is it?"

"I can't swim."

"What?"

"I'm scared *shitless* of water."

The giggles started clambering their way back up his throat. "Oh, good," he finally managed. "I had worried that our passage to Hexos would make a devilishly dull trip."

They both laughed, and if either of them wept, the other did not see fit to make note of it.

# 16

*"Nothing should ever induce me to aid you," said Resalind, biting
her lip with scorn.*

*"And your aid was never asked for," returned Govran. As he
said this, a flash of anger glowed on his cheeks; but such stains of
sentiment were foreign to one whose life had been so little marred
by discord, and they soon passed as wisps of cloud before the sun. The
elegant youth brought his dark brows over his wide bright eyes and
thrust his hands in the pockets of his velvet skirt. He thought Resalind a very headstrong, hectoring girl, and her reproving glances
struck him in no pleasant manner . . .*

—The Trials of Resalind *by Sora Gebowa*

The evening after their journey to the troll neighborhood, Onna
sent a little note to Captain Run updating her on her progress in
conducting interviews, and asking if she would mind if she spoke to the
young man who was rumored to be a witness. Captain Run responded
promptly that she would be glad of Onna's assistance in the matter: the
young man in question was somewhat wary of the police and had refused to speak with them. Loga, of course, was keen to involve himself
in the adventure, and the next day he once again brought out the palanquin to take them to the young man's address. After some time they
stopped on a quiet, very genteel-looking street. Loga advanced confi-
dently toward one of the doorways and knocked.

The half-troll gentleman who answered took Onna by surprise. She
had expected him to be like a troll, but smaller; instead he was like a
handsome Esiphian man, but bigger. His features were strong and even,

his eyes large and dark brown, and his skin a very decided shade of blue. She thought, for a moment, of how difficult that must be to look so clearly unlike most of the people around oneself. Then she thought of the smug, knowing looks of the owls at her examination when they saw her dress and heard her accent, and she felt ashamed of herself. This young man hadn't asked for her condescension.

The troll bowed when he saw Loga and spoke softly in Nessoran. Loga interrupted him. "Excuse me, I'll just set a translation."

He spoke to the troll, and when the troll responded, Onna could understand. "It's an honor to have you here, Magister." He was wearing a black tunic like Loga's house dress, though it was much less fine. His feet were in slippers. "Can she understand me now?"

"She can," Loga said. "Might I first compliment you on the poem you wrote on the occasion of the Directress's birthday? I admired it exceedingly."

The troll inclined his head. "It was only a little trifle that I dashed off, sir."

"Don't be so modest! I agree with Magister Wazir that you're one of the greatest poets in Hexos."

They continued in this very polite manner as the troll ushered them inside, invited them to sit on the floor beside a low table, and served them each a cup of very strong Hexian coffee. After a few more exchanges of pleasantries Loga nodded toward Onna. "We have just a few questions for you. Onna? Please proceed."

Onna took a deep breath. "What is your name?"

"Stetanwyntsumelle. Most people call me Tsumelle."

"Oh," Onna said, hoping dearly that she wouldn't need to call him by name before she'd had the chance to practice the pronunciation in secret. "Do you spend much time with other trolls?"

"With trolls, yes," he said. She noticed how he discarded the word *other*, as if he didn't quite consider himself to be one of them. "I've been trying to spend more time in the quarter, learn more about my papa's culture. Some of the vahns have been teaching me a little Nasener." He spoke politely but directed his words to a point somewhere past her head.

"Are you from their great-clan as well?"

"I don't know." He paused. "My papa died when I was nine. I never asked about his clan."

Onna nodded. "I should think that's very natural. My grandparents are from Awat, but I never really asked much about what their home was like, when I was a little girl."

Tsumelle finally met her gaze. "Then you know."

"Yes," Onna said, and she thought that if she didn't know exactly then at least she could imagine. She swallowed. "Have you made many friends in the troll quarter?"

"Yes. The vahns have been very kind to me."

She pressed on. "Miss Teiranwynartur said that you had seen the murderer."

"Yes."

"Could you tell me what you saw?"

"It wasn't much." He paused. "Are you with the police, Magister?"

Loga shook his head. "Not remotely."

"I'm glad, my lord. Aorwynbahnoc came to visit me by himself at around eleven o'clock, four days ago. He brought me some choke and we smoked it together, and he sang me some troll songs. I had a few cups of wine. Then I tried to kiss him. He stopped me and told me that I should have my first time with one of the blood while I was sober. The next I remember was about two or three. I woke up and saw that he was gone, and I heard a door open outside. I went after him and saw him going around the corner. I followed and saw the wizard kill him."

Onna caught her breath. "What did he look like?"

"Human. Tall. He was wearing trousers, like a foreigner. It was too dark to see much else." His voice quavered slightly. "I ran."

Onna nodded, trying to speak gently. "Of course you did. He's a very strong wizard, you know. You wouldn't have been able to do anything to stop him, and he could easily have killed you."

"She *is* right, you know, darling," Loga said, in his careless way. "You did the right thing to run away. You wouldn't have been a bit of use to us as a corpse."

"Loga!" Onna said, horrified.

Tsumelle gave a smile that looked more like a wince. "I'm glad you think I'm more useful than a corpse, my lord."

"Of course. You strike me as an *intrinsically* useful young man." Loga examined the nails of his left hand and frowned. "I don't suppose you remember anything else about that wizard?"

"No, my lord. I'm sorry."

"Don't apologize. You've been *dreadfully* helpful. Hasn't he, Onna?"

Onna nodded. Loga gave a little bow. "Then we'll say good-bye to you, Tsumelle. Please do come see us at the Lamp if you think of anything else, or if you'd like to pay a visit."

Tsumelle returned the bow with a much deeper one of his own. "Thank you, my lord. I'm honored." He straightened. "I would be pleased to exchange poetry with you someday soon."

Loga smiled, looking him straight in the eye. "I can't tell you how pleased I would be."

They returned to the floating carriage, and Loga slumped back against the cushions with a soft groan. "My head is positively *throbbing.* I despise translation spells: I'm certain that they have a cooling effect on my brain. Would you be so kind as to draw the curtains?"

Onna did so, and the carriage made its silent way down the street. Loga closed his eyes and seemed to doze for a few minutes. When he eventually shifted position, Onna cleared her throat, deciding to make a little test of one of her theories. "Loga?"

He opened his eyes. "Yes, darling?"

"I've been thinking, and I hope you won't be very angry with me— I know that you're very fond of him, but have you thought at all that Mr. Finnbair—"

"Jok is not a suspect."

"But—"

"You heard what I said, Onna." His voice was clipped and hard, all of the languor and playfulness gone out of it.

She swallowed. "More people might die."

"I *know* that," he said. He scrubbed at his eyes with his knuckles and cursed softly in Sangan. "Give me some time. If I'm to have him arrested, I want to know for sure that I'm doing right. It might be someone else, after all. And it might be—" He fiddled with his cuff, rubbing at the embroidery with his thumb. "Give me time."

They were quiet for the rest of the journey back to the Lamp. Loga seemed distracted, almost dazed, though Onna supposed that was reasonable enough for the circumstances. His distress, at least, seemed genuine. Then again, he had been on the stage. It could be a pose, meant only to misdirect her, to turn her attention away from his friend or from himself. She knew so little about either of them, so little about anything in this strange city: How on earth was she ever supposed to detect a lie? And if she had no way of knowing what was being concealed from her, how on earth could she be of any use to anyone? To Teiranwynartur, who had spoken to her like an equal? To Tsumelle, who had looked at her and expected that she would understand?

Onna felt her own head begin to ache.

When they arrived, Loga did not at first realize they were home, and Onna had to tap him lightly on the shoulder to get his attention. His face was strangely gray. As they walked through the garden, she ventured a question, a little probe to see if she could elicit a scrap of honesty about a topic that seemed particularly sensitive. "I'm dreadfully sorry to be so impertinent, but I've been wondering. What happened to Mr. Finnbair's brother?"

Loga turned to her and seemed as if he would answer. Instead he dropped to the ground. Onna gave a little scream of shock. He was so still, his lean body crumpled in an awkward heap, elegant robes twisted up to expose his legs to the knee. He looked so fragile, and maybe *dead*, and she found herself tearing up as she shouted for help, since it was horrible to see him so still when she had only ever known him in motion. Then she heard footsteps, and a group of people came tearing around the corner: two servants and Mr. Finnbair.

The servants stopped dead in their tracks when they saw their master on the ground, but Mr. Finnbair continued to his side, dropping to his knees and checking his pulse. Onna swallowed. "Mr. Finnbair, is he—he *isn't*—"

Mr. Finnbair sat back on his heels. "Just fainted, Miss Gebowa. He'll come around in a moment." He frowned. "He didn't tell you about his Genoit's?"

Onna's eyes went wide. Genoit's arrhythmia was what ordinary people called the wizard swoons, a condition that cropped up in wizards who had used powerful magic for many years, especially those who had done so in their childhoods. But she couldn't imagine how Loga could *possibly* have Genoit's: If he knew that he had it, then how could he continue to work as if it couldn't kill him at any moment? And how could the Lord-Mage of Hexos have an illness that was most often seen in poor souls who had worked in wizard-lamp factories since they were twelve years old? She shook her head. "He never said a thing."

Mr. Finnbair's frown deepened.

"No wonder you were frightened. Look, see? Coming around now."

Loga was stirring. Mr. Finnbair drew his head into his lap. "Feeling all right now?" He spoke in a tone of such tenderness that Onna had to look away. "You scared the starch out of poor Miss Gebowa."

Loga mumbled something indistinct. Mr. Finnbair leaned in closer. "What is it, then?"

Loga opened his eyes. "Elgarson?"

Mr. Finnbair only shook his head. "Nah. Only Jok."

He smiled up at Onna. "My old da thought it was a fine joke to call his twins Jok and Elgarson, like we could have been any old fellows. We never thought the joke was so funny."

He helped Loga to his feet. Loga leaned up against the bigger man's chest, his face gone very gray. He clutched at Mr. Finnbair's shirt with one hand. "Jok? Why are you here?"

"You dropped your pin in the street." He drew from his pocket the object in question, a very expensive-looking little trifle set with rubies at one end. "I thought I'd bring it back for you."

"Oh," Loga said, and then mumbled something in Nessoran.

"Are you now? Then we ought to put you to bed," Mr Finnbair said, and began steering Loga toward the Lamp, Onna trailing disconsolately behind them.

Once Loga was delivered into the hands of his manservant, who promised to get him into bed and keep him there, Onna walked Mr. Finnbair to the door. "Will he be quite all right, do you think? He seemed very—unlike himself, just now."

"He's always pretty funny when he first comes out of a faint. He'll be good as new once he's had a rest. Maybe a little touchy." He paused. "I haven't killed any trolls, you know."

Onna's face went hot and her hands went cold. "I—I beg your pardon, Mr. Finnbair, I—"

"I know how it must look, especially with my past. But I swear to you now on my brother's grave that I don't have any reason to hurt a troll. My research doesn't need it, and I wouldn't have the stomach to do it. They're fine hardworking folks, all the trolls I've met. I hope that you find the man who's doing it and stop him before he hurts anyone else." He bowed. "Good afternoon, Miss Gebowa," he said, and left.

After this rather excessively exciting interlude, Onna's life at the Lamp became quite ordered for a time. There were meals, and healthful strolls, and many, many hours of work in Loga's study. Captain Run made her appearance exactly at the appointed hour.

She certainly seemed to take her responsibility in teaching Onna very seriously: she talked her through the construction of a miniaturized longeye step by exacting, excruciating step, and then made Onna explain it back to her, correcting her mistakes along the way. By the time they were through, Onna felt strangely exhausted, as if her brain was trying to ride a bicycle through a tub of molasses. This, perhaps, was how the other students at her Weltsir exam had felt. She wasn't sure if she felt challenged and excited or just worn out and annoyed. In any case, Captain Run left looking just as crisp and soldierly as she had when she arrived, and Onna dragged herself with enormous anticipation to bed.

The next few days continued on in just about this fashion: hours and hours of slogging away on astoundingly difficult parametrical work until Onna's brain ached, interrupted by nothing but meals and the rambling afternoon walks that Loga insisted upon. The meals and walks, at least, were lovely: Loga chattered away while bringing her to all of the fascinating little nooks and crannies in his part of Hexos that he thought she might like to see.

They went to an Awati restaurant, something which she had never heard of in Daeslund, and visited an enchanting little doll's house of a walled garden overflowing with thousands of roses. They visited an art gallery where Loga taught her how to seem as if she knew what she was talking about when she commented on the art. Her work was so difficult that these little diversions were extremely welcome. She was, however, still quite taken aback when Captain Run appeared at the Lamp one evening and said, "I'm sorry for the short notice, Miss Onna, but if you don't have any plans tonight, we could use you as a spy."

Onna, cheeks heating, glanced toward Loga. "I don't know," she said. It suddenly struck her that engaging in clandestine police work was another thing that was much more amusing to contemplate from a distance. "I suppose that I ought to—finish that bit of language that was giving me trouble this afternoon, Loga?"

"Oh, no," Loga said, in a very bright and cheery tone of voice. "That will keep, surely! You ought to go out and have your adventure."

Onna narrowed her eyes at him—she was quite sure that he knew *exactly* what he was up to and was making mischief intentionally—but he continued to smile in a very innocent sort of way, until Onna was forced to concede this round to him. She swallowed a sigh and smiled at Captain Run. "Then of course I'd love to help, Captain. Just tell me what you'd like me to do."

Captain Run did, indeed, tell her what to do. She was to wear a dress that was pretty but not too expensive or new—Onna decided not to point out that this would hardly present a challenge to her or her wardrobe—and then present herself as a friend of Mr. Cadwell Bix and attempt to draw Mr. Wail into conversation about his politics and thoughts on trolls. She was *not* to attempt to elicit a confession, only to engage him in conversation that might produce some useful information that the officers could pursue later. Captain Run, Sergeant Bato, and several other officers would be waiting close at hand. If the atmosphere grew tense and uncomfortable to the point that Onna felt concerned about her safety, she should say the word *elderberries*, and an officer would enter to rescue her. The sheer degree of specificity in the plan seemed to imply security and professionalism. The details piled up on top of Onna like layers of heavy blankets until she felt utterly sure that she wasn't in the least bit of danger, and she headed off to get dressed for the evening with only the merest suggestion of nervousness to disturb her sense of comfort.

The party, she soon discovered, was being held in a part of town with which she was unfamiliar. "Student flats, mostly," said Captain Run. "That's why Loga's never taken you down here. Not posh enough for him." The palanquin they were in came to an abrupt jolting halt. "You'll get out here, and we'll take our positions nearby. You remember the house number and who to say sent you?"

"Number fifteen," Onna said. "Cadwell Bix. We met at the exams at Weltsir."

"There you are," Captain Run said, and she gave Onna's arm a comforting pat before she heaved her big belly out of the palanquin. "Remember, just give us an *elderberries* and my old man will swing in to rescue you, if you need it."

"Yes, ma'am," Onna said, and nervously adjusted her longeye—she had built it into a pretty Sangan brooch in the shape of a bat that Loga had given to her as a gift—and marched toward the flat that contained the party.

She knocked at the door and was admitted by a stocky young man with a shock of thick black hair, who seemed very pleased to see her and ushered her in without asking for any particular explanation. The flat was hot and dark and crowded inside, thick with the smell of cigarette smoke. The gathering of mostly young men parted for her and closed around her again in a rush of gentlemen offering to pour her a glass of wine or light her a cigarette. She accepted the wine and declined the cigarette—*goodness*, she couldn't *possibly*, she'd never once in her *life*—and then she started to chat and flirt her way through the assemblage. The party was quite unlike anything she'd ever experienced before. Everyone was either a wizard working in some obscure sort of theory or a painter or a poet with alarming political views. After a few minutes she found herself deep in conversation with a very tall, slender fellow—who was attempting to construct an artificial symphony that could spontaneously compose its own music—when she suddenly recalled that she was meant to find Mr. Wail, so she extracted herself with the excuse of wanting another glass of wine.

She was in luck: Mr. Wail himself was refilling a glass from a bottle that someone had carelessly abandoned on an end table. She sidled up and affected surprise. "Oh! Excuse me, I don't mean to be a bother, but have we met? You look *terribly* familiar."

He frowned at her, but his expression cleared and he smiled. "Of course," he said. "The beautiful young lady in the public square. I think I shocked you with my politics."

There was an irritating smugness to his assumption that she found him shocking, but Onna forced herself to smile just as she ordinarily did when speaking to a gentleman. Or ordinarily as of a few weeks ago, perhaps. It occurred to her that she hardly ever bothered to smile at Loga when she wasn't in a smiling sort of mood, and he took it with good humor and didn't seem at all offended by a young woman looking less than overwhelmed with joy to be in his presence. Mr. Wail, however, was not Loga, so she smiled and ventured a small giggle. "Not *shocked*, sir," she said, in a tone that she knew suggested that she found him very delightfully shocking, indeed.

"Offended, then?" he suggested, and took a sip of his wine. "You didn't like at all that I was saying disrespectful things about trolls. That's very natural, you know. We're raised from childhood to treat them like they're gods. Like they have more than us because they *deserve* it somehow, in the same way that we're meant to think that headmen are headmen because they're further on in their relivings."

Mr. Wail was patronizing as well as smug. She hated how he made her uncomfortable. "Are you an Elgarite?"

"My parents are," he says. "I'm an atheist. I've read a lot of troll philosophy. You see, I don't *hate* them. I just believe that the headmen and their lickspittles ought to be dragged from their manors and made to labor in the mills while their possessions are sold and the proceeds used to build houses for the poor." He looked her straight in the eye as he spoke, not so much as blinking. Then he threw his head back and laughed, his golden curls flying about his head like something quick and living.

She ventured a smile. "You're joking?"

"Oh, no," he said, smiling back. He had a crooked front tooth and eyes of a peculiar indeterminate pale color, somewhere between gray and green and blue. "I'm just proud of myself for really having shocked you this time."

She felt her smile shift into something more natural, even though she was shocked at *herself* for that. It was only that she'd never met anyone like him before. She could understand now why Captain Run thought of him as a leader among this crowd of silly boys with dangerous ideas. He made everything sound both less silly and less dangerous, as if it was all a very wonderful clever game that they were playing together.

"So you don't actually *believe* in all of that," she said. "You're just saying it to be shocking."

"I believe every word of it," he said. "Whether or not bringing all of my principles into action is *practical* is another matter."

"I see," she said. "How *would* you bring your principles into action?"

She refilled her own wine glass and then, on impulse, offered him some more as well.

He accepted the wine with an air of surprise, then gave her a confiding little smile. "Armed insurrection, I suppose," he said.

"And have you very much experience in leading armed insurrections?" she asked.

He gave another of those big, head-thrown-back laughs and smiled at her for a moment. "You're very wonderful," he said. He was blushing. "No, you're right, I'm a fragile man with soft hands. I might be of more use doing the paperwork for the generals."

The self-deprecation didn't seem put-on. Neither did the laughter. She smiled back, then let her expression go grave. "I didn't like what you said about trolls," she said. "It didn't seem right to stir up that sort of thinking with what's going on right now."

He didn't look shocked, upset, or exaggeratedly puzzled. He only looked as if her indirect statement lacked explanation, and his face fixed into a polite look of feigned interest. "With what that's going on right now?"

"The murders," Onna said. "The murders of trolls."

He frowned, then comprehension dawned. "Oh, you mean all of that horrible stuff going on in the north of Daeslund? That was all a setup, you know. The human and troll governments banding together to get the poor going after each other instead of banding together."

She could only stare, astounded. "But you were saying all sorts of things about how awful the trolls are the other day yourself."

"I meant the kind that come to *Hexos*," he said, as if that should have been patently obvious. "It isn't as if those poor border-trolls they're slaughtering up there are booking nice comfortable cabins to sail overseas and compete for positions at our universities purely because they think it seems like a bit of a lark, the way that the rich ones do."

"Mr. Wail," Onna said, with a sudden flash of temper. "I'm sure that you heard that there was another body found in Hexos just the other day."

That stopped him talking, at least for a moment. He licked his lips. "Oh. Really? Here?"

She rolled her eyes. Perhaps she shouldn't react this way, as it didn't assist the investigation, but she was so *angry*. "It's been in the *papers*, Mr. Wail."

"I don't read the papers," he said, chewing on his lip. "They're all owned by the rich."

Onna had to concede that the newspapers were, as far as she was aware, all owned by the rich: the most widely read morning paper in Cordridge-on-Sea was owned by a second headman who lived in Aufdom Mare. It had never before occurred to her that this might influence the paper's contents. She found herself feeling annoyed again and irritated that this silly boy had made a point that she hadn't thought of on her own. Eventually, she said, "That doesn't mean that they're entirely inaccurate, Mr. Wail. I saw the body myself." Then she nearly bit her own tongue off. She wasn't meant to tell him that she was *involved with the investigation*. Her ears went hot, and she was on the verge of darting out of the room shrieking *Elderberries!* when Mr. Wail spoke. He'd turned the slightest bit green.

"You saw a *body*?"

"Yes," she said, thinking quickly. "Back in Leiscourt, after my Weltsir exams. A woman—I think they were householded—she was wailing over the body, and there was blood *everywhere*. It was absolutely horrible. I had nightmares for *weeks* about it. So of course—I'm sure you think I sound like a silly little girl, but it *did* bother me when I heard you speaking about trolls like that. I hate to think of anyone getting *ideas*." She cast her eyes downward, doing her best to look meek and worried and embarrassed, and *not* like she wanted to light Mr. Wail's skirt on fire with her eyes.

"*Oh*," he said, looking markedly less green. "How absolutely horrible for you. No wonder you felt upset. It's only natural that you would have sensibilities about these things. And—if they have been finding bodies, you might be right." She wanted to kick him in the knee at how *astonished* he sounded at the thought that she *might be right*. "If trolls are being murdered *here*, I probably ought to be watching my mouth. I don't want to be the next man hanged for his politics in Hexos."

Onna was fairly certain that she had read quite recently that there hadn't been a hanging in Hexos for *any* reason for almost twenty years, but she didn't say as much. Instead she twittered delicately at him. "Oh, goodness me, how awful! But surely you don't *know* anyone who might do anything so terrible?"

For a moment he looked truly, actually troubled. Then he shook his head. "No," he said. "No, nobody—nobody I know." He swallowed down the rest of his wine, refilled his glass, and pretended to notice a friend. "Ah, there's Jok Kelweg," he said. "If you'll excuse me, miss?"

Onna excused him and made the rounds about the room, deigning to extend her attention for a moment or two upon whichever young gentlemen expressed interest in a bit of conversation. She was starting a third glass of wine and feeling very much like a cunning, beautiful young headwoman disguising herself as a nun in order to infiltrate the rebellion (this was, in fact, the plot of one of her mother's most heart-rending books) when she felt an odd itch behind her eyes. Someone was trying to use magic on her—or if not on her, then at least very, very near to her, indeed.

She turned in the direction that the itch was coming from and felt her heart pound and her face go hot. Mr. Wail was coming back, accompanied by another young man. This fellow was short, with thick straight black hair in a severe Hexian crop to his shoulders and an equally severe expression. The air around him buzzed with magic. He might just be doing that to intimidate her, she thought. She despised the fact that it was working. "Miss," he said. "Might I ask where you got that brooch? It's *very* pretty."

"It was a gift from a friend," she said, smiling at him. "Do you *really* like it? I didn't know if it quite matched my dress." Then she took a sip of her wine and gave an airy little giggle. "My, isn't this wine lovely! It tastes a bit of elderberries, don't you think?"

At that, no officer of the law came crashing into the room, though judging by the expression on the boys' faces she'd succeeded, at least, in momentarily distracting them. "I just bought the cheapest I saw," said Mr. Wail, who then withered in the face of a stern look from his friend. "Erm, yes. Is that brooch enchanted in any way?"

"*Enchanted?*" Onna twittered. "Oh, no, I'm *sure* I would have noticed if it was enchanted." She was suddenly very aware of how crowded the room was and how closely everyone was looking at her.

"Would you mind letting me look at it?" the other man asked.

Just then, a clamor at the door interrupted: some young men were shouting, and a familiar, Awati-accented voice boomed out, "Where is she, then? Where's my little sister?"

Onna was so relieved she thought she might faint but endeavored to appear the exact opposite. "My brother," she whispered. "He'll be *furious.* Oh, *hide* me, please, I'll lose my allowance for weeks!" She made a game effort to conceal herself behind a curtain. A moment later the curtain was whipped aside by Sergeant Bato, who had his braids hidden under an enormous hat and was also wearing an exceedingly unconvincing-looking false mustache. He bellowed at her a bit in Awati. She responded in beseeching tones with one of the only phrases she could say in that language, which was, "Happy new rains festival, grandmother!" This sent her protective elder brother into a brief coughing fit before he—very gently—dragged his reprobate of a younger sister out of the house by her elbow.

Once they were outside, Sergeant Bato bundled Onna swiftly into the palanquin, where Captain Run was waiting. "Good work, miss," she said as the palanquin jolted into motion. "We'll make a copper of you yet. Had *me* worrying about your allowance."

Onna's ears went hot and she shivered. She felt somehow very cold and as if she would like to run around and around as fast as she could or hit something, scream, or weep. "Did I—*really* do well?"

"You did," Captain Run said, and patted her shoulder. "Just take deep breaths, miss. Takes a minute for the battle nerves to wear off."

Onna took a few deep breaths while Captain Run and Sergeant Bato politely looked away. Once she was settled, Captain Run said, "So what do you think of our Mr. Wail?"

"He's awful," Onna replied promptly. "I don't know if I think that he's a murderer. But I don't know if I've ever met a murderer before, so I couldn't say exactly. And I'm afraid I didn't manage to get him to say anything *very* useful."

"We didn't expect a sudden confession," Captain Run said. "Just wanted to plant some seeds. Start getting someone in with that crowd. I thought that some of the things he said seemed right suggestive, though. Might be that we've been looking at the wrong fellow but the right orbit. What do you think, Bena?"

Sergeant Bato gave a small grunt. "Maybe. I'd keep an eye on him either way. We'll at least be able to use her again, I think, with Wail. He's more featherheaded than his friends, even though he's a better talker."

"I wouldn't send her right in again," Captain Run said. "Make it an accident. Have her just happen to be where he is. Lots of apologies. Explaining that she didn't know that her brother had put a tracker on her brooch."

"Oh, I like that," Sergeant Bato said, and then the two of them occupied themselves so thoroughly in strategizing that Onna could at last uncurl her shoulders from where they'd gotten stuck beside her ears.

Eventually, Onna ventured to interrupt them and mentioned a few of her suspicions regarding Loga and Mr. Finnbair. In response to this, she earned a matched set of raised eyebrows.

"I know you're new in town, miss," Captain Run said eventually, "but I'd take care before I go saying things against Lord Zilon. He's eccentric, all right, but he's a real pillar around here. Done us a few good turns at the force."

"He's the only reason we can afford to use longeyes in our investigations," said Sergeant Bato. "I don't mean you any insult, but there's a reason the missus let you get so involved with our investigation, after he

said you were interested." Then he stopped speaking, cut off by a pointed
look from his wife.

"You're a real help, like I said," said Captain Run. "Glad to have you.
But it was his good word that made me want to take a chance on you.
He's a good man, miss. No reason to waste resources going after him or
his friends when we have more likely tigers to hunt."

"I see," Onna said. She felt queasy. She lapsed into silence.

They dropped her back at the Lamp—Loga, fortunately, was out at
some party, which preserved her from having to give him a detailed
summary of her evening—and she retreated to her own rooms. She still
felt on edge. Everything seemed so dreadfully muddled. She had suspects but no evidence, suspicions but no facts. It was one thing to wonder about Mr. Wail, or one of his associates, or some anonymous wizard
who worked as a surgeon at the hospital, and another to make accusations. Worst of all, she had no one to consult with about the problem.
Captain Run and Sergeant Bato had all but said outright that they
would refuse to investigate anyone who had donated money to the Hexian police, and Loga was both acting suspiciously himself and clearly
trying to protect his suspiciously acting friend. Who on earth was she
to turn to? Mrs. Cordram? Surely not.

She longed, suddenly, for Sy. As hapless as she found him at times,
he was at least clever enough to help her think through a thorny problem. Then, all at once, it occurred to her: she knew someone in Hexos
who was clever, and not being paid off by Loga, and she had wanted an
excuse to write to him in any case. And so, with a mixture of excitement
and enormous relief, Onna sat down to write a note to Haran Welder.

# 17

**DR. HARAND GORDRICK'S BLUE OIL
FOR HEALTH AND VITALITY! ADDS
FLESH TO THE THIN, RESTORES
VIGOR TO THE AFFLICTED!**

*I, Dr. Harand Gordrick of Leiscourt, have Studied for many
Years with a famous Troll Doctor, of Cwydarin, who has Instructed me in the Art of Troll Medicine, Long Forbidden to Human Wizards! For only 25 SEN PER BOTTLE, restore your lost
Vitality, Reduce Pain, ENJOY HEALTH AND HAPPINESS!*
                    —*Patent medicine broadside, Leiscourt, 6572*

The captain—who had introduced himself as Groton—looked
Tsira up and down. "My cousin died at Coldstream," he said.
Then he leaned over and spat off the edge of the dock. "I'm not trans-
porting any trolls."

Jeckran sucked in a breath through his teeth. "Tsira isn't a criminal,
sir. I can vouch for his character myself."

The captain curled his lip. "Sure you can, with that accent. Wasn't
your kind getting killed in the streets at Coldstream. My boys need to
be able to sleep at night without worrying about some headmen's plot
to kill off poor men and reduce the surplus population, *sir*."

"Oh, *honestly*, if you really believe—"

Tsira cut him off. "Put me in irons."

"*What?*" said Jeckran, whipping his head to look at her.

"If it's needed," said Tsira. "I don't give a fuck. Put me in irons. Chain me to the fucking mast. Just get me to Hexos."

She did give a fuck, really. Didn't like how she and her vahn were being treated like mad dogs that might bite. Problem was, she didn't have any room to put her nose up. She needed on that boat. Didn't care too much what it took.

Pink started to argue with her. She stared down at him. "Quiet," she told him in Dacyn, and he was quiet. She looked at the captain.

"Forty tocats," she said. Twice the asking rate. "Thirty here, ten when we arrive safe. I'll be in irons the whole way. Your men won't have anything to worry them. That sound fair to you, Captain?"

The captain thought for a while before he nodded. He was brave enough to meet her eyes. "Sounds about right."

"And you'll vouch for us when we get there. So someone will be willing to take them off."

He paused. "Yes."

She held out her hand. He didn't take it. Took a step back.

"I like an honest man," Tsira said, and watched the captain's face go paler.

Leiscourt was a cold city. Cold and wet and dark. Pink limped as they walked back to the little room they were letting. She put her hand to his back. "All right?"

"Yes," he said. "I'm rather tired." Then he slipped on a wet cobblestone. She caught him. Held him a bit longer than she had to.

"All right?"

"Yes."

Later, in the room, he got out his sketchbook. She'd bought it for him before they left Monsatelle. He'd almost cried when she gave it to him. When he drew, his face went still and easy, like he'd never seen a friend lying on the floor with his heart cut out.

While he drew, she sewed. He'd lost some buttons off his shirt a few nights back, from her trying to get his clothes off too quickly. Once she finished sewing them back on, she went to see what he was drawing. It was a picture of a stranger. Big hands, broad shoulders. Strong nose and jaw, light eyes, light hair. A hard crease between the eyes from frowning. She frowned.

"You made me handsome."

He looked surprised. "You *are* handsome."

She picked him up and fucked him sitting in the room's single straight-backed chair. He pressed his face into her chest. She could feel his sweat on her skin. "*Yes*," he said. "Yes, yes, *yes*, Tsira, *God*, I love you—"

When they were finished and had washed up she carried him to the bed and tucked him in and watched him for a while. He noticed. "You're staring at me."

"Yeah."

"Why?"

"Like staring at you."

"Why?"

"Want a compliment?"

"And if I did?"

She lay down next to him. "You're the prettiest fucking thing I've ever seen."

"Oh," he said.

"Night, Pink."

"Good night." There was a pause. "I love you, Tsira."

"Night," she said again, and fell asleep.

When she woke up, he was getting dressed. It didn't happen often that he'd wake first. He put a cup of coffee on the side table near her head. "We have to clap you in irons today."

She sat up and took up her coffee cup. "Thanks."

"For the leg irons?"

"For the coffee."

"You're welcome, boss." He kissed her cheek. He smelled like soap and tobacco. Must have had a smoke while she was still sleeping. She smiled and caught him by the shirtfront to kiss him properly. He made a soft little sigh into her mouth, then pulled away. "You'll pull off my buttons again, if you keep doing that."

Once in their old room at Mon Del Ras's place, she'd moved the dressing table closer to the bed so he could watch his own face in the mirror while she fucked him. She held him so he couldn't get away and kept whispering in his ear the whole time about what all of his friends would think if they saw how good he was for her, how he did whatever she told him to do. He'd come so hard that he screamed, but he wouldn't look her in the eye for a while afterward.

She finished her coffee, then stood to dress. "Where do we have to go?"

"I'm afraid that I haven't the faintest. A blacksmith? A farrier? Perhaps a prison."

She looked out the window. Gray and wet. "Fine day for it," she said, and startled him into a laugh.

They found a farrier's shop not far from their boardinghouse. Pink explained to the man what they wanted. When he was finished, the farrier looked at Tsira and touched his finger to his cap, then gave her a clumsy little greeting in her own language. She smiled at him, startled. Sounded sweet when he spoke like that, like a little vahn just learning to talk. "You speak Dacyn?"

"Only that. My grandda used to say that we've got some troll blood, on account of his being a headman's bastard, and I should learn to say a how-d'ya-do in case I should meet a relative." She could believe it. He was a big fellow for a pink. He was keeping his eyes down, too, like a good vahn. "You're a reig."

"Yeah."

"I could tell." He sounded surprised at himself. "How?"

She considered. "Smell, maybe."

"I'll be damned," he said. "Begging your pardon, ma'am. Only I've never met a troll before."

"I'm half," she told him. "I've never met a human with some of the blood before."

Jeckran shifted from one foot to the other. "So will you do it, or shall we be on our way?"

The farrier looked surprised. "I'll do it, sir."

They haggled over the price. Once that was settled, it took a while to get the chains ready, even though the farrier was using a bit of magic to speed things up. She could smell it on him: a cold smell. She let her mind go quiet for a while.

Jeckran touched her arm and said, "Where do you go?"

"Mm?"

"When you go blank like that. Where do you go?"

"Just woolgathering."

The farrier watched them. Jeckran noticed and got snappish. "Are you nearly finished, then?"

"No, sir. You might take a walk. Come back later."

Jeckran glared. "I will not."

There wasn't much to say to that. The farrier went back to his work. She nodded at him. "What's that magic you're doing?"

He looked up. "Nothing much, ma'am. Just what I learned while I was apprenticed."

"You could get trained more, if you wanted. You don't have enough of the blood to be let in at a Cwydarin school, but they'd take you in a border-clan. Mine's about three, four days' ride northwest of here. North of Coldstream. Called Cynallum. The clan wizard doesn't have anyone to teach. Takes about ten years to get any good at it, but I guess it's worth it if you want to learn."

He was staring. "He'd teach me to be a wizard?" He dropped his voice. "Would he have me bring the dead back? I won't do that. I'm an Elgarite, ma'am."

"We don't do that. Our wizards are just good at making sick people better. You want to learn?"

He hesitated. "Might that I would, ma'am."

"Good. Tell them that Cynallumwyntsira sent you to apprentice to Marden." She paused. "Can you read?"

"No, ma'am."

"That's all right. He'll teach you that, too. Repeat what I say."

She had him say her name, and her clan's and Marden's, until she thought he would remember them. She hoped he would use them. Marden needed an apprentice, true enough, but they needed new blood in the clan more. It might be that he'd take to one of the young reigs who was still living.

A few minutes later he'd finished work on her chains. She clanked a bit when she stood. The farrier shook his head. "Sorry about this, ma'am."

"Not so bad. I can still can do some damage this way." She showed him. Moved real quick and got the chains at her wrists around his throat. Didn't squeeze, but got close enough to let him feel the heat of her. Saw his eyes go dark. Good.

She let him go, grinned at him, and slapped him on the shoulder. He gave his head a little shake and laughed. She nodded to Jeckran. "Pay him."

He was funny, Jeckran. He liked getting treated like her sweet little vahn until he hated it. He glared at her now instead of reaching for his purse. She tried again. Spoke in Dacyn, dropped her voice down a bit. "*Mind.*"

She could tell that got him a little hot, and it annoyed him that it did. He paid the man. She set her gaze on the farrier. "You'll make a good wizard," she said.

He ducked his head. "Thank you, ma'am."

She and Jeckran got out on the street. The chains rattled when she moved, and people crossed to the other side of the street when they saw her. That was all right. That way, no one could hear as she and her vahn fought.

He started out fast and got a few good hits in. She was faster than him with every part but the tongue. "You *humiliated* me. Was it intentional? Have I done something to offend you?"

She just looked at him. The air was so cold and wet that he looked smeared at the edges. "What?"

"Flirting with him. *Touching* him. Ordering me to pay him as if I were a servant. Telling me to *mind*."

It made her tired just to listen to him. She didn't know if he was done yet, so she decided to wait. That just made him madder. "*Say* something!"

She spoke like she did when he was hurt or scared. "Sorry. Didn't think it'd bother you."

"Good *God*, what I would do if it would keep you from speaking to me in that *voice*, as if I were a fucking *child* who needed to be soothed back into bed!"

She nearly sighed but choked it back. That would be the end of her, all right. She tried again. "Pink," she said. "Sorry. We need a new wizard. Need new blood in the clan. That's all."

"Ah, well, if it was for the sake of harvesting more young human men for your pleasure, then how could I *object*?"

"Pink," she said. "Don't be an ass."

There was a moment of quiet, and she could hear the sound of cartwheels and other people talking. He pulled in a breath. "Yes. All right." He swallowed, looked away. "I can't stand looking at those things."

The chains. She grinned at him. "That's it?"

"I think it's enough!"

"Think I can't burst them?"

He looked startled. "Could you?"

"Sure." She smiled at him again. "The chains might be all right, anyway."

"How? Even if you *could* break them in an emergency, you'll be stuck in them for weeks."

"Yeah. Damn awkward. It'll be hard to get on top of you. We'll have to try something else. Keep trying until something works."

"*Oh*," said Jeckran, the rest of the fight dropping out of him. "I see. We *will* have to apply some thought to the matter, won't we?" He looked a little more cheerful. "I've heard that in Hexos they have an entire book on the topic. It's called something like *Various Approaches to an Interesting Subject*, which I suppose is about what one would expect from an island full of wizards."

Tsira smiled.

They had to board the ship early the next morning. At night they ate, packed, fucked, couldn't sleep. Had a glass of brandy each. Jeckran read aloud with his head in her lap. Dawn crept up slowly. They left in the dark and the quiet. There weren't any people out on the streets.

They held hands for a while.

The docks were already full of men shouting and cursing, loading crates off and on the ships, exchanging money, starting arguments. They found their ship and stood by the gangplank. Tsira stared down at the narrow boards and the black water. "Pink," she said. "Don't know if I can go over that."

"Of course you can," he said. "Have you ever fallen off a sidewalk?"

She snorted.

"This is just as wide as a sidewalk. You won't fall. They push freight over it. It will hold your weight. I'm going to walk across first, and you'll follow and keep your eyes on me and not look down. You'll get across, and none of those asses staring at us right now will have any cause to be amused."

A pretty good crowd had gathered to stare. She stared right back until some dropped their gaze, then she looked at Jeckran and nodded. "Go. Now."

He shrugged his pack up onto his shoulders and walked. She followed. Kept her eyes on the back of his head. Her stomach dropped when the fucking plank moved under her. Then she got on the ship and met his eye again. "Shit." Her knees were shaking.

"Well," he said. "You won't have to do it again for almost three weeks."

"Shit," she said again.

"Are you the troll on board, sir?" said a sailor, staring at them. No fight in his voice, just curiosity. Short fellow with curly black hair and fat cheeks like a child.

"Yeah," she said, wondering why he'd have to ask, when he was looking straight at seven-odd feet of her.

"I grew up near Coldstream," the boy said, like he wanted her to apologize for it. "I know a fellow whose grandmother got killed there, and the government gave his family twenty tocats and told 'em to stop complaining."

"I didn't have anything to do with that," she told him.

"I did," said Jeckran. Spoke in the way he did when he wanted someone to know that he came from the sort of family that other people knew about. Bit slower and stupider than his normal way of talking. Like he was so rich he could afford to be a real dunce. "I fought at Coldstream. Nearly died for all those poor people. I'll give you my word as a soldier that Tsira had no hand in it. Not *all* of us trolls and headmen are the bad sort, what? And what do you do here?"

The sailor looked a bit embarrassed. "I'm a cook, sir."

Jeckran smiled. "Well, then. You're just the sort of man one wants to meet aboard ship." He held out his hand, and the cook shook it, looking pleased. "What's your name?"

"Pip Williams, sir."

Jeckran smiled at that, too. "Dashed pleasant to meet you, Williams. My name is Smith. This is my partner, Cynallumwyntsira." He could say her name right, now. She liked hearing it. "Tsira, if you're short on time, what?"

Pip Williams gave them each a salute. "Glad to have you aboard."

"I don't suppose you know where we'll be sleeping? From Captain Groton's gimlet eye, I imagined it might be the brig. Or in a bunk below a fellow with a weak stomach."

The cook grinned. "You're lucky. No other passengers in steerage, so it'll just be you and the molasses barrels."

"I don't suppose you'd have the time to show us the way?"

He had the time. Led them down into the black gut of the ship.

Tsira hated it straight off. It was like her cave, but wet and stinking and moving under her feet. Like the insides of a sick animal. A few bare bunks in a corner, and the rest full of barrels. There was a smell of sweet rot and vomit. The cook went back up again and they were alone.

Jeckran looked around. "I think we should each take a top bunk. I'd prefer not to be brained by a rolling molasses barrel in a squall, and there's more room to sit on top."

She waved her wrists at him so the chains clinked. "Rather not try the ladder in the dark with these on, more than I have to." She sat on the closest bunk. "This one's fine."

They unpacked. Lay down their blankets and pillows and strapped their packs to their bunks. There was more shouting from above. Jeckran looked up. "I think I'll go up there."

She followed him. Didn't want to go up, but didn't want to stay in that stinking hole.

On the deck, pinks were everywhere. She held fast to the rail and watched them swarming the rigging like ants up blades of tall grass. She thought that living over that black killing water must pull the life from you somehow. The sailors had young bodies and old faces, wrinkles so deep around the eyes that they might have been born that way. She looked toward the dock, then looked down fast. The ground was moving away. "Fuck. Pink."

"Are you all right?"

"No." The sick rose in her gut. She swallowed. "It's a lot of water."

"And a very big boat. And a fine time of year for the passage." He touched her wrist. "You've gone very pale. Are you feeling ill?"

"Yeah."

"Keep your eyes on the horizon. I've heard that it helps." He was quiet for a bit. "I wouldn't really know, myself. I've always been a good sailor."

Prideful little shit.

She lasted half an hour before she was sick off the side of the boat.

Jeckran kept saying it would get better. Kept wiping her face off with wet rags and bringing her cups of water. Kept saying she'd feel better once she got her sea legs. She didn't know what the fuck that was supposed to mean. *Sea legs.*

She was sick for days. It was hard to keep down water, even. She lay in her bunk and tried not to move.

On the fifth night he stirred molasses into water and made her drink it. "Try to finish it, boss. You're losing too much weight."

He touched her arm. She could see where she was getting jagged. The skin tight over the muscle, each piece of her cut out hard and sharp. She got like that when she was starving. "I can see your veins," he said.

"You like it?"

"Why would you ask me that?"

"You like me looking tough."

"I like you looking well."

"Then get me off this fucking boat."

"If I could, boss, I would cheerfully drain the Osten Sea for you, but I'm afraid that it's beyond my meager power to do so." He wedged himself into the bunk next to her, lay his head on her shoulder. Slid a hand between her thighs. "Are you feeling any better?"

Between the chains and her being sick, they hadn't fucked since they'd been on the boat. Used to be they'd manage once or twice every day. She shook her head. "No. Sorry."

"Don't apologize." He pressed his head closer into the crook of her neck.

She was about to doze off when he leapt back like he had touched something hot. Stood still, for a moment, listening. Shook his head. "I thought I had heard someone at the ladder."

He went back to her. Pressed close.

"Think they'd kill us if they knew, Pink?"

His face went dark. "I—I don't suppose that they would go so far. It's *unusual*, but there are no laws against it, that I've ever heard. It's only that most men would find it very . . . peculiar of me. It isn't as if you're my wealthy householder."

"So you're not scared. Just ashamed."

He swallowed. "It's not—I'm not ashamed of you."

"Yeah? Wouldn't mind telling the fellows you went to school with that you're fucking me? That you're mine?"

He flinched. "Please. Let's not talk about this."

"Why not?"

"We're contented enough, aren't we? I don't see the use of—of worrying over things that will only serve to bring us grief. I could easily ask you why it is that, in all of the times that I've told you that I love you, you've either ignored me or said 'hm!'—which *does* make a man feel like a great silly ass." He wasn't looking her in the eye. "I won't ask for what you can't give me. I would be grateful if you could grant me the same consideration."

She didn't see there was much she could say to that.

She stayed sick. He kept tending to her. She might have hated that, if she hadn't been so tired all the time.

One day he came down the ladder from the deck and knelt next to her bunk. The bridge of his nose was sunburned. She couldn't remember when that had happened. "Boss," he said, "come up above deck. The fresh air might do you good."

She did. Seemed easier than arguing. It took a lot for her to get up the ladder. By the time she saw him at the top he had gone pale. "Tsira, are you—you're not well at all."

She just looked at him. "No."

It was too bright up above. The sun made a hot path from the boat to the horizon. She closed her eyes. Jeckran touched her elbow, and she shushed him. "Just the light. Wait."

When she could see again, she made her way to the rail and leaned on it. Ship wasn't rocking too badly. She'd stopped smelling the stink down below after the first few days, but now the air smelled stronger and brighter, like air after the rain. Nothing but water as far as she could see, and no fish jumping in it like in the streams back home. "You ever see any fish out here, Pink?"

"Sometimes. I think that I saw a whale once, in the distance, but it may have been my fancy. I'm more taken by the sunsets. You should watch it with me tonight."

"Got them at home, too. Sunsets."

"You're terribly pragmatic. Doesn't it touch you at all to see something beautiful?"

She shrugged.

Sunset started not long after that. They watched it together. He cupped his chin in his hand. "One thing that I must say for the modern metropolis is that it makes for better colors in a sunset. You don't get those lovely purples farther away from the smokestacks."

"Yeah? They got more colors in the city?"

"Yes, they have. Didn't you notice when we were in Monsatelle?"

"I don't see so many colors."

"*What?*"

She shrugged again.

He frowned, glanced around, then pointed to his cravat. "What color is this, Tsira?"

She hesitated. "Purple?"

"Good God. No. Green. How is it possible that I never knew about this? Were you born color-blind?"

"Yeah. I get reds all right, mostly. More trouble with yellows and blues."

"Why did you never tell me? You told me that you liked my eyes once. What color do you think they are?"

"Earth."

He looked startled, then smiled. "I suppose you're right." He looked at her for a moment. Spoke gently. "What other secrets have you been keeping from me, boss?"

She noticed something moving out of the corner of her eye. Turned her head to look. Group of sailors standing around, laughing with their hands over their mouths. One of them pretending to be sick.

She went hot.

Jeckran noticed the second after she did. "Tsira—" he said, but she was moving. Sailors mostly scattered when they saw her coming, but she managed to grab the one who'd been making the fucking joke. Hauled him to the rail, got him by the ankle, dangled him off the side. She heard a lot of shouting. Didn't pay much mind. Wanted to rip him to pieces. Wanted her teeth in his throat.

Jeckran punched her in the ribs.

She hauled the man back and dropped him on the deck. He curled himself into a ball. "Please, sir, please don't—"

She nudged him with her toe. "Get up."

He got up. She stared at him. "Rude. Making fun of people behind their backs."

Captain came charging over then. "What the hell is going on over here?"

Sailor answered real quick. "Nothing, sir. Just had a little bet on whether or not he could lift me with one hand." He glanced up at Tsira. "I lost, sir."

Being on board ship got a bit better after that. She got sick less, and when she went up on deck, sailors came by to talk. She did a lot of arm wrestling. Pink played a lot of cards. Days got easier to swallow.

Then after two weeks, one morning they saw land—Hexos.

One port in the world, Tsira thought, must be close enough to another. Same rush. Same stink. Same splashing and banging and shouting. Then they got off the boat and heard languages she couldn't understand. Saw people wearing clothes she'd never seen before. Everything the same and everything different. Like the same place from midwinter to a hot day in spring.

Good that they'd gotten to know some of the sailors. She didn't know what they'd have done without a guide. Lots of people in this city: more than she'd ever seen in one place before. Looked all right, though. She saw some pinks with good troll embroidery on their tunics, and not so many people looked hungry here as she'd seen in Leiscourt. It was warmer, too, like it was still summer. Someone had planted trees and flowers along the streets like they were making a garden. She'd seen a few streets like that in Monsatelle, but just in places with big houses and no people. Not like here, with ordinary people walking all around.

The captain himself took her to get the irons struck off, but some of the men did the rest. The place the sailors showed them to stay was all right. Clean enough. She saw Pink's eyes go wide when they told him the price. He paid. A young boy helped them to carry their packs up to the room.

Once the boy left, she lay down on the bed. Pink frowned. "Are you tired?"

"Yeah."

He knelt next to the bed. Took her hand. "No wonder, after you were so sick on the ship. You should rest. You'll feel better after a good sleep."

"Yeah."

His frown got harder, but he didn't speak. He just climbed into the bed next to her.

When they woke, it was dark, and she still felt like she could sleep for a week. "Feel better."

He brightened. "Do you really?"

"Yeah." Wasn't a lie. Sick feeling had passed. "I could eat."

They went out. The night was warm and the streets were crowded. They served all kinds of food in Hexos, except the kinds Tsira knew about. They didn't walk long before they found a whole street of little food carts. Jeckran said he thought most of the people were speaking Nessoran and Sangan, along with a few other languages he'd never heard before. They all seemed to know what they were doing, going straight to the cart they wanted and ordering without hesitation. The street smelled of onion and meat and coal and vinegar.

Jeckran bought some of this and some of that, pointing at what others in front of him ordered. Told her what he thought everything was. "Rice," he said. "With mutton and spices." It tasted all right. Next were fried noodles and little pouches of meat that burst when she bit them and filled her mouth with soup. Jeckran got grease on his suit, but he just laughed.

They found a stand with a man scooping some multicolored stuff into dishes and pouring syrups with fruit in them on top. Jeckran smiled when he saw it. "Oh, lovely. I haven't had ice cream in years. Have you ever tried it?"

She shook her head. He bought one and handed it to her. "Here."

"That for me?"

"Yes." He smiled. "You'll love it."

It was so cold it made her head ache, and it tasted like all of summer at once. She finished it and had another. The man behind the stand laughed and put a few extra bits of fruit on the second one. Asked her a question she couldn't understand. She shook her head. "Sorry."

"Fatsein tu dach?"

Nasener. Not her tongue, but close enough. *Is it good?*

She smiled. "Tsa." It was.

They kept walking. The streets were clean and brightly lit. The air smelled thick and honey-sweet. When they reached a crossroad, she felt the ground change under her feet. They'd changed the pattern of the paving stones from one street to the next. She nudged Jeckran and showed him. "Look. Road's different running east to west than it is north to south."

"Good God. In Leiscourt they barely manage to have roads at all."

Some people stared at her as they walked, but most didn't seem to mind her so much. "They got other trolls here?"

"Yes. Quite a few. There have always been a number of troll wizards here, but I believe that there's been a rush of trolls moving to Hexos since all of the trouble started back home. There's even a troll quarter out on the western end of town."

She looked down at him. "How do you know so much?"

He flushed. "I only read the papers."

She gave his shoulder a squeeze. "We can go talk to them tomorrow. Those trolls."

"Good."

They walked into a quiet neighborhood. A chicken walked past. The streets were lined with tall, thick trees. There was the smell of green sap, of hot earth, of hard rain about to come.

"It's bad luck," she said.

"What?"

"What you want me to say. It's bad luck."

"Tsira, what in Elgar's name are you talking about?"

"You said it made you feel like an ass. Saying it and me not saying it back. But we try not to say it. Think it cheapens the meaning. Some people say it brings bad fortune. I know it's bad logic. I just can't help thinking it."

He looked confused, then smiled. Laughed. "After all of this time, and my making myself such a miserable wretch over it, you won't say that you love me because you're afraid of *bad luck*?"

"Knew you'd think I was being stupid." She swallowed. "You asked me once. If I'd ever loved anyone." She took a breath. "I said only my ma."

He stopped walking. "*Tsira*," he said. "You must know that your saying that you loved your mother had nothing to do with her—"

"Not our way, saying that kind of thing. She wouldn't have liked it. Didn't like most of what I did. How I am. Always smiled too fucking much." She bit the inside of her cheek. Did it hard enough to taste blood and ease the ache in her throat. "Doesn't matter now. She's dead."

He didn't say anything. Grabbed her by the hand. She didn't think. Just bent down and kissed him right there in the street.

There was a chorus of shouts.

*This*, she thought, *would be a damn stupid reason to die.*

She straightened and squared her shoulders, trying to look big and mean. She felt a bit better when she saw them. Just a crowd of skinny boys trying to feel like they were tough and grown. Laughing and hollering and keeping their distance. Jeckran shot her a look. "Are you going to do anything stupid, boss?"

"No. Let's go." She turned. Kept her body between the boys and Jeckran. Tried not to think about how good it would feel to kill every last fucking one of them. The boys hooted louder. She ignored them. Kept walking. Swallowed her temper until she nearly choked on it. She wasn't too surprised when the rock hit the back of her head.

At first she thought it was just her vision swimming as the wall of magic closed around her.

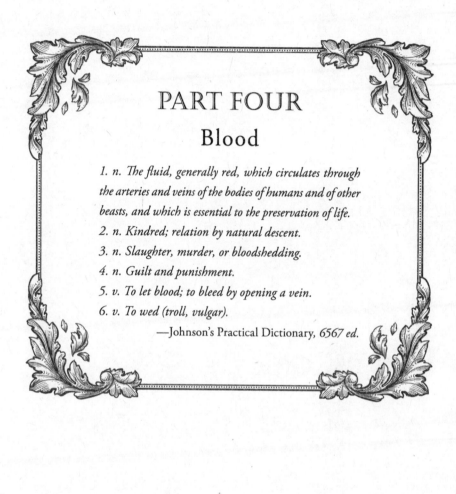

# PART FOUR
## Blood

*1. n. The fluid, generally red, which circulates through the arteries and veins of the bodies of humans and of other beasts, and which is essential to the preservation of life.*

*2. n. Kindred; relation by natural descent.*

*3. n. Slaughter, murder, or bloodshedding.*

*4. n. Guilt and punishment.*

*5. v. To let blood; to bleed by opening a vein.*

*6. v. To wed (troll, vulgar).*

—Johnson's Practical Dictionary, *6567 ed.*

# 18

*Elgar himself, the founder of the religion that represents the very heart of Daeslund, was the son of a merchant who most scholars now believe to have been of Mendani extraction. Born Aman Agara, he took the name Elgar as a child in Leiscourt, which was at the time the walled city of the Grewick clan. Known to be extraordinarily gifted from an early age, by twelve Elgar was taken under the tutelage of a troll magister who instructed him in mathematics, argumentation, and basic wizardry. By the age of sixteen Elgar had broken away from his teacher, and by twenty he was traveling the country delivering the speeches that would later become his letters. His philosophy, which spoke of new messages from the ancient God of Daeslund and rejected troll philosophy and troll authority, was taken up by human youth who called themselves the New Dawn, and identified themselves by wearing sprigs of holly on their clothing . . .*

—A Brief History of Daeslund, *Melton Grote*

Haran Welder set the paper down and sighed. "It's not *definitive*," he said. "Though I admit it does look suspicious, doesn't it?"

Onna and Haran were sitting in his office at the hospital the day after Onna found Loga's notes, a pleasant, airy room overlooking the central courtyard, going through the notebook together. Onna had explained the situation to him and asked for his help with the translation, and he had listened with sympathy, though he kept saying over and over that he didn't like to think such a thing of either Loga or Mr. Finnbair. Now he sighed again and gently disentangled the hand of the little girl in his lap from his hair, speaking to her gently in Nessoran. Matti, who wasn't yet two, scrubbed at her eye with one tiny fist. "Hawan," she said, and closed her eyes, rubbing her face against his shirt. Her cheeks were very pink, and her eyelashes wet with tears. Haran had just retrieved her from one of the nurses when she refused to be put to bed for her nap until "Hawan" held her first.

"She'll be asleep soon," Haran said to Onna, with an apologetic air. "I know that it's a dreadful nuisance, but she's grown awfully attached to me since I've started dropping in on her in the ward."

"It isn't a nuisance at all," Onna said. "I have a sister her age. It must be so terrible for her to be so ill."

"She's better now," Haran said. "One of the lucky ones. She'll be able to go home to her parents soon." He kissed the top of her head and said, with what Onna thought was very charming frankness, "I'll miss her. It's very selfish of me, but I miss them when they get better and go home. It makes my dull work even duller."

"It isn't selfish at all," Onna said. "I'm sure it's very natural to grow fond of them." Matti had spent a few minutes in Onna's lap as well, and the warm, damp solidity of her little body had been enormously comforting. "And she's such a cunning little thing." She paused and said, "You're *quite* sure that there's nothing about trolls in his notebook?"

"Not as such," Haran said. "There's a bit about research done on pig brains that notes that work on a human or troll brain might result in more precise results, but he didn't pursue it. Not in any way that he recorded, at least. If I'm very honest with you, I'd say that Wail seems like the better suspect, in terms of personality. I've spent plenty of time with his set at parties, and he's frightfully easy to wind up. I can imagine him murdering someone just to feel important. He's dim lights as a wizard, though, so I don't know if he could manage it. Maybe one of his friends? Or Finnbair, I suppose, though I really do hate to think that of him."

Onna sighed. "I know. It's such a terrible muddle. I'm glad to hear what you said about Loga's notebooks, though. If it was him, I don't know *what* I would do. And now Captain Run's baby has come early, so I don't even have her and Sergeant Bato to consult with." Sergeant Bato had sent Onna a note early that morning about the baby, saying he and Captain Run would be on leave for the next few weeks. She had written a note of very enthusiastic congratulations in response, and then sat at her desk and cried briefly over how *unfair* it was that she should have to keep working on this all alone.

A grim silence fell over them both. Matti seemed to have fallen asleep. Haran said, "I think that we could both use a cup of coffee."

He put Matti to bed, then boiled coffee in a tin pan and served it in beakers. Onna laughed at him, but he only smiled, content to be found absurd. They talked about their families.

"My father doesn't approve of my working in medicine," Haran said. "Especially in something as unglamorous as sanitation protocols. He thinks I ought to go into politics."

"I think it's wonderful," Onna said, "to do something that saves lives without wanting any credit for it." Then she said, "I'm quite sure that my parents never expected me to go quite this far with wizarding. They wanted me to be successful, but I don't think they ever imagined I'd go to such lengths to pursue it. My mother was an authoress, but she stopped publishing her work after she was married. I think they expected wizarding was going to be that for me. Like watercolors or pianoforte. Just something to distinguish me and help me find a good husband."

Haran smiled. "Forgive me if I speak out of turn, but expecting any man to occupy all of that enormous brain of yours would be, I imagine, an unfair burden on the poor fellow."

"You *are* speaking out of turn," Onna said, but she smiled a little into her beaker and bit her lip. "I do hope you shan't be too offended, but you know that I must ask. Do *you* know anything that might have to do with the murders? You *do* work at the hospital, after all, and it *does* seem that there may be some sort of medical or research motivation for the killings, and if Mr. Finnbair is correct about the peculiar qualities of troll blood, perhaps someone in the hospital could be using it in their work. Perhaps you might have—seen something or heard something, and not wanted to say anything? If whoever was involved was a friend, perhaps?"

He looked very grave for a moment, then said, "I'm not offended. Of course you should ask. And no, I can't think of anyone who's behaved oddly. They run a very tight ship here, especially since I've started the new protocols, so I think it would be very difficult for anyone to get up to any funny business." He paused. "Would you like to read through all of my notes I've taken on my research? I've been logging everything that the doctors and nurses track down about how infections are spread. If you look through them with an eye for anything that seems suspicious, you might catch something that I haven't."

Onna looked him in the eye, trying to gauge his sincerity. "Yes, thank you. I should like very much to have a look at them."

He didn't look startled by this, nor frightened or annoyed. He only nodded and went to his desk to retrieve a thick ream of paper. "Take all the time you need. Shall I make some more coffee?"

He did, and Onna spent over two hours reading through his notes. By the time she finished the pile, she felt at once invigorated—there was something very bracing about reading so many sets of such beautifully written parameters—as well as somewhat tired and rather foolish. She had found nothing in Haran's observations that wasn't perfectly logical and appropriate. Everything was in order: the parameters, his notes on the patients' diets and the doctors' and nurses' daily routines, and the observation reports from his supervisor. "I'm sorry," she said eventually. "I oughtn't have doubted your observations."

"Of course you ought," he said. "We're both only doing our jobs. You're investigating murders, and I am properly documenting my research so I won't have to toss it all out and try for a position in the Assemblage." He gave her a confiding little smile that made her feel as if she were tumbling happily down a grassy slope.

They said their good-byes not long after. Onna started to return to the Lamp but changed her mind, flagging down a cab to visit the troll quarter instead. Perhaps people would speak to her differently without the presence of the men, all *three* of whom she had found reason to suspect of involvement in the murders at one point or another.

Teiranwynartur greeted her very politely, considering the fact that Onna had arrived at her home unannounced. However, she only repeated what she had said before: none of them knew anything about who the murderer might be. She did, however, kindly take Onna on a brief tour of the neighborhood in case she might find some sort of clue. Their last stop was at the learning hall, where about two dozen children were having their lessons. Watching them, Onna felt an ache rise up in her throat. They were just children. Just sweet little children whose nightmares must be full of death and stolen blood.

The injustice needled at Onna as she rode back to the Lamp, and by the time she arrived she was so toweringly furious that she thought she would happily wrestle Loga to the ground and *force* him to cooperate. Fortunately, he had had another fit that morning and was flat on his back in bed when she stormed into his room. Mrs. Macosti was there as well, pouring a steaming bitter-smelling liquid from a clay pot into a cup for Loga to drink. Onna waited for Loga to take his medicine and for Mrs. Macosti to depart before she slammed down the notebook, open to the page with the note about troll brains. "Loga," she said. "If you are not honest with me this *very* instant about what exactly all of this is about, and why exactly you're defending Mr. Finnbair, I'll tell Teiranwynartur about you and let her sort you out herself."

He gave an unnatural little laugh. "How deliciously forceful you are, darling! And perfectly right, of course." He pushed himself gingerly into a sitting position and looked her straight in the eye. "Those notes are about my attempts to figure out how to save my own skin. I'm very ill, darling. I have the swoons—I've had them since I was a child—but being the Lord-Mage has made it much worse. It's from all of the magic that we take on. My predecessor as Lord-Mage, Lady Bawu, used to get terrible headaches from it. I get those as well, along with the fainting spells, but those are happening more and more often." He smiled slightly. "Which is the real reason that I needed an assistant so urgently, darling. It seems that I might not last as Lord-Mage quite as long as the nation might hope. Or as a personality for quite as long as I myself would like."

"Oh," said Onna.

"Oh, indeed. I suppose that it's all very just in a way, that I should die young from too much magic, since it was magic that I used to murder Jok's brother."

Onna stared, her irritation abating in the face of this awful confession. "*What?*"

He sighed. "I think I'll have Mrs. Macosti bring more tea, darling. I like to have something to do with my hands whilst I describe the worst moments of my life."

Onna frowned, not sure whether to feel abashed or defiant. Loga made it very difficult to trust him, with his love affairs and secret keeping, and she thought it unfair that she was expected to take him at his word on everything while he skirted the truth. Once more tea was delivered and poured, Loga propped himself back onto his pillows, as if he didn't want her looking down at him quite so directly.

He began, "I told you that I was on the stage when I was a child. My parents entrusted me to an opera company because they couldn't afford to send me to school, and they wanted me to learn to read and write. It wasn't a particularly easy life." He was gazing at his hands, but he spoke clearly and calmly, as if he was describing the plot of a sensational play he had seen many years ago. "I always tell people that I turned a man into a toad when he tried to rob me. I always thought that was an amusing story." He paused.

"I was fourteen. My manager grabbed me. He often hit me and usually I would never protest, but that day I pulled away from him, and he started to beat me. It just kept going and going until I thought he would kill me. And so I immolated him." He took another sip of tea. "I burned him, and I burned everything around us. We were in a small village theater after dark. I stayed inside the building as it came down, but when they found me, I was in perfect physical health. Later I was told that I didn't speak a single word for almost three weeks. I can't remember that."

He picked up the teapot, added more to Onna's cup, refilled his own cup, set the pot down, and continued.

"There was some question of my being put on trial. Lady Bawu stopped it. She came as soon as she heard about the little Sangan boy who burned a two-story building down with nothing but natural magic. She already had the twins, but she wanted me, too. She was Sangan herself, from a poor family as well, and I imagine she felt some kinship with me. I remember feeling very dull about it. I don't know that I understood what was happening. But she was wonderfully kind to me." His voice grew softer, remembering. "I was terrified of the twins, when I first met them. You've met Jok, so you know how he is, but I couldn't understand why they were so kind to me. I can only imagine what the twins must have thought of me: this little creature who didn't speak a word of Nessoran or Daeslundic and screamed like a cat whenever anyone touched him. But they never acted as if there was anything strange about me. Never once remarked on me unless it was to pay me a compliment, which Elgarson did almost every day."

He picked up his teacup, brought it to his lips, then set it down again. "Heavens, I could use a cigarette. Do you smoke at all?"

Onna shook her head.

"Do you mind if I do?"

She shook her head again. He reached into his sleeve and pulled out a cigarette, which then lit itself. She couldn't help but laugh, and he smiled.

"I know that it's almost too rich of a joke for a wizard to go about pulling things out of his sleeve, but when I was thinking of a place to fix my parameters for retrieving a cigarette, I couldn't think of anywhere else that amused me so much." He took a drag and gave a soft little sigh. "I picked this up when I lived in Monsatelle. They do know how to to live, the Esiphians, even if they can't manage a sewage system."

Onna frowned. "You lived in Monsatelle?"

"Yes. For almost ten years. After I killed Elgarson. That's why I speak Daeslundic so well. And Esiphian, though I'm afraid that my accent isn't what it could be."

She spoke gently. "You haven't told me about Elgarson yet."

"Ah, yes. Well." He took another drag, tapped the ash onto the floor, and continued.

"I worshipped him. I loved Jok as well, but I *worshipped* Elgarson. Most people who met him did. He was like some minor god; this wonderful, handsome, laughing boy. The two of them were quite different, but they did everything together. Even their magic came from the two of them together. When they were children, they somehow figured out how to direct energy into the same parametric channels simultaneously. They were actually *studied* at Leiscourt, but no one could pick apart how they managed it. It made them extremely powerful. I was already extraordinary, with the little education that I had, but the two of them together could outmatch me.

"It was too much of a hothouse, when I look back on it. We spent too much time studying and too little time around other people. We were too wrapped up in one another. We used to work all night and then fall asleep on the same bed together. Elgarson had a very beautiful mistress then, but by the time I was sixteen, I fancied myself in love with him, and like the silly child I was, I told Jok about it. It devastated Jok. I think he was afraid of losing both of us; Elgarson to his woman, and me to Elgarson. They started arguing with each other more and more often.

"They were working on some major project then; something that Elgarson was interested in. Extracting valuable minerals from deep underground. Something went wrong. I'm not sure what. In any case, Elgarson almost died. He didn't wake up for three days, and when he did he was—" Loga stopped and took a long drag of his cigarette.

"His magic was gone. Or blocked, somehow. He could still work a bit with Jok, but he was incapable of performing any magic on his own. He was absolutely beside himself at first, and then he fell into melancholy, and then he became obsessed with finding a way to get it back. We all went along with it for a time, but when it became clear that nothing was working, Jok stopped wanting to help. Elgarson was such a bright young man; he had any number of other avenues available to him. Jok would rather have him happy as a solicitor than miserable as a failed wizard. But I was still mad to do anything Elgarson asked of me, so when he came up with a plan to have me direct a strong burst of energy to a certain part of his brain, I did exactly as he asked. He fell to the ground and never moved again."

Loga drew a long breath. "Jok—" He stopped. Swallowed. Tried again. "He wouldn't believe he was dead. He kept asking about him. *Where's Elgarson, where's my brother?* They had to put up guards around the body because Jok kept trying to wake him up. First just as if Elgarson was sleeping, and then, when he understood what had happened, with his magic. He wanted to bring him back. His parents wanted his body sent back to Daeslund, but at last Lady Bawu had them burn the corpse because it was the only way we could ensure that Jok wouldn't try anything terrible. She had to lock Jok in his room and surround the whole room with bindings so he wouldn't try to keep them from taking Elgarson away. He screamed for days. *Days.* Until he couldn't make a sound anymore. I still heard him, even then."

He stopped speaking. When Loga raised his hand to take a sip of tea, Onna noticed the fine tremor in it. "Lady Bawu sent me to Monsatelle to complete my schooling at the academy. After my first few weeks, I got my first letter from Jok. He never blamed me, not for a moment. Never accused me of anything. He came to visit me at school, two years later, and was just as sweet to me as he had ever been. We've stayed in touch ever since. But there are still times when he seems to— drift. Especially when he sees me have an attack. He's so frightened of my dying, too, and leaving him alone."

He swallowed. "You must see now why I don't want him chased down like some criminal. If it does turn out that he is somehow related to these deaths, it may be that he's—" Loga's voice cracked slightly. "I'm afraid that he's the one who's been doing this. I'm afraid that he thinks he might be able to bring his brother back, or keep me from dying as well, and I *won't* put him down like a mad dog, I *can't*—" He closed his eyes for a moment. "If it's him, I will be responsible for him. I have an estate in Sango, quite far away from everything. I'll keep him there with me. I'll keep him away from the world for the rest of my life. But I won't turn him over to the authorities. I won't see him executed. I've killed two men, and I live like a prince and do as I please. It would be *just* for me to make a prison for the two of us, if my murdering his brother has—" Loga stopped short and closed his eyes. His face had turned very gray.

Onna grasped his other hand. "Loga! Are you going to be ill again? Is there anything that I can do?"

He was grinding his teeth. "I—take it, take some of it, *please*—" He squeezed her hand harder, and her face went numb. There was a single instant in which she seemed to be looking at herself through Loga's eyes. Then a wonderful, breathless rush of energy and joy and mindless animal pleasure. She laughed. "Oh! Oh, *golly*! What was *that*?"

Loga let go of her hand and leaned back against his pillows. Some of the color had already returned to his face. "I gave you some of my magic. I hope that you don't mind, darling."

"Mind?" Her skin felt as if it was shimmering. Fireworks were going off behind her eyes. She wished that he hadn't let go of her hand. "*Goodness*."

He smiled—more toothily than usual, she thought. "Ah, yes. I remember when it felt like that. Unfortunately, it doesn't last." He covered a yawn with his hand. "*Heavens*, but I feel better."

"I'm very glad," she said. "What do you mean that you gave me some of your magic?"

"Exactly what I said, darling. The Lord-Mage of Hexos takes on a certain amount of magic as a burden of the position. There's an alarmingly large pile of parameters in a vault under the Directress's palace to back up the whole system: I'll show you one day, if you like. In the ordinary course of things, I would have preferred to start this process twenty years from now, but one must make allowances for circumstance, mustn't one? I'm so glad that you've already proved yourself such a gem: I would have had to start transferring my magic over anyway, to avoid dropping dead in the next six months or so, but it's wonderfully comforting to know that I am not transferring the terrible and wondrous power of all of the wizards who came before me to a dithering ninny."

As always, when Loga spoke, Onna had to ignore a great deal of what he said in order to identify the bits that weren't silly nonsense, and as she managed this, her eyes widened.

"You're making me the Lord-Mage?"

"I'm beginning the process. What on earth are you looking so shocked about? What exactly did you think being my apprentice entailed?"

"I—I don't know! I didn't think it entailed *that!*"

"Oh, don't play at disliking the idea," he said with a little smile. "You wouldn't have come across the seas to Hexos to audition for the role if you weren't ambitious to the bone. I always find this sort of thing dreadfully unconvincing in novels. 'Oh *no*, I couldn't *possibly* marry you and become a duchess, for I am but a simple milkmaid and so long promised to the butcher's boy!' What terrible rubbish. In any case, you *must* take my magic at some point if you want to stay on as my assistant—I need someone who's willing to take the job on—though you *do* always have the option of wallowing in self-satisfaction over your own virtuous martyrdom on my behalf, if reveling in your triumph doesn't suit."

Onna stared as a giddy smile tugged at the corners of her mouth, though part of her was more inclined to burst into tears. "I suppose that it must suit."

He smiled back. "I thought so."

She reached for her piles of paper, which had remained on the floor, forgotten, as he told his story. "Are you well enough now to talk about parameters?"

"Always, darling. Do you have anything brilliant to show me?"

She managed a smirk. "Always, darling."

She was, in fact, proud of the neat little set of parameters she had made. They were based on the work of a Daeslundic wizard—here Loga interrupted her to say that she should leave acknowledging the work of other people to a footnote at the very end of her presentation—who had been hired by a headman farmer to create a better way to keep track of a flock of sheep. What he had come up with was simple enough: a massive grid laid out over the headman's property and corresponding to a scale version of the same grid kept in the farmer's office. Each sheep was fitted with a collar that set off a signal in the grid whenever an animal moved into a new square. This was, of course, an utter absurdity as a way to track livestock—for the expense of keeping the thing running, the farmer could have hired a dozen able shepherds—but perfectly suited to Onna's requirements. The principal difference was the trigger that would communicate with the grid: in Onna's version, the signal would be set off any time a troll shed blood, and a protective barrier would appear around the troll—and expel any human standing near at hand—until Onna arrived to disable it.

Loga approved, broadly, of her plan, though he added some notes to the margins of her work. Once satisfied with his alterations, he said, "Have you made any allowances for half trolls?"

She frowned. "What do you mean?"

"Well, darling, if your parameters demand that humans be expelled from inside of your protective barrier while trolls are trapped within, and if our half-troll friend Tsumelle we met the other day were to slip and skin his knee within your grid, mightn't we find ourselves the inadvertent perpetrators of a vivisection?

Onna winced. "Oh, goodness. But how shall I account for that?"

"I leave you to that problem; I'm afraid that I'm dreadfully tired. Besides which, it isn't good for you to have answers handed to you."

She drew herself up slightly. "I've never in my life had answers handed to me. It was always *me* who was expected to hand answers to everyone else, and smile while I was doing it."

"And look ever so grateful for the opportunity to do so! I *know*, darling. That's why you will be the Lord-Mage of Hexos one day. But I won't allow my admiration of you to spoil you on the vine." He slipped down under his blankets. "Wake me tomorrow morning, and we'll discuss your brilliance over breakfast."

The next few days for Onna were comprised chiefly of devilishly hard work. After a few days of drearily laboring over her parameters, she at last was satisfied with what she had written, and she asked Loga to check them for anything that would cause accidental vivisection. He declared them perfect, and then she moved on to the next step: laying out the grid itself, which necessitated a great deal of trudging about the city and stopping every few yards to solder a small battery (these had been designed with Loga's assistance) to the nearest stable bit of cobblestone before filling it with a small amount of her own magic.

She had expected to be completely alone in this endeavor, but to her astonishment Loga threw himself wholeheartedly into assisting her in her labors every afternoon after luncheon. He claimed it was a new way to introduce more healthful exercise into his day. In any case, after long, dreary mornings of working on her own, she was always very pleased to have his chatter to amuse her through the afternoons, especially when the exertion of filling the batteries made her cross and light-headed.

One evening Loga pulled her away from her labors to attend a dinner party, and she was surprised—and quite delighted—to be seated next to Haran. He was dressed in what appeared to be the same suit he had worn to Loga's auditions, and he talked with a great degree of animation about his work at the hospital. In fact, he said, he was organizing a tour of the surgical ward for potential sponsors of his research in two days. "Finnbair has been good enough to arrange for Judge Schutts to be there, so there's hope that my funding will be increased, if the old man takes it into his head to be generous." He sighed and raked his hand through his hair with a rueful little grin. "As my budget stands I can barely afford to continue the program. I can't train everyone on the new protocols all on my own, so I'll need at least a part-time assistant. I'll have to reduce my living stipend to make up the difference."

"That's *terribly* good of you," Onna said admiringly.

"Oh, no, it's all very selfish," he said, smiling. "If the infection rate goes up again because I couldn't properly train the nurses on ward six, then that's two years of research that have been contaminated."

"Couldn't you ask your father for help?"

"Never!" he said. He laughed a little. "I've made a vow to only accept the charity of strangers, like any other academic. I would never be able to respect myself if I was reduced to going to my father with my hat in my hand."

Onna nodded, but she privately thought that, though it was very noble to stand on one's own two feet and refuse support from one's wealthy father, all things being equal she would have preferred having wealthy parents whose support she could refuse, rather than being denied the option entirely.

Haran then inquired about her own project, with a meaningful glance. She leaned a little closer, confiding. "I spoke to Loga," she murmured. "I *believe* that he was honest with me. He's only studying his own brain, nothing else. I'm afraid that he's very ill."

Haran nodded, his shoulders relaxing slightly. "I'm glad," he said quietly. "Not that he's ill, of course. But I wouldn't want to think of him mixed up in something like that."

"He may still be," Onna said, just as soft. "Not directly. But—the other person."

"Oh," Haran said, with a little frown. "I do hope not. He's always seemed like such a kind man. Very gentle, you know. He's lovely with the children at the hospital, when he visits."

They changed the topic then to a louder and drier discussion of parameters, which would be incomprehensible to most of their fellow guests and thus perfectly safe to speak about in public. Haran asked a great number of intelligent questions about the grid and the batteries and her parameters for identifying troll blood. Her mouth became very dry from all of this discussion, but the party was blessed with a supply of very fine Esiphian wine, so it did not remain dry for long. They talked and drank for so long and so happily that they barely noticed when the other guests began to leave the dining room for the garden, until at last they were alone with the empty dishes, and, overwhelmed by a moment of perfect accord on a point of somewhat controversial theory on preventing energy surges in long-term constructions, Haran leaned over and kissed her.

Onna had never been kissed before. It was interesting, she thought, how the mouth of another person could be sour from wine and still make one's whole body light up like a lamp.

She giggled. He apologized. She demurred. He clasped her hand and said some very silly, very fervent things. She giggled some more. Loga appeared, as if attracted like a fairy by the scent of young love, and caused a great deal of consternation. Haran went very pink and stammered all sorts of even sillier and more fervent things to Loga.

Loga, for his part, laughed himself sick, told Haran that he was a precious puppy, and told Onna that they were going home immediately.

They walked back to the Lamp—Loga said that the fresh air would do Onna good—and she leaned heavily on his arm and sighed. It was raining, in a fashion, a sort of warm mist that couldn't quite decide whether to turn into one of Hexos's sudden, hair-soaking downpours.

"Haran wants to *court* me," Onna said.

"So I heard, darling! And do you want to be courted by him?"

"He's *very* handsome."

"He is!"

"And *very* clever."

"Indeed!"

"But I don't know if I *shall* only walk out with one gentleman just yet. Maybe I shall live in the Lamp and have heaps of lovers, like you."

"Gracious, darling! Speak more softly: you're only confirming the public's darkest impressions of my moral influence on Hexos's youth." They reached a puddle, and to spare her slippers, Loga scooped her up and carried her over it. She giggled.

"How did you do that? I'm bigger than you are."

He set her gently back onto her feet. "You are *not*. I'm *slender*, not *diminutive*. And I used magic, of course. What's the good of being a wizard if one must still put one's back out in the name of chivalry?"

"Do you do that with all of the girls you walk home?"

"Only the ones who are as dazzlingly brilliant as they are devastatingly attractive."

She cast him a suspicious look. "I'm not nearly as pretty as your young lady." Loga's young lady was beautiful in a very elegant and grown-up way that Onna despaired of ever achieving for herself.

"I never made the claim, darling, though you are quite as pretty as any other fresh-faced seventeen-year-old girl. I said that you were *attractive*, which is something different entirely. *Pretty* is what one calls a pair of silk slippers or a potted orange tree. It loses its interest. No one is *pretty* after one has stared at them for fifteen years over the breakfast table. *Attractiveness* is a function of personality. Prettiness is lent to you by youth; attractiveness is purchased with experience."

She giggled again. "You do talk nonsense, Loga!"

"I know," he said. "I've been told that there are those who find it very charming."

"I suppose that *you* think it is. Will you have a lover visiting tonight?"

"What cheek! I shall not, in fact. I abandoned a very lovely young lady in the garden when one of the servants told me that my protégée was making very radical choices about her evening's entertainment in the supper room. Though I would never deny you the right to make your own decisions in these matters, I thought you would be better served by making them sober, especially since you are only seventeen."

"I'm eighteen in three weeks! And you needn't have worried, you know; Haran is a perfect gentleman."

"Exactly. There is nothing quite as hazardous to the happiness of young girls as a perfect young gentleman."

"Or the Lord-Mage of Hexos."

"You wound me! To virtuous young girls I am a very lamb. I only present an amusement to their wicked elder sisters."

"How old must their elder sisters be?"

He raised his eyebrows. "Much, much older than seventeen, pet. Decades older. *Centuries*."

"You needn't talk like *that*. You shan't seduce *me*. Don't think *you're* so very impressive, Loga!"

"I certainly would never be foolish enough to make such a mistake! It would take a very impressive creature indeed to deserve *your* attention."

"You're awfully old, anyway," she said—he was in his early thirties, at least, which if very young for a powerful wizard struck Onna as a very *paternal* sort of age for a gentleman—and at this he only laughed.

When they arrived back at the Lamp, Onna was stumbling too much to manage the magical stairs, so Loga escorted her into her rooms. She flopped down into one of the elegant chairs. "Stay and talk more nonsense, Loga!"

He shook his head and smiled. "You should go to bed. I suppose that Mrs. Macosti is asleep. Can you manage to undress yourself?"

"I suppose that I did without servants for the first seventeen years of my life!" she said pertly, and nearly fell out of her chair trying to undress herself.

"Stand up and let me help you with that, darling."

She did so, though she continued to be pert. "You are *very* scandalous, Loga. What would Mrs. Cordram say?"

"Though I have never met that worthy lady, I can imagine that she would say any number of things entirely uncomplimentary to my person. There, darling, I've undone the back for you: the rest will be easy enough for you to manage alone."

"But I don't want to be alone," she said, and grasped at his hand. "I'll be lonely."

He looked at her, his eyebrows drawn together. "Are you often lonely, darling?"

"Sometimes," she said. "Are you?"

"Always," he said quietly, and kissed her cheek. "Good night, Miss Onna. Dream well."

She smiled foolishly at him, pleased to have been kissed twice in one night. It struck her that perhaps she should have attended better to what had just happened, but the thought escaped her. "Good night!" she said, and promptly crawled into her bed to fall asleep fully dressed.

She woke up the next morning feeling somewhat ill, fairly delighted, and very foolish. This was not helped in the least by Loga's relentless teasing about Haran, especially when an invitation arrived for both of them to attend a formal hospital tour the next day. Still, when she fretted over what to wear—she had only her own worn dresses and her party clothes—he called in his tailor to make up something that would create the proper wizardly effect. The three of them concocted a neat little dress of black silk with white trimmings, which echoed the severe black Leiscourt suit without making her look as if she were trying to disguise herself as a man.

"You look *wonderfully* academic," said Loga, surveying her with great satisfaction before they left for the tour. Loga himself was wearing an extremely frivolous-looking concoction in pale pink. She supposed that, in his case, it wasn't that the right costume made him look like a wizard, but that whatever he wore had no choice but to surrender to the inevitable and look like a wizard's costume.

The hospital tour was surprisingly enlightening. It was less than edifying in terms of the research itself, as it was intended for donors, not wizards, and focused largely on the great advancements some of the surgical wizards were making in their techniques and how Haran's systems for improved sanitation were ensuring that more patients made it home alive and well. They visited the children's ward last, and Matti looked so sweet and cunning in her tiny pink tunic and hospital slippers—like a miniature Lord-Mage—that Onna felt quite sure that the entire program would be funded on the spot.

To Onna, more interesting than the tour were three of her fellow participants: Haran's supervisor, Magister Dorabri, who was tall and elegant and greeted Onna with warmth and kindness despite his frosty reception of Loga; Judge Schutts; and his personal wizard, Mr. Jok Finnbair. Mr. Finnbair gave Onna and Loga a little wave of greeting when he entered, but he had no time to exchange pleasantries, as he was far too occupied with his employer.

Onna had heard very little about Judge Schutts, and all that she had heard was bad. She was pleased to have the chance to observe him in the flesh and made sure to position herself so that she could stare without being discovered. He was a short, stout, gray-haired gentleman in what seemed to be robust good health, with a broad face and a slow, highly enunciated manner of speech. He had a curious way of walking, with his arms held very stiffly at his sides, and a face that seemed capable of expressing no emotions outside of boredom or mild, ironic amusement. He spoke only in Nessoran—at one point Loga informed her that he was perfectly capable of speaking Daeslundic, but he generally did not like to do so, even when Onna was standing directly in front of him—and as he was the richest man present, everyone else followed suit, so Onna was forced to float along in a state of dull incomprehension. Matters were only made worse by the clouds of perfume that wafted in Judge Schutts's wake, which were strong enough to make Onna feel quite giddy whenever she was caught behind him. Fortunately, he walked very slowly, so she managed to keep herself a pace or two ahead for most of the tour.

Loga offered to cast a translation for her, but she flatly refused, fearing it would trigger another of his fits. In lieu of the translation spell he simply whispered into her ear whenever Judge Schutts said anything he found particularly amusing in its awfulness, such as, "The *children* are all well and good, but what's the benefit of investing in this program?" Or, in reference to a passing nurse, "I had a girl who looked like her when I was last in Mendosa."

Onna watched him talk for a time with an irritating sense of recognition. She had a strange sense that he had been at her examination at Weltsir, but this of course was nonsense: he couldn't possibly have been there. Then she remembered: he was the man in the square when she first came to Hexos, haranguing the students about how trolls oughtn't be allowed to participate in Loga's audition. She glanced toward Loga and whispered, "Did you know that your friend's employer gives speeches against trolls in the town square?"

Loga looked taken aback and shook his head, murmuring, "I'm not surprised. He's been lobbying the clan-heads of Cwydarin for years to try to get one of his representatives into a troll medical education institution as part of his immortality project. Making Hexos inhospitable to young trolls might be an attempt on his part to apply pressure on Cwydarin."

When Haran described how certain healing techniques used by medical wizards could inadvertently cause rapid growth of bacteria if proper precautions weren't taken, Judge Schutts pricked up his ears. "Ah, Finnbair," he said suddenly in Daeslundic. "It's like what you were saying about the troll blood."

For a moment Onna thought that Mr. Finnbair looked embarrassed or annoyed, but the moment passed quickly. "Yes, sir. It does sound as if it's similar," Mr. Finnbair said.

Judge Schutts addressed Haran. "Finnbair is of the opinion that troll blood could be used to stave back aging. What do you think of that, Welder?"

Poor Haran looked nonplussed. "Well, I suppose—I must say that I haven't done any research into—"

"I'm afraid that I may have been unclear about my theory, my lord," said Mr. Finnbair, his voice clipped. "I think that it might be possible to learn more about *why* trolls are so long-lived by studying how their blood is different from ours. I don't think it's *unicorn* blood, sir. It won't make you younger to drink it."

"Well, what's the damn use of your leaving all of that blood around my house, then?"

Then Loga said something airy in Nessoran that made everyone laugh, and the tour continued. However, at the first opportunity, Onna walked up to Mr. Finnbair—doing her utmost to appear sweet and artless even as she was practically shaking with nerves, since she had no idea how Loga might respond to what she was about to do—and said, "Mr. Finnbair, I thought what you were just saying was terribly interesting. Do you suppose that you might let me take a look at your research notes?"

Mr. Finnbair frowned, but before he could respond, Judge Schutts broke in, speaking Daeslundic so perfectly that Onna found herself even more irritated about his earlier refusal to address her: "Certainly not! I know how you wizards operate. If you get a peek at his notes, the next thing I know your employer will have published his findings in some journal, and all of my investments in this project will go to waste."

Loga raised his eyebrows and gave a lazy, ironic smile that Onna thought would make most people regret their every transgression, from a second helping at breakfast to the lies they told their mother when they were six. "Really, sir, I'm insulted by the suggestion that I'm anything but *entirely* ethical in my academic dealings."

She barely heard a word of what was said for the rest of the tour, but she kept herself well enough in check to hold her tongue until she and Loga were safely concealed within his palanquin, at which point she whirled upon him.

"It must be Mr. Finnbair. Or his employer, probably, with his assistance."

Loga shrugged one shoulder. "I must say that I wouldn't be entirely *surprised* to learn that Schutts was involved in a series of murders. He's the sort of man I imagine would stop at very little to achieve his goals."

"And what are you going to do about it?"

He picked at a stray thread on his robe. "Nothing."

"*What?*"

He looked up. "*You*, darling, will activate that charming grid system we've been working away at so diligently. And *I* will wait to see who we scoop up in our little net before I take any drastic actions."

"So you'll wait for someone else to die before you do anything to stop them."

He met her gaze. His face was very still, more still than she had ever seen, with a strange coolness, and it seemed to her that she was really seeing him for the first time. He said, "I killed two men by the time I was sixteen. I'm sure I'll find myself in hell in any case."

"In the prophet Elgar's letters he wrote that there is no hell. There's only the baser urges of our own hearts, which we can struggle against."

"Well, darling, Elgar never came to Hexos."

She swallowed and began to feel ill. She expected Loga, the very person who had encouraged her to investigate these murders, to immediately swoop in and end this dreadful injustice, not to shrug as if it hardly mattered at all. "You're not—it's not right. It's wicked."

"I suppose so. But listen, darling. Judge Schutts is investing in the schools I'm building in my home region in Sango. As it is, we have no evidence other than vague suspicions against him, and if we start throwing out wild accusations, we might end up with nothing to show for it but dozens of very disappointed little children who will never learn to read. As far as Jok goes, I absolutely refuse to accuse him of anything without proof. I value our friendship far too much for that." He gave another disinterested little shrug. "It's funny, really. One can be the greatest wizard in the world and still be dreadfully afraid of dying. I want there to be someone with me at the end to hold my hand, and I'm afraid that if I accuse Jok of murder unjustly, it will ruin my chances."

Onna's throat felt very tight. "You're not going to die."

He smiled at her. "Oh, Onna," he said. "Aren't you the one who's so opposed to the concept of immortality?"

None of this was right. Not his refusal to become righteously furious on the behalf of the trolls who had been killed, and still less his refusal to become angry on his own behalf, to rage against what was happening to his own brain and body. Onna's eyes stung, and she swallowed hard. Then she smiled back at him because for the life of her she didn't know what else she ought to do. "Well," she said. "You mustn't die just yet. We have work to do."

Back in the Lamp, Loga helped her to activate the grid. It took more power than she thought it would. When they were finished, he slumped against the huge table, his breath coming in short gasps. The wizard-lamps in the room had flickered on as the sun set, and they made it very evident how gray his skin had gone and how terribly sunken his cheeks were. He had grown thinner in the few weeks that she had known him. She spoke lightly. "I do hope you haven't made any social engagements for us tonight. I'd much rather eat those special noodles that Mrs. Macosti made the other day with you here at the Lamp."

He nodded and sat down with a thump. "That sounds lovely." He brushed a strand of hair from his face with a shaking hand. "Should I call Mrs. Macosti?"

"No," Onna said quickly, "I'll do it."

He smiled. "You don't know how."

"Then *teach* me, or I'll just wander all about the Lamp calling her name until I find her."

"My," he said, "how forceful you are, Onna! Just a few weeks ago you were so overawed by me that you could barely look me in the eye. How things do change!"

"Well," Onna said, "when it comes to talking overconfident nonsense, I've had a very accomplished teacher."

He laughed, and at the same moment one of the little bells above the miniature grid rang.

Onna looked up in a panic. "But I haven't planned yet what to do once it goes off!"

Loga raised his eyebrows. "Are you joking? No, I can see that you're quite serious, I beg your pardon. Do you know how to teleport yourself?"

"Are *you* joking? No one in Daeslund has managed that in fifty years! I would end up as a fine spray!"

"Actually, you'd be more likely to lose track of yourself midway and end up—elsewhere. Fortunately, I'm very good at it. Hold on, darling," he said, and before Onna had the time to do so much as shriek in horror, they were on a dark street that Onna didn't recognize.

As soon as she could focus her eyes—her head was spinning so badly that she thought she might be sick—Onna looked around and immediately saw the troll. He was standing very still inside the dome of magic, illuminated by the light of the street lamps, watching quietly as a man flung himself repeatedly against the barrier. A human man just about the size and shape of Mr. Finnbair.

Though he bounced violently off of the barrier, the man seemed prepared to do it again and again, and Onna couldn't help but shriek, "Oh no, *stop!*"

The man whirled to face her. She started.

He was a stranger: a tall, handsome man wearing a fashionable Daeslundic suit and gripping a cane in one hand. His hair was long and dark brown, and his skin quite pale. He would have looked like the romantic hero of one of her mother's novels if he didn't also look as if he wanted to get his hands around someone's neck. As it was, she took an involuntary quick step backward.

Then he saw her, and the corners of his mouth curled up into a vacant smile. He spoke in a soft drawl. "I say, are you Daeslundic? How *frightfully* good to see you here! My friend has gotten himself trapped inside of this demmed thing, and we're having a devil's own time getting him out, what?"

Onna could only stare, utterly nonplussed. She didn't know what she had expected to find—she had hoped, at least, not Mr. Finnbair—but certainly not a frightfully handsome, rather silly member of the Daeslundic headmanship.

Eventually she gathered her wits enough to speak. "I should certainly be very glad to assist your *friend*, sir, since I am the one who made this barrier."

The man's eyes narrowed, and the silly smile vanished. "You did this?"

She addressed the troll. "Excuse me? Do you speak Daeslundic?"

The troll nodded. "Yeah."

As Onna regarded the troll fully for the first time, she saw that he looked like Tsumelle, the young half-troll gentleman she and Loga had met previously. This troll was, like Tsumelle, handsome. His face made Onna think of one of Elgar's knights: a strong, stark-looking face that was made more intimidating by the gray-blue skin and sharp teeth. He would, she thought, make a very inspiring general or assemblor. There was an air of command to his wide-legged, straight-backed stance and to the level way his yellow eyes met Onna's. Then something occurred to Onna about the boldness of his gaze. "May I ask your name?"

"Cynallumwyntsira," said the troll. "Tsira."

"I beg your pardon, but I don't suppose that you're a *Miss* Tsira?"

The troll grinned. "Yeah."

Onna turned to face the man. "I would think, sir, that you would know the actual sex of your *friend*." Her heart was pounding. "I am arresting you in the name of the Lord-Mage of Hexos."

"*What?*" The man looked incredulous. "What *crime* have I committed—misstating the sex of a troll to an officer of the law? Who in the releft *are* you, anyway?"

"She's my protégée," Loga said, stepping forward, "and I would be *delighted* if you would be so kind as to speak to her more respectfully, darling."

The man glowered down at him, which was not especially difficult, as he was an athletic-looking man, much bigger than Loga. "I deal respectfully with those who deal respectfully with me, sir, and I will thank *you* not to address me as your *darling*, when you have not so much as introduced yourself to me, and your so-called protégée has attempted to arrest me in the absence of any charges."

Loga looked delighted, which Onna thought boded ill for this gentleman. "Lord Wuzan Zilon, Lord-Mage of Hexos, *at* your service. This is my charming young successor, Onna Gebowa. And *your* name?"

The man colored slightly and gave a stiff little bow. "Jeck Smith, your grace."

Loga raised an eyebrow, clearly enjoying himself immensely. "Oh, are we using pseudonyms? How delightful! But had I only known I would have said my name was Topsy Borrowsworth. *Come* now, try to be serious before I become impatient."

The man's flush deepened. "Phillim Kail Jeckran, sir. If you would only let my friend out of this—cage, we would be glad to be on our way."

Onna addressed the troll again. "Miss Tsira, is this man really a friend of yours?"

She nodded, still grinning. "Yeah. My partner."

"And did he attack you just now?"

She shook her head. "No. Some local boys did. Threw a rock at my head." The sound of Tsira's voice made the anxious rolling of Onna's stomach ease. All trolls had deep voices, of course, but Miss Tsira had quite the loveliest voice Onna had ever heard.

Onna could see Mr. Jeckran relax as well, though his brow was still furrowed. "She's injured," he said. "And I can't do anything to help her as long as she's trapped in that magic *box* of yours."

Onna, satisfied at last that he wouldn't try to kill any trolls *straightaway*—at worst he might irritate Miss Tsira a bit—mentally ran the parameters to disable the wall. As soon as it came down, Mr. Jeckran was at the troll's side, suddenly as sweet as someone's nice old auntie. "Kneel down for me, boss. I need to look at the back of your head."

"I'm fine."

Mr. Jeckran's voice was still oddly quiet, and the drawl seemed genuine. Definitely a member of a headman's clan, Onna thought, but one who was silly when it suited him. He said to Miss Tsira, "I'm sure that you are, but I would appreciate it if you could humor me nevertheless."

Miss Tsira mumbled something in her own language, and he, to Onna's surprise, shot back in kind. The troll sighed and went down on her knees in one smooth motion, like a cat jumping down from a window-sill. He inspected the wound on the back of her head. "It's stopped bleeding, at least. We'll need to clean it." He punched her shoulder.

She stood, and Onna was struck again by her enormous height and how comfortable Mr. Jeckran seemed to be in her presence. In her brief experience with trolls, Onna had always found herself very aware of their proximity—and how much *bigger* they were—and she had noticed Loga and Mr. Finnbair maintaining a certain distance from them. This man, on the other hand, seemed to think nothing of bossing about and punching a person who was almost two feet taller than him and had a grin like a crocodile.

Both the human and the troll, she realized, with a sudden thrill of discomfort, were now staring at her. Mr. Jeckran lifted his chin slightly. "Are we free to go?"

"Well, my moonbeam, you were never technically under arrest, but we would rather like to have a word with the both of you before you continue," Loga said.

Mr. Jeckran slid his eyes toward Loga with a look so magnificently frigid that Onna was quite sure it could transform a vapor into a solid. "What about, *sir*?"

Onna had never before heard the word *sir* pronounced so much like *you vile little beast*.

Loga smiled placidly. "About your attackers. Did they seem wizardly or at all villainous in aspect? Did you note any degree of interest in your vital organs? *Do* think carefully, honeypot; it's important, and we are pressed for time."

The troll spoke. "Murders happening here, too, then?"

Onna's eyes widened. "What? You know about the murders?"

"They're why we came to this damned island in the first place,"

Mr. Jeckran said, followed quickly by, "I beg your pardon, Miss Geb-owa, for my language. I'm afraid that it's been a long time since I've been in the presence of a young lady, and my habits of speech have become rather coarse."

"*Thanks*," said Miss Tsira.

Mr. Jeckran looked up at her and smiled. "Don't be clever, boss," he said. "I didn't say anything about being in the presence of a great hulking reig of *incredibly* advanced years."

Onna gaped at this, but Miss Tsira only laughed and cuffed him on the back of the head. "*You* like it all right."

Mr. Jeckran grinned, and it struck Onna that there was something very unfair about the ways in which people were matched with their faces. Haran, who was always smiling, was at his handsomest when he was looking thoughtful and grave, while the perpetually scowling Mr. Jeckran had the sort of smile that was used to sell patent medicines.

Loga steered the conversation back to the topic at hand. "I'm afraid that this is all very deep going for me, darling, so you must bear with me while I endeavor to comprehend. What do the murders have to do with your coming to Hexos, precisely?"

"They killed my ma," Miss Tsira said. "We tracked them here."

"I'm so sorry," Onna said, shocked despite herself. Though she understood the seriousness of the riddle she was trying to solve, Miss Tsira's obvious grief still hit her like a bucket of ice water.

Loga nodded. "And so you're out for vengeance, of course. And you, Mr. Jeckran? What reason do you have to involve yourself in this particular intrigue?"

Mr. Jeckran answered at once. "Tsira is my partner, your grace. I go where she goes."

Loga raised his eyebrows. "Your partner in what business, exactly?"

Again there was no hesitation. "Private security."

"You're *mercenaries*!" Loga said. "How wonderfully romantic. I suppose that you must be the brawn, Tsira, and I daresay you provide the majority of the brains of the operation as well. What exactly is your partner's role?"

"Mostly talking posh and looking pretty," Miss Tsira said. "And he can put a bullet through a playing card at fifty paces."

"Heavens," Loga said, "how wonderfully virile of you, Mr. Jeckran. I may swoon."

"If you do, your grace," Mr. Jeckran said, "I would recommend doing so in my partner's direction. I can make no assurances that I would catch you."

His partner, for her part, seemed amused. "You flirt like that with everyone, wizard?"

"Oh, no. It's only that your partner is so wonderfully charming and pleasant to converse with," Loga said.

Onna couldn't help but giggle, though Mr. Jeckran scowled. Loga arched an eyebrow at Tsira and gave her half a smile. "In any case, you must call me Loga, Tsira. *You* may carry on calling me *your grace*," he said to Mr. Jeckran. "It makes all of the little hairs on the back of my neck stand up."

Mr. Jeckran's expression at this was so comical that Onna giggled again, then decided to intervene. "You mustn't mind him, Mr. Jeckran. He's only doing that to make you uncomfortable."

"How *dare* you question the depths of my sincerity, Onna," Loga said, and then winced and swayed slightly on his feet.

Onna barely saw Tsira move, but suddenly she was at Loga's side, steadying him with one enormous hand to his shoulder. "You all right?"

"Of course, I—" Loga went a terrible grayish color and collapsed. Onna yelped, but Tsira scooped him up into her arms before he hit the ground.

Onna rushed to her side. "Is he all right? He isn't—"

"Just fainted." She cast Onna a look. "Sickly, ain't he?"

"He's the greatest wizard in the world," Onna said, indignant. The troll gazed at her in silence until Onna had to look away. "Yes. He's ill."

"Where d'you want me to put him?"

"I, ah—oh, gracious," said Onna. "I don't suppose that you might be able to help me carry him home, Miss Tsira?"

"I suppose that would depend on you, Miss Gebowa," said Mr. Jeckran.

Onna turned to him. "What do you mean, Mr. Jeckran?"

"I mean that if my partner is to carry your employer to safety, then I think she should be able to expect some consideration in return."

"And what sort of consideration would that be, Mr. Jeckran?" Onna snapped. She was tired and worried about Loga and repulsed by such naked greed. "I suppose that Lord Wuzan can pay you for your time, if that's what you mean."

Tsira was the one to answer. "Don't give a shit about money."

"Watch your language, Tsira," Mr. Jeckran said, sounding so much like Mrs. Cordram that Onna was tempted to laugh. Mr. Jeckran, for his part, did not look at all as if he was in the mood for jokes. "If you're investigating these murders, Miss Gebowa, you should involve us. We've encountered at least one of the killers."

It was like being struck. Onna took a step backward to steady herself. "At least one of them? There's more than one? But that's—how do you know?"

"We killed one of them," Mr. Jeckran said.

"Didn't slow them down none," Tsira said, and in her deep voice Onna thought she heard the edge of something like exhaustion. Loga stirred slightly, and Tsira glanced down at him. "Hey."

"Yes, quite," Loga said, his voice a weak thread. "Be a dear and don't put me down just yet. I doubt I'll stay upright." He wrapped an arm around the troll's neck to steady himself and said, "Are you wearing *cologne*?"

"No."

Loga closed his eyes and rested his head against her chest. "Really? How fortunate I am to have swooned in the arms of someone who smells so naturally expensive."

Miss Tsira grinned. "Thanks."

Mr. Jeckran, who had been gritting his teeth through this, snapped out something in Tsira's native language. She responded very calmly in the same language and adjusted Loga slightly in her arms. "We going somewhere where we can talk?"

"I suppose so," Onna said. "We're going to the Lamp."

# 19

*A bit of boiled mutton is all right by me*
*Just feed me a scrap and how happy I'll be!*
*Not Nessoran sweets or rare Sangan stews*
*Show me trollish dainties I'll turn up me nose*
*Just a dry crust of bread and a girl on my knee*
*A bit of boiled mutton is all right by me!*
   —*Music hall song, "A Bit of Boiled Mutton," Leiscourt*

Jeckran would not give that wretched man the satisfaction of looking impressed.

The Lamp was a wonder, of course, from the perfect miniature world of its gardens to the elaborate carvings and vaulted ceilings of the main hall to the endless curving steps that would bring them to the glass-walled study. It was the grandest place he had ever seen, and in his childhood he had visited the home of a Daeslundic first headman. That old pile now seemed absurd, in comparison, like something a child would piece together out of building blocks. This place was a miracle. But Lord Wuzan kept watching him from the corners of his eyes, his lips quirked in a way that Jeckran found intolerable, and he would *not* satisfy that look by marveling at his home.

It was for the best, he supposed, that they had fallen in with the Lord-Mage. It would end this sooner, get them home more quickly. Still, he chafed at having to bow and scrape to a smirking ass like Lord Wuzan. Everything about the man set Jeckran's teeth on edge. He was exactly the sort of cocksure, well-dressed fellow who had tormented Jeckran to distraction at school, only to start a glittering career in the

Assemblage the day after graduation. It made Jeckran want to punch him in the nose.

The Lord-Mage seemed to fall asleep in Tsira's arms as they climbed the stairs, which spared Jeckran from having to conceal how the climb made his limp worse and set him panting. It also gave him an opportunity to examine the Lord-Mage without having to listen to him talk. His face was handsome and youthful, though Jeckran suspected him of being older than he looked. His hair was black, a shade darker than Jeckran's own, and his skin a light brown. Jeckran sped his climb slightly to get closer to Tsira's side and spoke in Dacyn, heedless of his grammar.

"Remember the game we played in Monsatelle?" They'd passed any number of boring hours tramping about Monsatelle playing "wed him, bed him, or throw him in the sea."

She grinned. "Yeah. You're bedding the wizard?"

He felt vicious, and expressed the sentiment in his dreadful Dacyn. "And then throw him in the sea. Talks too much."

She cast him an amused glance. "He talks like you."

"*Fuck off*," he said, and nearly said it in Daeslundic before he remembered the girl. She, at least, was pleasant enough, and too much of a proper young lady to be subjected to his bad language. He wondered that she should be so attached to the Lord-Mage, who had no qualms about making disgusting innuendos within her hearing.

They finished the climb in relative quiet, and Jeckran was glad for the Lord-Mage's continued unconsciousness, which allowed him to gape freely at the glass-walled study at the top of the Lamp. He walked slowly around the edge of the room, marveling at the sight of Hexos spilling out in every direction below. The city was like a second night sky beneath his feet, the twinkle of oil and gas and candles and the steady red glow of the wizard-lamps continuing until they faded into darkness at the horizon.

"It's a lovely view, isn't it?"

Jeckran leapt nearly a foot into the air and pressed his hand against the glass, his heart pounding. Lord Wuzan had woken up. Jeckran steeled himself for laughter over how easily he started, but the man ignored it and kept talking, as if it was perfectly ordinary for grown men to leap about like midsummer's night dancers. "You've a wonderfully good head for heights. Most people can't manage to look out for so long the first time they come up here."

Jeckran was surprised to realize the Lord-Mage wasn't mocking him. "Thank you, sir."

"Have you eaten? Miss Gebowa and I were about to order dinner before we had the pleasure of making your acquaintance."

"We've eaten, thank you," he said, just as Tsira said, "Could eat." She had moved to stand next to him, and rested her hand briefly on his shoulder. He leaned into the touch for a moment, then stepped away, hoping neither of the wizards had noticed. "You could always eat, Tsira." He said to the Lord-Mage, "I'm sure we wouldn't want to trouble you, Magister."

The Lord-Mage smiled. "Really, *no one* calls me by my title. And it isn't any trouble. Do you like Hexian food, Tsira?"

She shrugged. "Like everything."

Jeckran noticed Tsira's flat expression had shifted from calm to rigid; she was uncomfortable. It occurred to him that her first meal of the evening probably hadn't gone very far to sate her after her weeks of being sick on board ship. "She generally prefers anything greasy or repulsively sweet," he told the Lord-Mage.

"Oh," said Miss Gebowa brightly. "I never thought of that, but of course that makes perfect sense, doesn't it? Miss Tsira, if you weigh about three and a half cask, you must need to eat about three times what a man of Mr. Jeckran's size would just to maintain weight if you're getting any sort of physical exercise. If you were to eat nothing but apples, you would have to eat, gracious, six dozen a day! So of course anything rich and stodgy would be much nicer, if you wanted to get anything done other than eating all the time. Do trolls eat a great deal of fat, traditionally? How do you keep yourselves fed if you're on the road?" She stopped in the face of Jeckran's amazed stare and looked away, fussing with some invisible bit of dust on the table beside her. "I'm sorry. I know that I'm a terrible bore when I go on like that."

"Not boring," Tsira said. "You can figure all that from looking at me?"

Miss Gebowa ducked her head and smiled. "It's a very silly little trick, really. I'm just—clever with numbers."

"Don't be modest, darling," said the Lord-Mage. "She's a genius."

Tsira nodded. "Thought so," she said. "We have special foods that we eat when we're doing a lot of work. Lots of nuts and honey in them, that kind of thing."

A middle-aged woman entered the room, and the Lord-Mage flourished a hand toward her. "Ah! Here is Mrs. Macosti." He entered into a spirited dialogue with the lady in question, who then departed. "Mrs. Macosti will bring us dinner shortly. Please, sit," the Lord-Mage said, with a precise gesture toward the huge table that dominated the center of the room. Jeckran and Tsira complied, as Jeckran studied the Lord-Mage curiously.

"Were you ever on the stage?"

The wizard looked surprised. "I was. Were *you*? It would certainly explain that accent."

"Why does everyone always remark on my *accent*?" Jeckran asked, nettled. "It isn't assumed."

"I'm sure they don't mean to laugh at you," Miss Gebowa said, with a quick, stern glance at her employer. "It's just that most people never hear that sort of accent in real life, so it sounds a bit like something from a play."

"Ah," Jeckran said. "I suppose that when one grows up surrounded with it, one doesn't attend to it at all. And you, Miss Gebowa? Where is your accent from? The Northwest, I should think? Near the coast?"

"Yes," she said. "Cordridge-on-Sea."

"Cordridge-on-Sea? Where they make the pencil erasers?"

She sighed. "Yes, that's the place."

"Jeckran," the Lord-Mage said suddenly. "Of course! Phillim Kail Jeckran. You're Fifth Headman Jeckran of Eastgate's son, the younger one." He raised his eyebrows. "You know, they really didn't do you justice in your obituary. How fortunate that you're not actually dead: you might make a few suggestions for improvements." He caught Miss Gebowa's incredulous look and shrugged. "I read the Daeslundic society papers."

Jeckran put his face into his hands. "My—good God. My poor mother." He raked his hands through his hair, then folded them in his lap. "Yes. You're right, sir. And you can see now why I travel under an assumed name. It might create—difficulties, if I was known to be alive."

He felt Tsira's hand at the small of his back, solid and reassuring. She stroked him with her thumb as the Lord-Mage made a dismissive gesture. "Of course, I shan't tell anyone about it if it's a matter of any importance. I'm perfectly capable of keeping my mouth shut if I have to, as unlikely as that may seem."

Jeckran was spared from having to articulate exactly how unlikely this seemed by the arrival of the food. They were each presented with a spoon, a fork, a knife, and a pair of chopsticks for choice. Tsira eyed the array with resignation. "Why do pinks always bring so many tools out to eat with? What do we got *hands* for?"

The Lord-Mage laughed. "You know, I was dreadfully alarmed the first time I saw someone cutting up their meat with a knife and fork at the table: I'd heard people in Sango say that Esiphians always keep a knife in their right hand so they can stab anyone who annoys them while they eat. But then I had a friend from Bundar tell me that her mother said people in foreign countries don't use their hands to eat because they never wash them, and after I was done feeling indignant, I tried to stop criticizing other people's cutlery."

Tsira cast Jeckran a look and served herself from a dish of spiced rice. "Well, *some* people never wash their hands."

Jeckran rolled his eyes at her. "You know perfectly well that I've fallen in line with your hand-washing requirements, Tsira, so you needn't look at me like that."

Along with various savory dishes, the servants had brought a platter of fruit, and the Lord-Mage began to eat a large yellow one. Jeckran was struck by its richly sweet, oddly familiar smell—which, he realized with a flush, reminded him partly of Tsira's sex. The Lord-Mage licked at a drop of juice rolling down his wrist.

Jeckran thought that he had best distract himself from that smell and that tongue. "Why do you bother eating?"

"What?" The Lord-Mage looked amused. "I'm a *wizard*, not a mechanical construct."

"I know that, but couldn't you—I don't know—do some type of spell that would keep you from having to eat regularly? Or just send nourishment directly into your body, or create a drink with everything you need in it so you wouldn't have to bother with actual food?"

"Heavens! I suppose that I could create something that would prevent me from starving to death, but why on earth would I want to? Where would be the pleasure in that? And in any case I doubt that anything like that would be *remotely* healthful. The body isn't an enemy force that needs to be suppressed. How dreadfully Elgarite of you."

"I suppose you're right. But I've often thought of how much time I would save if I didn't have to think about hunger or thirst or cold or that sort of thing."

"They have that," Tsira said. "Called being dead."

"There's more to life than eating, Tsira," Jeckran said.

"Yeah," said Tsira. "But it's one of the best parts. Along with reading and fucking. Sorry, miss," she added, with a nod toward Miss Gebowa.

The Lord-Mage threw back his head and cackled. "Hear, hear!"

Miss Gebowa cast him a disapproving look. "I agree with Mr. Jeckran. Think of everything that we could accomplish if we didn't always have to attend to our physical needs! I always hate to have to stop to sleep when I'm working."

"*Pinks*," Tsira said.

"*Daeslunders*," said the Lord-Mage, at the same moment. They grinned at each other—Tsira very toothily—and Jeckran glanced at Miss Gebowa and caught her look of commiseration. Tsira tapped a finger on Jeckran's spoon.

"Eat something."

"We've eaten."

She switched to Dacyn. "You look too thin. Eat."

"You're a dreadful mother hen," he said in Daeslundic, but he heeded the command and took an orange from the bowl of fruit. He hadn't had one in years and allowed himself to enjoy it: the sensation of his thumb breaking through the peel, the sudden perfume in the air, the way that the first segment burst between his tongue and the roof of his mouth. It was just like he had remembered.

He was startled by the Lord-Mage's laugh as he said, "So you *can* experience enjoyment, after all."

He flushed. "I haven't eaten an orange in years."

"Whyever not?"

"They're too dear," he said shortly.

Miss Gebowa looked startled. "But—aren't you a headman's son?"

The Lord-Mage smiled. "You don't read many terrible Daeslundic novels, do you? The impoverished headmen are just as thick on the ground as simpering shepherdesses who don't know how to recognize an opportunity when it presents itself in a crimson doublet."

Miss Gebowa finished chewing, swallowed, and dabbed her lips daintily with her napkin before replying. "My mother is the authoress of several popular three-volume novels, so I imagine that I know *almost* as much about them as you do, Loga. I always thought that the impoverished headmen were meant to be poor because they had only the cook and two housemaids and had to economize on footmen."

Jeckran laughed. "I know a few fellows of that sort as well. I think I'm more of a poor relation, the sort they always have sitting by the fire and listening in on conversations."

"Nah," said Tsira, suddenly. "You're a foreign duke in disguise. With a wounded expression and a noble brow and all that. And a dagger in your boot."

The Lord-Mage practically choked, he laughed so hard.

"Surely *you* don't read three-volume novels, Miss Tsira," Miss Gebowa said, smiling at Tsira in a way that made Jeckran decide that he quite liked her. So many humans were suspicious or in awe of her: this girl's warm, friendly regard was lovely to see.

"She's absolutely mad about them," Jeckran said. "She's read the second volume of *The Trials of Resalind* three times."

"Why only the second?" asked Miss Gebowa.

"They only had that one at the boardinghouse," Tsira said. Miss Gebowa smiled.

"But I have all three! My mother wrote them, and she insisted that I bring them when I came to Hexos."

"Your ma wrote them?" Tsira's eyes were slightly wider than was usual, and Jeckran almost laughed: she was like a girl waiting behind a theater for a glimpse of her favorite actor. "Could I borrow them?"

Miss Gebowa smiled. "Of course!"

The Lord-Mage said, "I'm dreadfully sorry, darlings, but if you've all finished eating, I really must bring up less pleasant matters. What can you tell us about the murders?"

They tried to get through it all quickly, but it took much longer than Jeckran had anticipated to provide all of the odd details that the two wizards demanded. They seemed very interested in Violet Chastonne's description of a young, handsome, thin man with a Hexian accent: Lord Wuzan seemed to take it as proof of something, while Onna insisted that it only proved whoever was responsible had hired several men both in and out of Hexos. It was their description of the wizard they had killed, though, that seemed to intrigue the Lord-Mage and his apprentice the most. Miss Gebowa sat up straighter in her chair. "You were unable to resist at all?"

Tsira nodded. "You ever dream about needing to run, but your legs don't work? Like that, but the other way around. Couldn't stop walking."

It had never occurred to Jeckran that Tsira might dream of being helpless. He wondered who those dreams might be worse for: her, because they were so beyond her experience, or him, because they weren't.

"How *terribly* interesting," said the Lord-Mage. "Did you hear, Onna? That means that it isn't necessarily someone who has had personal contact with the trolls so that they might recognize him. It could, indeed, be any wizard at all."

"I *did* hear, Loga," Miss Gebowa responded. She sounded pert. "But we've already established that it certainly must be someone who graduated from Weltsir because I recognized the magical signature."

"Indeed, Onna," the Lord-Mage said. "It could easily be any one of the *hundreds* of graduates of Weltsir who live here in Hexos. One simply *shudders* at the thought of the sheer number of potential suspects, don't you agree?"

"*Certainly*, Loga. Though there won't be nearly so many once we reduce it to only highly accomplished wizards who have recently been in Daeslund."

"As I am sure you will do *very* thoroughly by personally examining the records in the customs office."

Miss Gebowa's mouth opened, then closed. She turned to Jeckran. "Mr. Jeckran, do you think you could recognize Miss Tsira's attacker if you saw a photograph of him? The one called Chastonne?"

"Absolutely," Jeckran said at once. He sometimes thought he would remember that dead man's staring face for longer than he would remember his own mother's. *The first person I killed off the battlefield*, he thought, and he was brought up short by the fact that he had to qualify the context of his kills to make them exceptional. How many had it been now? The Mendosans, Chastonne, the girls at Catleen's—had it been more than a dozen? A score? They were substantial numbers, *alarming* numbers. What did numbers like that make a man?

*A monster*, some helpful part of his brain supplied.

Miss Gebowa spoke again. "Loga, did you know that Weltsir takes a photograph every year of the graduating class?"

The Lord-Mage's face went very still. To Jeckran he looked

completely terrified, which seemed an odd reaction to a class photo that presumably did not contain himself. Jeckran was always horrified by the single extant photograph of himself—it made him look the very image of his mother's mink stole—but he didn't see why anyone should be frightened by other people's class portraits. "No," the Lord-Mage said eventually. "I didn't know that."

"Well," Miss Gebowa said, with a sort of ferocious cheerfulness, "they do. Why don't you write a letter to the appropriate authorities and ask them to send you a copy of each picture from the past thirty years or so? If the wizard who attacked Miss Tsira was a student, then he'll appear in one of those photos, and we'll know his real name. Along with the names and faces of all of his classmates, men who might be associated with him."

"Clever," Tsira said, in tones of great admiration. If Jeckran didn't know better, he would suspect her of having developed a little schoolgirl pash.

"Yes, fine. Very good, Onna. Aren't you *wonderfully* clever." The Lord-Mage stood, though he had to steady himself with a hand on the table. "I'm going out for a cigarette."

"You smoke?" Jeckran said, before he could remind himself to keep his mouth shut.

The wizard gave him a look. "Yes. But not in my workshop. The particles in the air wreak havoc on my experiments."

"Oh," said Jeckran. The thought of a cigarette made his mouth water, and he swallowed, trying to look disinterested.

The Lord-Mage of Hexos smiled like a cat in a fishmarket. "Would you care to join me, Mr. Jeckran?"

*The bastard.*

Jeckran followed him out.

They went down to the floor below the workshop, where an observation platform wrapped around the exterior of the tower. Jeckran leaned on the railing, a lacy wrought-iron confection that was the only thing between himself and an impressive drop, and stared out toward the city. He heard the rustle of the wizard's robe and smelled the smoke.

The Lord-Mage said, "I'm not sure at this point, Mr. Jeckran, whether it's an excellent head for heights or a reckless disregard for your own safety. I've never seen *anyone* lean on that rail."

"The first, sir. I imagine that the greatest wizard in the world wouldn't invite a man from whom he needs a favor to smoke cigarettes on a death trap. Will the rail give out?"

"It won't," the Lord-Mage admitted, and passed Jeckran a lit cigarette. "How dreadfully calculating of you."

"Sharpshooting isn't actually my major contribution to Tsira's and my business relationship. I earn my keep by being calculating, sir." He took his first drag on the cigarette and sighed, then turned to face the wizard. "May I be very direct? Tsira will pretend that she isn't, sir, but she's rather concerned with her honor and with making it clear that she's only doing this in the name of defending her clan. I, on the other hand, haven't the honor that God granted to wild dogs. I'm only involved in this because I didn't want to let Tsira put her life in danger all alone, and I'm the one who keeps track of our finances. We are, frankly, completely strapped. I've paid for a few days at a rattrap down by the docks, but when that's done with, we'll be out on the streets unless we find some paying employment. Prizefights, probably, which are often somewhat—messy. She always wins, of course, even six against one, but with those odds she sometimes comes out worse for wear. Her nose didn't always have that bump at the center, and her damn right *ear*—" He paused and gathered himself. "It's that or legitimate employment as bodyguards or something of the sort, which won't leave time for amateur policework, and even with only prizefighting, you would lose us for the time it will take for her to recover from getting her face smashed in—"

"Heavens, darling," the Lord-Mage said. His tone was very mild. "You really *have* had a dreadful time of it, haven't you?"

"Sir. I served in Mendosa. I was shot in the shoulder and watched any number of good men die over the rights to a *cod fishery*. I was at the battle of the white rocks, and I've shot more than half a dozen people since, generally because they were either shooting at me first or attempting to murder my business partner. It hasn't been a seaside holiday."

There was a pause. The Lord-Mage smoked calmly, one hip cocked, his eyes half-lidded. "Room and board here at the Lamp," he said finally. "Along with your normal fee for full-time work. Which is?"

Jeckran, without any hesitation, named a sum more than twice what they had ever earned, and he cursed himself for not aiming higher when the Lord-Mage only nodded in response. "Wonderful, darling. I'll send a boy to pick up your things from the rattrap."

"Oh," said Jeckran. "Yes, well—thank you, sir."

The Lord-Mage shot him an amused look. "Must I make your calling me Loga a term of your employment?"

"Yes, sir," Jeckran said. It came out simultaneously more militaristic and more playful than he intended.

"Very well. I'll write it into your contract, poppet."

"Yes, sir. Loga."

They reentered the Lamp, and Loga immediately issued directives to the servants, which gave Jeckran the opportunity to explain the situation to Tsira. She made the face that was her public smile: her eyes narrowing slightly, the left corner of her mouth ticking upward. "Whose cock got sucked out there?" she said in Dacyn, and Jeckran felt his whole face go red.

A servant ushered Jeckran and Tsira down the stairs—which were, Jeckran thought, almost certainly enchanted—and down a few twisting hallways to a door, which the boy opened with a flourish. Jeckran thanked the boy—not that they had any language in common—shut the door, and locked it behind him, giving him and Tsira the first real comfortable privacy they had enjoyed in weeks.

They looked at each other. Tsira suddenly grinned. "*Shit.*"

Her glee made him laugh, and looking around the enormous sitting room made him laugh harder. The Hexian furniture with its dark wood and curving lines, the vases of flowers, the massive smoking couch with its elaborate scrollwork: all of it was mad, absurd, ridiculous. Tsira was practically giggling. "How many rooms do we got?"

They inspected the two bedrooms before discovering a sort of closet off the second one, into which they both crowded. Tsira stared at the central piece of furnishing, nonplussed. "What's that?"

Jeckran stared for a moment before his eyes went wide. "Ah! It's the privy! They call them water closets. They have them in some of the great houses in Leiscourt now."

"Shit," Tsira said, eyeing the thing with apparent skepticism. "In Cwydarin, too. My ma said she saw one once."

It was a very grand-looking affair, with wooden carvings at the top and ceramic tile for the seat. Jeckran investigated it for a moment, then found a lever on one side, which he pressed. There was a roar, and they both watched with amazement as the water flowed. "Magic," Tsira said.

"Well," Jeckran said, upon reflection, "though generally I believe that they do it with pipes, in this case you may be right."

"You sit right on it?"

"I believe so."

"I'm going to try."

Jeckran left her to it. The roar of the thing was loud enough to hear through the heavy wooden door. Then a quieter hum, and Tsira's delighted voice. "There's water to wash your hands!"

"I think you'll find you can fill that tub by yourself as well," he called back. There was a bathtub in the little room. He considered suggesting that they bathe together, but gave up the idea as an absurdity: even two humans couldn't fit without being crammed like stuffing in a goose.

As it turned out, another, identical bathtub was attached to the other bedroom, so Jeckran was able to bathe alone. The water came out hot, which was a strange sort of shock, though he didn't know what exactly he had expected. Certainly pipes that delivered baths full of icy water could be of only limited utility: perhaps for devout and self-denying Elgarites and very devoted hammerball players. He luxuriated in the hot water and expensive scented soap, letting the ache soak out of his muscles. When he returned to the other bedroom, he was greeted by the sight of Tsira, resplendently naked, reading a book on the bed. She nodded. "Hey, Pink."

"Hey, boss," he said. "When did you learn to read Nessoran?"

She gave him a fond look, and he felt enormous self-satisfaction over his conviction that he was the only person on earth at whom she had ever made that face. "Looking at the pictures," she said, and waved him over.

Jeckran lay down beside her and nuzzled his face into the side of her neck, inhaling the sun-and-leather smell of her under the flowery soap. "I've missed you," he said.

"Haven't been anywhere."

"You've been ill. I've, ah, *missed* you."

She laughed and tapped at her book. "This the one you were talking about?"

"Mm?" He ran a hand up her thigh by way of distracting her. She just grinned. He sighed and turned his attention to her book. "What— *oh.* You found a copy." He frowned. "You know, I would find it very odd that the Lord-Mage keeps a copy of *Various Approaches to an Interesting Subject* in his guest suite if I hadn't already met the man." He looked more closely at the pictures. "It seems to be rather heavily focused on the . . . phallus."

"Clever, too," Tsira said, tapping one of the figures with her finger. "See? Got straps to hold it on."

"Oh," Jeckran said. "*Oh.*"

She laughed. "Hey. Pink."

He swallowed. "Yes?"

"Think I'm feeling better."

# 20

---

### YOUNG MAN SEEKS HOUSEHOLDER 35662

*I am a Young man, tall and strong, brown eyes and brown hair,
I am seeking a gentleman who would like to household a young
man of seventeen who is good looking and has good habbits. I am
from Coldstream village and have lost my Father in the Massacer
of last winter with his business where I worked with him, and my
village is destroyed, so I am now newly come to Leiscourt and have
been seeking work but with no good results. I am a good Elgarite
boy and only Seventeen this month, I will be very good in your
household. I can read and write and bake. My father was a baker
and I am trained in baking and am hansome. To respond please
write to the number in the subject in the care of this newspaper
and God bless you.*

　　　　　　　　　　　　　　—*Personal advertisement,* Leiscourt Crier, *6572*

Onna slipped out in the night after Loga and their two guests had
gone to bed.

She put on her new black frock and a big black Hexian-style hat that
covered much of the top half of her face. Then she proceeded toward
the home of Judge Schutts, the location of which she had managed to
casually extract from Loga whilst they were on the hospital tour.

She was a little nervous about what she was about to undertake. She
had a little writ in her reticule that said she was Loga's agent and that
any molestation of her person should be taken as an assault of the Lord-
Mage himself, but she doubted very highly that anyone who was

annoyed by the presence of a strange young Daeslundic lady slinking about in his back garden would take the time to examine her paperwork before turning her out on her ear. With this in mind, she dressed herself all in black and went out into the dark to investigate.

Hexos was very pleasant after midnight. The night air was warm and soft, and the few people out on the streets drifted along in states of pleasure or anticipation, as if everyone was on their way to or returning from some delicious entertainment. It took a bit of effort for Onna to focus on the task at hand, which almost immediately presented some difficulties. Judge Schutts's home, she discovered, was surrounded by a stout wall, about ten feet high and topped with very discouraging-looking metal spikes. This, she thought, might require some good parametrical thinking.

First, she needed to scale the wall. This would be difficult: although she supposed that *Loga* might be capable of simply floating into the air like a very well-dressed hot-air balloon, she did not think that she should like very much to attempt it. Instead she circumnavigated the building, pondering. Eventually she came upon some slender vines creeping up the far southeast wall. For a moment she had a vision of herself as a figure in an old Daeslundic story, whispering to the plants to make them grow thick and strong. Speaking to vegetation not having been covered by Cordridge-on-Sea's basic system of magical education, she needed an alternate solution.

Petrification, she thought, might do the trick, though one never *really* liked to go about forming dangerous acidic compounds on the side of a public street. There was also the little matter of the rapid petrification of wood being more of a theoretical idea than something wizards were accustomed to doing. Still, needs must, so she clasped her Elgar's Circle for a moment and then set to her task.

About halfway into creating a humid acidic atmosphere in a sealed field around the vine, she realized she had made a terrible mistake, and by the time she was raising the temperature within the field until it was as hot as an enormous kiln, she was weeping quietly and cursing herself

for her silliness in attempting such a thing. She struggled desperately to
maintain everything, convinced to her bones that it would collapse and
she would set the entire street alight. Then, quite suddenly, it was over.
Her ears were ringing. She leaned against the wall for a long few minutes, breathing slowly and waiting for the shaking to subside. Her heart
was pounding, and after a moment she identified what she was feeling.
She hadn't just overexerted herself. She had been absolutely terrified.

Naming the feeling was the trick that allowed Onna to catch her
breath, and soon she was hitching up her skirts and beginning a very
unladylike scramble up the stout lattice of petrified vines she had created. To descend the other side of the wall was far more straightforward:
though floating *up* was beyond her, she was quite capable of slowing her
progress *down*.

Onna alighted on the ground with a satisfactorily ladylike little
thump and moved toward the main building in what she hoped was a
very stealthy fashion. She crept about to the back and tried what she
thought was the servants' door. It was locked, but not magically. She
made quick work of the mechanism and slipped inside.

Once indoors she quickly ran the parameters to identify the greatest
nearby source of magical activity and was immediately flooded with
information. There were wizard-lamps, dumbwaiters, a lift, fountains,
a swimming pool, and what seemed to her like every possible magical
construction necessary to keep a very wealthy man's household running. Then, at last, she managed to find it: the distinct combination of
organized parameters and half-formed experiments that indicated a
wizard's study.

She found Mr. Finnbair's office on the third floor of the mansion. It
was a little corner room near the stairway that led to the attic where the
servants slept. She was startled to find that the doorknob turned easily
when she tried it, though upon reflection she supposed it wasn't all that
surprising: they didn't anticipate thieves scaling the walls, breaching the
outer doors, and forgoing the expensive and beautiful items elsewhere
in order to rummage about in this dark and musty-smelling closet.

It really was grim in the little room. She triggered the wizard-lamps and felt a peculiar tug at her heart. There were no windows, so Mr. Finnbair had made his own: an artificial view of a pleasant day on a rocky coast, the sun glinting off the breakers. He must be horribly homesick, she thought: a Daeslunder from the cool and pretty and wild Gallen Islands stuck here in the hot, crowded city where his twin brother had died years ago. She suddenly found herself longing a little for Daeslund—for green hills and little brooks, and for her mother. Then she shook herself and set back to her work.

She didn't have to look long. It was almost *disappointing* how blatant it was. There were books on troll magic that had been banned in Daeslund, Nessoran books on medical and life-extending magic, and several volumes that Onna thought must be troll originals, printed in an angular, unfamiliar script. She pulled one off the shelf just to see if she could make anything of it, giving a startled little hiss when she saw the illustrations.

It was a book of troll anatomy.

As she looked for his personal notes, she at last found herself defeated: Mr. Finnbair had set a cunningly designed magical lock on his desk drawer, and Onna was quite certain that if she attempted to open it, she would at the very least be discovered and at worst find herself at the wrong end of a nasty curse. She decided to leave, since now she had some fairly solid evidence once it came time to arrest him. She could only imagine that whatever he kept locked in that drawer was even more damning than what she had seen outside of it.

By the time she made her weary way back to the Lamp, the sun was rising, and she was looking forward enormously to her bed. However, before turning in, she decided to check the parameters on her grid one last time to ensure that it was functioning correctly after being triggered by Miss Tsira. She was yawning her way over her notes when one of the bells began to ring.

She shrieked and looked for Loga, but of course that was no good: he was still in bed, and in no state of health to help her in any case. For several seconds she could only stare, utterly at a loss. Then she remembered that she and Loga were no longer alone in the Lamp, and she was off like a shot, pounding down the twisting staircase to the visitors' suite.

She hammered at the door to Mr. Jeckran's half of the suite and was alarmed to hear a loud series of thumps and muffled yelps emanating from within the room. It occurred to her just then exactly how early in the morning it was, though, she supposed, that couldn't be helped now. The door flew open, and she was greeted by an enormous expanse of gray-blue pectoral muscle. Miss Tsira, looking unhappy. Onna had picked the wrong door and found herself struggling for words. "Oh *goodness*, I, ah—"

"*What.*"

Onna managed to gather herself. "There's been another attack, Miss Tsira. I wanted to ask if you and Mr. Jeckran might—oh. *Oh.*"

Mr. Jeckran was crouched on the floor next to the bed, desperately attempting to cover himself with a blanket. She hadn't knocked on the wrong door, after all. For one long, horrible moment they looked directly into each other's eyes. Then Mr. Jeckran stood, only the blanket still grasped in his hand preventing Onna from seeing portions of the male anatomy that she had only previously encountered in textbooks. "We would be happy to accompany you, Miss Gebowa," he said, "if you would only give us a moment to dress."

She closed the door so quickly that it created a very forceful little breeze, leaned against it, and reflected on how, after all of her work to control every aspect of her parameters, people *would* insist on confounding everything by acting exactly as you never thought they would.

Miss Tsira and Mr. Jeckran wasted no time in getting their clothes on, much to Onna's enormous relief, and within minutes, the trio reached the street, which was bustling despite the early hour. Mr. Jeckran looked puzzled. "Is there always so much construction on the streets of Hexos at dawn?"

Onna shook her head. "There's a festival in ten days. Everyone competes to build the most fantastical-looking sculpture out of paper flowers, and everyone sings and dances and parades the sculptures down to the harbor, and then they put them into boats and set the boats on fire so the gods can enjoy them and send real flowers down to Hexos when the spring comes. It's supposed to be great fun." Loga had been looking forward to it, and Onna felt a little pang at the thought that he might be too ill to enjoy it.

"Going to be a great pain in the ass," Miss Tsira said. "That many people around while we're trying to hunt."

Onna put her head down and walked faster.

When they arrived, it was already far too late. The victim, a big strong troll far bigger than Miss Tsira, was freshly dead at the back of a narrow alley. The magical bubble that should have protected the troll was missing, which immediately put Onna into an even worse temper. She sucked in a breath. "Oh, *damn*," she said, without giving a damn that she had used bad language, either.

Mr. Jeckran raised his eyebrows, but didn't comment on her vocabulary, which was the only thing that saved him from a very bad fate, indeed. "I take it that the barrier is still meant to be in place?"

"It is," she said briskly. Then, more quietly, "This shouldn't be possible."

Tsira knelt beside the corpse. "Human magic," she said. "Not the same as I smelled before."

Onna knelt beside her, heedless of her skirts. She closed her eyes for a moment and found the same crisp magical signature that had become familiar to her over the past few days. "It's the same as last time. The same wizard." She opened her eyes. "It has to be someone who knows Loga or myself. Someone familiar enough with our magic to be able to quickly intuit how to break through our work, and someone powerful enough to manage it." Someone powerful enough, perhaps, to have once been the protégé of the Lord-Mage of Hexos.

Tsira leaned over to sniff at the corpse. Mr. Jeckran wrinkled his nose. "Must you, really?"

Tsira rocked back onto her heels and ignored him, speaking to Onna instead. "Daeslundic."

Onna's eyes widened slightly. "I beg your pardon?"

"The murderer. He's Daeslundic, maybe Esiphian. Wears a shirt with starched cuffs. I can smell the starch."

"Oh, *no*," Onna said, and stood. "Oh, Elgar bless us. We have to get back to the Lamp."

Mr. Jeckran frowned. "Why? What is it? Have you found something out?"

Onna took a deep breath and nodded sharply. "I know who's doing this. And if we can't talk sense into Loga, I'm afraid that no one will be able to stop him."

# 21

---

*What are we to the humans? Should we call ourselves their ances-*
*tors? Shall we demand their fealty? Can we say we know their*
*clans when we knew them in their infancy? Can we say we know*
*a people when we've never known their children?*
　　　　　　　—*Grandmother-book 7, clan Cynallum, annotations by*
　　　　　　　　　　　　　　*Cynallumwynreigan, page 63*

N o," said Loga. "Absolutely not. You haven't a shred of actual evidence against him."

Tsira watched the girl's face. She looked like she wished she had
some nice troll teeth to rip his throat out. "Then you're condemning
more trolls to die," she said. "You're letting them die because you're
more interested in letting your friend roam around loose than you are
in protecting innocent people."

Loga tried to sit up. Didn't manage it. Tsira looped an arm under
his shoulders and hauled him upright. "Thank you, darling," he said.
He looked even tinier propped up against the red embroidered cushions. Fragile. Tsira liked a pretty little vahn as much as anyone, but this
one made her nervous. Body like a newborn rabbit. The whole heart of
him burning like a lightning-struck tree. His face twisted up like all
that fire was hurting him.

"I'll invite him to dinner," he said. "I'll invite him here to dinner,
and I will *speak* to him, and I'll ask him for an accounting of where he
was this morning."

He swallowed. Jeckran watched him, watched the movement of his throat. Made her want to laugh. He always got real nervous looking when he wanted someone, like a child sneaking sweets.

Loga spoke again. "I've received those photographs that you wanted, Onna."

Onna looked startled. "Already?"

He waved his hand through the air. "I'm the *greatest wizard on earth*, darling. They're in the sitting room on the tea table."

Onna bounded out of the room like a spooked deer and moments later came running back in with a big stack of papers. She shoved them at Jeckran. "Do you recognize anyone in these photographs?"

Jeckran raised his eyebrows and flipped through them. Tsira looked, too. Didn't see how anyone could pick someone out of that lot. Just a bunch of male pinks with short hair and matching dark suits. No way to tell one from the other. None of them beautiful like her vahn.

He stopped flipping through the pictures and tapped his finger on one man's face. "Tsira, look!"

She looked. Just another human. Pale face, pale eyes, darkish hair. Nothing to notice. Not so much as a real chin to his name.

"It's Chastonne," Jeckran said. "Algad Chastonne. Don't you recognize him?"

Then she did. Remembered those pale eyes staring out of his dead face. He'd had a beard when they'd killed him. It was gone in the picture or not grown in yet. She tapped his face with her finger, glancing at Onna. "That's him," she said. "Wizard who tried to kill me."

Onna looked at the picture. Then her eyes went wide. She stabbed her finger at it. Not at Chastonne, but at two other men. "And them? Do you recognize either of them?"

Two big, tan-skinned, broad-shouldered pinks. Brothers, probably. One handsome and smiling like he could see his future and felt good about it. The other plainer and turning his face toward his brother.

"No," she said. Jeckran shook his head.

Onna went to Loga and showed him the picture. "Loga," she said. "*Please.*"

"Fuck," Loga said. "*Fuck*." His face was gray, his breath coming fast.

The air smelled like a lightning strike. Then a wind sent the pictures flying, a hot wind with the smell of smoke. Onna grabbed Loga by the shoulder and shook him. "Stop that! Stop it at once! You're going to give yourself an attack!"

He took a gasping breath. "I'm sorry, darling," he said. "It wasn't—it wasn't intentional. It's just that it's bigger than I am, sometimes." He swallowed. "I suppose—I suppose that I'll have to bring in Jok."

He used some kind of magic to call his friend that Tsira didn't understand. Onna didn't either, from the look on her face. Then a new pink came through the door, the plainer one from the picture. Not so plain, really, when his brother wasn't next to him.

"Land sakes, Loga, you haven't pulled me in like that since the time you created a process for speeding up fermentation." His voice was nice. Low for a pink. Warm and steady. "What is it?" He didn't smell exactly like what she'd smelled at the scenes of the murders. Like metal, but different. Then again, he wasn't killing anyone right now.

"Where were you early this morning, Jok?"

Jok frowned. His fingers flexed. "I took a walk late, when I couldn't sleep. Then I went back to bed. I woke up again about forty minutes ago. The hours I keep are a little irregular. I've only just gotten dressed."

Loga's voice came out as more of a croak. "Did anyone else see you?"

"Like who? My lover? My half a dozen servants? No, Loga. No one saw me." He shoved his hands into his pockets. "Why am I being asked to account for my whereabouts?"

"Another troll died this morning, Mr. Finnbair," Onna said.

"And you think I'm the fellow who killed him," Finnbair said. "Well, I didn't. I was asleep in my little garret."

"You went to school with a man who Miss Tsira and Mr. Jeckran say attempted to kill Miss Tsira several months ago," Onna said. She held out the photo, pointing to Chastonne.

Finnbair squinted at it. "Coller, I think. Jacob Coller. Nervous little fellow. Haven't seen him in years. Am I free to go?"

"No," Loga said. "I'm so sorry, Jok. You'll have to stay here. Just for little while, until we get all of this sorted out."

"Until we get this sorted out," Mr. Finnbair said. His face was pale. "What in the releft does *that* mean? Am I a prisoner? How exactly am I supposed to prove I *didn't* kill a man?"

"Darling, please, don't." He sat up. "You'll just be staying here as my guest, no one will have to know—"

"I'm not your *darling*. Don't you *dare* call me that. I'm not some ambassador's wife you're trying to get up to your rooms. I've known you since you were *fourteen*." He clenched his fists. "I'm not Elgarson. I'm not my brother."

"I never said you were. I never once said that you were Elgarson. Please, Jok, there's no need to make a scene. This can all be sorted out so quickly if you would just—"

"If I would just what? Roll over and show my belly, let you treat me like a criminal?" He was shaking. That big body all wound up with anger. "You're right. You're not treating me one bit like Elgarson. You would have given him the benefit of the doubt."

"Jok, please—"

"I'm leaving, Loga. If you want to make me your prisoner, you'll have to treat me like one." He started toward the door, but it slammed shut first. Loga gave a quiet hiss. There was a bad smell in the room. Blood and burnt hair.

"I'm sorry," Loga said. "About your brother. About everything. You never deserved any of this. I know, Jok. *Fuck.* I'm so sorry. I'll—I'll put you in the best guest suite. Jok, I swear, no matter what happens, I'm not letting anyone lock you up. I swear to you that I'll protect you however I have to. But I have to do this, I have to be able to prove—"

"I don't care about your *promises*, Loga," Finnbair said. "I care that you don't *believe* me."

Loga flinched. Finnbair vanished.

Onna gave a little cry and rushed to the spot where Finnbair had been standing. Loga waved his hand. "No, darling. It's—it's all—I moved—" His head lolled back. The smell of burning hair was stronger.

Onna moved to his side. "Loga? Loga, you *stupid* thing, did you teleport him?"

"And—locked the room. He can't out. He. Jok." He started to cry. "I'm sorry. It *hurts*." He said something in Sangan, then made a retching noise. Onna jumped back. Tsira grabbed a vase of flowers off the table, dumped the flowers out, and held the vase under his face just in time for him to sick up his guts. There wasn't much. Water. Not eating, probably. Would make sense, with how skinny he was. A quill of a man, and flickering out like a burned-down candle.

Onna crumpled her skirt in her hands. Crushing the cloth in her fists so you could see her ankles, then letting it drop, wet and wrinkled. "Loga. Loga, you have to give more of it to me. Let me take it, please. Your heart—"

"*Please*," he said. His voice was high and rising, a chattering shriek. Tsira wanted to cover her ears. "Please, take it from me, take it, *take it*—"

Onna reached out for him. There was a sound like a bonfire blazing up. Then both of them screamed.

Terrible screams. Tsira had never heard anything like it before. It just kept going, two voices turned into one, rising and falling together. Insects. Cicadas. A line of ants moving. Pink pressed against her side, grabbed her hand. "Good God," he said. "Good God, Tsira, what is this, what's *happening*—"

She put her arms around him, pressed his face into her chest. Loga's eyes were rolled back in his head. Blood trickled out of Onna's nose. They wouldn't stop screaming. "I don't know," she said. She wanted to be sick. She squeezed him tighter. "Let's go."

They went to the door. The handle wouldn't turn. "Oh *God*, of course," Jeckran said. "He closed it, he closed it with magic—"

She could smell the fear-sweat on Jeckran's body. That *screaming*, fuck, she couldn't *think* anymore. "The window," she said. "We can use the window." She knelt. Her heart was pounding. "Get on. Get on my back."

"Tsira—"

"*Now.*"

He climbed on. Then the screaming stopped.

She looked toward the bed. The two wizards were both limp. Lifeless. Loga sprawled out sideways across the bed. Onna in a crumpled heap on the floor.

It was quiet. Tsira heard the sound of a fly beating itself against the window, wondered how it had gotten inside.

Onna stirred. Sat up. Wiped the blood from her nose with the back of her hand. She looked at Tsira with Jeckran on her back. Then she smiled. "Good *heavens*, darlings, what on earth are you doing over there?"

"Elgar save us," Jeckran whispered.

Onna shrieked. "*Loga! Get out get out get—*" She smacked the side of her head.

Loga, on the bed, rolled over, sat upright, and said, "Get out of my *head*, Loga, you've no business, you've no *right*—oh, no." Then Loga went pale and said, "*Do* calm down, darling. I know that it's dreadfully annoying, but you're only making it worse."

"*Annoying?*" said Onna. "You're mad, you're completely mad, I—I am *not* being hysterical, I have every *right* to be hysterical! You saw me in the bath!"

"I didn't *intend* to see you in the bath, darling, it was an honest accident, and I only saw your toes in any case." Then Loga burst into tears.

Onna stood and put a hand on his shoulder. "I really am *frightfully* sorry, darling," she said. "But if you would only calm down, I could sort this out in a moment. Just close your eyes and breathe."

"Close *whose* eyes and breathe?" Loga said. Then they both closed their eyes, and the room went quiet.

There were new smells. Books, at first. Then blood. Then night-blooming flowers, all thick and sweet. Bread. Licorice. Tobacco. Apples.

New grass being stepped on and the rain falling. Garlic cooking. Sulfur and smoke.

Onna made a high little sound. Then Loga gasped from his chest. A drop of sweat rolled down the side of his nose. Onna groaned and her eyes flew open.

"Oh," she said. "Oh, my goodness."

Loga laughed. He sounded different. Like maybe he'd been talking with his face under a blanket all this time, and now his voice was coming out clear. "I quite agree, darling!"

Onna sat on the edge of the bed. Seemed funny for a nice Daeslundic girl to sit on a bed with a man. She was laughing, too. "Goodness!" she said again.

"Would either of you mind explaining to us what in the name of God just happened?" said Jeckran, who always hated not understanding stuff. Tsira was pretty mad herself. Onna and Loga were giggling like they'd found a new toy when they were trying to catch the man who killed her mother.

"I'm the Lord-Mage," Onna said. "Or, well. I suppose that *we're* the Lord-Mage, now. Together. At the same time. He still has the *title*, I'm just sharing the power. Oh, *stop* that, Loga, what a pest you are!"

Loga wasn't doing much of anything, as far as Tsira could tell. He said, "You know I'm not doing it *intentionally*, darling." Then neither of them spoke, but after a few seconds they both laughed.

Pink glared. "So you've—made yourselves into a single person. It sounds dreadful."

"We have *not*," Onna said. "It was an accident. And we're two *very different* people. We're just very—close now."

"*Very* close," Loga agreed. Onna smacked his arm. Then he added, "It will make our work go wonderfully smoothly, won't it? Think of the *research opportunities*, darling!"

"I *am* thinking about them," Onna said. "I can't help it, with how loud you are. Will this last *forever*?"

"I should certainly *hope* not," Loga said. "It's a side effect of you taking on too much of the Lord-Mage's magic too quickly. It hasn't had the chance to grow accustomed to you as its host yet, that's all. I've read of it happening before, when the Lord-Mage's life is in danger and the process happens too quickly. It ought to wear off in time, as you take further control of the magic. And my Genoit's is vastly less likely to send me to an early grave if I'm only dealing with my own innate magic, which is very comforting to *me*." After another few moments, he said, "There, I think I've shut you out now. It doesn't seem very difficult. It's just all so thrilling."

"You're right," Onna said. "And it *is* better. I can't hear you rattling around at all now."

"Yeah, real fucking thrilling," Tsira snapped. "My ma's dead. Maybe your friend's the one who killed her. I'm not feeling too fucking thrilled."

That made Loga shut up. Onna pursed her lips and said, "At least this terrible business with Mr. Finnbair is finished with for now."

"Is it?" said Jeckran.

Onna frowned. "What do you mean?"

"Have we really dealt with anything, or are we just soothing ourselves into feeling that we've done something by locking him up? And what exactly are we meant to do now? Just sit about and wait to see if any other trolls die? That seems a careless way to go about preventing a series of murders. What evidence do you have against that poor man?"

Tsira raised her eyebrows. "You don't think he did it?"

"All I know is that you two apparently know him and thought of him as a suspect before you considered any of the other men in that photograph. Don't you have any way of telling whether or not a man is lying? It seems the sort of thing that a wizard ought to be capable of."

Loga shook his head. "It's more complicated than simply waving one's hands about and saying *fiddle-dee-dee, don't lie to me*. One of the essential, elementary points of writing magical parameters is defining your terms. Could you explain to me exactly what a lie is? If you, for instance, told me that because I was born poor I will endure fewer relivings and am thus closer to paradise, would that be the truth or a lie? You might perceive it to be the truth, but I would know it's a lie because Elgarism is absurd superstitious nonsense. Would my theoretical spell of lie detection, in this case, tell me that you're lying or not? Or what if, for instance, I ask you what you think of my new summer tunic, and you tell me that it's lovely, when in fact it's not to your taste? Both could be true: you might objectively believe that many would find it charming while personally feel that it's absolutely frightful. Are you lying or not?"

"Despite your implying that I'm a fool for respecting the noble faith of my ancestors, I take your point," Jeckran said. Then he repeated, "A fool. Where—" He frowned, reached into his jacket pocket, and pulled out a coin. A second later he pulled out another. He stared at them both for a long, long time. Then he said, "*Elgar.* I've been a fucking *fool*, of course—"

"Pink," Tsira said, impatient. "What."

"It's *fake*," Jeckran spat out. "This damn coin that *brought* us here, it's a damn *fake*. It hadn't occurred to me before, but I just remembered that damn inscription."

Onna took the two coins from him and stared at them both, frowning. "Which one do you mean? They both look in order to me."

"The one that says it was minted under the leadership of *Director Balach.*"

Loga frowned. Onna looked blank. Jeckran groaned. "Of *course*, you're *wizards*, you speak the damn academic Hexian Nessoran. I went to school with a Nessoran boy who taught us all of his favorite dirty words. I don't suppose that Hexos has ever had a *Director Fool* or— *Director Asshole?*"

"Give me that," Loga said, and held out his hand for the coin. He frowned at it, then snapped his fingers. "Two years ago, the last time the Nessoran delegation came, they threw an enormous party at the Esiphian consulate in honor of the Festival of Fools. They gave out these coins as a prank. For a while they were all over. They're actually parametrical constructs, you see. If you apply a bit of magic, they—"

A loud bang made Jeckran jump and Onna yelp. A shower of little bright sparks exploded around Loga's head.

"Pretty," Tsira said, in the silence that followed.

"Then—it *did* come from here," Jeckran said. "We haven't been chasing the damn thing to the four corners for *nothing.*"

"It did," Loga said. "Someone must have been here then and taken it out of Hexos almost immediately. It was all the rage to make them pop in people's faces for about a week afterward. I haven't seen one since. We ran through them very quickly. I suppose, if a wizard never activated the trick, it could very easily knock around without exploding for years."

Onna frowned. "Was Mr. Finnbair in Hexos at the time?"

Loga's expression brightened and he sat up taller. "No," he said. "No, I'm quite sure that he wasn't. I remember writing to him about the party."

Onna clenched her fists. "It doesn't prove anything," she said, but there was an edge to her voice.

Jeckran said, "I don't like the idea of sitting on my hands like an ass while Tsira is still a target. Begging your pardon, Miss Gebowa." He paused. "And there is still the matter of the thin young man that Mrs. Chastonne mentioned. He hasn't been accounted for, even if Mr. Finnbair *is* involved."

"I don't see why you always apologize for your language if you're just going to curse in any case," said Onna. "My grid is still working, isn't it? If anything else happens, it will trigger the alarm."

"And then we can waste half an hour getting to the scene and arrive just in time to inspect another corpse," Pink said. "Forgive me if my concerns aren't utterly dispelled."

"You don't need to be so *ironical*," Onna said, and she turned to Loga. "You *have* been trying to teach me more about your methods for teleportation."

"I have, indeed," he said, smiling. "I imagine, with your newfound talent for creating miniaturized constructions, that you might be able to work out a way to introduce a contingency for instant transportation into the grid itself."

She smiled. "Those awful old owls at Weltsir would have to give me a prize for research."

"The Ismael Prize, I should think," Loga said. "And one for me as well, as your coauthor. How perfectly charming. I haven't won a major award in years. One does like to have something to do when one is convalescing, don't you think?"

"My auntie used to knit hats for babies," Onna said. "I'm sure that performing original scientific research is *almost* as soothing for invalids. Should we start after lunch?"

Loga grinned. "I would be *overjoyed*, pet," he said.

Tsira glared pointedly and Loga tried to look as though he wasn't enjoying himself quite so much.

The next four days passed pretty quietly. Tsira spent some time with Onna. Talking and watching her work. Tsira taught her some Dacyn, talked about her culture, showed Onna how to fight a little. Grappling and eye gouges, choke holds, hits to weak spots. Pink walked in on it and screamed like a bee-stung child, and Onna let her skirts down and laughed.

Onna wanted to teach Tsira a little wizardry. "Of course you can do it, Tsira. If you can smell magic, you can memorize a few simple parameters."

"That's toff shit."

Onna giggled. "Goodness, Mr. Jeckran would be very shocked by your language."

"He's worse, when you're not around."

"Of course he is. Why do men always act as if women would never know what anything was if they didn't say the word in front of us?"

Tsira grinned. "Never had that problem."

"Oh," Onna said, and found something to do so Tsira wouldn't see her look embarrassed.

On the street they were building wire sculptures covered in paper flowers. Tsira liked to walk around and watch them going up. They came in all kinds. One was a giant leaping horse with a saddle covered in jewels. One was a castle with a whole little garden inside that you could see when you looked through the doors. One was a pale tree with paler leaves. "Blue," Jeckran said. "It's bright blue, Tsira, and the leaves are yellow."

*Good to know.*

Onna got her little magic troll trap set up. They tested it out. Tsira cut herself with a knife, and Onna and Jeckran came blowing in like seeds in the wind while the magic walls went up around her. Jeckran sicked up his breakfast a second later. Onna fussed. Tsira laughed at him. "What happened to your sea legs?"

"I'll leave you in that bubble," Jeckran said. "I'll abandon you to your fate, Tsira, and no one will fault me for it."

"He shan't," Onna said, and let her out. "I think that went *very* well, don't you?"

"I despise you both," Jeckran said. "Why is it my fate to be tormented by terrifying women?"

"Behaved well in your last reliving," Tsira said.

"My *last reliving*? You're an atheist! Why am I being lectured on Elgarite theology by an atheist?"

Tsira said, "Didn't behave *that* well in your last reliving."


Two nights later it happened.

It happened while they were getting ready for bed. The ringing sound warned them. Jeckran grabbed his pistol off the table, and the room stretched and melted.

They hit the alley and the air smelled like war. Blood and burning. Onna was in her nightgown, a cap on her head. Her small feet were bare against the slick warm stones of the street. In front of her was something that shouldn't exist. Magic that had been broken and not cleaned up. A circle of light where Onna's work should be, too bright and flickering into black like the space between stars.

Onna said, "This isn't—but this can't be *possible*, Loga and I are the only ones who know the parameters to break through the barrier—"

The body at the center of the circle looked like a pink at first, until Tsira saw how he was too big and his skin the wrong shade.

"Pink," Tsira said. "He's like me."

She went through the flickering light. She didn't listen when Pink and Onna screamed. She went through it and felt something strange and hot go through her gut. The light went out. Onna made a sound like she'd taken a hard hit.

Tsira went down on her knees. He'd been stripped, the little vahn. There was a long neat line cut halfway down the center of his chest, like the murderer had run off before he could finish slicing into him. He was beautiful. He could have been her brother.

He stirred.

He said, "*Mama?*"

Tsira said, "I'm right here." Then she called out, "He's alive. Get over here. Help him."

Onna said, "I can't, I don't know how. I'm not a medical wizard—"

Tsira said, "*Get the fuck over here and fucking help him.*"

Onna got the fuck over, knelt, and said, "*Loga, Loga wake up please help me, help me I don't know what to do—*"

Then, as if talking to herself, Onna said, "I *know* that I don't have to speak out loud, shut up and *help me*—" She turned to Tsira: "Loga thinks that you ought to stand back, Miss Tsira. He says that you might be vaporized."

Tsira retreated as Onna went to work, waves of power flickering through her, in and out like a lightning bug. It smelled like meat cooking.

Onna sat back on her heels. "He won't bleed anymore, but I don't—there's no way to replace the blood he's already lost. He needs rest and water, and to be somewhere safe. He might pull through, yet."

"What if I gave it to him?"

Onna stared. "What do you mean?"

"Our wizards do it when one of us gets hurt. Take blood from one troll and give it to another."

"But that's impossible," Onna said. "It's been tried ever so many times, and the patient always dies."

"Works for us. Don't know why it shouldn't for you. Put it in pinks sometimes, even. Helps you heal faster."

"But I don't know how to—it helps trolls heal faster?"

"Not me. You. Pinks."

"Oh," Onna said. Went a little gray. "That would—certainly be of very great interest to someone who worked at a hospital." She swallowed. "No human wizard has ever managed it, Tsira. I won't risk trying it without a troll wizard to consult. We need to bring him to the hospital, as quickly as we can. They'll do their best for him there. And then—I think we need a new plan."

They took him to the hospital. Onna had Tsira hold back and stay out of sight while she and Jeckran struggled to get the poor little vahn inside. Interesting.

They got back to the Lamp and washed up before they gathered around that big table. Onna took a deep breath. "I have an idea. I spoke about it with Loga just now, before he had to rest again, and he thinks it could work. It might be—rather dangerous, but I think it's our best chance of catching the man who's doing this."

Tsira and Pink both nodded. "I can't speak for Tsira, but I trust your judgment, Miss Gebowa," Pink said. "I haven't been able to talk her out of putting herself in danger to stop this man, but I can only imagine that we'll be safer if we work together."

"What he said," Tsira said.

Onna looked surprised but pleased, then covered it up pretty quick and went on. "I think that we ought to use Miss Tsira as bait."

"*No*," Pink said, just as Tsira said, "How?"

They glared at each other, until Pink sighed and slumped in his chair. "I don't know why I damn well *bother*."

Tsira patted his hand.

"I am sorry, Mr. Jeckran," Onna said. "But the magical traps aren't working. He just notices them and rips right through them. We need to draw him out, and Miss Tsira is a troll, which is what he wants. She's new in town, and he doesn't know she knows Loga and myself. My idea is that we establish her as someone who has recently arrived in Hexos alone and who—I'm sorry, miss—doesn't have very much money and is looking for work in the neighborhood around the hospital."

Jeckran frowned. "We were attacked once before, for asking questions about the murders in Monsatelle. They might know of us here, as well. Your plan will only work if we make sure no word gets out that Tsira came here with a human man matching my description. And how will you keep her safe?"

"In that case, they may already be suspicious of you," Onna said. "I'd still like to try. There's a device called a longeye that she could wear. We could stay nearby, Mr. Jeckran, and rush to her as soon as someone suspicious engages with her, and we will see his face on the longeye, either way. And—I think I could create a very small construction of some kind that would track where someone went. If Miss Tsira could affix it to him somehow, we would know where he went once he ran away, and we wouldn't have to waste time messing about with trying to trap him all over again."

"Affix it to him," Jeckran said. "How? Ask him to stand still while she ties it around his neck?"

Onna's jaw went tight looking. "I don't *know*," she said. "I'll think of something, or Loga will. There's no need to make sarcastic comments if you haven't anything *useful* to say."

"Could you make a burr?" Tsira asked. "With those tiny hooks. They'll stick to anything."

Onna looked blank, then frowned. "Tiny hooks," she murmured. "That's *brilliant*, Tsira."

"Thanks," Tsira said. She liked it when Onna forgot the *miss*. Tsira figured that you shouldn't be too formal with someone if you were going to put your life in their hands.

For a few days after that, Tsira felt about as useless as a pig's tail. All she could do was sit around and wait for Onna to be ready with her little bits of magic. Tsira wasn't even supposed to leave the Lamp. Onna was afraid of the killer spotting her and figuring out she was involved in the investigation. That meant pretty much the only thing left to do was nap, eat, and fuck, which was mostly all that she and Jeckran did.

One night she was holding him him close, his small body all warm and sweaty and soft from tiredness. He put his head onto her chest. "I think I'd like you to household me, Tsira."

"Oh," Tsira said, like an ass. "Yeah? I could. If you wanted."

"I do," he said. "I'd like to take your clan name. If you don't mind me arranging it in the Daeslundic way."

"Phillim Kail Cynallum," she said. It made her chest ache. A good, warm ache. "Sounds good."

"I thought so, too," he said, and fell asleep pretty quick.

The next day when they went up for breakfast, Onna came jumping up at them like a little cat.

"I *did* it," she said. "I made the little burr. It's all ready."

"And I looked it over for her," Loga said. "Though I confess that at her extremely tender age she's already far surpassed me in her ability to create constructions, so I don't know that I was really of all that much use." He paused. "There's also the matter of my own ability to use magic being a bit . . . temporarily limited."

That sounded pretty damn bad. "Thought you were better," Tsira said.

"Physically, vastly better," Loga said. "*Magically*, still somewhat . . . depleted. I've given a great deal of power to Onna which I'll never get back, and using any more than ordinary household magic while I'm still recovering from the swoons would be deeply unwise in any case."

"Oh, wonderful," Jeckran muttered. "It's good to know that we'll be going into this with backup, then."

"More backup than we had before," Tsira said, and nodded toward Onna.

"*Thank you*, Tsira," Onna said. "And Loga will still be able to advise me, in any case, so with him having . . . *given* me some of his magic, I'm sure that you might find me *almost* as helpful as him."

"*More* helpful," Loga said. They all glared at Jeckran until he apologized.

That night, Tsira went out with all of her new wizard-tools on her. The longeye pin on her shirt collar and the little burr in her pocket. She went to a cheap inn near the hospital and booked herself a room for the week. She sat around in the bar talking to anyone who'd talk back about how she was a troll of clan Fwynnad, down on her luck and looking for work. She slept in the narrow bed in the musty room all alone. Pink was nearby, she knew. Somewhere close at hand with Onna. Watching out for her.

She still missed the sound of his breath in the night.

She spent a few days bored out of her skull. Talked to plenty of people in the bar, but none of them seemed like they wanted to cut her heart out of her chest.

One night she decided to try something different. Drank a little more than she usually would. Not enough to really get drunk, but enough to make a human think that she might be. Talked with a few people about how much trouble she'd been having finding work. Then she said, "It's too fucking hot in here," and walked out. She made sure to sway a little as she went.

She'd done it to hook a fish, but her guts still went icy when she got a bite on the line. "Excuse me!"

She stopped and turned. A young man came toward her. Handsome pink. Dark hair to his shoulders, bright light eyes. He was smiling. "I'm sorry," he said. "But I couldn't help overhear you talking in the bar. I might be able to help you find work."

"Yeah?" Tsira said, and rubbed her torc. It was hard to get the word out. She could smell it on him, the rising copper. She palmed the burr. If she died, her vahn would be able to kill this man in her name.

He reached out a hand to shake. "Yes, I think so. Your name is?"

"My people don't shake hands," she said, and clapped him on the shoulder, setting the burr. Their eyes met. She tried not to flinch. She was never scared. She wasn't going to let him see that she was fucking scared.

His eyebrows drew together. Tsira couldn't tell if it was anger or plain puzzlement. Then he said, very gently, "I'm sorry. This won't hurt," and Tsira dropped to the ground and rolled away from the hot bolt of magic aimed at her chest just as Onna and Jeckran came tearing around the corner.

"*Haran Welder!*" Onna screamed out. "I'm arresting you in the name of—" There was a loud crack and the man was gone.

Pink helped Tsira up. She was shaking. Onna was shaking, too.

"I *know* him. Oh, God." Onna covered her mouth with her hand. "Oh, *God*. I *kissed* him."

"Fuck that," Tsira said. She felt cold. Didn't give a shit about pinks, and their crying, and their fucking *kisses*. Her ma was dead. Her ma was dead and burned. "We're going after him."

# 22

*Why do some perform evil acts, and others behave with virtue? It is the age of the soul.*

*Here there's a headman's son. He is a young soul: he has not learned through reliving. He goes to the beds of strangers, he drinks mead, he neglects the needs of his clan. Beside him is the son of another headman. He has lived this life many times before. He has learned from his failings. He has learned from the prayer and fasting of his relivings. He has grown more modest, more frugal: he eschews the body. He has relived and his soul remembers, and every retreading brings him closer to God.*

—*From* Elgar's First Letter

This couldn't be real. This wasn't happening.

Onna kept thinking about Haran, trying to make herself understand. She couldn't, though; couldn't reach it, couldn't grasp it. She could only think about how good he was, how polite, how handsome and clever and kind. How he helped the sick little children. How he had access to every process that occurred in the hospital, and his research always gave him an excuse to enter a room. How very, very interested he had been to talk with her about how she meant to catch the murderer.

She wished that she could swoon, like the heroine in one of her mother's novels. She wished that she could faint dead away and be carried off to some cool quiet room where she could sleep and be gently looked after.

They were walking quickly, Tsira charging ahead, Mr. Jeckran's limp growing more pronounced as he tried to keep up with them. The burr, at least, was working: Haran had teleported himself straight to his rooms at the hospital. Onna guessed that he wouldn't have the strength to make another jump like that. They would be able to catch him, if only Onna could keep her wits about her.

As they ran toward the hospital, Onna heard a swell of noise: music, people shouting, the bang of drums. When they turned a corner from a side street, they ran straight into the festival celebration, which filled the broad avenue.

The festival for the coming of spring. Onna had forgotten all about it. Down the center of the street came the flower sculptures, all lit up with candles and miniature wizard-lamps. Between each sculpture marched the dancers and musicians, each troupe led by a banner with the name of whoever or whatever had funded them. The troupe directly ahead of them was made up of dozens of girls dressed in costumes that shimmered green and blue in the glare of the lamps; one girl was dressed as the queen of the city and held aloft on a litter, and the rest were dressed as her honor guard. Two of the guards ran ahead and executed a series of flips, and the crowd erupted into cheers. They were wonderful, and Onna stopped, momentarily transfixed, until Tsira grasped her arm and broke her out of her reverie.

It was like something out of a very strange dream. The fear, and the hurry, and the darkness of the night mixed with the glaring lights of the procession. There were so many people in the street that it was nearly impossible to move forward, so Tsira charged ahead, shoving and snarling until people made way. No one seemed frightened of Tsira or even took much notice as the three of them galloped headlong through the street. Perhaps they thought it all part of the spirit of the evening.

Then the crowds thinned, they turned off the avenue, and the streets grew darker very quickly until they were at the hospital gates, the grand building looming before them, lit only by the thin crust of the moon and a few candles held by shouting, running people inside. Onna's eyes went wide. "He destroyed the wizard-lamps."

"Charming," Mr. Jeckran said. He was limping terribly. "I always do prefer to confront murderers in the dark."

"Fix it," Tsira said to Onna. Then she knelt and motioned for Mr. Jeckran. "Get on my back. Slowing us down."

"I *can't*," Onna said, just as Mr. Jeckran said, "I will *not*."

"*You fucking will*," Tsira said to both at once.

For a moment Onna thought and felt nothing but a sort of dull, aimless panic. She called out for Loga in her head, tugging hard at the thin rope that connected them until he was there. *I taught you how to make a light, darling.*

She pulled in a deep breath, thought through the parameters, and watched as the light poured into her palm. Tsira stood with Mr. Jeckran on her back. "Let's go."

The hospital was strange in the dark. Nurses were rushing about on their rounds, candles in their hands, but none tried to stop the three intruders. Perhaps they recognized Onna—Loga's apprentice was well-known around the capital by now—or perhaps they, like Onna, felt as if this was all a dream and the usual rules didn't apply.

Onna led them to the back of the complex, to the little door that Haran had pointed out as his private quarters. It opened when she tried the handle. Someone had clearly rummaged the place and grabbed things in an enormous hurry. Onna sensed a strange snarl of broken parameters and noticed the remains of the burr on the floor. Onna said, "*Shit.*"

Tsira balled up her fists and said, "Onna, can you find him without it?"

This time Onna didn't dither. "I can damn well try."

She closed her eyes.

It was all too much at first. Everything was a snarl of thread, an ocean, a barrel of rice with a universe inside each grain, and Onna was forced to struggle frantically to keep from drowning in the rush of numbers, measurements, impressions, until finally she made her way out of the chaos and looked down at it from above.

Hexos, drawn in magic, was a map composed by an incompetent cartographer. Some places were as neat and regular as a formal garden; others were spread as naturally as moss; and others were barren and eerily empty. Some of the magic was new and bright as a fresh bit of ribbon, all of the common household parameters that ordinary people used to keep the wagon wheels turning smoothly and the dough rising fat and white in its wicker baskets. Some magic was so old that its parameters were written in a language that Onna couldn't understand. At the center of all of it blazed the lamp, all power and precision and sheer audacity, casting everything beside it into shadow. In all of this, she was searching for a single man.

She thought of the numbers. The geographical size of Hexos, its population, its population of wizards, its population of wizards who were young men in their early twenties, the speed at which Haran might be walking, the influence that stress might have on his body temperature. Then Loga stirred at the back of her mind.

*There's no time for a statistical analysis, Onna.*

She sent him her panic, the rush, the danger, the hopelessness of what she was trying to do, how she could only solve this with magic. She felt his amusement. He sent her his hand opening, the little light blooming. He sent a naked, terrified child in a house consumed by flame. He sent the crackle of lightning. He sent a troll wizard putting the beat back into a still heart.

*I trust in your will. It's gotten you this far.*

She thought about Haran. She thought about the soft waves of his hair, his sturdy wrists, his one good suit and how it was growing shabby. She thought about him with a little girl at his heels. She thought about the taste of his mouth.

She opened her eyes.

"He's almost to the harbor," she said, and held out her hands. "We can beat him there."

Tsira and Mr. Jeckran grabbed ahold of her hands, and she let the magic tear through her.

When they hit the ground at the harbor, Onna crashed to her hands and knees and was painfully, violently sick on the ground. She gave a little sob and wiped her mouth with her sleeve. Her head was swimming, pounding. She could feel the ground list under her. "*Tsira*—"

Tsira placed her big hand on Onna's back, rubbing little circles. "Can you stand?"

She did, with Tsira's help. Then she swallowed. "I don't—I can't find him again, I can't—"

Tsira shook her head. "You did good," she said. "*Shh.*" She stood very still and drew in a deep, long breath. Mr. Jeckran kept very still as well and held up a warning hand when Onna tried to speak. Tsira nodded and gestured in the direction of the water.

All of the lights went out.

Mr. Jeckran cursed softly and drew his pistol. Onna put up her hand and tugged at the light. It came, weak and flickering, casting strange shadows on the huge stacks of crates that surrounded them. She could hear the slap of the waves against the hulls of the ships. She could hear footsteps.

"Haran?" Onna said.

The footsteps stopped, then sped into a run. Tsira cursed and lunged after him, quicker than any human could run, and vanished at once into the gloom between the piles of freight. A man shouted, followed by a blaze of light and a dreadful, monstrous roar.

"*Tsira!*" Mr. Jeckran screamed, as if her name had been cut from him with a knife, and he sprinted toward the source of the light. He fell almost immediately, his bad ankle buckling under him, but he was up and running again in an instant, with Onna close behind, her bare feet sliding a little over the slick wet ground.

As they rounded the corner, they saw Haran standing a few feet away from Tsira. Tsira was on her knees, groaning quietly, the sound almost a growl. It was too dark to see Haran's face, but he was shaking slightly. Onna could feel the magic crackling between them: his application of will against her wild, furious resistance.

"Onna," he said. His voice was almost steady. "Just let me go. Let me go and I won't kill her."

"I can't do that," Onna said. "You're a murderer." Her voice cracked. "You killed so many people, Haran, you killed them like *animals*. There needs to be justice. If you'll just come with us—"

"They don't *care* about us, Onna," Haran said, and now his voice broke. He was crying. "They won't even teach humans their magic. They can heal and they *don't*, they *refuse* to: they'd see us all die before they'd put out a hand to help us. Do you have any idea what it was like, all of those months, all of those *years* working in a hospital on petty *shit*, watching little children die and not being able to stop it? Once I figured out what the trolls' blood could do, it was a *crime* not to use it. One dead troll can save six human children, Onna. One of them for *six*. More, maybe, if I could only research properly instead of skulking around in secret. *Think* of it, the organs, the *brains*—"

"*Stop*," Onna said, sickened by his words, sickened by her sympathy for his intentions. For the dying children in their little beds. For sweet tiny Matti in her slippers.

"Onna—"

"*Don't call me by my name*," she said, and threw a ball of fire at him.

He caught it and extinguished it in his hand.

"Your magic's changed," he said. "Loga's done something." She felt a barrier go up, a crackle of heat and energy. A Morgan's wall and a field of electricity together, impervious to magic and deadly to touch. He started to back away. "Just let me go."

Onna threw her whole mind against it, all of her force: no parameters, just will and fear and fury. She felt it rebounding against her, felt her whole body ignite in agony. She shrieked, staggered, barely managed to catch herself on Mr. Jeckran's shoulder.

Tsira stood slowly, her legs shaking, her teeth bared. Haran hissed. Tsira's voice was a rasp.

"My ma," she said. "She was one you killed."

He looked, for a moment, genuinely surprised. Then he shook his head. "I'm sorry," he said. "But I did what I had to do. It was right. She died for good."

Tsira started to walk toward him. "Don't give a fuck about *good*. Don't give a fuck about *six lives for one*. Don't give a *fuck* about your *fucking reasons*," she said, and launched herself against the barrier.

She screamed. It was a sound with nothing mortal in it. She screamed. Her hair smoldered and her clothes smoked. Mr. Jeckran gave a panicked cry. "Good God, Tsira, *stop*—"

She ignored him and kept going, pressed forward through the barrier till she grabbed Haran by the throat. "*She was my mother*," she said, the magic burning her, her skin blistering. "She was my *mother*, you took my mother, you *took* her—"

Haran scrabbled at his throat with his hands, his eyes wide and terrified. He didn't look handsome anymore. He looked young and frightened and helpless. Tsira's hair burst into flame. Mr. Jeckran fumbled with his pistol, cursing, "Fuck, *fuck*, it's *jammed*—"

"Tsira," Onna said. "Tsira, please, *stop*, don't do this, it will make you a murderer, too. *Stop*—"

Mr. Jeckran gave a muffled shout and flung his pistol, which bounced off Haran's shoulder. Haran gave a yelp of surprise, and for just a moment, the Morgan's wall flickered. And in that moment, Tsira thumped Haran soundly over the head.

# 23

*"Oh, Govran," said Resalind. "We shall be happy, shan't we? As happy as we always dreamed we might become?"*

*"Yes," Govran said, and gazed down upon the face of his young bride, as the light slipped from her bright eyes, and the dark lashes began to drop down upon her cheek, and his tears spotted the silk of her wedding gown. "Yes, my darling. I do believe that there could be no other pair in the world who could be happier than we shall be."*

—The Trials of Resalind *by Sora Gebowa*

The murderer was arrested. Tsira's ma stayed dead.

Tsira and Jeckran stayed at the Lamp. They thought it was just for a few days. But Loga kept telling them that they should stay and rest. So they did. Mostly Tsira lay on their bed while Jeckran pressed cool cloths to her burns. He was startled by how fast she healed.

She wasn't all that impressed with herself.

Onna and Loga had to heal, too. Loga said that they'd both used "more magic than the human body is really capable of enduring when not in the grips of heroism." This made Jeckran laugh. So they stayed, and Tsira asked questions about what was going on with the people who'd been working with the Welder boy. Loga told her about the forger who'd written fake receipts so Welder's father would keep sending money to fund the killings. About the wizards who'd done the murdering. About the supervisors at the hospital who ignored his creeping about the children's wards at night. About all the others who'd traded money for her ma's life. Some got arrested. One shot himself.

The governments of Cwydarin, Daeslund, and Hexos were all arguing over where Welder's trial would be held. Tsira figured that was better than all of them going to war, at least. They'd had more than enough of that.

Tsira tried not to ask about it too often.

She thought Pink was doing all right. He and Loga seemed to be getting on just fine. Loga always seemed to know how to make him laugh. She didn't mind too much. She liked the sound of his laughing. She liked seeing how pleasure made him blush.

He had nightmares, but she did now, too. They held each other through them. They drank wine at midnight. They put their mouths to each other and licked a little pleasure out. They cussed and punched holes through the walls. Jeckran stood on their balcony and smoked, leaned hard against the railing, his body pushed up close to the long drop.

"Don't you die," she said. She kept him naked when she could. Locked up with her in their room. Safe. She stole his cigarettes. She hid his boots. She pressed him into the bed and bit at his shoulders. "Don't you ever die, Pink. Don't you fucking go. You stay here. You stay with me."

"Whatever you say," he told her. "Whatever you like. I'll live for five hundred years."

She said, "That's right."

She knew about it before she told Jeckran. Walked around with a question in her body. She let it sit for a while. Then she went to Loga in his study at the top of the Lamp.

"I'm pregnant," she said.

He raised his eyebrows. "Are congratulations in order?"

She thought about it. Then she said, "Not sure."

"Ah," he said.

She said, "Can you tell if it's all right?" She wanted to know now if its heart was beating.

He brought her down to his rooms so that they'd have some privacy. Told her to lie down and put a hand to her belly. Then he made a yelping noise and jerked back. She frowned. "What?"

He shook his head like he was clearing it. "It's healthy," he said. "It's also a girl—and a wizard. I mean, she has innate magical ability, not that she's living in a freezing garret and complaining about how her research isn't being funded."

Tsira stared, her mind blank. Then she said, "*Shit.*"

Loga raised his eyebrows. "You would prefer her to be living in a freezing garret and complaining about her research not being funded? Because if so, all you need to do is give birth, raise her to the age of six or seven, and send her to an unutterably expensive wizarding academy. The rest should sort itself out."

Tsira sighed. "Makes everything more complicated, if she's a wizard."

He blinked. "Really? Why?"

"Clan needs one," she said. She stood. "I'm a clan-chief's daughter. If my daughter's a wizard, it's good for the clan. She'll have that weight on her, like I did. Duty to her clan. Can't get out of it." Then she leaned against the table and said, "*Fuck.*"

She left Loga to think about it a while longer. Carried it with her. Turned it around in her hands.

Her ma would ask her to make an argument.

Mark: It would be in custom for her to have this child and raise her in the clan. Bringing more magical blood into the clan was a good act. It would help her people. Marden would have a student, and a reig wizard from a clan-head's line would be a good candidate to be head herself one day.

Countermark: Tsira's daughter would be practically a pink. More human than troll, anyway. Small and fragile, short-lived and short-tempered. Raising her in the clan would be a damn pain in the ass. Too little and delicate to keep up with the troll children when they played. Probably would look big and strange to pink children, too. Nothing would ever come too easy to a child like that.

Countermark to that: She didn't see how having a child with Jeckran could ever be too bad.

*Fuck*, she loved him.

It was harder to make reasonable fucking arguments now that she had to think about love.

She told Onna to go get Jeckran, then sat down in the garden under a cherry tree to think some more. Loga's trees bloomed year-round. She wasn't sure how she felt about that. Pretty, sure, but after a while you stopped seeing the beauty, like how the last bite of cake was always worse than the first. She sat under the blooming cherry tree and thought, and didn't see that it was beautiful. By the time Jeckran found her, petals covered her lap and her hair.

"Tsira," he said. "Is everything all right?"

She said, "I'm pregnant."

He sat down hard on the grass. "I thought—"

"Me, too."

They stared at each other.

"I asked Loga to check on her," Tsira said.

"Oh."

"He said she's healthy. And a wizard."

*"Oh."*

She leaned her head back against the trunk of the tree. "If she's born looking troll, we can go back together. Raise her in the clan."

He smiled big and happy, like he liked the sound of it. Then he frowned. "If she's born—but what if she looks human?"

"Then that's how you'll raise her," Tsira said. "Pink name. Pink school. Everything that she'll need to survive with pinks, if that's how she decides she wants to live when she's grown. Like my ma wished she could've done for me. When she's grown and come into her magic, she can decide what she wants for herself. If you raise her up right, she'll be able to choose easier than I could. A quarter troll makes her troll enough for the schools in Cwydarin, if she wants that, but you pinks have more rules for girls. I want her to be able to have either, if she wants. Whatever she wants."

Jeckran nodded slowly and sat for a while, quiet, thinking. That was new for him. A good thing that he'd learned how to sit and be still with his thoughts.

After he'd thought for a while he took a deep breath. "That sounds perfectly reasonable. I'll take charge of her learning Daeslundic and Esiphian and her basic Daeslundic-style education, and you can teach her what a troll of the same age would need, and we can send her to a girls' school at the right age so she'll be able to conduct herself well in human society, if she wishes. A school here in Hexos might do very well. It's less traditionally Daeslundic than Leiscourt, but I would say that from all reports the quality of education is quite good, and it isn't as if traditional Daeslundic values are particular concerns to either of us in any case."

She shook her head. "I'll be with the clan soon as she's weaned. You'll be wherever's best for the child. Here, probably."

He shook his head right back. "No. Absolutely not, I don't accept that. I won't allow you to *leave* me, you can't—"

She put her hand to his cheek. "Won't *leave* you. But you'd hate living with the clan. You're rankless. Don't have a place there. You'd be bored as hell. Get to hating me for it, after a while." She took a breath, thinking. "Monsatelle, maybe, for you and the baby. I could . . . go back and forth. Until a new head's in place, at least. There's a young reig or two who might do all right, if I train them up some. I think one of them can barely fucking read." She laughed. Shook her head. "This is stupid, Pink. Us trying to raise a child together. Stupid thing to do."

Jeckran smiled up at her. Squeezed her hand. "Well, boss," he said. "In that case I would say it's rather beautifully in our ordinary mode of doing things, isn't it?"

Loga and Onna were both pretty funny about it when Tsira told them she was going to have the child. Onna spent a lot of time reading pink books about pregnancy so she could give Tsira advice. Tsira mostly ignored it. Onna also spent a lot of the time at the children's hospital, and she spent the rest of her time knitting little hats and shoes. Tsira thought that was nice of her. After a few days of watching Onna knit, Tsira asked her how she did it. Tsira picked it up pretty quickly, and once she had the trick of it, she and Onna spent a lot of time knitting together. Jeckran thought that was pretty funny. He always laughed when he saw them. Tsira wasn't too sure why, but she figured anything that made him laugh had to be all right.

Loga had his own ways of showing that he cared about her and the child. He was always trying to get her to drink bitter-smelling Sangan medicines, which he brewed up in his study, and telling her all of the things that she should and shouldn't eat. He invited her and Jeckran to big parties while saying she shouldn't tire herself by staying out too late. Mostly Tsira just laughed and did whatever she liked. Loga didn't seem to mind too much.

Loga threw a big party at the Lamp for Onna's birthday. Tsira found herself a seat and watched the people go by. She talked a little to anyone who greeted her. Jeckran sat next to her drinking too much Hexian liquor and trying to make her laugh. Then Loga came to sit with them and started telling stories about different people who came by. Turned out that rich pinks did a lot of the same cheesebrained shit that rich trolls did. Jeckran and Loga cackled like two old chickens together. Then Jeckran slopped some wine on himself, which made Loga cackle even harder.

The two of them were smacking at each other and laughing when Finnbair walked up.

Loga stood when he saw him. "Jok. You came."

"I had thought of not coming," Finnbair said. "Out of spite."

"I would have deserved it," Loga told him. "I've been an absolute beast."

"You have," Finnbair agreed. "You looked fine while you did it, though. You've got real style while you're being a bastard."

Loga's face creased in on itself. Finnbair stepped closer, then stopped. Loga reached out to grasp his friend's shoulder. "I'm so sorry, Jok."

"I know," Finnbair said.

"Will you forgive me?"

"Probably will, to my deep regret," Finnbair said. "Might have to give it some time."

Loga wiped his eyes on his sleeve. "There's someone here I'd like you to meet."

He set off through the crowd with his arm linked through Finnbair's, that smiling face he wore in public locked in place. She and Jeckran followed after them at a distance, elbowing each other and grinning over how damn nosy they were. Loga stopped next to a handsome pink with a short black beard and a bright, hard-looking smile. Loga smiled back. "Kosson, darling, may I present to you my dear friend, Mr. Jok Finnbair? Jok, this is His Royal Highness Kosson Zahir."

Finnbair bowed. He looked nervous enough to turn and run. "Kosson," Loga said, "Jok is the gentleman who wrote those Angus Finnwake translations you enjoyed so much."

That hard smile changed, went warmer and more natural. The prince had a low voice for a pink and a way of talking like he was purring. "Mr. Finnbair! I'm a tremendous admirer of yours. *The Red Collection* is my one of my favorite books. Of course I'm sure that the work is vastly better in the original Gallen, but I'm afraid that I've never even heard the language spoken."

"Oh, but that's a real pity," Finnbair said. Tsira tried not to grin. He was making his accent stronger, same as she always did when she was trying to impress a pink. "It's an oral tradition we have in our islands, Your Highness. Those poems are meant to be read aloud."

"Can you recite?" the prince said. He sounded more eager about it than Tsira figured most folks would get over poetry reading. He let his eyes run down Finnbair's body and back up again.

"I can, Your Highness," Mr. Finnbair said, ducking his head. "But it's too loud for it here, with the crowd."

"Then we should find somewhere more private for your recitation," the prince said, and he put his arm through Finnbair's to lead him off.

Finnbair shot a happy owl-eyed look over his shoulder at Loga. Looked like he didn't really know what was happening, but he wasn't too mad about it, either.

"Heavens!" Loga said once they had gone. "That took even less time than I thought it would."

After that, time passed quickly and quietly. They all had their jobs to do.

Onna spent months going over Welder's work at the hospital with the blood from his victims, trying to find some way to make a medicine that would act like troll blood in a human's body. Welder had been using it on children who'd just had surgeries to help them heal faster and fight off infection. Tsira thought it seemed like rough work, but if any pink could do it, that was Onna. She found some troll texts a young troll wizard had snuck out of Cwydarin, and Tsira helped translate the text from Cwydacyn. They all spent a lot of time in the hospital, visiting Onna and bringing her food so she didn't forget to eat. When Tsira stopped by, half the time Loga was quietly working with a child curled in his lap.

Once when Tsira was there, two strangers came with their own baby. Onna introduced them as Captain Run and Sergeant Bato. They wanted Onna to join the Hexian police. She said no, she was too busy as Loga's apprentice—they hadn't told anyone she was halfway to being the Lord-Mage, yet—even though she was pleased to be asked. She was even more pleased when they invited Onna to the blessing of their child's name.

Sometimes Onna looked sad when she worked with the children. Sometimes she watched Tsira and Jeckran together and looked away fast when Tsira caught her watching. One day at the hospital, Jeckran brought Tsira some sandwiches, gave her a kiss, and patted her slightly rounded belly. Onna looked sad again, so after Jeckran left Tsira said, "First vahn I ever fucked once told me he hoped I would freeze to death in the mountains and then get eaten by wild dogs."

Onna looked a little ruffled. "*What?*"

"Just saying," Tsira said. "Welder was a murderer, but he didn't try to murder *you*. Could've been worse." Then she said, more gently, "You'll find another."

Onna looked like she didn't know whether to laugh or look offended. She settled on both. Then she said, "It's not that I'm concerned with *finding a man*."

"More that you think it says something about you that you liked a bad one."

Onna looked embarrassed. "I'm sure I have much more important things to be worried about," she said, and looked back to her books.

She did, Tsira thought. She was a good, tough girl. Every day she worked on her projects, she got madder. "He was *lazy*," she kept saying. "He was just *lazy*. He could have found some other way to replicate some of the effects without the troll blood, I *know* he could have. It's only going to be a matter of doing the work." That's what she did, day in and day out. The work. Using those clever brains in her head to try and make something good of all the shit that Welder'd started, all of that pain and blood. When Loga said anything to her about schools and academics and prizes, she looked a little surprised that they still existed.

Sometimes she even looked happy about that.

Tsira asked her about it once, while they were sitting in the study drinking tea together. "Do you like this? The medical stuff?"

Onna leaned back in her chair and cocked her head. "I don't know if I *like* it," she said finally. "But it's very difficult. More difficult than anything. It takes up all of my time, so I can't think too much about— other things. And it's about stopping people from dying, not chasing after the dead. So I think that it must be . . . enough. At least for now."

"How about after now?"

"I think I should like to go home and see my family," Onna said quietly. "And then—" She smiled and shrugged. "Back here to Hexos, or Sango, or *anywhere*. I have some of Loga's power now, but he's still the Lord-Mage, and I have a few years before I'll have to start taking on some of his official duties, so I need to learn as much as I can while my time is still my own. Loga has said he thinks I should take on a fellowship in Bene to learn about some of the alternative parametrical languages they're developing. And while I'm there—I'll meet the glamorous set, I suppose, and go to parties, and talk to unsuitable gentlemen, and have all sorts of wonderful adventures that don't have *any murders* in them." Then she hurriedly added, "And then come back here again to see you and Phillim and the baby, of course."

Tsira laughed and refilled Onna's teacup. "I'll drink to that."

A few weeks after that, they were all gathered in the garden. Onna and Loga were playing a game, making a ball of light that changed colors when you touched it the right way and shocked you when you made a mistake. They seemed to think it was pretty funny. Tsira didn't like games that stung, especially since she couldn't see all the colors. She was reading an awful novel instead and eating Nessoran sweets Loga had purchased for her. She had to rub at her belly sometimes when the muscle ached.

She'd swelled up big, now that she was about seven months along. Jeckran liked it all right. Always looking at her and blushing, waiting to get her alone and get his hands on all the changed parts of her.

Jeckran wasn't staring now, though. He was sitting in the grass surrounded by ledgers. Loga had invested in a small shipping company that belonged to the father of some girl he'd been chasing, and he hadn't bothered to check the balance sheets. Jeckran had told him the company's manager was cheating the hair off his balls, so Loga made Jeckran the manager. He seemed to like it all right. He could tell her every night about all the clever things he was doing to make everything run right, and she could rub his back with one hand and say that she was proud of him.

They were having a nice time that afternoon. Later, Jeckran made up a new game where Tsira had to read parts of her books aloud without smiling. Sometimes she had to bite her cheek when she got to bits like, "The faintest stirrings of Hope, which flits from heart to heart upon wings as fragile and gossamer as those of spring's first butterfly, fluttered delicately within my breast, though I quailed before the lightning flash of his darkly wicked eyes." The rest of them just fell over laughing.

Onna laughed the hardest, which was nice to see. Usually she acted like taking time to enjoy herself was the same as if she'd given cancer to those kids at the hospital herself. Onna was almost crying from laughing over a part in the book where the characters wrote bad love poetry to each other when a servant came up and said there was a guest for Miss Gebowa.

The guest was young, good-looking, a scar on his lip. Tsira started. She'd seen him back in Monsatelle: he'd spoken in a strange voice and said he was sorry about her mother. Onna leapt to her feet when she saw him.

"Sy!"

They embraced, both of them laughing. Onna pulled away first. "What on earth are you doing in Hexos?"

He rubbed the back of his neck. "Well," he said. "It turns out that the reason my parameters were always such rubbish compared to yours was that I was never meant to be an academic wizard. I'm, ah, within the faith. They call us Clear Voices." He ducked his head. "It turns out that I'm religious after all. And very good at helping people who are unhappy. My father's rather puzzled by the whole thing, but I feel as if I finally know what I want to *do* with myself."

"You're traveling about in a riverboat having adventures, aren't you?" Onna said. She was smiling like it was the first warm day of spring.

"Sometimes I just sit and hold sick people's hands and listen to their stories. But the riverboat *is* awfully fun." Then he looked toward Tsira and met her eyes. "I'm so sorry about your mother."

Onna introduced Sy, and they all talked for a while. He was shy around Loga, being a wizard himself, and Loga kept teasing him until he looked like he'd like to dig a hole in the ground and hide inside it. Before Sy left, he took Onna's hand. "I'm sorry," he said. "For having been a condescending little ass all those years, and not appreciating you, and using you to get what I wanted. I was so wrapped up in trying to do what everyone expected of me that I didn't know how to admire anyone else. You're—you're remarkable, you know. You always were."

"Yes," Onna said, smiling. "I was, wasn't I?"

Once he was gone, Tsira ate some more of her sweets and said, "You could take him tomorrow, if you wanted."

"*Really*, Tsira," Jeckran said. Pretending like he was shocked. Tsira winked at him.

"Well, I certainly shan't accept any proposals just *now*," Onna said. "Loga is bringing me to Nessorand this winter after I get back from visiting my family. We're going to attend a conference of illusionists, and I need to apply for fellowships. I shall be far too busy to think about *marriage*."

Tsira raised her eyebrows. "Wasn't talking about marriage."

Jeckran squawked. Onna's eyes went wide.

Then she smiled like a grown reig would.

The final weeks passed quickly. Tsira was a little surprised when the pain started.

She let a pink nurse in the room with her because Jeckran begged her to. Sat her down in the corner and told her to keep quiet. This wasn't the worst thing she'd ever done, but it sure as shit wasn't the best, either. She sorted it out in her head, and then panted and sweated and dug her fingernails into her thighs. Better than seeing her mother's corpse. Worse than being shot three times.

She'd rather not fucking well do it a second time, either way.

When it was over, the nurse made herself useful getting things cleaned up a little. Tsira figured Jeckran might faint if the room looked too much like people had been murdered in it. Tsira lay still and rested. Her baby rested, too, safe and warm on her chest, tired out from screaming. She was tiny and angry and perfect.

Tsira figured she took after her da.

The nurse went out, and Jeckran came rushing in. When he saw them, he looked like he was seeing the world's first sunset.

"*Oh*," he said. "Oh. There you are." He touched the baby's dark hair with one finger.

Tsira smiled at him. Her face did it without her asking for it. "You can touch her," she said. "She won't break."

"Oh," he said.

"She's a little reig, too, maybe. Like me. Her troll name is Cynal-lumwynsurai." She paused. "She needs a human name, too."

He hesitated. "Winifer? After my grandmother? She was always very kind to me."

"Sounds fine."

They were quiet for a moment, just looking at her.

"What will we do, Tsira?" he said. "What will happen to us? To her? Elgar knows we're not the most usual of parents."

She shrugged one shoulder. "We'll fight. Eat. Fuck. Worry. Earn money. Raise her up. Might have to split up. Be apart for a while if money gets tight and we've got to find work. Do things we don't want to. Doesn't matter."

She reached for his hand and squeezed it hard enough to hurt. She looked him in the eye and smiled. "We'll get by."

# ACKNOWLEDGMENTS

There are so many people who carried me through publishing my debut novel (and kept me from changing my name, moving to a distant forest, and becoming a simple woodland beekeeper) that it would take another book to list all of them. Briefly, though, here are some people I need to thank:

My husband, Xia Nan, who always knows where my glasses are, told me that I was an author before I was fully convinced, and keeps trying to sell my book to strangers.

My parents, Jean and Jeff, and my sister Ellen, who are consistently more impressed by my efforts than is probably warranted.

My big sister Rosemary, who's been providing thoughtful critiques since I was fourteen.

Deborah Marinelli, my first writing teacher, who read my stories and told me that she thought I could go somewhere with this.

Catherine Lewis, Bob Stein, and my wonderful creative writing classmates at SUNY Purchase for reading the first chapters of my initial attempt at a novel and giving me the feedback I needed to do better the next time.

Many, many thanks to my heroic pals Chloe Heintz and Emily Fitzgerald. You're the most dedicated readers, fans, emotional support columns, and unpaid publicists anyone could ask for.

I also had some amazing pros on my team: a million thanks to Jennifer Udden, agent extraordinaire, who guided me through edits, talked me through the entire publishing process, and provided lots of handholding phone calls whenever I started to panic. Just as many to my editor, Jessica Wade, who found every single weak spot I was too lazy to fix on my own and really whipped this thing into shape. Special thanks also to Nia Davenport, who made amazing suggestions to strengthen the characters and worldbuilding that I hope I was able to successfully work into the story.

Finally, I'd like to thank the wonderful folks who volunteered to read my very first draft: Lisa Kuppler, Iris Chamberlain, Sharay Setti, Zoe Polach, Vale Aida, and Philippa Hewlett. Your incredibly thoughtful feedback and all the conversations that followed were so important to getting this thing to achieve its final form. I can't wait to see what projects come next for all of you.

**C. M. Waggoner** grew up on an old sheep farm in rural upstate New York. She studied creative writing at SUNY Purchase and lived in China for eight years before moving with her husband to Albany, NY. In her spare time, she volunteers with a local HIV/AIDS organization, talks to strangers, and gardens badly. *Unnatural Magic* is her first book.

Ready to find
your next great read?

Let us help.

**Visit prh.com/nextread**

Penguin
Random
House